W9-ANJ-740

AN IMPERFECT PAST

EVE SEYMOUR

OTHER BOOKS BY EVE SEYMOUR

Beautiful Losers

AN IMPERFECT PAST

EVE SEYMOUR

MIDNIGHT INK
WOODBURY, MINNESOTA

FIRST EDITION
First Printing, 2017

Book format by Cassie Kanzenbach
Cover design by Ellen Lawsom
Editing by Nicole Nugent

Midnight Ink, an imprint of Llewellyn Worldwide Ltd.

Library of Congress Cataloging-in-Publication Data
Names: Seymour, E. V. (Eve V.), author.
Title: An imperfect past / Eve Seymour.
Description: First edition. | Woodbury, Minnesota : Midnight Ink, [2017] |
    Series: A Kim Slade novel ; #2
Identifiers: LCCN 2016033192 (print) | LCCN 2016054080 (ebook) | ISBN
    9780738748672 (softcover) | ISBN 9780738750354
Subjects: LCSH: Clinical psychologists—Fiction. | Women
    psychologists—Fiction. | Missing persons—Investigation—Fiction. |
    GSAFD: Mystery fiction. | Suspense fiction.
Classification: LCC PR6119.E973 I47 2017 (print) | LCC PR6119.E973 (ebook) |
    DDC 823/.92—dc23
LC record available at https://lccn.loc.gov/2016033192

Midnight Ink
Llewellyn Worldwide Ltd.
2143 Wooddale Drive
Woodbury, MN 55125-2989
www.midnightinkbooks.com

Printed in the United States of America

For Sarah Vincent, friend and best writing pal.
Thanks for listening to many tales of my imperfect past.

ACKNOWLEDGMENTS

Lots of people were involved in the creation of this novel. I couldn't have written it without Detective Inspector Jo Tidmarsh from Avon and Somerset Police. Jo was immensely patient and meticulous in explaining to me the finer points of police procedure. Any mistakes made are mine alone or are the result of choosing the dramatic over the strictly authentic. It should be stated here and now that she is nothing like the fictional female police officer in the story.

In common with most of my novels, Cheltenham plays a starring role. Unusually, I used the real Battledown Guesthouse on Hales Road as setting for a couple of key scenes. And yes, Sarah and Simon generously gave me permission to play themselves in the narrative, with a walk-on part from their daughter, Isabella. Look no further if you're planning a visit to the town; there is nothing fictional about the hospitality displayed in the story. In a similar vein, cafes I frequent are mentioned, as is the excellent independent bookshop in the Suffolks.

I was reliant on Paul Britton's *Picking Up the Pieces* for information about multiple personality disorder, so thank you. As ever, I'm indebted to Broo Doherty, my agent, for suggestions, revisions, and her legendary enthusiasm. Ditto big thanks to the entire team at Midnight Ink, including Terri Bischoff, Nicole Nugent, and Katie Mickschl, for their continued and much appreciated support.

PROLOGUE

"My name is Kim Slade. I'm thirty-six years old and a clinical psychologist. I specialise in treating eating disorders. My mother abandoned me when I was three. My lover is dead, murdered by his best friend, the man who stalked me. My father and one of my brothers are also dead—the former from old age and hard living, the latter through accident and no fault of his own. Rarely, but sometimes, I lose a client. You could say that people leave me abruptly. Death has a habit of snapping at my heels."

"Does it scare you?"

My heart gallops in my chest. I look straight ahead and meet the therapist's eye. "You bet."

ONE

Not the kind of woman to cut and run, right now I wanted to get the hell out, flee, hide under a dirty great rock and stay there. Then Jim Copplestone shambled down the corridor banging on about psychopaths.

"According to the most recent American study, brain scans indicate that certain regions of the brain, areas that govern empathy and morality, for example, are entirely closed off. Rather proves the point that it's all down to genetics," he added with a provocative expression designed to get me going.

I muttered something, sucked in a deep gulp of air, and tore into my consulting room. Undeterred, Jim followed and parked his bony rear on the edge of the desk, folded his arms, and drew his big louche eyebrows together. A psychiatrist and clinical director of Ellerslie Lodge, a fifteen-bedded residential home for anorexic young women, Jim was my boss. We shared history. A staunch ally, he had once cut me slack when others would have shown me the door. Not to put too fine a point on it, I'd found him to be fair-minded when the need arose. We got on well as professionals and colleagues, more so as friends, even if sometimes he annoyed the heck out of me. When the direct line phone blared, he stayed put. Maybe he was checking to see if I was up to the job.

Shrugging off my coat, I picked up the call and spoke in my best professional telephone voice, no hint of a Devon burr, no wobble in the tone. "Kim Slade."

"Kim, it's Georgia."

I brightened. We'd been mates and regular lunch chums for years.

"Hi," I said. "Great to hear from you."

"Cut and rewind."

"Oh?"

"Look, I'm sorry to drop this on you," Georgia said, grim finality in her voice.

"Drop what exactly?" Obviously this was no prelude to a social invitation. My first instinct was correct. Returning to work this soon and on a Sunday, no less, had been a rubbish idea.

"Hasn't Jim got you up to speed yet?"

The thought of getting *up to speed* crushed me. I'd had what most people commonly refer to as a nervous breakdown, a phrase never used in medical circles and too crude a description for a condition that embraced anything from depression to high anxiety state to schizophrenia. I regarded it as my crash-and-burn episode, a textbook response to traumatic events. Not good news for a shrink. I was better now, or so I'd been told. Clamping my hand over the receiver, I mouthed *Dr. Thorne* to Jim, who pulled a face and slapped his forehead. "Hell, I forgot."

3

That's what happens when you get carried away with chat about psychopaths. Important stuff careers out of the door and onto the road where it gets hit by a truck. I flashed him a checkmate smile, to which Jim responded by sticking out his tongue.

"Sorry, Georgia," I said, "He hasn't had the chance. What's the problem?"

"Mimi Vellender."

I have an almost photographic memory. At once I recalled a shy, darkly pretty, quietly spoken, intelligent teenager. She had the most amazing chocolate brown eyes. I'd treated her four years earlier and as far as I knew she'd made a good recovery from anorexia nervosa. Shout lines in her background were as follows: family dynamics dysfunctional with a mother clinging to a colour supplement lifestyle; father a fully paid up workaholic; older brother gone AWOL.

"She's been admitted to the high dependency unit at the hospital," Georgia said.

Shocked, I glanced up at an earwigging Jim. "We decided to section her while you were away," he murmured.

I frowned big-time. "How bad is it?" I said to Georgia.

"Late stage, I'm afraid. She barely weighs fifty pounds." The normal weight of a seven-year-old, I registered.

I briefly closed my eyes. Thankfully, this kind of scenario was rare. It didn't lessen the impact. I gathered myself. "Where do I fit?"

"She's drifting in and out of consciousness. In her more lucid moments, she begged to see you."

"*Begged?*"

"It's important to her, otherwise I wouldn't have bothered you."

"Will it make a difference?"

"It might, but probably not."

Georgia was nothing if not honest. I looked up questioningly at Jim. "We haven't booked any clients for today," he said. "Thought we'd give you a chance to settle, get the feel of things, ease yourself back to normal."

Normal? For a consultant psychiatrist, it seemed a singularly inept description.

"I'll come straightaway," I told Georgia.

"Give it an hour. The critical care team are all over the shop at the moment."

"Okay, but what about the parents?" There was bound to be a bedside vigil.

"Leave that to me. They mustn't know."

"What? But..."

"Mimi insisted on it." One thing I'd learnt about anorexics during my career as a clinical psychologist, even when tapping at death's door they were stubborn and determined. To take the slow and agonising road to starvation demanded tenacity of epic proportions. If Mimi insisted, she meant it. No compromise. No negotiation.

I glanced at my watch and swallowed. Mending minds should be classed as a dark art. "About eleven then—would that be all right?"

"Perfect. And Kim..."

"Yeah?"

"Welcome back."

TWO

I SAT IN A cold and empty family room with anaemic-coloured walls, poor lighting, and soulless Swedish furniture. I felt nervous and disengaged. Professional enough to know that sometimes I failed, that sometimes women—and they were mostly women—died, I was not immune from guilt, from asking myself if I could have done more. If I got through this with any degree of sanity, I could class myself as officially "cured."

My coat wrapped tightly around me, I physically focused on my scuffed and sturdy boots and mentally concentrated on the highlights of the file notes I'd dug out earlier.

Mimi Vellender was fourteen years old when I first encountered her after a referral from her GP. She exhibited classic symptoms of an eating disorder: low body weight, crushing exhaustion, intolerance to cold, a tendency to faint, dry skin, thin hair, and she hadn't had a period for a year. There was an extra complication. A vitamin D deficiency, significant enough to be noted and treated when she was tiny, meant that her bones were especially at risk of complication.

The family had responded like most families, with bewilderment and incomprehension and, in this case, spirited denial. I didn't blame them. Mimi's parents were a toxic combination of personal fitness trainer and Michelin-starred chef—lethal for a child obsessed with exercise and anxieties about food. Initially, an acrimonious divorce between the parents and a father hardly ever on the scene appeared to provide the trigger for Mimi's downward spiral. I soon jettisoned that idea.

"Nick disappeared," Mimi blurted out after a particularly gruelling session.

"Nick?"

"My big brother." Her large button-brown eyes were blinded with frantic tears.

"When?"

"A year ago. He'll be almost nineteen now."

"Do you know why he decided to leave home?"

Indignation tightened her features into lots of angry little points. "You make it sound as if he took off because he wanted to."

"People do." Especially young men.

"Dad drove him away. He was always on Nick's case. And now something has happened to him. I *know* it."

Alarmed, I'd followed it up with Mimi's mother who, fixing me with a blank stare, confirmed that her only son had, indeed, gone missing, that he'd left without leaving a note.

"There were tensions," she added, "between my son and his father."

"What kind of tensions?" I said.

"People fear what they don't understand. My ex-husband never understood Nicholas."

Whatever the reason for Nicholas's continued absence, it seemed that he was strongly motivated to cut family ties. For Mimi, who was close to him, it had been a devastating decision. I treated her appropriately, as if she had suffered a bereavement, which in a way she had.

The door opened. Georgia, wide-hipped and wide-smiled, stepped inside. I stood up and she gave me a hug. She felt solid and reassuring. A mother of four kids, two girls and two boys, all under the age of ten years of age, she offered me a glimpse of Georgia in full-on mummy mode. "So sorry to do this to you on your first day back."

"Nothing like being thrown in at the deep end." I forced a smile and raised my voice a little to make it sound light, bright, and unburdened.

Not easily fooled, Georgia held me away and studied my face in the same probing manner she viewed her patients. "Are you all right now?"

All right for a woman whose life had been turned upside down by murder and mayhem. If anything, I missed Chris more now than in the grim aftermath. I still found myself about to tell Chris something unusual, or even commonplace, only to remember that he was dead. It's tricky to forge a life for one when you've been accustomed to creating one for two.

I assured her I was.

"Good." She linked her arm through mine, clasped me close as if I might run away given half a chance. Perceptive of her, I thought. "I'll take you in. Unfortunately, Mimi suffered a seizure after we spoke."

"Fluid loss?" I said.

"Afraid so. Bear in mind we've had to stabilise her."

"You mean she's not really with it?"

"She's lucid enough to have a conversation."

I wasn't so certain, but we walked together down a corridor towards a closed door. Mute and impassable, it might as well have been a large boulder at the entrance to a cave. Georgia paused, her hand hovering over the handle. She turned towards me. My heart thumped against my rib cage.

"Ready?"

I braced myself. "Yes," I lied.

THREE

A BODY DEPRIVED OF food over a long period of time turns rogue, breaking down and devouring vital organs in a doomed bid to create energy and sustain life. Cannibalism personified.

My eyes fixed on the chest drain, nasal drip, saline, cannula, plugs, and monitors before they focused on the pitiful, bloated mound in the centre of the bed. Mimi's once pretty face was now a shrunken head. Wisps of hair, like twists of black cotton, clung to her skull for dear life. Bruised and yellow skin signified liver damage. The back of one claw-like hand, speared by an intravenous drip, looked too heavy for her fragile arm to support it. Exposed skin revealed deep scars that formed a pattern, bold as a tattoo, as if someone had tried to turn her into a human piece of conceptual art that packed a negative message.

I wanted to run, say it was all a mistake and confess that I was an impostor. I wanted to cry out about the suffocating cloud of sadness that hovered too near, directly above my head. Instead, I drew up a chair, sat down, and closed one hand over Mimi's. I felt the chill and bone, and leant towards her. The scent of impending death came off her in waves. I suppressed a shiver.

At my touch, her eyelids flickered, her cracked lips parted. "You came," she rasped. Altered by the damage to the larynx and oesophagus, her voice sounded ancient, salty, and prematurely aged.

"You wanted to see me, remember? You wanted to tell me something."

Her tongue, dry and furred, darted out and tapped the corner of her mouth. With a supreme effort, she opened eyes that once were beautiful and brown and were now haloed with yellow. They looked bush baby huge against the shrivelled features of her face. "I saw him," she said.

"Who?" I strained forward, lowered my face, my ear next to her mouth. I tried not to breathe in the foul, decomposing odour of approaching death that tainted her breath.

"Nick."

"Your brother?"

"After all this time." Mimi's thumb hooked over my hand with surprising force and strength. "He came back."

"That's wonderful."

"But it's not. Don't you see?" Her face screwed into despair.

I didn't and neither could I fathom the reason for Mimi's steep physical decline. Perhaps the silted residue of depression still clogged my brain.

"You don't believe me. Nobody does." Dismay at my dismal lack of insight shrouded her eyes.

I stroked the thin papery skin on her arm. "Mimi, I'm trying to understand, that's all."

"They said it wasn't true, that it couldn't be, that I'd made it up."

"They?"

"Mum and Dad."

"You spoke to them?"

"Yes."

"Individually?"

"Yes. They both said the same."

"But you actually saw Nick, right?"

"It was dark, but I knew it was my brother. You have to find him," she said, agitated again, digging into the soft flesh of my palm with the point of a bony finger. "You have to protect him, make sure he's safe. Can you do that for me?"

"Mimi, just hold up a moment. Are you—?"

"Listen to me," she hissed, "it was Nick."

Anorexics are often confused and judgements skewed due to chemical changes in the brain, but there was something disturbing and compelling about Mimi's claim.

"It's all right, I absolutely believe you."

She let out a breath. I could almost hear the air rattling through the ragged and bony remains of her chest cavity. "I knew you would," she said. "That's why you have to do something."

Do something? Do what? Me? I was the last person. "I'm sorry. I don't quite follow."

Mimi sighed, as if she were talking in Italian when I only understood German. Her energy fully expended, she shrank back into the pillows, drifting out of the here and now. I waited, turning over what she'd told me. Mimi had admitted that it was dark. I know only too well how easy it is to imagine seeing the person you love the most, even when that person is no longer alive. Feeling fragile or vulnerable makes illusionists of us all.

After a time, Mimi's eyes half opened. "I saw Nick speak to Mum outside our house."

"Did you hear what was said?"

"I was too far away."

"And you said she denied it?"

"She said he was dead."

"She didn't mean it in a literal sense, Mimi."

"She said my father killed him."

FOUR

STUNNED, I JUMPED AT the sound of raised voices outside a door that suddenly wrenched open. Paris Vellender shot inside like a racehorse released from the start line at Cheltenham racetrack. Her hair, a glossy mane of gleaming chestnut brown, flashed like a banner behind her. Trailed by Georgia, she crossed the room in a cloud of dense perfume. Beneath a red leather three-quarter length coat, she wore a steel-grey cashmere sweater over straight-leg black jeans and boots. Her painted face failed to conceal dark shadows underneath her eyes, which made it all the more remarkable that she looked considerably younger than she did four years previously. It wasn't simply due to her athletic figure, honed, no doubt, by hours of pumping and jumping. Fine-boned, skin taut for a woman in her late forties, her heart-shaped face retained an enviably sculpted jawline. Automatically, my hand shot up to the damaged side of my cheek, touching the not-so-smooth skin and ragged scar tissue that bordered what remained of my left ear, the vestiges of a childhood accident with a firework.

"What is she doing here?" Mrs. Vellender's chilly question was addressed solely to Georgia.

I opened my mouth to respond but, like a ventriloquist with a dummy, Georgia answered for me. "I realise that this is an upsetting time for you, Mrs. Vellender, but as I already explained, Kim has a professional interest in Mimi's case and—"

"She's the reason my daughter is in this state." Paris Vellender spoke in such a low, reasonable, and even tone, I almost missed the cold venom contained in her accusation.

Mimi let out a feeble rasp of protest and Paris Vellender, resting a hand on her daughter's brow, told her not to worry, that the "nasty, stupid woman" would go away.

Barely able to process what Mimi had confided, I now had Mrs. Vellender using me as an emotional punching bag. Watching my accuser fussing over her daughter, I reminded myself of the enormous pressure she was under.

"I realise how distressing this is for you."

Her head flicked up and her dark, flashing eyes met mine. "Don't. Just don't. You have no idea what this feels like. You think you do, but you haven't a clue."

Fear does weird things to people and deep down I knew that Paris Vellender was justifiably unhinged. It wasn't pleasant and I wasn't thrilled, but I understood her anger and the need to blame someone. The other silent, insidious part of me wondered whether her fear was for something else—fear of discovery, perhaps, fear that someone was about to shine a light on a dark and dirty corner. I didn't have time to consider it, because she was back on my case. Relentless should have been her middle name.

"Had you done your job properly—"

"That's neither true nor fair." To my astonishment, the words were mine.

"Really?" she sneered. "Why don't you do us all a favour? Go. Leave."

I stood, or rather sat, my ground. Georgia flashed an awkward smile in my direction and made a shooing gesture with the tips of her fingers. Paris Vellender glowered, pouted, and sighed, in that order. Finally, she stared me out and said to nobody in particular, "Troy will be here at any moment."

Whoever Troy was, I got it. Only two visitors allowed at any one time. This was the equivalent of giving me my marching orders. I wouldn't be sorry. I gathered up my bag and, leaning in close to Mimi, whispered, "I'll do my best," then stood up and left.

FIVE

I STUMBLED DOWN THE corridor, cheeks flushed the same red as a traffic light on stop. All I could think of was Mimi's last words to me: *She said my father killed him.*

At the sound of footsteps, I glanced over my shoulder, fully expecting to see Georgia offering apologies. How wrong could I be?

"Miss Slade?"

I winced at the thought of another round of abuse, stopped walking, and slowly swivelled. My day had barely begun and already I felt weary and dog-tired.

Mrs. Vellender, inches from me, grabbed hold of my arm and almost sank to her knees. Her burgundy-coloured nails dug into me like poison-tip darts. I attempted to pull away, but she clung on.

"I'm sorry," she said, her eyes great pools of sorrow. "I was terribly rude to you. Please forgive me. Will you accept my apologies?"

Many would be moved. Me, I swear she had a theatrical bent. "Mrs. Vellender, honestly, please, there's no need." I could afford to be magnanimous—just. Frankly, I was confused and embarrassed.

"It was unforgiveable to doubt your professional judgement."

"It's all—"

"The thing is—"

"There's really no need to explain," I cut in awkwardly. "I'm not a mother so I don't pretend to know exactly what you're going through, but I'm not a stranger to grief, Mrs. Vellender." Nor am I immune from despair.

She bit down on her bottom lip. "Of course, silly of me, in your job you must see all kinds of misery, but the thing is," she said, her voice tearing, "it was my fault."

"What was?" I tried to maintain my confusion rather than express suspicion.

"Mimi's condition."

"It's nobody's fault." I smiled to prove I meant what I said, but her eyes shone with fresh tears that splashed at an alarming rate down her cheeks. "I feel so guilty. I should have prevented it. I know I should."

"You couldn't." Feelings of parental guilt were a normal reaction but, nine times out of ten, misplaced. "For a whole host of reasons, trust me, there was nothing you could do. Look, do you want to get a cup of coffee, a breath of fresh air?" I cast my eyes towards the end of the corridor and sneakily wondered if I could persuade her to talk about her elusive son.

Torn, she took a long, wistful look back to the room in which her daughter lay dying. There was no doubt in my mind that Paris Vellender's distress was acute and genuine.

"Five minutes won't hurt," I said.

She put a hand to her temple, briefly closed her eyes, and smiled in a way that indicated she'd be glad of someone to talk to before abrupt hesitation in her manner told me that she'd changed her mind.

"I'd better not," she said.

I wondered whether to push it, whether to ask, maybe even challenge Mrs. Vellender about Nicholas right there and then in the corridor. Should I? Could I?

Suddenly, eyes aflame, she released her grasp. "Here's Troy now." She glanced up ahead, her eyes lifting over my shoulder.

I stepped aside. In spite of the January chill, Troy wore a plain black T-shirt with *God is an Astronaut* proclaimed across it, jeans, and beat shoes. I thought I detected an aroma of garlic and meat cooked in red wine, as though he'd recently prepared for a dinner party and the smell of cooked food had attached itself to his clothes. His head was shaved and, unlike many men with bald heads, it complemented and accentuated his strong facial features. He was around six-two, broad-shouldered, and seriously ripped with a physique that could only be obtained through sweat and serious working out. He exuded animal heat and, although I'm not accustomed to imagining men without their clothes on, I could picture this guy. I pegged him at no more than thirty, almost twenty years younger than Mrs. Vellender, but it was obvious from the way he crooked a knuckle under her upturned chin and kissed her parted mouth that they were lovers. My heart creased with an unexpected pang of envy and loss. In the wake of Chris's death, a universe of dreams, through which I'd longed to travel, were denied me.

Mrs. Vellender introduced me to Troy Martell, who gave me a big wide smile, his teeth so perfectly whitened they looked fake.

"How is she?" he said. He had an American accent.

Paris Vellender looked to me in anticipation of a professional answer, which I found irritatingly inconsistent. Wrong-footed, I cleared my throat and said, "Not great."

"Do you figure you can do something?"

"Well, I'm not sure. What I'd really like to…" I stalled. If I said something, I'd betray Mimi's confidence. I'd break her trust. Yet, if I kept silent, I'd have less chance of establishing the truth and carrying out Mimi's dying wish.

"Yes?" Paris broke in, expectant.

"If you remember," I said, starting again and choosing my words with care, "Mimi's condition began when Nicholas left home." I was careful not to say the more emotionally loaded *disappeared*. "I was thinking, wondering really, whether Nicholas has returned."

Paris Vellender didn't move a muscle and I didn't think it was down to Botox. Martell's features, on the other hand, sharpened into a moving picture of animation.

"Yeah, what is it, four, five years?"

She didn't glare. She looked right through him in the way warring couples do when one half says the wrong thing in front of others. There would be trouble later and, although I regretted pressing down so hard on an exposed nerve, Paris Vellender's deadpan reaction revealed more than if she had lied or prevaricated. Something was afoot.

"No," she said, stony. "I haven't heard anything since the day he vanished."

"I'm so sorry," I said.

"For all I know, he's dead." Then she turned on her kitten-heeled boots and stalked away.

Troy Martell stiffened in apology. "Catch you later," he said, and followed her.

SIX

WISHING I'D KEPT MY mouth shut, I walked outside. Underneath a black and blue sky, a chill, blustery wind blasted me in the face, stinging my eyes. It was easy to see how Mimi could have misinterpreted her mother's words, although it didn't explain how Mimi was so certain she'd seen her brother talking to her mother. Neither did it explain Paris Vellender's closed-down, hands-off expression. It gnawed at me as I crossed from Sandford Road onto the Bath Road and headed back to Ellerslie Lodge. About to cross again, my phone rang. I prised it out of my bag and glanced at the number, which I didn't recognise.

"Hello?" I said.

"So you're back."

I stopped walking. "Kyle?"

"Have you missed me?"

"Erm…" The image of Kyle Stannard, which had been crouching in the hippocampus part of my brain for several months, catapulted into my frontal lobes and, unleashed, went on the rampage.

Stannard the beautiful; Stannard the damaged, depending on which side of his face you saw first; Stannard the jester and saviour and seducer. He had once been a male model, his career destroyed through malice. The operation to correct the facial damage had been a disaster due to medical negligence, for which he'd sued. A property developer, he ran a successful estate agency in town. Our paths had crossed when I suspected him of stalking me. I'd been wrong, but there was definitely something obsessive about him. Deep down, I knew that our last goodbye was in reality an au revoir. I simply hadn't wanted to admit it.

Brash as ever, he said, "I gather you did the mental equivalent of crashing into a wall."

"That's one way of putting it."

He let out a laugh. "Glad to see you haven't entirely lost your sense of humour."

Glad that I've entirely fooled you.

"But are you sort of okay now? I mean I know what hap—"

"Sort of," I said, sparky, heading him off. "How's life treating you?"

"Not bad, that's the main reason I need to see you."

Need?

"Thing is, I've got you something."

"For me?"

Despite standing in a public place, cars whizzing past and people scuttling by, heads down, faces chilled, I closed my eyes briefly and thought *Shit.*

"Don't sound so surprised. Treat it as a housewarming present."

"Right," I said, my voice slack with unease.

"Thought I could drop by with it."

Honestly, I almost fell off the pavement.

In a chemically induced haze, I'd sold the flat near Lansdown and moved into a candy-coloured terraced house in a private enclave in the centre of town. It had the extra benefit of a car parking space and was handy for the shops, convenient for a high-end supermarket, practical for work, and close to the rhythmic sound of running river water, which pleased me. One huge plus: Stannard no longer knew where I lived.

Improvising madly, I said, "How about we meet for a drink at Blancs?" Somewhere neutral. Somewhere you can't talk about our past. Somewhere you can't scare and intrigue and tantalise me.

"That would be tricky."

"Why?"

"My gift is way too big."

Too big? What was it, an elephant? Anything was possible with Stannard. A heavy sigh escaped from between my lips.

"Christ, Kim, most women would be pleased."

"I'm not most women."

"Darling, I know that."

"Sorry," I said, exceptionally tense. "When?"

"Tonight."

Tonight?

"I'm leaving for the States in three days."

This perked me up. If Kyle Stannard was heading for the other side of the Atlantic, he couldn't exercise his obsessive bent on me. "What time?"

"Seven, seven thirtyish."

"Fine. See you then."

"Kim?"

"What?"

"The address?"

"Oh sure," I said, mumbling the number and name of the street. "Want me to bring a bottle?"

"Not necessary." Alcohol and antidepressants weren't a great mix, but I indulged in the odd glass of wine without side effects. That evening, I had the strong suspicion I was going to need it.

SEVEN

I thought the world had moved on without me, but it hadn't. Not really. Same old.

Doggedly refusing to think about Nicholas Vellender and the allegations made by his sister and denials by his mother, I read through notes on our latest intakes, got myself "up to speed" as Georgia had suggested, and sorted out my client list for the following day. Prior to life throwing me a hissy fit, I'd split my work between Ellerslie Lodge and another clinic in town, but during time off on "compassionate grounds," I'd jacked in my other job and arranged to increase my hours at the Lodge. It suited me. I'd always preferred the more hands-on approach demanded there.

Minutes before I was about to set off home, Georgia called full of apology.

"I'd no idea Mrs. V would show up. I should have handled it better and saved you a bashing. She's so damn highly strung."

"Poor woman is in a rotten situation."

"Well, yeah, but she didn't have to maul you in public. What happened in the corridor?"

"She apologised."

"Really? She never said a word. I thought she'd gone after you to dish out another verbal thrashing."

"On the contrary."

"Oh?"

"She feels responsible."

Georgia snorted. "Guilt isn't part of her mental makeup."

"What makes you say that?"

"*Sorry* doesn't figure in her vocabulary. Arrogance is her middle name, any admission of failure weakness. You must have picked up on it when you first treated Mimi."

I thought back. If I'd been pressed to describe Paris Vellender, I'd have said that she was ambitious, single-minded, and focused, in common with most women running their own enterprise. Anybody serious about obtaining the body beautiful in Cheltenham attended Mrs. Vellender's fitness centre close to the Suffolks. The town had around forty millionaires, in other words men and women prepared to pay top dollar in their bid to sculpt the perfect physique. A savvy businesswoman, she was also vain, terrified of growing old, and defined herself by the man she was with. Even then, she'd had a penchant for younger males, according to her daughter. Did it make her a bad person? Not in my book.

"Less of Mrs. V," I said. "What about Mimi? Any improvement?"

"Too early to say, but her heart rate has settled and she seems more comfortable." Georgia paused. "Did Mimi talk to you?"

"Yes."

"And?"

"It's private."

"Was it a confession?"

"No."

"A secret?"

"No."

"Are you telling me to mind my own business?"

"I wouldn't be so rude, but yeah." I hoped my smile translated down the line.

"Think it helped?"

Only if I can trace her brother. The thought of what might lie ahead made me queasy. "I have no idea. I hope so."

Afterwards, I walked home, put a bottle of Macon in the fridge, lit the wood-burner, and cobbled together an omelette with leftovers. The whole time my mind was consumed by Mimi, Mrs. Vellender's chill response, Nicholas Vellender, what if anything I could do to find him, what I'd do if I didn't, how this would impact Mimi. The weight of expectation that she had placed on my shoulders practically bent me double. I strained to think until my brain hissed and spat fire and my head hurt. Desperate for a diversion, I reached for my CD selection. A rock chick at heart, I hadn't been able to listen to anything loud and raucous since Chris's death. Power chords and a dirty bass beat brought back too many happy memories, reminding me of what I'd loved and lost. It took time to tame the obsessional nature of grief, to remember with fond and warm recollection without the pain. I wasn't nearly there yet. Lately, I'd got into classical music and selected a popular piano piece by Schubert.

I cleared away, applied another coat of lipstick and, bang on time, Kyle's charcoal grey Maserati purred into the close. Nobody paid it attention. Cheltenham was the kind of town you'd see Astons and Bentleys parked up, two wheels on the kerb, behind a rusting dust-bucket, Smart car, or the ever popular Fiat 500.

As I opened the front door he turned his good side toward me and beamed. In spite of my mashed-up feelings, I couldn't help but beam back. He leant in and kissed me lightly on the cheek. A waft of expensive cologne, warm and earthy, ghosted around me.

"You're looking good," he said.

"You're looking empty-handed." My bullshit-detector on high alert, I thought the present a ruse to find out where I lived. In a trice, he'd fooled me into allowing him access to my life once more. Like a mug, I'd allowed myself to be hoodwinked.

He laughed, tipping his head back. I didn't tell him that his eyes shone with pleasure, that he looked more rested and confident than the last time we met, that his beautifully cut suit could only look this good on a body like his. Jesus, what was the matter with me? Hadn't I throbbed with that same instinctive desire when introduced to Troy Martell? I thought of Chris once more and ached.

"Hey, why are you looking at me like that?"

"I'm not looking at you like anything."

"Well, are you going to invite me in for a drink or are you leaving me to freeze to death out here?"

I burbled something and stepped aside, pressing my back against the wall as Kyle marched in. "This is very nice, Kim," he said, giving the downstairs a professional once-over. "You've done well for yourself. How much did you pay, if you don't mind my asking?"

"I do mind you asking." I threw him a sweet *mind your own business* smile. There was only one way to treat Kyle and that was to keep him at arm's length. "White wine, or do you fancy red?"

"Whatever you've got open."

He parked himself on the sofa, loosened his tie, spread his feet apart, and basked in the heat from the wood-burner while I poured out two glasses then joined him. To prevent him from assuming too much control—it was my house for goodness' sake—I took the initiative and threw him a question.

"So is the trip to the States a holiday, work, or what?"

"Or what," he said, his tiger-eyes dancing in the firelight.

I hiked an eyebrow and took a sip of wine. Silence had always been my best ally. Stannard was bursting to tell me his news. He wouldn't be able to hold out for long.

"I'm having an operation," he said, still with the smiling eyes.

"Oh," I said, surprised. "Nothing serious, I hope?" I was concerned and, frankly, curious. "You look remarkably pleased and relaxed for someone facing the knife."

"I wouldn't put it quite like that. Let's say I'm hopeful."

That's when I knew. "Your face," I blurted out.

"Yep," he said. "I've found a plastic surgeon prepared to correct the previous botch-up."

"God, are you sure? It's one hell of a risk."

"So is crossing the road."

"But, Kyle—"

"I'm not like you."

"You don't know me," I bridled.

He let out another amused laugh. "That came out all wrong. Your scars are barely noticeable." It was true. A good haircut and clever make-up largely disguised the damage to the left side of my face. "What I meant," Stannard said, for once in his life inelegant, "is that my disfigurement is something I've failed to come to terms with. If there's a small chance of success, I'm willing to take a gamble. Besides, plastic surgery in the States is no big deal."

"It's always a big deal."

"I meant that it's more commonplace."

"Repairing a facial nerve is not common." I probably looked as stern as I sounded.

"Nerve grafting followed by electrical stimulation produces significant improvement."

"Were you warned of the possibility of post anaesthetic psychosis?"

"Posh term for going bonkers," he said, hugely pleased with himself. "Happens in around two percent of cases—not exactly a game-changer."

I was impressed. "You've done your homework."

"Extensively," he assured me. "Might even get my teeth fixed at the same time."

"There's nothing wrong with your teeth."

"It was a joke, Kim. Lighten up."

"It's not exactly a laughing matter." I sounded prissy and hated myself for it. Kyle Stannard always seemed to get me to say things I didn't mean and do things I didn't want to. I took another swallow of wine and said, "You have every confidence in the surgeon?"

"He's a master of reconstruction and, critically, he reckons he can repair the intricate nerve system damaged by the previous butcher. The only good thing to come out of that little episode, the compensation awarded me will fund the operation."

I wondered whether the new wonder surgeon would be able to manage Kyle's ambitious expectations and said something to that effect.

To my surprise, he became utterly serious. "I know I'm not going to look like the man I was before the attack, but I'm hopeful this guy will be able to balance me up a little, so that the damaged side will tally up with the good side." The beautiful side, I thought. "Less Beauty and Beast," he added with the kind of self-deprecation that I admired.

"Then I respect and salute your courage. I genuinely hope it's a massive success for you."

"Strange," he said, fixing me with an uncompromising expression. "I wasn't sure you'd be pleased for me."

"Why ever not?"

"I won't be part of the club any more."

"Bloody hell, Kyle, you really think I'd be that mean-spirited?" I snatched at my drink to conceal my irritation. Some club I was in.

Rather than apologising, he said with uncanny insight, "Shit day?"

Was he clairvoyant or something? "I've hardly been back long enough for it to get going."

"Well, yeah, but after what happened, it must feel strange to be at work again. Tell me, when you were off your trolley, did the shrink get a shrink?"

I frowned. I didn't mind referring to myself as a shrink. I disliked the term when used by others. "If you mean did I have any professional help? The answer is yes." It had felt uncomfortable to be on the receiving end. Up until that point, I'd resigned myself to accepting the hand of cards life had played me and got on with it. It was disturbing to discover that heartbreak was not an isolated episode in my life, that I still mourned the loss of a mother who'd abandoned me when I was little, that an overbearing father had only hardened and roughened my exterior, while the interior part of me remained a jellied mess. My almost chameleon ability to be whatever people wanted me to be had ensured my survival. Despite regular psychological assessments, a requirement for my career, I'd

31

duped the best. Up until that particular devastating moment of truth, that is.

"Should give you more insight into your clients," he said, practical as ever.

Not wishing to get bogged down in my mental health, I changed the mood music and said, "So when do I get my housewarming present?"

He let out a delighted laugh and handed me his glass. "Stay right there. Trust me, it's perfect and you're going to absolutely love it."

I issued a weak smile and hoped neither of us would be disappointed. As he vanished from the room, I thought with a streak of amusement that we were both what could be colloquially described as cracked.

EIGHT

"Dear God," was all I could manage.

"It's perfect, isn't it? Do you like it?"

I gaped. "I can't accept this."

"Why ever not?"

"Because," I stammered, "because it must have cost a small fortune."

"So? What I do with my money is up to me."

"But, Kyle—"

"Don't be so small-minded and parochial."

"I'm really not—"

"Kim, it's something to add to your collection."

I couldn't dispute it. Jack Vettriano's limited edition print of *Beautiful Losers* was probably my most, if not *the* most, valued possession I owned. I didn't give a toss about its monetary value. It was all about the narrative it conveyed. And here was Stannard offering me another painting, another story.

"Do you get it?" he said.

Of course I got it. My eyes devoured the seated woman in the cocktail dress, louche cigarette in one hand, a solitary male standing behind her, lights down low. A strong beam from a projector directed the focus of their gaze, the film with its flickering images out of shot. I wondered what so captivated them—something damning, visual evidence, perhaps, that could undo one or other of them? The footage had a sexual element. For me, *An Imperfect Past* bore all the trademarks of Vettriano's unique style.

"It's fabulous," I admitted. "I love it, but it's way too much."

"Nonsense."

"It's undeserved."

"You're in no position to make that judgement," he said, a steely edge to his voice. "And if you think I'm carting it all the way back to my place, you have to be kidding."

"I don't know what to say."

"*Thank you* would be a start."

I broke into a ragged smile. "I'll borrow it, gladly."

He waggled a finger, giving the strong impression that he would not take no for an answer. I wondered what he'd want in return.

"Well, I…"

"For God's sake, say yes and kiss me."

"Kiss you?"

He placed a finger on his cheek, good side. "Here," he said.

It was probably one of my craziest decisions but I caved in, glanced across his face with my lips and was profuse with my thanks. "I'll treasure it," I added. It was true.

"Good," he said, all business-like. Part of me wondered whether he was disappointed that I hadn't put up more of a fight.

I only topped up his glass. I still had plenty in mine. We chinked in celebration and Kyle settled back into the sofa and gave me a long hard look.

"What?" I said, shifting position.

"So about your shit day." The hint of a mischievous smile tipped up one side of his mouth.

I sipped my drink to play for time. Was Kyle Stannard a magician, too? My expression must have said it all. He laughed again with his firelight eyes and, before I knew it, I'd embarked on edited highlights. Why the hell I opened my mouth to Stannard when I hadn't squeaked one word to Georgia defied me.

"The poor girl," he said when I finished. "Do you think there's any truth in the mother's allegation?"

"A play on words, I'm sure."

"But you think the mother is lying about contact with her son?"

That's what troubled me. I didn't believe Paris Vellender, yet a mother's first instinct is to protect her children. My own mother, admittedly, bucked that trend. Why would Paris cause her daughter so much pain by denying Nicholas Vellender's return?

"If, as you say, her daughter's life is hanging in the balance," Stannard continued, mirroring my thoughts, "why doesn't her mum come clean and give the girl every reason to live? It doesn't make sense."

"Unless she's protecting her son."

"From what?"

I shrugged. Something dangerous or life-threatening, I assumed, although I didn't squeak a word of this to Stannard; he was far too apt to speculate. And there was something else. If someone wants to disappear they can, but paper trails and technological footprints are almost impossible to conceal. We all leave digital debris. Nothing and nobody can remain secret forever. Our twenty-first technological world doesn't allow it. Then, again, if he'd had help, his mother, for example…

"What are the politics of the family set-up?" Stannard said, breaking into my thoughts.

An intelligent question and so typical of the man, I filled him in on the background. "The father was rarely on the scene even when the couple were together."

"Maintaining a Michelin star is a bugger of a job, sixteen-hour days standard."

"Yet it's the mother who's the driving force."

"*Cherchez le femme.*" The fervour in his voice was a clear reference to his own mother. I'd met her once. Olivia Mallory's scream of protest at what she considered my vile attack on her son's reputation would be branded on my brain for a lifetime.

"What's she like?" Stannard asked.

Without naming names, I described Mrs. Vellender in broad terms. "She has a taste for toy boys and drama," I finished.

"My kind of gal," he said with black humour.

I opened my mouth to quip that Stannard's taste was for much younger types and stopped myself in the nick of time. Probably unfair and unkind of me. I said, "The only thing you two have in common is a penchant for cosmetic surgery."

"That's low. Mine's not cosmetic."

"True. Sorry," I said with less grace that he deserved. Truth was, I'd given away too much and felt guilty for it.

He looked thoughtful. "Wouldn't be Paris and Otto Vellender, by any chance?"

"Who?" I got up and headed for the kitchen under the guise of retrieving the wine from the fridge.

"You're a lousy liar, Kim," I heard him call after me.

I choked off a groan, retrieved the bottle, and returned brandishing it like a shield. "Forget what I said."

"Easy for me, not so easy for you," he said with infuriating logic. "What are you going to do about it?"

"Honestly?"

He nodded.

"I don't know. Another top up?"

"Depends."

"On what?"

"Whether I can leave my car here and pick it up tomorrow."

"Okay," I said, thinking, oh my God, he wants to make a night of it.

He smiled, extended his glass, and settled back into the sofa. "Have you talked to the girl's father?"

I shook my head. "It's not that easy. If I go blundering in, all kinds of questions are going to be thrown up into an already highly charged emotional atmosphere. I'd be breaking client confidentiality."

"But she's no longer your client."

He was right, yet it would take a massive degree of subtlety on my part to pull it off without leaving a maelstrom of wreckage behind. "I guess I could try."

"Of course," he said, viewing me over the rim of his glass, "if the girl got it wrong—if she didn't see her brother, and there's any truth in the allegation that the father murdered his son—you could walk into a world of trouble."

Something dark snapped inside. "You think that's likely?"

"All things are possible."

I gave a weak smile of agreement. As usual, Stannard was maddeningly right.

NINE

I GOT UP THE next morning, fragments of the previous evening charging through my mind with the velocity of a runaway train. To be sure I hadn't dreamt it, I shot downstairs to the sitting room to check on Stannard's extravagant gift. The painting stared back at me, as if challenging *my* existence. I briefly wondered where to display it. Until I had a better idea, it would hang in the bedroom.

I ate breakfast, poured myself a glass of water and downed 20mg of Fluoxetine, a drug with which I was already familiar because it was sometimes proscribed for bulimics. Aside from lifting the serotonin levels in my brain, it had a zingy awakening effect. By the time I downed my first and only mid-morning cup of coffee, I'd be flying.

Intending to get to work early, I set off. It was one of those inert days when the weather, damp and grey-faced, looks as if it's got a hangover and the sun, in sympathy, refuses to crawl out of bed. Determined it wouldn't stall my mood, I told myself that my job was what I got paid for, that work was knowable and quantifiable, that I was pretty damn good at it. Every time the Vellender problem popped into my head, I swatted it. Nothing you can do till later, maybe in your lunch break, I told myself, intending to pop around to the restaurant and seek an audience with Otto Vellender, a man I'd never met.

"Hey," I heard from the other side of the street.

I glanced across and spotted Troy Martell jogging on the spot, eyeing the traffic. He waved a raised hand that clutched a plastic bottle of water. Seconds later, he dodged between two cars. His chest, pressed into a white T-shirt, looked even wider than it had the day before. Running shorts revealed tanned legs, the muscles in his meaty thighs rippling with oil or sweat or both. It felt as if the street had filled up with neat testosterone.

"Hello," I said. "You look hot." As soon as the words left my mouth, I wanted to grab them back. As a conversation opener, at best it was bereft of originality; at worst, easily misconstrued.

"Not nearly hot enough," he said, failing to spot my verbal gaffe. Before I sank any deeper with *do you run here often?* Troy said what he'd come to say and nearly punched the air out of me.

"For what it's worth, Paris is lying."

"That's a strong statement."

"For a heavy situation."

"Why are you telling me?"

"For Mimi." Perhaps it was my suspicious mind, but I had the odd instinct that Troy Martell cared more for Mimi than he did for the woman with whom he slept. Troubling.

"Where's your proof?"

An explosion of car horns blasted his words across the road and into the next street. I caught the last bit: "… she wasn't mad or losing it, is all."

It wasn't what I'd call compelling evidence. I glanced at my watch. My early start sabotaged, I suggested we find somewhere to grab a coffee.

"Can't," he said, dancing from one foot to the other. "On my way to train a personal client."

I took out my phone. "Give me your mobile number. Can we meet later?"

Troy gave a furtive look both sides of the pavement, as if he expected Paris Vellender to materialise from behind a tree. "Paris has an aerobics class at one. I could get away then."

"That would work for me." We exchanged contacts. My visit to the restaurant could go on hold.

"It will have to be somewhere out of the way, where we won't be seen."

Had Paris Vellender's theatrical side brushed off on her lover, or did Troy Martell also have something to hide? I looked up into his eyes but couldn't read him. Disorientated, I complied and suggested that we met in a less affluent part of town. I didn't think a café serving all day breakfasts would be Paris Vellender's favourite haunt. I had her down for an egg white–only omelette, and lactose-free soya milk type of diner.

Troy agreed, jinked sideways, and jogged off back towards town. I, meanwhile, headed into work and saw my first client in several months, a bright seventeen-year-old in danger of flunking her A levels. Before her admission, she'd lost thirty-five pounds from her nine stone five-seven frame and existed on 300 calories a day for the past three months in spite of putting herself on a punishing exercise schedule. Her name was Eleanor, or Ellie, as she preferred. On a first meeting clients can often be defensive and hostile, but Ellie was neither. Straightaway, I had every hope that I could get her through this difficult stretch in her life. I fleetingly wondered whether Jim and Cathy, the practice manager, had engineered my safe and easy passage back into the world of work by putting softly smiling Ellie at the top of my list.

My next client was similarly well disposed to treatment. I'd finished the session when my phone rang. It was Georgia. I recognised in an instant that something was wrong from the sound of her voice, which was thick and nasal, as if she'd been crying.

"Mimi died half an hour ago."

I did the mental equivalent of screeching to a halt. "What? How?"

"Heart attack."

"But you said she was stable, that her heart rate had settled."

"That was last night."

What occurred this morning? "Did something happen?"

"What do you mean?"

"Something upset her?"

"Like what?"

"I don't know," I bluffed, "a wrong word, a ..."

"Things like this crop up, Kim. You know they do."

Well, yes, but this was different, I wanted to say. Circumstances made it unusual. "Did anyone visit her?"

"Only the doctors, why?"

"Are you sure?"

"Yes, I think so."

Think? "Did her mother visit?"

"Kim, what the hell are you driving at?"

Questions. Mine. Had I stirred the bottom of a dank and muddy pool? Had my enquiry about Paris Vellender's son the previous afternoon set off a train of events? Had Paris Vellender followed it up and spoken to Mimi? I lowered my voice and denied driving at anything.

"Is this connected to what Mimi told you?" Georgia didn't sound like Georgia. Her voice was nervy. It rattled with alarm.

"Of course not, I'm simply trying to get it straight in my head." Thank goodness I was on the other end of a phone line and not on Skype. If Georgia could have seen my face, she would have spotted the visual sidestep. "It's such a shock, like it came out of nowhere."

"There's nothing to understand." She was tense and terse. "You know how these things can pan out. There was too much strain on the girl's heart. It could have happened at any time."

But it didn't and Georgia couldn't be sure that Mrs. Vellender hadn't visited that morning. I wondered whether Troy Martell was better informed.

TEN

THE TEXT FROM TROY Martell came through twenty minutes later. Unsurprisingly, our meeting was off.

Jim caught me as I nipped to the loo in between clients. "I heard the news, Kim. I'm sorry. Are you holding up?"

"There are days when I absolutely detest this job."

He looked at me with kind eyes, and rested a hand lightly on my shoulder. "We all do."

As soon as I was behind the safety of a locked door, I bawled my eyes out—for Mimi, for the waste of a young life that had barely got cracking and had ended in decrepitude. I also cried a little bit for myself and wasn't proud of it. Tempted to increase my dosage of pills— I could take up to 60mg although not desirable—I resisted and urged myself to calm down. Splashing my eyes with cold water, I patted them dry and repaired my face with the special make-up I used to conceal the scarring. Then, fortified with coffee, I worked through the rest of the morning, lost myself in it, too numbed to string together any coherent thoughts about Mimi. Five minutes before the end of my last session with Imogen, a girl with dead white skin, a history of self-harm, and who had uttered three *fuck you* sentences in almost an hour, Cathy tapped on my door and popped her head round.

"Someone to see you." Spirits lifted, I thought of Troy Martell. Then, with apprehension, Stannard.

"Who?"

"She wouldn't say."

I said, "Wouldn't?" I thought *she?*

"It's supposed to be a surprise, I think."

My stomach snagged at the thought of Mrs. Vellender. No, foolish, it couldn't be. "But I'm not expecting anyone."

Cathy rolled her eyes. "That's *why* it's a surprise."

"Young, old?" As Imogen was disinclined to utter another syllable, I saw nothing wrong in using up the last five minutes. It would be a relief to both of us and maybe my client would follow my example, even catch on to the subtle art of conversation.

"Hard to say," Cathy replied, "possibly in her sixties."

Oh no. Olivia Mallory, Kyle Stannard's possessive mother. Had to be.

"Sorry, Cathy, I don't want to put you in an awkward position but, unless this woman gives a name, I'm not seeing anyone." And I was most definitely not doing battle with Mrs. Mallory.

"I quite understand," Cathy said. "It's been a sad morning for all of us."

The saddest, I thought.

"Leave it with me," Cathy said.

And I knew I could. Cathy Whitcombe's mild and charming manner disguised a will of cold rolled steel. As fiercely protective of staff as she was of residents, if Cathy couldn't sort out my unnamed visitor, nobody could.

I turned back to my client and forced a bright smile. "I appear to have done all the talking." Which wasn't strictly true. Most of the hour had been spent in silences I couldn't read. "You said you wanted to work on overcoming the urge to binge. Have I got that right?"

Imogen dropped her gaze and took an avid interest in the carpet.

"Good," I said, stilted, "we've made progress. I'll see you next session and we can talk some more."

She nodded furiously, eager to bolt.

"In the meantime, jot down any notes in your record book about how you're feeling, your mood, and attitude to your body, particularly when you want to purge. Can you do that for me?"

Imogen issued a fake smile. Contained and clutching her secrets tightly inside, she scarpered. I updated my records on the computer and tidied my desk. Cathy returned, only this time she closed the door behind her.

My eyes met her troubled gaze. "What is it?"

"The woman outside in Reception."

"Yeah?"

"Her name is Monica Slade."

As if tectonic plates had shifted beneath my feet, revealing a death-defying plunge into a sinkhole, I all but gasped. Giddy, I peered at Cathy. "No, that can't be right."

"Kim," Cathy said, with finality. "She's definitely your mother."

ELEVEN

"SHE ONLY SAYS SHE is. It means nothing." I was flushed and furious.

"Well, I have to say, you look like her."

I remembered. Same nose, same mouth and similar shade of brown eyes. No scars.

"Do you want five minutes?" Cathy said with concern. "You've gone quite pale."

And my scars itched like crazy. I ran my fingers through my hair.

A couple of decades ago, I'd have killed for this moment. I'd waited so long for it, prayed she'd come back to me, to us. My one anxious, tentative attempt to make contact had ended in disaster in a tearoom in Exeter when I was fifteen. She hadn't wanted to see me then so why now? A few reasons sprang to mind. She was sick, broke, or in trouble. Did it soften my rage? Did it help? She'd abandoned our family for over thirty years.

Cathy poured a glass of water and handed it to me. "Drink this. Calm down and let me know what you want to do." She made to go.

I took a tentative sip and called her back. "It's all right. I need to get this over with."

"Are you absolutely certain? I can fob her off. Perhaps you could meet later?"

"No," I exploded. "Sorry," I said, flashing a fragile smile of apology. It wasn't poor Cathy's fault. "I'd like to do it now." It won't take long, I thought. "Send her in."

I was fiddling with the contents of a box file when a straight-backed woman with a retired ballerina's gait walked into my office. I glanced towards her, took a long hard look, checked it was really my mother—yes, no doubt about it—and with great deliberation pushed a stack of papers into a pile. Her coat was good quality, probably expensive, as were her knee-length boots, which were black with a pointed toe and cute heel. A racy tiger-print snood indicated that she was a woman who cared about fashion. This was my first impression. I was so disconnected from what was happening I was like a huge surveillance camera positioned on the ceiling, roving through the eye of a lens from above. I wasn't really in the room with her at all. Surreal.

My mother had filled out in the intervening years, the hard edges vanishing from both her body and face. She wore little make-up, enough to make a difference and enhance her wide forehead, straight nose, turned up a little at the tip, and generous mouth. Her hair, once as blonde as mine, was flecked with grey at the hairline, the remnants of a tint growing out. Overall, she looked less careworn than the last time we met, as if life had treated her better than it had me. As she walked towards me with a tender, shy smile on her face, her arms outstretched, I found myself longing to become a ghost and walk through the nearest wall. I slid around to her side of the desk and stood stiff as a piece of hardboard, sharp elbows tucked in

47

and pressed to my side, while she kissed me on each cheek. She smelt of good-quality soap and light cologne.

"What a lovely place to work," she said. "I'd no idea."

Now I had proof that she was no impostor. Her voice, so different to my father's Devonian accent, was cultured, melodic, and memorable. I'd been staggered by it the last time we met.

"Take a seat," I said, distant and formal. She did and I retreated to my big power chair. The leather complained as I sat down. It was very shrink and client, no hint of mother and daughter. She smoothed down the creases in her warm woollen coat and, tugging at the fingers of her soft leather gloves, one by one, took them off and rested them on her lap. It was a studied gesture and I suspected that she had rehearsed the moment many times. She must have wondered how I'd react. Did she expect a fanfare? All is forgiven? A *how wonderful we can pick up the shattered pieces of our relationship and become mother and daughter once more?* Was she about to reveal that she was sorry she missed out on my childhood, my growing years and transition from child to woman with all the messy emotional steps in between? Whatever my mother had predicted, my silence floored her. She was nervous and I did nothing to put her at ease mainly because I was struggling to breathe. Someone had done the equivalent of thrusting me into a dark, airless vault, slamming the door shut and turning the key. Abandoned. Lost. Forever.

"I expect you're wondering why I'm here," she said in the crawling silence.

The thought had more than crossed my mind. "How did you trace me?"

"Easily, Kim."

I frowned in incomprehension.

She smiled. "I never really went away."

"Forgive me if I beg to differ." My own smile was glacial.

The light faded from her eyes. "Yes, of course, I see that."

I nodded with more neutrality than I thought myself capable of.

"It's difficult to know where to start."

"How about with missing Guy's funeral?" It was a calculated low blow and it had the desired effect. She gasped. The soft features of her face cracked into crevasses of pain. Her hands clenched.

"I watched from a distance."

"Really?" My voice was cold, hard, and flat.

"'I waited in the graveyard."

"Why? You could have come inside."

"Kim, I wasn't welcome. Your father made it perfectly clear."

"I don't believe you."

"There's a lot you won't believe, but it's true. Can't you imagine how I felt to lose my son? No parent should lose a child. It's not part of the natural order."

I didn't know what to say. On an intellectual level, I could imagine a mother's pain, but not *this* mother's. "It must have been extremely difficult for you." I only said it because I wanted to give the impression that I wasn't devoid of empathy or kindness.

"It rated as one of the saddest days of my life."

I nodded my agreement once more. There seemed to have been rather too many of those. "Why are you here?"

"There are certain things you should know."

"What things?"

"About the past."

I had enough past with which to deal. The present was all that mattered to me now. "Why didn't you tell me these *things* when we last met?"

"Because I couldn't."

"Couldn't?"

"It wasn't appropriate."

I had to hand it to her. She was a mistress of meaningless one-liners. "I was fifteen. I came to you. I needed you." Emotion leaked into my voice despite my best efforts to contain it.

"Your father had custody."

I knew this. How could a mother sign away her kids? There were some mothers who discovered, too late, that they didn't have a maternal bone in their bodies; some who selflessly, in the best interests of their children, gave them to others who would love them in a way they knew they never could. But this was *my* damned mother. She'd had two boys for over ten years and then me. "And your point?"

She flushed and swallowed. Intolerant, I didn't help her out. "He wasn't master of your thoughts and actions," I said. "He didn't hold us captive with ball and chain. You could have visited, taken an interest. You—"

"It wasn't that simple." Her hands, peppered with liver spots, twisted in her lap. Flushed with emotion, I was merciless.

"Remember the café in Exeter? You had an opportunity to talk to me and you passed on it. In fact, you treated me with stunning indifference." And that was the bit that had really hurt.

"Kim," she said, "it wasn't as straightforward as you make out."

I was tempted to say *enlighten me*, but I was no longer interested in her defence. I specialised in complexity, yet, for me, my mother's behaviour was simple. "The truth is you didn't want to know."

"Kim, I—"

"You commiserated about my scars, as if I had an incurable disease, thrust ten quid into my hand, and cleared off."

"I know how it seemed," she said, flustered now. A nervous tic tugged at the corner of her right eyelid. "But it was important that you didn't become emotionally attached."

"So you thought that, by being cruel, you'd be kind?" My voice was one big jeer.

"I did it to protect you. Your father would never—"

"Let's leave him out of it, shall we? He's been dead for several years." I felt venomous towards her. "You had a choice and you took it. I have no idea what you're doing here now. I suspect it's because you're in some kind of trouble." She paled and I pounced. "Does Luke know?"

She lowered her eyes, bit her bottom lip, and shook her head. Maybe she thought I'd be more vulnerable and pliant than my brother. Well screw that. "I don't see that we have anything to discuss, either now or in the future."

I thought she'd get up and leave. She stayed put, raised her head, and met and held my gaze. Silence cast a long shadow over the room, sucking out all the light. I read all kinds of emotions in her face, but the one most evident was desperation. It was present in her eyes, which were wide and shiny and fragile. I didn't want it to, but it hit home. It made me see her as less of an enemy and view her as a human being in genuine distress.

"You're right to feel as you do," she said, slow and guarded. "I robbed you of your childhood. What you went through must have been confusing, bewildering, and painful, unimaginably so," she added, her voice scorched with guilt. "But I wanted you to know that I'm truly sorry for all the pain I've caused. A day has never passed without my thinking of and missing you. I so wish things could have been different, but I had my reasons. I'd like to explain, if you'll let me."

51

I wanted to close my eyes and make her disappear. I wanted it all to go away and leave me in peace. I wanted to smoke again, cadge a cigarette from a stranger, better still to roll my own, light up, puff away, and lose myself. "Monica," I said, weary now, and wholly unable to call her Mum, "how can you explain away half a lifetime?"

"Won't you give me that chance?"

I stayed silent. Why should I give this mad prophet houseroom? We stayed looking at each other for I don't know how long. Here was my flesh and blood, my only connection to her biological and tribal. And yet how could I reject it? It must have taken balls to come to me, I realised then. Was there a chance I'd misread the situation? Had I got her wrong? I wasn't exactly doing a U-turn, but I've never been good with finality, or black and white. When it comes to the spectrum of human behaviour there are so many subtle shades of grey. To her credit, my mother did not exploit my weakness. She didn't appeal to my curiosity, my need for closure or anything else. She took my failure to speak as a negative.

"If not, I accept what you say and I'll never trouble you again." Resigned, she put on her gloves and, shoulders bowed, stood up. Fishing a card from her handbag, she placed it flat down on the desk and, fingers splayed, pushed it across. "I'm staying here for the rest of the week. If you change your mind, you know where to find me."

I think she would have liked to give me a hug, but didn't know how to go about it. She shifted her weight uneasily from one foot to the other, looked at me one last time, as though memorising every feature on my face in detail in exactly the same way Chris had done the very last time I saw him. As I watched her leave I had a huge undignified and instinctive urge to tell her to wait, but I said nothing. The door closed after her. For the second time that morning I broke down in tears.

TWELVE

I phoned Luke in New York at his office in East 42nd Street. A newly appointed partner in a firm of accountants, he would have been at his desk long before my 8:00 a.m. US time call. I came straight to the point. Astonishment didn't really cover his reaction. My brother rarely swears but he did this time. After a run of expletives, he calmed down enough to ask questions.

"Did she give any prior indication that she was in town?"

"None—turned up out of the blue."

"Well, I'll be damned. Why now?"

"Search me. To be honest, I didn't give her much of an audience."

"Any ideas what she came to say?"

"To plead her case and put the record straight, according to Monica Slade, that is."

Luke said nothing. He was probably in shock. My mother's prolonged absence in our life wasn't a subject with which we were comfortable. There had been an unspoken message at home: we don't talk about her. The person who should have been the cornerstone of our family became the ultimate taboo and my father's legacy was the familial equivalent of Omerta.

"She inferred that Dad was the problem," I said. "That he blocked access."

My brother still didn't speak. It made me uneasy. "Luke, is there something you're not telling me?" Older than me by over a decade, there had only been two years between him and my other brother, Guy. At thirty-six years of age, I was still the baby of the family and, it seemed in the threatening silence, still young enough to be kept in the dark. I had a sudden moment of misgiving.

"Luke?" I said, appealing to him, my mouth very dry.

He let out a huge sigh. Miles of Atlantic Ocean between us did not prevent me from cottoning on to my brother's inner struggle, which of itself was unusual. Luke didn't do regret or waste energy or emotion. A numbers guy, his mind was Cartesian. If you do this you get that. "You were way too young to notice," he said, "but there were a lot of rows back then."

"Not uncommon in warring couples destined to divorce."

"I think she sometimes had a raw deal."

I flinched. "What do you mean exactly?" And why didn't you say so before?

"Kim, it's ancient history."

"It's our past," I insisted and instantly felt panicked that I hadn't cut our mother any slack on the subject. Instead, I'd wanted to stay in the present, dwell in the moment, and run away from something that might challenge my simplistic worldview. "Come on, Luke, spit it out."

"Dad would often have too much to drink."

I almost laughed. "Don't be soft. He only started drinking after she left."

"Who told you that?"

Blood belted through my brain and found a connection to my heart. "Dad," I spluttered.

"Not true," Luke said.

I gulped in disbelief. Surely not, surely... I dropped my voice. "Luke, did he abuse her? I mean did he hit her?"

"God, no, but you know what he was like."

I did. My father could be cruel. A believer in reverse psychology, something that might have worked on the boys but never on me, he could fell with one look, shrivel your soul with a few select words. I lost count of the times I tried to be good enough, to please, to be part of the gang, but often I was *never bloody good enough*, quote unquote. I'd clashed with my father on everything, from sweating the small stuff to big picture, creed, race, colour, and the corrosive and corrupting power of money. He thought me a bleeding heart liberal, but excused my febrile nature because I couldn't help being female. I thought him more right wing than a dyed in the wool fascist. Over the years I'd cut him slack. He was a man alone with two sons and a young daughter. Out of his depth, he did his best. Hurt, he couldn't help being emotionally distant. It didn't quite square with the other junk—the numerous random women in his life and in his bed—but even that I'd rationalised. He couldn't be expected to live like a monk. Why should he? If there was a degree of domestic carnage, it was my mother's fault for leaving. I was so busy playing the blame game, I almost missed Luke's next question.

"What are you going to do?"

Moments ago I would have said, "Nothing." Now I wasn't certain. In less than a minute, Luke had overturned one small deeply held belief. Were there others to be dismantled? Was my faith in my past about to be challenged and tested? "She's in town for the next few days."

"Are you going to see her?"

"I hadn't planned to."

"She isn't getting any younger."

Yes, and I knew from bitter experience that most regrets in life are as a result of *not* doing things rather than from doing them. "Do you think I should?"

"That's not for me to say."

Classic Luke: always measured.

"I don't want to meet her at home," I weakened.

"Best you find somewhere neutral."

He was right, of course, but I wanted somewhere I could let off steam. I didn't care for being silenced because of the strictures of sitting in a public place. "If I make contact," I said tentatively, "do you want me to pass on a message?"

Luke didn't hesitate. "Tell her to get in touch. Tell her I'd be glad."

THIRTEEN

FEELING AS IF I were drifting through cobwebs, I returned home after work and found Stannard's Maserati sleek and poised outside the door. It hadn't moved an inch since the previous evening. Key in the lock, and about to scuttle inside, I started as Kyle shot around the corner bearing a bottle of wine. I wondered whether he'd been skulking in the shadows awaiting my return. Paranoid me.

"Pleased I caught you," he said. "I really didn't want to go without saying goodbye properly."

"I thought we did goodbye last night." He'd even jotted down the name and number of the clinic.

He affected a perplexed demeanour. "Did we? Well, anyway, I wondered how you got on with your little problem."

Which one? Neither seemed little to me. "I didn't."

"Why ever not?"

Concerned about being overheard, I glanced both ways, peered into the shadows, and walked inside. "Come in for a moment."

I flicked on all the lights, went through to the sitting room and told Stannard what had happened. This time, I didn't disguise Mimi's identity. No point. I didn't mention a single word about Monica.

"Christ! To have one child go missing is bad; to lose another is terrible. Does this sort of thing usually happen in your line of work? I mean, do kids die?"

"Fortunately, not as often as you might expect."

He thought for a moment and turned as if to go. I stayed where I was, watched the good side of his face in profile. He had impossibly long eyelashes for a man, straight small nose, razor-sharp cheekbones, and a solid squared-off jawline. He turned back and, from the way he brandished the booze, I knew what Stannard had in mind.

"Kyle, I've had a pig of a day and I'm tired. Haven't you got packing to do?"

"All done," he said, marching through to the kitchen and rifling through a drawer, presumably rooting around for a corkscrew.

Next, I heard an enormous pop and the sound of running water. Dammit, he was rinsing the glasses we'd used the night before. I opened my mouth in protest. Stannard with his nimble brain and agile spirit was too quick for me. "You've only been back in action a day or so," he said, pushing a glass of white wine into my hand, "and someone is dead."

I snatched at my drink, a perfectly chilled Bourgogne, hints of vanilla and toffee, classy. Must have cost Stannard at least thirty quid. I might as well have been swigging cement. "You make it sound as if she were murdered, or as if something dodgy is going on."

He issued one of his incisive looks, all the more penetrating when he revealed the damaged side of his face. "But isn't that what you really believe?"

I stared at him, dazed. "Absolutely not."

"Why don't you take off your coat?" he said.

Stannard had a habit of inducing amnesia in me. This was my sitting room and I felt as if I were a guest in his. Exasperated, I put down my glass and did as he asked.

"You said you spoke to Paris Vellender yesterday." He sounded like a barrister for the prosecution. I blamed it on the fact that his stepfather was a QC. "Do you think Paris argued with Mimi about your conversation?"

That's what really bothered me. Had I initiated a terrible chain of events by openly enquiring about Nicholas? My blood didn't run cold. It froze rock solid. "Why would she do that?"

"To shut her up, warn her off."

"It's too far-fetched." Uninvited, my mind flashed back to Troy Martell. What was so important that it was worth hijacking me on my way to work? "Anyway, according to the doctor in charge," I continued, "Mimi was more comfortable in the evening, heart rate settled. Her mother didn't visit this morning so Mimi wasn't especially stressed."

Stannard took a long deep swallow and appeared to consider and accept my explanation. "Rather good, isn't it?" he said, then changing tone, "When do most heart attacks take place?"

"You have the same stubborn nature as a dung beetle."

"Not like you to go all Kafkaesque on me."

Kyle had no idea just how Kafkaesque, as he put it, my life had become.

"Well?" he said.

Ignoring his jibe, I clenched a smile. "There are exceptions, but most occur during the morning, sometimes during the latter part of sleep. Satisfied? And can we talk about something else?"

We did. The property market mostly. Reluctantly, Stannard got my *I don't want to talk about this any more* message and, after an hour of me steering the conversation through a sea of trivia, I told him that I needed to eat and he needed to go.

"This is it then," he said, hovering in the hallway, his coat slung over his arm. I thought he seemed nervous, which, given the prospect of a life-changing operation, wasn't unusual, but it wasn't that.

"It is," I said, meeting his gaze. We were in a confined space. I could feel heat from his body and from his mind. "Good luck, Kyle. I hope the op is a brilliant success."

He leant towards me, chest to chest, crooked a knuckle under my chin, tipped up my face, and planted a single soft kiss on my lips. Against my will, I felt a small shiver of pleasure. "Take care, Kim," he said. "Stay safe." Then he was gone.

With the door closed behind me, the sound of the Maserati's purr in my ears, I broke out in a cold sweat. Kyle's gesture mirrored perfectly Troy Martell's with Paris Vellender. The only difference: Stannard and I were not lovers. Never could be.

FOURTEEN

Sleep was fine until around three thirty a.m. After that my mind jolted into action. Random, scary thoughts careered at a hundred miles an hour through the motorway of my mind and refused to slow down. I remembered my dad shouting, the time the boys had remonstrated with him not to send me away. Me cowering in the downstairs loo, cheeks shiny, red hot with crying, ear pressed to the door. *Please, please, listen. Please let me stay at home with you and the horses and my friends.*

I punched the pillow, turned it over, pressed my burning skin against the cool weave, tossed from one side of the bed to the other, feeling cold then hot then ...

I gave in, got up, and stamped downstairs. Simply because I'd implied to Luke that I'd see our mother didn't mean I would.

With no early recollections, my memories of her were scavenged from others. Loose snatches of overheard conversation were hardly enough to form an accurate picture of the woman who had carried me for nine months, given birth, and then handed me over, a toddler, to an older dad ill-equipped for the business of rearing a child, let alone a daughter. I possessed no photographs with which to remember her by and few mementoes unless one included a beach towel and a butter dish, both rescued from destruction. It was easy to see how I'd cast her in the role of villain. All the evidence pointed in that direction. We never received gifts, communications, or any indication that she cared. *Indifference* was her watchword, yet I knew enough about people to understand that they do not fall into neat, easily labelled boxes even when those boxes turn up years later packaged in glossy wrapping paper, tied up with a bow of satin ribbon.

Still uncertain how to respond to her sudden entrance into my life, I put on the kettle and parked the dilemma with my mother only to be confronted by another: Mimi's dying wish.

In theory, I was off the hook. I could forget the whole thing. I had enough with which to deal. Any thought of foul play, as Stannard suggested, was plain ridiculous. Besides, what could I do? I was hardly going to approach two grieving parents and stir up a shitstorm of trouble in the middle of funeral arrangements. Bang on cue, my mind took a balletic leap and flipped straight back to my mother. *I waited in the graveyard.* Would Nicholas Vellender, if he were alive, do the same? Would he watch from afar, too afraid to show himself, but unafraid to creep up close and hang around in the shadows? If he didn't show, was it proof that he was no longer alive?

Firing up my laptop, I scoured the Internet for newspaper reports following Nicholas Vellender's disappearance five years earlier. A picture of him appeared instantly. The similarity between brother and sister was striking—almost Mediterranean looks, strong brown eyes that looked as if they could stare right through a person, straight symmetrical features, pointed chin, and intense expression.

Nicholas had the whisper of a moustache that sat passively underneath his nose. But there was nothing halfhearted about his stance. He brimmed with teenage arrogance and invincibility. I could well imagine him clashing with his father, a man I'd never met but heard plenty about. Sons on the brink of manhood had locked horns with their dads since time began. With a shudder, I recalled my brothers arguing with my father about some woman he'd taken up with. Once or twice, it had descended into thrown punches and flying fists, always raised voices. I wondered what had transpired between Otto and Nicholas, how things had got so bad between them that Paris felt the need to step in. Or was I way off beam, was there something more sinister going on?

Newspaper articles followed a traditional and well-trodden route, each headline escalating the degree of concern: HAVE YOU SEEN THIS TEENAGER? POLICE BECOME INCREASINGLY CONCERNED FOR THE WELFARE OF ... POLICE LAUNCH A FULL INVESTIGATION INTO THE DISAPPEARANCE OF ... Right until the last: HOPES FADE. But no body was ever found.

Nicholas would be roughly twenty-two or -three now and a man can change a lot in those intervening years, particularly if he's been sleeping rough or getting into things he shouldn't.

If he were alive.

I scanned his photograph and printed it out. Feeling flat, I padded back to bed with a cup of tea, drank it in the darkness and finally fell into a deep sleep unimpeded by dreams or nightmares or ghosts from my past. By the time I'd showered, dressed, breakfasted, and taken my medication that morning, the problems of the last couple of days hadn't bottomed out but receded. I had both clarity and focus. As I stepped out into the chill morning light, I even spared a thought for Kyle driving to Heathrow to catch his flight to the States. Roughly twenty-four hours from now, he'd be under the knife. I gave a small involuntary shiver. Rather him than me.

Reaching work and before I changed my mind, I phoned The Battledown in Hales Road, the guesthouse in which Monica was staying. Despite calling right in the middle of breakfast service, the woman's voice on the other end was relaxed, upbeat, and friendly.

"You have a guest staying with you, Monica Slade," I said.

"Yes, she's in the dining room at the moment."

"Is it possible for me to speak to her briefly? I won't take up much time."

"Not a problem. Who should I say is calling?"

I hesitated. Factually true, *her daughter* sounded false and too intimate. "Can you tell her that Kim is on the line, please? She'll know who it is."

My heart drummed a tattoo against my ribs. What was I going to say? *I think we should meet. I'd like to drop round because I'm angry/confused/curious. I've been thinking about what you said and I've decided to give it a miss.*

"Hello, Kim." Tentative. Wary. Wondering which way the conversation would play.

"Oh, hello, the thing is can I come and see you?"

"Of course you can." Her voice tripped with pleasure.

"Would after work suit, say around six o' clock?"

"We could meet in the lounge here. It's quite private and I'm sure the owners won't mind. They're absolutely lovely. Nothing's too much trouble. Would that be all right?"

"Perfect," I said, wondering why I sounded so effusive.

I ploughed through my morning sessions. With a few minutes to spare before heading out for lunch, I called Georgia. "Are you free?"

"Terrific timing as it happens. Meet at Moran's?"

"Great and, to save time, could you order the usual?" Working at the hospital, Georgia always beat me to it.

"See you in ten."

As I guessed, Georgia had already snaffled a table for two at Moran's in the Bath Road. Dark and cosy, with a log fire, the bar resembled a smugglers inn on the Helford River. Our table was tucked away next to a window that overlooked a small yard of tables and chairs facing the road. A few hardy smokers sat outside with their drinks and smokes, their breath making circles in the freezing air.

I shrugged off my coat and sat down.

"You look tired," Georgia said. Did I? "Are you overdoing it?"

I wasn't sure what she meant by *it*. "No."

Georgia's eyes fixed on mine and narrowed. "Has something happened?"

I stifled a smile. I'd arranged to have lunch for a reason—to fish. I very much got the impression that Georgia was doing the same. My best response was to give her what she wanted, but not in the way she wanted it.

"My mother came to my office yesterday."

"Bloody hell."

That shut her up. Our food and drinks arrived, buying me more precious time. I tore off a piece of pitta and dunked it into a pot of spicy tuna pate.

"How long since you last saw her?" Georgia fell on a jaw-defying chicken and avocado stuffed ciabatta.

"Twenty-one years."

Her eyes popped. Another enormous mouthful of food prevented further comment. While she chewed with gusto, I gave forensically edited highlights.

"So you're going to see her?" she said, breaking off to drink.

"This evening."

"Very wise," she said, munching thoughtfully. "Without understanding the past, it's impossible to jettison and embrace the present, let alone look forward to the future."

"God's sake, Georgia, you're not in the consulting room now." Privately, I wasn't certain that the talking cure worked in all cases. Sometimes, unearthing secrets and flushing them out into the open could be so destructive it was better to leave things buried.

"Sorry," she said, taking another bite. "God, I'm ravenous."

I flashed a grin. "I'd never have guessed."

"I'm on the 5:2 diet, you know two days of restricted calorie intake and—"

"Then five days of chocs away," I butted in. "Hope you don't tell your clients you're on 500 calories two days a week."

"As if."

There is no easy way to ask when a date for a funeral is set, so I simply came out with it.

"Tuesday week." Georgia met my eye line a bit nervously, I thought. "One o'clock at South Chapel, Bouncers Lane."

"Are you going?" I said.

"Yes. You?"

"Not really appropriate."

"No. Best not."

Did I detect a note of relief? She glanced away. "What's up, Georgia?"

"Nothing." She attempted a smile but it died.

"I'm a shrink, too, remember?"

She made a strange frustrated noise, part way between a growl and a curse, and ran her fingers through her dark hair. Thick and wiry, it stuck up in tufts. Now was not the time to tell her that she looked as if she were having a bad hair day.

She leant towards me, eyes locking onto mine. "Okay. But you are not, I repeat *not*, to get the wrong end of this and run with it."

I placed both hands against my chest in *a cross my heart and hope to die* gesture.

"Promise?"

"Sure." Which, to my ears, was not the same as swearing on oath.

"You asked me whether Mimi's mother had visited the morning she died."

I started forward.

"See, I knew you'd get worked up."

"I am not worked up." I strained every sinew in an effort to mute all my physical responses.

"Right," Georgia said, stern as hell. I imagined this was the tone she used when catching one of her kids in a lie. "Remember, I told you that Paris Vellender hadn't visited, well, I was right. Except…"

Others might be tempted to dive in but part of my job was to inhabit the silences. If you wait long enough, most people gab.

"Except," she spluttered, "Otto Vellender, Mimi's father, visited an hour before she died. I'm only telling you," Georgia raced on, "because I didn't want it leaking out and you getting any weird ideas."

… my father killed him… "I understand," I said. "Nothing unusual about a father visiting his sick child."

"Quite." All dutiful, and done and dusted.

I watched as she reached for her coffee and drank. She swallowed it as if it were neat whisky.

"And?" Now I'd hooked on I wasn't letting go. I needed to reel her in.

She took another long swallow. This time she refused to meet my gaze. Georgia glanced to her right, as if checking to see if anyone at the counter could hear. She dropped her voice a semitone.

"I'm told there was some kind of dispute."

"A row?"

"Possibly overstating it," Georgia said. Shifty, I thought.

"Do you know what it was about?"

She shrugged her broad shoulders.

"Does it bother you?" My voice was even. I could afford to be calm and in control, mainly because I was. I was the one with the information, not Georgia.

"Should it?"

"It might explain why Mimi had a heart attack. Shouldn't the coroner be informed?"

"Informed of what exactly? Jesus, I knew this was a bad idea. I'll get the bill, my shout," she said, casting around.

"Hold up," I said, pushing my plate away. "Look, I take your point."

"Mimi's underlying condition was the cause of her death, not a row," Georgia said with slow deliberation.

A lot of people have arguments or differences of opinion with loved ones before they die. A hard knot formed in the pit of my stomach at the memory of the horrible period preceding Chris's death. I nodded in acquiescence.

"Good," she glowered.

"I'm sorry," I said. "Got a lot on, what with my mother and everything."

Georgia's expression softened. I think she felt sorry for me, which was something I found detestable, but I smiled, played the game. We gathered up our things and Georgia went to settle the bill. Me? I was virtually hopping from one foot to the other to escape.

"Kim?" she said, as we bowled out onto the pavement together and walked back down the road.

"Mmm?"

"What did Mimi say exactly?"

I gave her a slow, sideways glance. "Nothing important, nothing to concern you."

FIFTEEN

I PARKED IN THE Battledown car park, stepped out into the chill night, and walked back around to the front of the spot-lit building, a handsome, classy double-fronted villa, French Colonial style, with a glossy black front door and portico. A wide flight of stone steps led up to the entrance.

I rang the bell. Almost immediately the door swung open and a woman my age greeted me. Her warm smile and friendly manner marked her out as the same person who'd answered the phone that morning even before she'd uttered a word.

"Hi," she said, "my name's Sarah. You must be Kim. Your mother's waiting for you in the lounge."

I gave a clumsy smile, wondering how much Monica had told a stranger, how much her story had emerged with edited highlights. I walked inside on legs made of tin, every step seeming to emit a slight squeak of resistance.

"Can I get you anything? Tea, coffee?" Sarah said.

"Tea would be nice, thank you."

She guided me into a room in which one half was set out for breakfast. Lovely paintings of Cheltenham adorned the wall. Monica sat on one of two sofas opposite each other near a front facing window. She stood at my approach, and did the same 'kiss kiss' thing she'd performed in my office. I forced a smile.

Sarah let out a genuine sigh of pleasure. "So nice, how long has it been, you two?"

We spoke in unison. "A while," my mother said.

"A couple of decades," I said.

Some of the shine vanishing, Sarah invited me to make myself at home and left us to it.

I sat down and looked into my mother's eyes. I'd already made my mind up that I would hear her out. We sat awkwardly for a few moments and exchanged a couple of pleasantries. "So?" I began, wishing I didn't sound so much like Blofeld quizzing James Bond in one of those old movies.

My mother took a deep breath. "I won't lie to you, Kim. I left your father all those years ago because I met someone else. I fell in love."

This was no surprise to me. An affair, my father had told me more than once. Tacky and sordid, is how it had been put across, which was fair enough. My mother had chosen her lover over us.

"I can't expect you to know what it was like being married to your dad," she continued. "But it wasn't easy. Older than me by almost fifteen years, it was very much a traditional relationship, more common in those days. He went out to work and I stayed at home with you kids. He was a good worker and provider, your dad," she said with fond recollection. "But, of course, being a vet he was out all hours in all weathers. Life was fairly unpredictable."

I resisted the urge to ask whether she really believed this a mitigating factor. I don't know whether she read it in my face, but she coughed and cleared her throat. "The thing is, I was lonely and, whatever you've been told, your dad wasn't happy. He couldn't have been…" She tailed off, swallowed, "And he liked a drink, or two."

So what Luke said was true. I leant towards her. "Did he ever hurt you?"

"Only with words."

A knock at the door and Sarah returned with a tray of tea and a plate of biscuits, homemade, by the look of them. I was glad of the distraction. She set it out and left. My mother did what mothers do. It must have been strange for her to ask her daughter of thirty-six years whether she took sugar in her tea, whether she liked it weak or strong.

"I'm not making excuses, Kim," she continued once we were settled again, "really I'm not, but I'd like you to have some idea what it was like for me."

I understood her need because I was no ordinary listener; it was what I got paid for. I nodded assent. She issued a short, grateful smile. "When I told your father that I wanted to leave him, he grew extremely angry. I've never forgotten it," she said, paling with the memory. "He told me that I could go, that he would be glad to see the back of me, but he also told me that if I tried to take any of you away, he would come after and kill us."

Most people would have jumped, but I knew my dad and his taste for the dramatic, which could be deeply unpleasant if you were on the receiving end. He'd owned two legally held licensed shotguns. Occasionally, I'd heard him issue idle threats to others, usually when he was in his cups. I'd never taken them seriously. Mouth and trousers, I'd thought. I'd also thought him a jerk.

"You believed him?"

"I did."

"You were afraid of him?"

"I was."

"Then how could you bear to leave three children in the care of a man who was that unstable?"

She glanced away, glanced back. "Your safety was never in doubt."

"That doesn't really answer my question."

She suddenly took hold of my hands, which felt soft and warm and, I guessed, motherly. "Kim, he threatened to kill me. I'd embarrassed him, brought shame on him. Where we lived, it was a small population. Close. Parochial. Incestuous." She didn't need to point this out. I knew only too well. I also recognised the law of unintended consequences when living in a semi-rural community and things went wrong. It could be very *Game of Thrones*, with one faction vying with another. "He wasn't having me back, but he would not let me leave with you. That was his punishment. He was of a different generation, do you see?"

Yes, I got that. All the dads at school were younger than mine, and with different generations come different views, some of them cemented in the dark ages, I'd thought more than once. "But a threat to kill?" I said in disbelief. I disengaged from her grasp as easily as she'd disconnected from my life.

"As long as I went quietly," she continued. "Mine and your safety were assured."

So that's why she'd treated me with such studied unease when I'd tracked her down. She was doing it to protect me, or so she'd have me believe.

I drew away. It was a difficult sell and I wasn't sure I bought it. She probably detected my resistance, which is why she changed tack.

"Do you still have the cottage in Devon?"

I nodded. My inheritance, I'd been trying to sell it for months, but it wouldn't shift and I'd taken the Slade family home off the market.

"Next time you're there, go up into the attic and check the floorboards."

"Check the—?"

Her eyes flashed. "Do it."

So you want to play the authoritative mother? I curled my lip. Her face fell. She knew she'd overplayed her hand. "I'm sorry, Kim. That was really unforgiv—"

"Dad has been dead for over half a decade. Why didn't you come before?"

She gave a world-weary smile. "For many years I moved around. I couldn't bear the pain of not seeing you. It was easier that way. I also worried how you would take it." And afraid of the reaction it would provoke, I thought. Well, now you know. "I hoped that you'd got your lives sorted. I had no desire to come back and mix things up."

But you have and the timing couldn't be worse. "This man," I said. "Your lover."

A shadow passed behind her eyes. She looked as vulnerable as a sleeping baby. "He died four years after we went away. Road accident," she said, bleak and sad.

I had become something of an expert in the lexicon of loss. Death tapped me on my back with a long, hard skeletal finger, and whispered *like mother, like daughter*. "I'm sorry. That's hard."

She didn't disabuse me. "Afterwards, I was forced to create a new life for myself. With few credentials, I took all kinds of paid menial work and finally managed to get a job as a live-in house-keeper for a judge and his wife. I've been living in Edgbaston in Birmingham for the past twelve years." Another shadow slipped across the back of her eyes. She didn't explain and offered me a biscuit, which I declined.

"I spoke to Luke after your call," I told her.

Her face immediately brightened. "Did you? Tell me all about him."

So I did and, before long, I realised that we were getting on well, that she was intuitive and interested and interesting. For a screwed up life, she hadn't done too badly. She had lived and for that I was glad.

"He asked me to tell you to get in touch." I gave her his number. She looked so pleased and grateful, I almost felt mean for harbouring such unpleasant thoughts about her. My biggest problem with her story remained. It's too easy to discredit the dead.

"Are you going back to Birmingham after your visit?" I said.

The shadow returned. I felt like one of those bomb disposal experts tentatively feeling the way for unexploded devices.

"No, my employment situation has changed."

"Oh?"

She put down her cup and saucer with a clatter. I realised that I'd done the verbal equivalent of stepping on a land mine. "A couple of months ago, Judge Hawkes discovered that he had terminal cancer. A few days ago, I went into his bedroom and found him dead in bed."

Fear trickled down my spine. Not death again.

"He'd committed suicide. Booze," she said, her voice empty, "I suppose to give him Dutch courage, and then he'd tied a plastic bag over his head."

Unbidden, I pictured a dead man's eyes and ruptured capillaries. I thought about air escaping and running out, polythene sucking in and sticking fast. Compression. Extinction.

"It made me think that life is too short," I heard my mother say. "It made me realise that I needed to see you more than ever."

Pain flashed through my shoulders. I changed position. As I snapped back to the present and looked into her face, I saw my own needy, haunted reflection. I got it. She was asking for my help and support without realising that I was the last person on earth capable of offering it.

SIXTEEN

I LEFT MONICA WITH the promise that I'd return the following evening, and drove back home. I couldn't be bothered to assemble dinner and took a fish pie straight from the freezer and shoved it in the oven. While it heated up I called Luke and told him everything Monica had said. He listened without interruption.

"Do you believe her?" he spoke, finally.

I wasn't certain and said so.

Luke was more forthcoming. "Dad was certainly capable of it. God, if even a fraction of what she describes is true, we've all been living a lie."

"But dead men don't talk, Luke, and without Dad around, we can't check her story."

"So your gut reaction is?"

I was uncomfortable at being put on the spot. How could I form a judgement based on so little hard information? "It's possible she's telling the truth."

He went silent for a few seconds. "We're in the middle of a massive audit at the moment. Soon as it's done, I'll get the next available flight back. Can you take care of things your end?"

"You mean look after her?"

"I guess."

"Sure," I said. Shit, I thought. Once we'd exhausted conversation, Monica was bound to ask questions about me. I didn't fancy taking a trip into the darkness of my past.

"Luke, do you know about something hidden under the floorboards in the attic?"

"Like what?"

"I don't know."

"No. Why do you ask?"

"Oh, nothing, I probably got the wrong end of what she was saying."

I signed off, ate supper, and felt unaccountably chewed up. On the verge of collapsing in front of the TV, my thoughts swivelled to Georgia and her revelation about Otto Vellender. Why would a father row with his daughter when she was so ill? Had Otto got wind of Paris Vellender's accusation? Was he denying it, putting the record straight, or what?

I ploughed through a programme on property and another on a food show featuring a trio of international judges with a keen script of one-liners. About to flick to the news, my mobile phone rang. I leant across, scooped it up, and clocked the number with a fresh flood of unease.

"Hello, Troy."

"Sorry I haven't been able to get in touch. Things have been …" He paused. "Difficult." I listened hard. Background noise suggested that Troy was outside, in traffic, walking down a busy street. "I told you Paris is lying."

I didn't respond.

"He's far from dead, or even disappeared," he insisted.

"Nicholas?"

"She's protecting him."

"From what?"

"Depends who you believe."

"Can you be more specific?"

"Paris says Otto is to blame."

"For driving his son away?"

"Worse, she reckons that Otto posed a serious threat."

I thought of my father, my mother's claim. "To Nicholas?"

"Right."

"You mean to his life?"

"That's what I figure."

I wasn't interested in what Troy figured. I needed facts, the same as I needed them to back up my mother's story. "What does Otto say?"

"Believe it or not, he's not high on my talk list."

Smart-mouth. "All right," I said slowly. "Are you saying that Paris is actively in touch with her son?"

"You bet."

"How do you know?"

"I caught a text on her phone."

"Caught?"

"Read. It was definitely from Nicholas."

Why was Troy snooping? What was it to him? "What did it say?"

He paused. "That they needed to meet up."

"Why the elaborate deception? It doesn't make sense."

"Like I said, Paris believes her son is in danger."

I glanced down, felt a sly shadow crawl across my feet. Tired, strung-out, my concentration wandered.

"Thing is," Troy said, ebullient now. "I believe Nicholas is right here in Cheltenham."

I snapped back to attention. Why remain in a place where you could be discovered? Answer: the best place to hide is right under the nose of those you are trying to escape. Recently, wasn't a hardcore terrorist found hanging out two streets away from his childhood home? And if Paris Vellender were protecting her son, as Troy inferred, it made sense for her to keep him close.

"Son-of-a-bitch," Troy said. "Paris is calling me on my other phone." I'd never got my head around two-phone syndrome. Unless you were running an empire, having an affair, or engaged in criminality, it seemed like an expensive waste of money and energy. "I'm going to send you something," he said, speeding up and keen to wrap up our conversation.

I didn't care for the sound of that. "Why are you involving me?"

"Because you care. I recognised it the moment we met."

"I cared about Mimi. Now she's gone—"

"It's a newspaper article," Troy cut across.

"I've already checked it," I began, but Troy had hung up.

I sat still for many minutes running through the conversation. If what Troy said was true, Nicholas Vellender had deliberately missed Christmases and birthdays and other important occasions to lead a life of lies. Effectively, he was playing dead. I couldn't help but wonder why Troy had latched on to me when Georgia was a more obvious choice. Again, what was in it for him?

I switched off the TV, washed and changed into my dressing gown, and hung around. The link to the article came through on my phone five minutes later and it wasn't what I was expecting.

Sixteen-Year-Old Receives Six-Figure Sum for Publishing Deal. Surprised, I read on, scanning the whole five-paragraph puff-up. As a result of Nicholas Vellender posting sections of his fantasy novel online, he'd attracted such a massive global audience that publishers had contacted him, offering a three-book deal with a six-figure price tag. I knew nothing about the publishing industry other than what I'd heard anecdotally. It boiled down to a writer standing more chance of winning EuroMillions than securing a chance of mainstream publication. So what had happened with that? Had Vellender's work sunk without trace? I switched to Amazon to check and found three books listed with moody covers involving blood, masks, and sensationalist titles. Reviews were mostly impressive apart from the odd vicious one-star offering, which was standard fare for anyone raising their head above the artistic parapet. Similar occurred in academic circles. Judging by release dates, it seemed that Nicholas's embryonic career had vanished without trace in much the same way as the writer. Unsurprisingly, a later headline read Fantasy Writer Vanishes followed by an article suggesting that Nicholas had not lived up to his early promise. Had he crashed and burned?

If Troy's belief that Nicholas had voluntarily gone into hiding and lived locally were correct, how had Otto failed to notice or even run into his son? Cheltenham was not a particularly big town. Yes, there were enclaves, but it seemed inconceivable to me that in almost five years their paths had never crossed, or that someone, a friend, hadn't run into Nicholas. I wondered how that had come about. I wondered if it were even true.

SEVENTEEN

"I FANCY HAVING A brain scan."

"Huh?"

"In the interests of research." For reasons unknown, Jim Copplestone had taken up residence in my office during the lunch hour. It was hammering down with cold, sleety rain outside and I'd decided to stay put and eat a sandwich indoors. It was supposed to be a peaceful oasis in my day and was proving to be anything but.

"Imagine how you'd feel if you found out that you had the same markers as a psychopath."

I looked up. "I can tell you for nothing you haven't."

For a moment he looked disappointed. "But imagine if one did." He pushed back in his chair, stretched out his legs, hitched his hands behind his head, in pontificating mode, and regaled me with a story of an eminent American psychiatrist who'd persuaded his entire extended family to have brain scans only to discover that one stood out from the crowd: his.

"Aside from being knocked sideways, he was pretty horrified to find out that his wife was the least surprised by his findings. She'd always known him to be a psychopath."

"Don't you mean sociopath?" I said.

Jim blew out his thin cheeks. "Ah well, now you're into different territory."

"True." Even if there were common denominators. "Look, Jim, it's really fascinating stuff, but do you mind?" I waved my sandwich, which was currently poised halfway between my plate and mouth. "I was hoping to have a quiet five minutes."

"Fair enough." He pitched forward, both hands slapping his skinny thighs. "Before I leave you to it, a quick word about Imogen Miller."

Defeated, I returned the sandwich uneaten to the plate. "What about her?"

"Did you get the impression that she was in imminent danger of self-harming?"

"It was tricky to get an impression at all. I'd hardly squeezed more than a few words out of her. Problem?"

Jim's eyebrows rose to meet his receding hairline. "She managed to get hold of a razor—we're looking into it," he said in reply to my astonished expression. We didn't run a draconian regime, but it was recognised that some youngsters with eating disorders could and did maim themselves. Accordingly, active measures were taken to guard against it. We were usually pretty good at policing. "Made a bit of a mess of her thigh," he said.

"Stitches?"

"Five."

Ouch. "When did this happen?"

"Last night."

"Honestly, Jim, there were no indicators." Were there and I'd failed to spot them?

"She didn't seem particularly distressed?"

"Didn't seem particularly anything other than bolshie. I'd put it down to run-of-the-mill teenage aggression."

"When are you supposed to be seeing her next?"

"Tomorrow."

"The hospital kept her in for observation. Apparently, an inch closer and she'd have hit a major artery."

I winced. "I'll reschedule. Would you prefer to appoint someone else?" Please say yes, I thought.

Jim looked pensive. "No, I think it best we keep things as they are. Simply thought you should be made aware."

I thanked him, watched him leave, and dropped my sandwich in the bin.

———

I was surprised to see a police car outside The Battledown that evening. Ringing the bell, I waited as Sarah came to the door, pink-faced and harassed. It wasn't lost on me. Cops don't look good for business.

"Sorry, have I called at a bad time?" I said.

Sarah glanced over her shoulder. I caught the sound of male and female voices drifting from the lounge, Monica's among them. "You'd best come in."

I stepped over the threshold with a deep sense of foreboding and looked to Sarah, who explained that two plainclothes police officers had arrived five minutes before and asked to speak to Monica in private. So did this explain my mother's rush to contact me? I'd imagined she might be in some kind of trouble, but nothing that involved the law.

"Did they say what it was about?"

"No, I'm sorry."

I made to go into the room.

"Should you be doing that?" she said with an anxious glance. "They seemed keen to be left alone."

I flashed a sheepish smile and walked straight in. Three sets of eyes locked onto mine. A male police officer stood up. He was all neck, no shoulders and he had a hard, defensive look on his face. The expression on Monica's was one of stunned disbelief mixed with gratitude at my arrival, but my full attention impaled on the female. I'd recognise those shark-like teeth and pillowy pink lips from a hundred paces.

"What are you doing here?" I said, bewildered.

"I could ask the same question."

My equally mystified mother looked from me to Detective Superintendent Niven and back to me. "You know each other?"

Regrettably, we did. I could almost see Niven pull me out of her mental pigeonhole and run my log number through its paces: stalking, murder, guilt and, joy unconfined, innocence.

"You're talking to my mother," I told her.

Did I imagine the chill, vengeful look on Niven's face? She'd so wanted to convict me of Chris's murder but instead, in the light of incontrovertible evidence, was forced to backtrack.

"What's this all about?" The question was to Niven, but it was the male officer, all spring and coiled energy, who answered.

"We're here to ask Mrs. Slade a few questions. Now, if you wouldn't mind allowing us to do our job."

"You've driven all the way from Devon?" I said, still not getting it.

Niven's smile was short and without warmth. "From Birmingham. I transferred to West Midlands Police."

"So, Miss Slade, if you'd like to step this way," the male police officer said, steering me firmly towards the door. His body and the punchy blocky way he moved belonged to a boxer.

"I'm sorry, I didn't catch your name," I said.

"Detective Sergeant Holst."

"Like the composer," I said without thought, his answering expression suggesting that a: he didn't have a clue about the connection and b: I was a smart-arse.

Back in the hall, I slumped down on the stairs. What had Monica got into? Had she lied to me? Was she on the run? And then it dawned on me. The judge's suicide. Naturally there would be questions. Pressure eased off, I accepted a small glass of wine from Sarah, who introduced me to her husband, Simon, a long, lean man with a sparky smile, and their small daughter, Isabella.

"Why don't you come through to our lounge while you wait?" he said.

I smiled thanks and stood up to move somewhere more comfortable. A loud shout of protest from Monica stopped me in my tracks.

"That's simply not true! I did not *take off*, as you put it. I gave an account. I spoke to you."

Chill crawled over me and I was mentally transported to a stuffy interview room that smelt of cold coffee and sweat, me feeling like a pressure cooker, as if my head would explode, and Niven bearing down and accusing me of murder.

All three of us stood mute, glasses poised mid-air. I didn't know these people and it felt embarrassing to be thrust among them in the circumstances. If I was lost, what the hell were they thinking?

After the outburst, things died down a little. At some stage my glass must have been refilled although I didn't notice when because I'd pushed it aside. Finally footsteps sounded and the door swished open, revealing Niven and Holst. Monica, grey and pale-lipped, remained seated.

"We'll need to speak to Mrs. Slade in a more formal setting," Holst said. "We'll also need a DNA sample."

"Can you tell me what this is all about?" I said.

Holst looked to Niven, who nodded. "Judge Michael Hawkes," he said, unblinking. "Your mother's former employer."

"He committed suicide."

"Who told you that?" Niven said.

"My mother." I glanced at Monica, who looked stricken.

"We believe his death is suspicious."

I felt as if I'd entered a country pub in the hope that it would be sweet and friendly, only to encounter a rank and dirty old boozer full of hostiles. "Is she under arrest?"

"No, but as you may be aware, your mother found the judge."

"That doesn't make her guilty."

Niven turned her cutthroat smile on me. "Nobody said anything about guilt. We simply want Mrs. Slade to assist us with our enquiries. Do you have a problem with that?"

"Of course not," I said, backing off. "Does she need a solicitor?"

Niven flicked a tailored smile. "Not at the moment."

EIGHTEEN

"What am I going to do?"

"Drink this." I handed Monica a cup of sweetened tea. Her shoulders and knees trembled. She complained that she was cold. Either she was in shock or eligible for a best actress award.

"What did the police say exactly?"

She snatched at her tea, helpless. The lines on her face seemed more prominent than they had the day before.

"They said that the judge's death was suspicious and that they needed to ask me more questions."

"What did they say about you leaving?"

Heat spread over her neck flushing it deep red. She hung her head. I thought it a guilty gesture. "Apparently, I should have stayed where they could find me."

"They think you ran?"

"It would seem so."

"Did you?"

Her head shot up. "No."

"Okay, let's take it from the beginning."

The nervous tic above her eye returned. "Do we have to do this now?"

"Yes." No damn question about it. "You said you found the judge dead in bed."

"That's right."

"Alone?"

"Yes."

"Where was Mrs. Hawkes?"

"They slept in separate rooms, had done for years. The judge snores."

"Did he leave a suicide note?"

My mother's features crumpled once more. "No. It was another indicator of something more suspicious, according to that ghastly woman, Niven."

"Not everyone leaves suicide notes," I pointed out reasonably.

"I tried to tell her that the first time."

Now I was confused. "You've talked to Niven before?"

"Yes."

I realised I'd made a classic mistake. I hadn't asked for a detailed account of events. "Talk me through what happened from when you found the judge."

"I called an ambulance."

"You didn't rip off the bag?"

"No."

"Why not?"

"I was too afraid and I knew he was dead."

"How did you know? You checked?"

"I felt his pulse. There wasn't one."

"Then what?"

"The ambulance arrived."

"Quickly?"

"I think so."

"So what did you do in the meantime?"

"I woke Mrs. Hawkes and told her what happened."

"What was her reaction?"

"The obvious one."

"She was distressed?"

"Very. She relies on him for everything. I helped her to his room. Mrs. Hawkes is virtually blind, macular degeneration."

Alarm flashed through me. Something didn't stack. "Monica, I have to ask you this, but why did you take off like that?"

Her eyes widened with indignation. "I already told you."

"You said Mrs. Hawkes is partially sighted. Why would you leave her, particularly at this difficult time? Doesn't she need looking after?"

Her cheeks flushed the same colour as her neck. "As soon as the family heard, they arrived en masse: two daughters, two sons-in-law, as well as the Hawkes's son. More than enough to look after her," she said, obviously narked. "I was told I could take time off."

But not beat it. "And you talked to the police before you left?"

She let out an irritable sigh and spoke slowly, with precision, as if I were difficult or stupid, or both. Instantly reminded of my father in one of his spiky moods, I did my best to kill the memory. "Police officers were called to the scene. When they arrived they asked me questions."

"Okay," I said, striving to keep an open mind. "Let's take it back a step, the ambulance arrived."

"Yes."

"*You* didn't contact the police?"

She shook her head. "The ambulance men did. They told us it was standard procedure with sudden deaths. Even terminally ill patients who die at home are scrutinised by the police."

"How many police officers arrived?"

"Two in uniform, a man and a woman. I forget their names," she frowned. "They were both very nice. They took notes."

"You gave an account?"

"Yes."

"And they were satisfied?"

Her face clouded. "They had concerns."

"No suicide note and the fact it was a judge who'd died."

She looked at me as if astounded to have bred a daughter who could follow such a garbled narrative and have an informed opinion. I didn't enlighten her that my smattering of knowledge was based solely on my own recent run-in with the police. As for the judge, I bet there were a few from his past who wished him dead. I put it to Monica.

"He's been retired for ten years. Is it likely?"

"No statute of limitation on revenge. He had no personal enemies?"

Perched on the edge of the seat, leaning forward, all bones and angles, Monica stared entranced, as if I were a soothsayer. "Of course not."

"Did you mention the judge's cancer diagnosis to the police?"

"I did and Mrs. Hawkes backed it up. We all assumed that it was the reason for him taking his own life. He was an immensely proud and capable man. Dying bit by bit was an intolerable prospect for him."

"But the police didn't rate it as a reason?"

She let out another bewildered sigh. "I don't know what they thought. They told us they were calling it in to CID. The male officer seemed to be on the phone for ages. When he came back he said two detectives were on their way."

"And that's when you first encountered Niven and Holst?"

"Yes."

"You spoke to them?"

"Yes."

"You gave a witness statement?"

She frowned. Her eyes fluttered with confusion. "I think so."

"Did you sign anything?"

"I, I don't remember." Deathly pale, she pressed a hand to her chest and turned her wide-eyed gaze on me. It was easy to understand her confusion and dismay.

"It's all right," I said, trying to soothe her while wondering about the veracity of her story. Was this why she'd come to me? If so, what had I stumbled into?

"When are you expected at the police station?"

"Friday morning, ten thirty. They muttered something about me giving a video statement."

"I'll cancel my appointments."

"No," she burst out. "I don't expect you to," she said, more measured. "It's my mess to clear up."

The knot of anxiety returned. A bad choice of words, perhaps, or had she given something away?

"I can catch a train to Birmingham," she said, bullish.

"It will take you at least forty minutes and then you'll have to cab it. Monica, I'll drive you there. I insist. Niven is not someone to meddle with." Ambitious, a woman who never took prisoners, I genuinely feared for anyone, let alone my own mother, becoming entangled in her battle lines. Niven had been born with a stick in her hand for the sole purpose of shaking it at people.

"How do you know each other?" Monica said.

I flicked a tight smile. "Long story."

NINETEEN

First thing next morning I spoke to Jim and explained the situation. Actually that's a lie; I explained *some* of the situation. Heavy on my mother's sudden return, light on the investigation by the police.

Jim is sometimes given to hyperbole. He leaned right back in his chair, crossed his arms, planted two feet on his desk, and stretched out like an adder enjoying the sunshine. "The return of the prodigal mother," he said, raising an eyebrow. "Fascinating."

The way his hooded eyes lit up, I had the nasty feeling that he was mentally doing the equivalent of rubbing his hands together in feverish anticipation, Monica lined up as a fitting subject for a case study. Jim couldn't help himself and *persuasive* was his middle name. He'd often wheedle his way round me and get me to do publicity stuff for the Lodge even though I wasn't that keen.

"So I need tomorrow off. She has to return home on Saturday," I fabricated, fronting it out.

"I see," he said. *Tell me more*, his voice inferred. "Where's home exactly?"

I opened my mouth to answer when a thud of realisation struck me hard. Given her sudden change in circumstances, Monica no longer had a place to call her own. "Um … Midlands," I bluffed, thinking it covered a large enough geographical area.

"And next Tuesday?" he said. I sometimes found it tricky to keep up with the way in which Jim's grasshopper mind worked. Then it dawned on me: Mimi Vellender's funeral.

"I'd hoped to pay my respects," I said, amazed by the ease with which I continued to tell porkies.

"Fair enough. I'll get Cathy to rejig your appointments. Terrible business," he muttered, shaking his head.

"Yes, thanks," I said before Jim had a chance to pick up and run with it. Escaping to my office, I closed the door and leant back against the solid wood, desperate to ignore the screeching in my head that suggested poltergeists had taken up residence and were messing with my brain. I'd swallowed my medication that morning and wished now that I'd doubled the dose. Warned that any extra stress when I was still in healing mode could cause me problems, I'd nodded blandly at the time, never envisaging that life could veer off and haul me onto a rodeo ride.

Pouring a glass of cold water from the dispenser, I quietly sipped and composed myself for my first client of the morning, Imogen Miller, the girl intent on expressing her pain by carving it into her thigh.

Gingerly lowering her gaunt frame into a chair, Imogen viewed me with exhausted, hollow eyes. Her thickly bandaged leg was visible beneath her leggings, an item of clothing routinely banned unless worn beneath a skirt.

"It must be sore," I said sympathetically.

She shrugged, like it was no big deal.

I didn't ask why she'd done it. No point. Unresponsive to direct questions, she needed a more nuanced approach. "Are you settling in okay?"

She nodded.

"Nobody giving you grief?"

She shook her head.

"Did I put pressure on you the other day?"

Another shake.

"Sure?"

"Yes."

A single word spoken and I felt as if I'd hit a bull's-eye. It was a start. "Talk to me about you. How are you feeling?"

Another shrug.

"You must have been pretty low to hurt yourself like that."

She gazed right through me, blank-eyed. It shrank my insides. A haunting image of Mimi dying in her hospital bed, deep scars on her arm, trophies of self-mutilation, loitered in the back of my mind. I pressed on.

"Your notes say that you're a gifted musician, is that right?"

"I play the piano a bit," Imogen said, toneless.

I smiled. "Grade eight with honours is more than a bit."

Imogen maintained a disinterested pose. Sprawled body, head lowered, but the flicker in her eyes told me that I'd piqued her interest.

"Recently, I've got into classical; listening, not playing," I added with another smile.

"Whatever."

"Got any favourite composers?"

Another world-class shrug.

"I love Rachmaninov," I coaxed her.

"Awesome."

"You play Rachmaninov?"

"Sometimes."

"I'm impressed. What a great gift." I paused, trying to connect with her. "Surely, it's worth getting better for?"

She looked momentarily startled then furious. "You sound like my mother." Her eyes darted to the door. If she wanted to get up and leave, there was nothing I could do to stop her. I made a note and waited while Imogen floundered in a deep, stagnant pool of her own creation. At last, she gathered herself, mentally regrouped, and glowered at me with defiant eyes. "I am not throwing it all away."

"I don't think I suggested you were." I spoke quite neutrally.

"Course you didn't," she said with a sneer.

"About the cutting," I said, trying to roll the conversation once more.

"It's fantasy, pretend. It's actually fun." She flexed one foot in a challenging motion and glanced down at her bandaged leg.

"Five stitches isn't a figment of your imagination. It's real. It hurts."

A brittle bright laugh escaped from between her dry lips. "That's the point."

"You feel more real when you're cutting than when you don't?"

"It's the *only* part that makes sense."

"You view mutilation as a valid activity?"

"Why not? It's what I do."

"For kicks?"

"For the buzz." She might as well have added *you stupid cow*, judging by the malevolence in her expression.

"And when you don't do it, you feel unhappy?"

Her face fell, a look of genuine despair flaring behind her eyes. In that fleeting moment she looked as fragile as a reluctant child left at the school gate on the first day of term. "It's the only way to connect."

"To what?"

She chewed her lip, looked straight ahead, stony.

"The fantasy side?" I said.

"I guess."

I twigged and almost let out a groan. Dismay rippled through me. "Imogen, are you talking about your online persona?"

Face drawn with rage, she braced and shrank back into the chair as if trying to make herself disappear. "Why do you say that? Everyone my age goes online."

"Not here." Those were the rules. No phones, no laptops, no cameras. She must have smuggled in a device. "You know I'm going to have to ask you to hand whatever it is over."

Her chin jutted out, mutinous.

"Is it on you?"

She shook her head.

"Okay, but you'll have to give it to Cathy."

"If you say so."

I took a drink of water. "Want some?" I gestured with my glass. Another shake of the head.

"Do you use self-harm websites, Imogen?" The proliferation of these and suicide websites targeting young people and offering them what they deemed valid life choices had become a major problem. It felt like the never-ending war on drugs. The only thing we could do as professionals was to treat the addiction.

"So what if I am?"

"But don't you see how destructive that is?"

She threw me a black, sullen look and snarled. "What would you know? I've got thousands of friends who follow my blog."

"I'm sure you have but these people are not your real friends, are they? You don't know them and they don't know you."

"So? Nothing is real."

"This is real," I said, glancing around the room. "Us talking here and now, together."

"You don't get it."

"Okay," I said evenly. "Help me out."

Her response was to fold her arms tightly across her flat chest, close her eyes, and tune out.

"Imogen, these people—"

"My friends."

"Your friends," I corrected myself. "They're only talking to one part of you, not all of you."

"That's not true. They encourage me."

"Encourage you to do what?" I needed her to spell it out, to say and admit it.

Her eyes opened. "To express myself."

"By cutting into your own flesh? What else do they want you to do?"

She glanced towards the door again, no doubt plotting a fast exit.

"They don't know the real you," I explained, "the talented and bright musician, the daughter and sister and friend. They're just engaging with one facet of your personality, the damaged side."

She pushed forward, making me jump, and bellowed, "It's no business but mine. You have no right to discuss or have an opinion on what I do in my time. It's private."

"Imogen," I said, keeping my voice steady, "I'm not here to interfere in your life. I'm here to help."

"Well, I don't want it so you can fuck off." She hauled herself to her feet. Awkward and disorientated, she staggered to the door, wrenched it open, and almost mowed Cathy down lurching to the corridor.

"What the hell was that about?" Cathy said, planting a mug of coffee on the desk.

"Another damn website. I wish there was something we could do to close them down."

Self-harm and Pro-ana (code for anorexia) forums and websites, promoting "thinspiration," remained a constant devil on our client's thin and bony shoulders. Jim had even made representations to our local MP. The real issue was that, as one website was taken down, another popped up to take its place. Intervention was critical but it was an uphill climb. Girls like Imogen were too sucked in to want to stop.

"I think she has a phone on her."

"I'll confiscate it," Cathy said.

"Good luck with that. She'll probably smuggle in another. Who does she hang out with?"

"She doesn't."

"To our advantage in some ways, I guess. This stuff is poisonous. I don't want any of the others seduced. I'll talk to Jim, see how to play it." I wondered whether to try and slide the Vellenders into the conversation, see if I could fish and find out if Cathy had heard anything on the grapevine about the Vellenders' missing son—or any information, come to think of it. I opened my mouth but chickened out. Openly messing with a family's DNA was bound to draw unwelcome attention.

"Everything else all right?" Cathy said, pausing by the door.

"Sure."

"With your mother, I mean."

"Fine," I said, curt. "Thank you," I added as if I'd forgotten my manners.

Her face widened into a broad smile. "I'm really pleased for you."

TWENTY

Under a bleak sky of fierce clouds swollen with hate and rain, I picked up Monica a little after nine Friday morning and drove to Birmingham. She wore a mask of calm inscrutability. Her hands gave her away. They perched in her lap like arthritic claws.

"Do nothing wrong, you have nothing to fear," she maintained, as she strapped herself in. I admired her jaunty optimism and hoped it would rub off on me.

Trapped for the next hour, I was prepared for her to take advantage of the opportunity to quiz me. Wise enough not to demand a potted history of what I'd done for the past twenty years, she probed with direct questions, to which I gave straight answers. I only faltered once.

"Nobody special in your life then, Kim?"

"No."

"The demanding nature of your work, I expect."

I looked straight ahead, flipped the windscreen wipers on to max, and switched on the radio to a music channel I thought she wouldn't care for. She fell quiet until we hit the motorway.

"I spoke to Luke last night. A wife and family, he's done marvellously well for himself." Her voice glowed with pride. "As have you, darling."

I didn't know Monica well enough yet to gauge whether her remark was genuine, or an afterthought. I accepted it at face value, with good grace. "I presume you told him about the police."

"No."

"Oh?"

"Why meet trouble halfway? It might all be a silly mistake." I glanced across at her in disbelief. She smoothed the creases in her coat. "I'm determined to remain positive."

In denial, I thought grimly.

We arrived with time to spare, but I hadn't bargained on the maze of narrow roads with parking restrictions. I got into such a sweat we were almost late. Eventually, I stuck the car in a side street and found the slab-sided building that was the police station. The wind had picked up, frantic and wild, and the sky had turned leaden with the promise of a heavy downpour. We went to the door and pressed an entry phone. A male voice answered: "Yes?"

"Monica Slade to see Hayley Niven."

I quelled a smile. Had Monica inadvertently dropped the DS's title, or was it a calculated move?

The door buzzed open and I followed Monica into a dingy corridor. The odour was more playschool than police station.

Holst greeted my mother and looked straight through me as if I were sheet glass, a calculated move to prove who called the shots.

I took a step forward. "You can't come in to the interview room," he said.

"I appreciate that, but can I wait?" I cast around the drab and depressing corridor.

He frowned. I smiled. He relented. "All right," he said as if the boss wouldn't approve. "In there." He gestured to a room filled with children's toys. The vibe was beige. Beige carpet, suspiciously beige seating, even the lighting gave off a grimy beige glow. I nodded at Monica as she was taken to another room. Gingerly sitting down, everything I touched felt sticky.

Doors opened and slammed. Voices, including Niven's, seeped through from the other side of a wall that was the same width as cigarette paper, then it fell quiet. With nothing to do, I got up, stretched, rolled my shoulders in a vain attempt to relieve the tension that had built up during the drive, and sat back down. Minutes ticked by. Wishing I'd brought a book with me, I pulled out my phone, thought about calling the hospital where Stannard was due to undergo his procedure but remembered, at around 5:30 a.m. New York time, it was too early. Scrolling idly through my list of contacts, I zoomed in on Georgia. As if another part of my personality had split off and was working its own agenda, I pressed Call.

"Hi, Kim."

"You sound jolly."

"Day off."

"Sorry to hound you."

"Not the Vellenders again." She said it with such a groan in her voice I had an image of her running her hands through her hair, as she had at the wine bar, and forcing it up into spiky tufts.

"A couple of questions and then I promise I'll leave you in peace."

Heavy sigh. "Go on then."

"I noticed Mimi had a number of scars on her arm."

"Yeah, her parents tortured her."

"What?"

"I'm joking," she said, as if unable to believe my gullibility. "They were self-inflicted, you muppet. You should have seen her legs."

"No evidence of self-harm when I treated her."

"Obviously stepped it up. It's not particularly outside the spectrum of dysfunctional behaviour."

"Do you know if she subscribed to online sites?"

"No idea."

"There was something strange about the scars on her arm," I said.

"Mmm?"

"They formed a pattern." *Human conceptual art*, I'd tagged them.

Another big hefty sigh billowed down the phone line. I was clearly ruining my friend's day off. "A symbol," Georgia said, as if this were her final pronouncement. "Make of it what you will."

"What kind of symbol?" I said. "Are you sure it wasn't a word?"

"Hell, I don't know. I wasn't looking for a human dictionary."

"Anything distinguishable?"

Georgia thought for a moment. "If my memory serves me correctly, it looked faintly Oriental."

Yes, it did, I now recalled. "That it?"

"Yep."

"Any idea what it signified?"

"No."

"Did anyone ask?"

"We were trying to save her life," Georgia said, tartly.

"Yes, of course, sorry."

"Next question?"

"Nicholas Vellender."

"The brother who went missing."

"Did Troy Martell ever mention him to you?"

"Paris Vellender's toy boy?" Georgia laughed.

"What's so funny?"

"I wouldn't take anything that man says seriously."

"You know him?"

"Not intimately, thank God. He's a fantasist."

My stomach griped in alarm. "What makes you say that?"

"The guy makes stuff up."

"Yes, I know what the word means," I said, testily, "but what are you really saying?"

"That American accent of his is fake, for a start."

"What?" I was floored.

"I knew someone who had a one-night-stand with him, back when he was plain old Duncan Wright." I clamped my jaw together to prevent it from dropping open. "Changed his name by deed poll and invented a whole new identity for himself."

"Is Paris Vellender aware?"

"Not a clue. To be fair, the guy went backpacking in the States for a year before travelling around half of Europe, so maybe he picked up the lingo there. Right, well, I have to go. Ironing and stuff."

Unsettled, I slipped my phone back into my bag as Holst, granite-faced, bowled into the room.

"Sorry, can I move you?"

"Why?"

"You'll be more comfortable."

"Is my mother all right?"

"Fine. A little excitable, but nothing to worry about."

I wanted to tell him that this wasn't like her, but then realised I had no idea what she was like, how she'd respond to pressure. In my experience, a police officer's definition of *excitable* was poles apart from the rest of the population's. Raise your voice one semi-tone and you're immediately met with defensiveness followed by the threat of arrest. Dutifully, I followed him. When he asked if he could organise a cup of coffee for me, I agreed despite not really wanting one, simply to appear willing. It was hours before Monica emerged, feeble and drawn.

"Get me out of here," she said, pushing past me, desperate to escape.

TWENTY-ONE

"They think I had a hand in it," Monica repeated in disbelief.

"Did they say that?"

"Didn't need to."

"You're a witness, not a suspect."

"You think?"

I wasn't sure whether she was overreacting or not. I tried to reassure her. "They conducted the interview by video to spare you the ordeal of reliving it again in court."

"I don't trust them."

And I'm not sure I trust you. The thought came out of nowhere. I blinked. "Run it all past me again."

I'd driven us away from the police station and into central Birmingham, parked in Brindleyplace, and walked into the first café I could find. Monica, meanwhile, remained mute. Taking charge, I ordered coffee for both of us and only then did she break her silence. Her account of the exchange came out in disparate fragments. I picked out the salient points and did my best to intuit the rest.

She put the cup down on the table in the same territorial way an explorer plants his flag and clasped her hands together, knuckles white, veins proud.

"They said that the judge had high levels of Zopisomething in his system."

"Zopiclone," I said. "It's a popular sleeping drug. Nothing for you to worry about." And mixed with anything he might have been taking for cancer, it could have had unintended consequences.

"They asked me if I took them."

"Do you?"

She stared at me as if I'd asked whether she used the services of gigolos. "No."

"Then that's all right then, isn't it?" I forced a bright smile.

"But then they asked me about the judge's drinking habits, as if I'd deliberately drugged him." Eyebrows high and tight suggested that she thought the whole idea absurd. "I explained that he always took a brandy and dry ginger to bed, helped him sleep."

"Did he drink anything else?"

"Scotch before dinner, as usual, and wine with Mrs. Hawkes."

"Quite a lot then."

"I suppose. I hadn't really thought about it like that." Her eyes glazed and she seemed lost for a moment or two.

"What else did they say, Monica?"

"What?" Confusion filmed her eyes.

"Was there anything else?" Of course there was. She'd been in there for the thick end of three hours.

She nodded vacantly, as if lost in the distant past then appeared to resurface into the present. "Bruises."

"What bruises?"

"Around his neck."

"How old was the judge?"

"Eighty-four."

"There you go. Old folk bruise easily."

She didn't look convinced. When she spoke next it was more to the wall than to me. "I had absolutely no idea that the police thought it was anything but suicide."

And neither did I. It pointed at an obvious conclusion. "Discrepancies must have been thrown up in the postmortem."

"And then there was the plastic bag he used to kill himself," she murmured, again, as if to nobody in particular.

"What about it?"

"I do all the shopping for the Hawkeses."

"You mean it was a supermarket bag?"

"I think so."

"You don't remember?"

"Could have been. I don't recall."

I thought it odd. Surely she'd remember if it was plain white, a coloured bag with a logo, or one of her own shopping bags?

"My DNA will be all over it," she added, suddenly breathing hard.

"So what?" I scoffed. "You had a legitimate reason. You were their housekeeper."

"Did I tell you the police swabbed the inside of my mouth and took my fingerprints?" She stared at me with genuine shock.

"Standard procedure."

"So you keep saying." Her sharp-eyed look matched the resentful note in her voice.

"I'm sorry," I mumbled. "This must be distressing."

Her hands embraced the cup she held as if it were a talisman, her knuckles standing white and pinched. Forehead creased, eyebrows like darts, the tip of her tongue nervously licked the corner of her mouth. The rest of her features remained slack with disbelief. "Although I might have worn my gloves, I suppose. I'm not sure I quite remember."

And so might a killer, although I didn't tell Monica this. There had to be a rational explanation. The police only said the death was suspicious. They hadn't stepped it up a gear. They hadn't arrested her. Yet.

She clutched the cup to her mouth with both hands, drank and put it down, spilling some of the contents. "They went on and on about there being no forced entry."

"Is it a big house?"

"Four bedrooms and annexe."

"How many entrances?"

She pulled a face. "I don't know."

"Think."

She did. Her eyes narrowed. Her brow furrowed. I half expected her to count up the number on her fingers. "Five in total."

"Could someone have entered illicitly? A door left open, perhaps."

She shook her head. "In this weather, doubtful."

"Any workmen visit the house, painters, decorators, electricians?"

"Well, yes, the Hawkeses have a regular gardener and there was the chimney sweep and"—she brightened—"a woman came to decorate the snug, their private sitting room."

"The police will be talking to them to eliminate them from their enquiries."

"I suppose that's what they meant by following up on a number of leads."

"Cop-speak," I said, blowing on the surface of my frothy coffee. "They'll primarily be looking for a motive."

"Judge Hawkes and his wife were extremely kind to me. Why on earth would I want to kill him?"

She made a good point. Without a motive, I couldn't see that the police had much to go on. Unless they knew things I didn't.

"Presumably, his wife will inherit?" I said.

Her eyebrows shot up. "Are you suggesting that she killed him?"

"I'm keeping an open mind."

"Ridiculous," she snapped.

I didn't try to explain that people did ridiculous things all the time, including abandoning and then tracking down long estranged children.

"Did his kids stand to benefit?" I persisted.

She stared at me as if she couldn't believe that she had bred such a cynical and cold-hearted daughter. "I'm only viewing it in the same way as the police," I explained.

"You never did say how your path crossed with Niven's." Gazing over the rim of her cup, she had a shrewd, calculating gleam in her eye.

"No, I didn't." And now wasn't the time. "I've got a contact, a solicitor. He's extremely good," I told her. "It might be worth having a chat with him."

"But I've done nothing wrong."

I let it lie. Like it or not, Monica had moved into the realms of a legal system that could cost a packet simply to defend one's innocence. We finished our coffee and I drove back to Cheltenham. On the way, Monica raised the spectre of needing somewhere more permanent to stay.

"I can't remain at The Battledown forever and I can't expect to take up my old position in Birmingham."

"Have you heard from Mrs. Hawkes?"

"No," she said, sounding dejected.

I did my best to quell the thought that there might be a more worrying reason for her employer's silence. "Another week or so won't make a difference and, this time of the year, it shouldn't be a problem for Sarah and Simon."

"I can't afford it," she said bluntly.

"I can help out." So could Luke.

"Kind of you, but no, and you understand as well as I that this is hardly going to be over in a week."

The thought had occurred and it made me despondent. I knew what she was asking of me—a roof over her head. It would be a kindness to offer, but the idea repelled. Selfish, maybe, but I needed my personal space more than ever, the freedom to move and do what I wanted when I wanted. If Monica came to stay, it would be like having a lodger with added emotional complication. Inspiration struck.

"Why not stay in the cottage?"

She screeched in horror. "In Devon?"

"Only during weekends. It's warm and cosy and—"

"I'd rather stick pins in my eyes."

I drove in prickly silence, feverishly thinking, hatching any plan that would ensure Monica stayed somewhere other than in my home. We were pulling into Hales Road when I said, "I've got a friend who may be able to help."

Her response was to issue a huge gale of disappointment. I refused to be moved.

"You never know, Mrs. Hawkes may welcome you back," I said, realising it to be a ludicrous suggestion and a measure of how desperate I felt about keeping my mother at arm's length.

"I'm not sure I ever want to return, not now."

I dropped her off with the promise that I'd be in touch. I didn't agree to meet, invite her for lunch, or suggest ideas about how she could amuse herself. Strangely, I think she was relieved.

TWENTY-TWO

Nipping into my favourite supermarket en route, I stocked up as if I were expecting a siege and spent an unfeasible amount of time browsing herbal remedies. In the fond hope that lavender and something called Panax ginseng would help lighten my mental load, I bolted when realising that any preparation screwing around with pituitary, hypothalamus, and adrenal glands might make an unhappy bedfellow with my current medication. As a halfway, if utterly reckless, measure, I stuffed a couple of bottles of decent wine into my shopping trolley instead.

Pushing supplies back to the car, my vision skidded and then snagged on the outline of a young man. I clocked low-slung jeans, leather jacket, and fancy trainers. Bent over, he stowed bags and boxes into the boot of a Mini. My legs wanted to run, my voice to call out. Breath sucked in, I quickened my pace, walked directly towards him, purposeful. He straightened up, caught the frantic expression on my face, and probably thought I was after a light or, worse, a date.

"Yes?"

"Sorry," I said, instantly realising my mistake. His features were just all wrong. "I thought you were someone else."

His laugh was easy, not how I imagined Nicholas Vellender's to be. "No prob."

"Fuck," I thought as I scooted past.

Back home, I stashed the shopping, lit the wood-burner and spoke to Luke, giving him a rundown of the situation with Monica. He responded in typical Luke fashion.

"The police are covering all the bases. It's bad luck, but that's the way it is. Wrong place, wrong time, unfortunately."

I grunted agreement. It was easier than being a dissenting voice.

"Odd coincidence about Niven, though."

"Another piece of bad luck," I said.

"You can handle it?"

No, not really. "Until you fly in."

"By then, it will be all over."

I jolted in alarm. "How long are you planning to take?"

"A couple of weeks should do it."

"Can't you get here sooner?"

"'Fraid not, little sister. Relax, things will be fine."

I wished I shared my brother's confidence. Fed up, I called the clinic in Florida.

"Hello, you have a patient who's recently undergone reconstructive surgery, name of Kyle Stannard."

"One moment, please."

The one moment took at least ten moments. Please God, don't let there be a problem.

"Sorry to keep you waiting. Yes, Mr. Stannard is here."

"I wondered how he is."

"And you are?"

"A friend," I said.

"I'm sorry, ma'am, I can't comment on his current status to anyone other than family."

"Of course, I understand." I felt crestfallen, not for me but for him. I really wanted Kyle to be okay.

"I can tell him you called."

"Thank you, I don't suppose it's possible to speak to him, is it?"

"Wait one minute."

I wondered how he really was, whether I'd been given a standard *he's fine and dandy, and you can whistle Dixie* line.

The receptionist came back. "He's in recovery."

"But the operation was a success?"

"You may be able to talk to him tomorrow. Want me to pass on a message?"

"Please. Tell him Kim called. Tell him"—I hesitated—"that Kim sends her love."

Stannard would be all right, I told myself. A force of nature, he had to be. The hospital was doing what hospitals do. I settled down to read with a sour taste in my mouth. When I'd covered the same sentence for the third time without taking it in, I closed the book.

Like Monica said, the Hawkeses had been good to her. She had nothing to gain by the judge's death and everything to lose. I ran again through everything she'd told me. Assuming she was telling the truth, the most likely scenario was that the killer had walked straight in and hidden, possibly for several hours, before he'd struck in a premeditated and carefully worked out attack.

Next I thought about the method of dispatch, which was unusual. More reminiscent of the kind of thing you watched in gangster movies, putting a plastic bag over someone's head and suffocating the life out of them required guts and determination. Doped up on brandy and drugs, the judge's instinct would still be to fight, hence the bruising. To asphyxiate requires a degree of force. Pressure would need to be applied for an extended period. Looking at it from a psychological perspective, I wondered whether the method chosen was important to the killer. Did he or she get off on it? Did covering the victim's face hold meaning or did it send a message: you've seen something you shouldn't or you were blind to something that hurt me?

I got up, poured a glass of water, and toyed with phoning Gavin Chadwick. A sharp-nosed criminal lawyer, he'd defended me to the police during Chris's murder investigation. He and I didn't particularly gel but I trusted him and Monica needed someone to trust, too. A small, mean part of me also wanted to hand over the reins to a professional who could remain dispassionate in a way that I knew I could not.

I scooped up my phone, went straight to Contacts and pressed Call and, almost simultaneously, cut it. Gavin would be entertaining or entertained, immersed in Devon life, or more likely Devon water, given the level of flooding in the area. And what would he think? *Hi Gavin, remember me, the police are questioning my mother in connection with the murder of her employer. Oh, and I forgot to mention, Detective Superintendent Hayley Niven is running the investigation.*

Convincing myself that Monica wouldn't welcome this level of interference, that I was jumping the proverbial gun, that the police had other people on their hit list, I contacted Troy Martell. No reason for Martell to know about my suspicion that he was a fraud, not yet. First I wanted to string him along and find out what his game was.

"Can you talk?"

"Uh-huh."

"How is the newspaper article you sent connected to Nicholas's disappearance?"

"You think he'd give up the limelight that easily?"

"I don't know. Maybe he didn't enjoy it. Some say that he didn't live up to the early hype."

"Nah, he gave it up because he was forced to."

"That's pure supposition."

"Well, it's what I figure," he said, surly with it.

"About Nicholas, are the police still looking?"

"Paris told me the investigation wound down after a year."

Yes, that fitted with what Mimi had said at the time. It seemed to me that if people didn't show up quickly, relatives were on their own. "Do the police stay in touch with updates?"

"Not any more, once in a blue moon."

"He's still officially classed as a Missing Person?"

"Sure."

"So Paris is still looking for him?"

"That's my point. You'd expect her to but she ain't."

"Are you certain?"

"Sure am. Mighty odd, huh? That's why I know that text was from him."

It wasn't conclusive to me. "You've actually seen them together?"

"If I had, believe me, we wouldn't be having this conversation."

"Who reported him missing?"

"Paris, but that was a cover-up."

"Cover-up for what?" I was as impatient as I sounded.

"I don't know, but something bad happened."

"So you keep telling me without the slightest shred of evidence. Let's face it, you can't know. You weren't even there."

"Look, I told you, I'd seen—"

"A message between them, yeah, I get that," I said, "but I'm struggling to understand why you're obsessed with Nicholas Vellender." And why you keep bashing me over the head with it.

"Obsessed?" He sounded shocked and angry.

"That's what I said." And I knew a thing or two about obsession. "Why would Mrs. Vellender go to all that trouble, get the police involved if, as you imply, something bad happened and she had something to do with it? And if Nicholas is still in Cheltenham, how come nobody has spotted him, including the police? People can't simply disappear." Or play dead.

"Well, I've spent the last twelve months searching and not found him."

"How?"

"Whatdaya mean *how*?" More of the pissy attitude.

"Did you go online, talk to his friends?"

"Some."

"Who?"

"Guys he went to school with."

"Girlfriends?"

"He didn't have any."

"A good-looking boy like that and no girls in tow? Come off it. You know that for a fact?"

"I didn't find any," he said, slow and insolent, which was not the same as there weren't any.

"And does Paris know of your activities?"

"Nope."

"See, I'm struggling here, Troy. I have to ask why? What's it to you?"

"I already told you." Now he sounded plain aggressive.

"For Mimi, right?"

120

"Sure."

"But she's gone. It's over."

"It's never over." His voice dropped several levels, the tone stark and chill. I was sitting in my own home, on my own sofa, safe and protected. In spite of the warmth of the room, I felt the crush of fear in my chest. "And that's why," he said, "you gotta do this, you gotta see it through."

"What makes you think I can succeed where you've failed?"

"Because you're a psychologist. You have an instant 'in' to people."

Designed to flatter, I wasn't flattered. "It doesn't really work like that."

His silence felt like a challenge. I should let it go, resist temptation, but found myself caving in. "When did Mimi start cutting herself?"

"What's this got to do with Nicholas?"

"Do you want my help or not?" Sharp-voiced, I had no intention of helping him; I was helping me.

"See, there you go, asking all those kinda smart, ditzy questions."

I scowled. His was a base method to get me to do what he wanted. Troy wasn't a fantasist. He was a deeply manipulative individual. "Truth is, I don't remember, a few months ago, maybe. Paris went crazy when she found out."

"Did you notice Mimi's scars?"

"On her arm? Sure."

"They portrayed a symbol."

"If you say so."

"You didn't notice?"

"C'mon, wasn't like she put them out there, on show."

"Do you know whether Mimi followed any self-harm, suicide, or pro-anorexia websites?"

He fell silent once more, but this time I got the impression he was giving it serious consideration rather than working a tactical move. "I don't think so. Maybe. Paris never mentioned anything like that."

"Would she have done?"

"What do you mean?"

"How much does she discuss her children with you?"

"Not as much as she should; not as much as I'd have liked."

I pulled a face at his creepy reply and hung up.

TWENTY-THREE

THE NEXT MORNING I awoke to a world that looked as if it had been coated in volcanic ash. More rain on the way. I made myself tea and took it back to bed to stare at Stannard's painting. What was on the film that so captivated the man and the woman in the picture? I wished I could view my own personal situation with as much transparency. That my mother had come back was not in dispute; cause for celebration or misgiving? Had she returned because she valued us, seen the light, feared growing old without making her peace, or because she was in a hole and knew it? Without answers, I cast her back into the past, to where she'd existed, sleeping and undisturbed, for most of three decades.

On a second cuppa, I fired up my laptop and studied the haunting image of Nicholas Vellender with his oloroso-coloured eyes and his jaunty smile. Troy Martell implied a cover-up, but according to Georgia, I couldn't trust a word he said. The problem with liars and manipulators is that they sometimes tell the truth. I hadn't spent more than a few minutes with Mrs. Vellender recently and had never clapped eyes on Otto, and yet every instinct shrieked that a conspiracy of epic proportions was in play. I had no idea how deep it went, or why. If I were wrong I could waste time and energy chasing a ghost.

Eager to achieve a modicum of control over my life, I got up, dusted, vaguely swung a vacuum cleaner over the carpet, and cleaned the loos. Armed with a copy of Nicholas's mug shot, I reached for my warmest jacket, put it on, and headed out.

I walked in a wide circle towards Montpellier. The wind had picked up, scything through me, and the air spat with rain. It was shudderingly cold. Even so, I meandered along the fashionable parade of shops, past a trendy interior design outfit with eye-wateringly expensive fixtures when, half frozen in shock, I stopped in my tracks.

Up ahead, a guy, over six feet tall, dark hair glossy with raindrops. I stared at his profile, entranced by the curve of his cheekbones, straight nose, square jaw. Gazing into the window of a gift shop with his hands deep in his raincoat pocket, he had a stance as familiar to me as if I had touched and explored the contours of his body. My heart lifted and then soared, one hand raised, mouth open ready to shout at the top of my voice. Before I cried out, he turned and the breath smashed out of me, vanishing into the atmosphere like smoke on cold water. As he strolled down the street and past me, oblivious to my pain, his name expired in my throat.

Rooted, I pressed a hand to my chest to stall a tributary of grief from surging and shattering my heart into a million tiny pieces that could never be reassembled. All the things I'd wanted to say but never had the chance to voice bubbled to the surface of my mind: the unspoken, the undreamt, the unshared. I felt so damn vacant. I *knew* Chris was dead. Of course I did, yet, for one fleeting moment, he'd seemed reincarnated, flesh and blood, as alive as me. Shaken, I recognised then how easily Mimi had fallen into the same poisonous trap, both of us seduced by imagining the dead, seeing them when they weren't really there *because we so desperately needed to.* And I had played directly into the hands of Martell, a fantasist and a man who'd reinvented himself to add colour and meaning to his empty existence.

I tightened my scarf, buttoned up my jacket and, against a squally wild wind, pushed one foot in front of the other with the same reluctance as if I'd encountered a minefield. In the space of two days, I'd twice imagined seeing those who weren't there. It was as if a malevolent force had grabbed hold of my shoulders, spinning me in reverse motion, deceiving and making a fool of me.

From Montpellier, I crossed into the Suffolks, intending to make a wide loop down to the Bath Road. My feet had other ideas. With no recollection of how I got there, I found myself in Casino Place, facing the back gate and garage of the Vellender family home.

In spite of it being Saturday, the street was deserted. I was there alone and in daylight. Nothing to worry about, so why the distinct thrum of fear?

I looked around: houses on both sides, wind whistling through a narrow connecting road wide enough for a car to pass through in single file. According to Mimi, this was where Mrs. Vellender engaged in a brief conversation with her son. It could easily have been an exchange with a neighbour or passerby, only Mimi's broken mind had visualised someone else because that was what she most desired.

Or…

I closed my eyes, pictured a clandestine meeting in the dark. Nicholas, hunched, deep in conversation with his mother, desperate to see his sick sister, keen to thrown off his cloak of anonymity. Or maybe, just maybe, he'd met Paris in terror, afraid someone had seen him, worried the game was up, that whatever he was running from had caught up with him.

Sound from the neighbouring street pulsed through me like a jolt of electricity. Over my shoulder, I glanced to where the tarmac petered out and disintegrated into a muddy puddled track. Which way would he have left, if indeed he had ever come?

Retracing my steps, I crossed into Great Norwood Street and walked past the front of the family home. Shutters were closed at the house in mourning, as if the Vellenders had decamped abroad, never to return.

People moved past me. All my judgements off, every face was Nicholas Vellender's. Neat adrenalin, like acid, burnt holes in my veins. Instinctively, I cut through St. Phillips Street and joined the bustling Bath road. Unique to Cheltenham, it had its own network of food shops, cafes and restaurants, even a couple of supermarkets so that it was quite easy to exist there without ever venturing into Cheltenham central. Shoppers out en masse, it had a jolly, busy, connected atmosphere and part of me began to come down from my manic state and feel more balanced. Monica would like it here, I thought, without knowing what she liked.

I ambled past Cheltenham College, from where I caught sight of the Playhouse Theatre up ahead in the distance. As I approached St. Luke's, a sweet residential area with a lovely church at the end, I turned right and stood outside the eponymously named Otto's restaurant. Triple fronted, with short wrought iron and ornate balconies on the upper storey, it twinkled with chandeliers, beacons of light in the middle of a dour, dismal day. Drawn inexorably towards it and cupping the palm of one hand across my brow, I pushed my face up against the smoky glass and glimpsed the same subtle shades inside as painted on the exterior, a combination of olive green and cream, the vibe quiet and unpretentious. Judging from the tasting menu, you'd need a hundred quid in your back pocket before ordering off the menu.

I couldn't imagine why Otto Vellender would discuss private grief with me. Undeterred, I ventured inside on the pretence of making a reservation.

It was as quiet as a museum on the coast in the middle of a heat wave. Directly opposite the entrance, a bar with a highly polished granite surface, behind which stood a petite woman with blonde hair and open features. She wore a simple grey shift dress that accentuated her slim build. Flat black pumps encased her tiny feet. Capable, in charge, with a quiet air of authority, she smiled, friendly with it. Front of house. Next to her, another woman dressed in kitchen whites clasping the neck of a bottle of brandy. She had hazel eyes and even features with a small downturned mouth. Her olive complexion bore the hallmarks of too much exposure to the sun. Late thirties, maybe early forties, I guessed. Deep lines scored the skin around her eyes and above her thin top lip. A smoker. Yet, she was undeniably attractive—the bone structure was all there—and would be more so if only she cheered up.

She watched as I entered armed with a smile that she didn't return, not even a cool tilt of her lips. It struck me that she was someone who had given up on being happy years ago. It caught my attention because it's really hard to ignore the warmth of a stranger, especially when the stranger is a potential customer. Scurrying into a back room, she left the woman in grey to make the running.

"We're not open, I'm afraid."

"I understand." Otto Vellender, a chef patron, was hardly likely to be working at a time like this.

"What I mean is that we're only open for dinner."

"This evening?"

"Fully booked tonight, but—"

"Gabriella, where the hell is that order from Markhams?"

We both swivelled in the direction of the voice. A man appeared with a wiry, lean, and powerful physique, creating the illusion of height, which, at a guess, was a couple of shades under six foot. He had short blond hair, cut with precision, pale eyebrows, pale side-burns, pale skin, and angular features suggesting Viking ancestry thousands of years down the line. His children, I realised, didn't take after him in looks. Heavy-lidded eyes, as blue as an iceberg on an overcast day, fixed on me. With his swagger and style, he looked very rock and roll. I likened him to quicksand because one look and you were sucked in.

"Sophia," he said, ignoring me. "Any ideas? Gabriella's got her Spanish head so far up her rear, she can't see for looking."

I coughed. The man swung around, looked me up and down, startled and, yes, pleased with what he saw. "Have we met before?" A smile glanced across his lips.

"No."

He inclined his head, as if trying to net a memory that wasn't there. I stayed silent, watching in fascination. Whereas Troy Martell was the type of man who checked his image in the mirror to reassure himself that he looked cool, Otto Vellender had no need. He knew it.

"I'm sorry," he said. "I'm Otto Vellender."

"I treated your daughter some years ago," I reminded him. "Kim Slade."

He flickered with recognition. "You've been in touch with my ex-wife." He came around the counter and took several steps towards me. That's when I noticed his hands, which were scarred and bunched up. I recoiled inside.

"I'm truly sorry for your loss," I said, eager to get in first.

"Is that all you came to say?"

I looked up into eyes that could burn, shrivel, and strip naked. An image of my father flashed across my mind. No wonder Otto Vellender's son had vanished.

"I wanted to talk to you."

"About?"

"Mimi." I meant Nicholas.

"Sorry, but I have a restaurant to run." He glanced towards Sophia and exchanged a belittling conspiratorial smile with her.

"I'm surprised to find you open at such a tricky time."

He stiffened as though I'd slapped his face. I expected a salvo of censure, but when he spoke his voice was tired and weary. "I am not a heartless man. My daughter is dead. She'd been dying for a long time. Sadly, I can't change any of that." He spread his scarred hands and, in the angled light, I registered sorrow, maybe even remorse.

"Of course, I'm sorry. I didn't—"

"If you want a shot at me, come for dinner tonight."

Did I see the suggestion of a smile? Was he flirting with me? "You're fully booked."

"I'm sure we could squeeze in a table for one somewhere." He glanced across at Sophia, who didn't seem the least fazed by the way her boss was behaving. Perhaps he always acted like this.

"Sorry, I've other plans." I should have said yes.

He shrugged, as if it were my hard luck. "Another time then."

I turned to leave, felt his eyes score the back of my jacket. I'd hardly reached the door when he called after me.

"I didn't kill my son, Miss Slade."

Staggered by his remark, I turned, looked back, and met his eviscerating gaze. Something in me sparked. He'd have to do a lot better than that if he hoped to intimidate me. I smiled as if confused. "I've no idea what you're talking about." And then I left.

TWENTY-FOUR

On Sunday morning a gap appeared in the rain, the sky a similar electric blue to Otto Vellender's eyes. Deciding to make the most of the decent weather, I did the noble thing and called Monica to invite her out to lunch. She seemed so made up by the prospect I winced at the memory of my mean-spirited and ugly thoughts. We agreed to meet for a late meal at 2:00 p.m., which would give me enough time to talk to Kyle and to investigate another area of town. Random, arbitrary, and naive as it was, I believed there was an outside chance that if Nicholas Vellender were alive, I'd simply run into him.

First, I took out a map of Cheltenham and divided it up into sectors. I'd already covered Montpellier and the Suffolks and decided to walk along the Honeybourne line, the old railway line connecting Cheltenham to Worcestershire. The route was flat, pretty and popular with walkers, cyclists, and parents with pushchairs. A lot of people seemed to have the same idea and there were lots of smiles and *good mornings* along the way. I should have found it reassuring that, after my tricky first week back at work, the world still worked and people got up in the morning and led, at least on the surface, uncomplicated lives, but my tendency towards paranoia remained unabated as my eyes raked the surroundings. Of Nicholas, there was no sign.

About to head back, my mobile rang. I recognised the number for all the wrong reasons.

"Hello Troy, what can I do for you?"

"How fucking dare you!"

My spirits didn't sag. They took a death-defying nosedive.

"To think I actually apologised to you, bitch."

I stopped walking and held my breath. Argument was pointless, contradiction a waste of energy.

"I saw the way you looked at him."

"Paris. Mrs. Vellender, I—"

"You're sick, you know that?"

"I can assure you that—"

"You're fucking mental."

Open-mouthed, I was unable to locate any words.

"You stay away from him, you freak. Got it?"

"It's really not—"

"Show some bloody respect. My son is dead and so is my daughter so stop asking your damn silly questions or—"

"Or what?" I said, finding the mettle in my voice.

"I'll make it my life's work to ruin you and your career."

"I don't respond well to threats, Mrs. Vellender. I appreciate you're upset, which is why I'm going to forget this call, but please—"

"You've been warned. Stay the fuck away." Then she hung up.

I stood mute in the sunshine. Heat spread across my shoulders and up my neck. Colour invaded my cheeks. Mood destroyed, I trudged back home and fumed like a child about all the things I would have liked to have said but didn't have the balls for. I could have turned the tables and told her that her anger was a weak and pathetic attempt designed to deflect me from looking into her son's life and disappearance. Most of my allegations were simply that—allegations, with little or no evidence to support them—yet Paris Vellender had stated her son was dead and had made a crude attempt to frighten me off with threats, and that put steel in my backbone. If only to honour a debt to a young woman I'd somehow failed, I vowed to find out what had happened to Nicholas Vellender, dead or alive.

But I needed to tread with more care.

Back home, I found one message on my answering machine. Mumbling and muzzy, as if talking from the depths of a tumble dryer, Kyle had left me a direct number. I glanced at my watch, 8:30 a.m. Florida time. I made the call and got straight through.

"How are you?" I said.

"Fucked."

"Nurses that hot, huh?"

"Don't make me laugh." His voice was a croak of *open my mouth only a millimetre* cadences.

"But it's been a success?"

"So they tell me."

Relief floated out of me. It was as if a bodybuilder had stood on my chest for a long, painful time and had suddenly stepped off. "I don't suppose you can talk much."

"No. Face numb, feel sick."

"That's the anaesthetic. Have you got any pain control?"

"A pump contraption. Don't get the wrong idea."

I flashed a smile that I hoped he could sense from across the Atlantic. "Look, I won't keep you long but I need a favour."

"Right now, I'd say yes to anything."

I laughed. "That's what I figured."

"Always hoped you'd take advantage of me."

In spite of the distance between us, I blushed. "The thing is I need somewhere temporary for my mother to stay."

"You haven't got a mother."

"She turned up." It seemed so weird to say it.

"Turn my back and look what happens."

"Shut up, you're not supposed to speak. Can you help?"

"Talk to Vanessa at the office. Tell her to let you have the studio flat in Pittville Circus Road. I'll email ahead, let her know."

"We'll pay the going rate, of course."

"Talk about it later."

"No, Kyle, I didn't mean that sort of favour."

"Gotta go. Too knackered to speak."

I smiled. He was a good man, a dependable friend. Forged in a random life-and-death situation, we had each other's backs, and for that I was grateful.

TWENTY-FIVE

I ANNOUNCED THE GOOD news to Monica as soon as we'd ordered drinks. Disappointment darkened her eyes. Her lips thinned and her mouth slanted down at the edges. She looked brittle and vulnerable, like a woman who has staked everything on receiving an inheritance only to be told it's been left to a cats' home.

"You don't have to worry about payment," I assured her. "Kyle is a mate."

"I don't want charity."

"It's not charity. It's a favour from one friend to another."

"A close friend?"

I faltered. How on earth could I explain my relationship with Kyle Stannard when I didn't fully understand it myself? "Not really, I haven't known him that long."

"Another of these individuals whose paths have crossed with yours," she said, her voice lightly rising while her eyes descended to the menu.

"Think I'll have the beef," I said in retaliation.

Conversation was horribly safe. Hot topics: the weather, Regency architecture of Cheltenham, shopping. I quickly discovered that my mother enjoyed cooking, which at least gave us something to rattle on about. Her passion for cakes and baking didn't chime with me but I gamely played along.

After we'd negotiated starters and mains there was a sea change.

Rosy with wine, she leant towards me, cosy and confiding. Resting one warm hand on mine, she said, "Is there anything you'd like to ask, something you'd like to know?"

"What about?" I felt instantly tense and wary.

"Me, perhaps?"

I blinked. Playing twenty questions wasn't going to work. I'd been dying to quiz her for most of my life, but I'd long ago accepted that there were no answers, that there would always be gaps in the narrative. I'd once fantasised about a last-ditch call from a deathbed and a confession of regret for a life not shared with mine. I'd never pictured this: flames and fire and ashes.

"Your lover…" I began.

"Steven," she said.

"How did you meet?"

"On a beach." Her voice was dreamy with reminiscence.

"Just like that?"

She nodded, shiny-eyed. "Sounds strange, doesn't it?"

"It's a little different." And yet it wasn't. I said nothing of long walks hand in hand with Chris. I remained silent about heat and blood and passion, and death by violence.

"Steven had a holiday home and he'd walk along the beach each day with his dog."

"Did we meet him?"

"Not really."

I jutted my chin out in disbelief. "But you were a mother with children. Where were we when you were … um … talking to Steven?"

She glanced down at the fine white tablecloth. In spite of the angle, I had a good view of the hot spots of colour on her cheeks. Like bloodstains. "You were with me," she admitted.

I slid my hand away. Hers remained, palm down, fingers extended, nails polished insipid pastel peach.

"Did Steven have children?"

The hand flinched as if I'd pressed the back of a heated teaspoon square against her skin. "He did."

"A wife?"

"Yes." She looked back up and met my flinty gaze.

"It isn't what you think."

"You don't know what I think." I didn't know myself.

A tic developed in her left eyelid. I thought dispassionately that she'd better learn to control it if the police interviewed her again. And if they did, would it signify a change, from witness to suspect? I didn't know what I thought about that either.

"So his family were holidaying in Devon while Steven chatted you up."

I had an odd detached feeling, as if I were having an out of body experience. Disconnected, I saw that I had put the blame squarely on a now-dead Steven rather than laying it on my mother. Interesting.

"There were problems in his marriage."

I nodded, indicating that I wasn't churlish, that I was sophisticated, that I understood. That tired old cliché, I thought.

"And afterwards?"

"The children stayed mostly with their mother."

"Mostly?"

"I didn't substitute one family for another, Kim."

I made no comment. I daren't. "Do you stay in touch?"

"Christmas and birthday cards."

Hot tears pricked my eyes. I bit down hard to prevent myself from saying words that could never be taken back. I think she knew then that her idea of *any* questions was a rubbish one.

"I'm sorry, Kim. I was being honest with you."

Ashamed to confess it, I wanted to hit her. She had more in common with my father than she knew. Brutal truth, he called it. "Would you like pudding?" I said, my voice brittle with barely suppressed rage.

"No. You?"

Feeling pale and cold and slightly nauseous, I shook my head. "Coffee?"

"Only if you're having one."

"I'm good." With haste, I asked a passing waitress for the bill.

My mother reached for her handbag, a big, solid, dependable affair. "Let me get it."

"But I invited you to lunch."

"I insist."

"If you're sure."

"I am."

I worked my mouth into the semblance of a smile, mechanically polite.

While we waited I chatted about the flat, anything to cover the tide of confusion and anger threatening to wash me away. "As soon as I get it sorted, I'll call you and we can go along and view it together," I said, far too chirpy.

"What about my things?"

"Your things?"

"At the house."

"It will be a crime scene. There will be protocols."

"But I lived in the annexe, nowhere near the judge's bedroom."

"Doesn't matter."

"Oh."

"Do you have much stuff?"

"Enough."

"Better have a word with Niven."

Her shoulders sagged. She glanced through the window. "I'd rather dance naked down the Promenade singing 'Rule Britannia'."

I have no idea why I found it funny, tension probably, but I burst out laughing. She joined in and, before I knew it, we were cackling like a couple of teenagers, tears streaming down our cheeks, helpless.

"You ladies having a good time?" the waitress said as she brought a card machine to the table, igniting another gale of giggles. God only knew why.

Afterwards when the hysteria died down, I felt betrayed and empty. We parted, not as mother and daughter, but as two people locked in an unholy alliance. It wasn't what I'd hoped for.

TWENTY-SIX

MONDAY WAS ANDROGYNOUS, NEITHER strongly one thing nor the other, a mixture of sorting out the personal with the professional. The pinnacle of my week would be Tuesday, the day Mimi Vellender was laid to rest.

During the only gap in the morning, I contacted Vanessa at Stannard's property company. Stannard proved true to his word. A done deal, I arranged to pick up a key at lunchtime after I'd seen my last client, Imogen Miller. Next I called Monica and left a message to the effect that I'd collect her after work to show her the flat.

As before, Imogen sloped in, collapsed into a chair, and viewed me with disdain. Her right knee twitched. The fingers on her left hand drummed a tattoo on the arm of the furniture. She presented a mass of writhing activity, like a prisoner doing time on a life sentence with absolutely no chance of parole. I made no mention of her verbal outburst in the previous session. We needed to push past it.

"How are you feeling?"

"Pissed off."

"Understandably," I said with a sympathetic smile. Cathy had cracked down on her. Taking away Imogen's phone was the equivalent of removing a bottle of booze from a seasoned alcoholic.

"This is all such a fucking waste of time."

"Is it?"

"You know it is," she said with a black smile.

"I know you're very angry. Want to tell me why?"

She clicked her tongue. I wasn't certain whether she thought me a fool for failing to notice something blindingly obvious, or whether she couldn't be bothered to tell me. At least she was talking.

"Are you angry with me?"

Her head shot back. "No."

"At the world?"

"Not especially."

"Your mum."

"Wouldn't you be? How would you feel if your mother nagged you all the time?"

Let's leave my mother out of it. "What does she nag you about, Imogen?"

"What I could be instead of who I am."

"And who's that?"

She scrubbed at her exhausted eyes with both fists. "Someone who wants to be left alone, who isn't pressured, who doesn't have to achieve."

Her mouth formed an ugly moue. "*Immy, have you practiced your Beethoven today? How many hours did you work on your scales this week? You won't get anywhere unless you stick at it,*" she said, scratchy and high-pitched, in ugly imitation of Mrs. Miller. "It's all she ever thinks about. She's stopped seeing *me*. I'm only a music machine."

141

And by starving yourself, you regain control and screw her plans. As double whammies went, it was brilliantly conceived and effective. Anorexics left most tacticians standing.

"Okay," I said, jotting a note, certain we were getting somewhere. "Obviously, your mum wants you to succeed. She believes in you. That's understandable, isn't it?"

Imogen resumed drumming her fingers. The shutters had come down again. I smiled. "If your mum told you that she didn't care what you did, as long as it made you happy, would that be okay?"

"She wouldn't do that in a million years."

"But if she did."

"What, give up music?"

"Do you have to give it up?" That was the other thing about my type of client—they dealt in straight absolutes and black and white.

She didn't answer.

"Is that what you want?" I pressed.

"I don't want the hassle."

"Fine, so if she agreed to let you play when you chose, at your own level, would that work for you?"

Imogen looked down, gave a tight shrug of her pointy shoulders. "I guess."

Breakthrough.

I sat back in the chair, gave Imogen space, let what we'd discussed sink in. She wasn't ready yet to strip off too many layers of protection, but I reckoned she'd cast off a couple.

"Will you talk to her?" she said, at last.

I nodded. Treating anorexia and other eating disorders was a collaborative process.

"Will my mother be told to sit here instead of me?" She flashed a rare grin.

"That would be something, wouldn't it?" I smiled.

We had struck an accord. As for Imogen's addiction to self-harm websites, I didn't push it. I wanted to enjoy a selfish moment of triumph, forget, for a split second, wounds, the missing and the dead, and the cloud of suspicion hanging over my mother.

If only because I knew it wouldn't last.

TWENTY-SEVEN

"It's small."

"Compact," I countered. It was, after all, a studio flat.

"Hmm," Monica said, sounding as doubtful as she looked.

I'd picked her up from The Battledown and driven over to Pittville, a leafy, genteel residential area north of the town centre.

The tour lasted minutes. It probably took us longer to walk across the drive to the chocolate box house and ascend the stairs to the top floor apartment than it did to view the accommodation. White bathroom suite. Large bedsitting room with kitchen off and laminate wood flooring throughout. Standard fare. Comfortable and functional. More bachelor pad than middle-aged singleton, but it came free.

"It's not forever. A temporary move until you get sorted."

She gave me one of those *heard it all before* looks. "I spoke to Luke last night," she said, breezy with it, in what I thought was a calculated divide and rule move. "He thinks I'd be better off nearer the shops."

I didn't point out that Luke had no knowledge of Cheltenham. "This is fine for now, particularly as you aren't paying a penny for it."

"Apart from council tax and utility bills."

"Which everyone pays, Monica." I pressed the keys into her hand. "You can move straight in." She viewed them with wary disdain. I was railroading her and she knew it. "Did you speak to Niven?" I said casually.

"I was informed she's on a rest day. I spoke to the sergeant."

"Holst?"

"He said that I might be able to collect a few things if I have a police officer with me."

"Progress. Did he say anything else?"

"Only that they needed to talk to me again."

"Did he say why?"

"No."

Worrying. Second formal interviews were designed to tie you in knots, to find holes and contradictions in original statements. Best advice would be to state the minimum. I told this to Monica, who looked at me as if I were being overly dramatic. I thought again about Gavin. "Did they say when?"

"Thursday at eleven a.m."

I briefly closed my eyes. I really couldn't take off any more time from work. She picked up on it.

"It's all right. I can manage. I'll go on the train and get a taxi the other end, saves all that messing about with trying to park the car."

I was sure she didn't mean it but every time she opened her mouth it felt like a criticism. "I'd feel happier if you weren't on your own," I said.

"It can't be helped." She presented a picture of injured pride and *get over it* petulance.

"What if you had some form of legal representation?"

"We've already discussed it." She pushed her hands into the pockets of her sensible coat. Matter closed.

"What harm would it do to make a phone call?" I aimed for a softly encouraging tone, to which her firm response was to cross her arms.

"I don't understand why you're so reluctant," I said in frustration.

Her eyes flashed with fire. "If you'd been at the butt end of solicitor's letters, you'd understand why."

"I'm sorry but I don't see—"

"You can't *possibly* understand. You've never been in my situation. You have no idea what it's like to have your name dragged through dirt, to be told you're an unfit mother, that you're unstable, to have the law make decisions about your future and to hell with what you think."

"I—"

"What forces do you think drove your father?" Her voice soared and roared. Before I had a chance to respond, she was all over me with an answer. "Revenge, Kim, and he used his lawyers like attack dogs against me."

Walk. Just walk out of here. Let me disappear through the walls, vanish among the trees, find somewhere nobody can see me. I actually don't know what happened next. I think I stuttered something about me being late and needing to go home.

Crashing gears, I drove back to the guesthouse in a trance, Monica unhinged beside me. When she climbed out without a word I felt a shard of fear embed itself deep in my heart. We didn't say goodbye.

Safe inside home territory, I locked the door behind me, went straight to the fridge, resisted the wine, and poured myself a soft drink. The cola sloshed about as I brought the glass to my lips and opened my mouth and swallowed. Bubbles fizzed unpleasantly down my throat and up my nose. Monica's hostile attitude towards the judiciary and the law provided the perfect motivation for murder.

Standing in the kitchen, still dressed in my jacket and outdoor shoes, I thought the unthinkable. Was I helping a killer?

TWENTY-EIGHT

DESPITE NOT TOUCHING A drop of booze, I slept the appalling sleep of a heavy drinker who, too drunk to drive home, kips the night on a friend's sofa. Tired, tetchy, dry-mouthed, and gritty-eyed, I surfaced through a prism of sludgy grey and emerged into consciousness.

Hiking my dose of antidepressants, I vowed to brave flood, plagues of locusts, and frogs, if necessary, and head back to Devon the following weekend. I'd check up on the old house and put as much physical distance between Monica and me as possible.

Feeling a bit more sorted, I picked out a pair of black trousers and chunky roll-neck. The temperature had dropped several degrees. Wind gusting. Muscular iron skies. Lightning and thunder and hail. Not a day for a funeral.

I drove to work, grabbed a coffee and phoned Gavin Chadwick's chambers. I needed help, even if Monica didn't. Asked for a name, I gave it. Asked with what it was in connection, I fudged. "Advice on a forthcoming case." The line went silent and I imagined wood-panelled walls adorned with muddy-coloured landscapes, shelves of dusty old tomes, dim EU lighting shining polka-dots of yellow on dark cobwebbed corridors, and that particularly old-money smell that you find in ancient legal practices.

"Kim." Gavin sounded pleased to hear from me. Probably mad with curiosity, wondering what I'd got myself into this time.

I didn't drag it out. Straight to the point, I gave him a rundown of events. I was factual and unemotional. He listened without interruption even when I mentioned Niven.

"So what do you think my mother should do?" I finished.

"You say they want her back?"

"On Thursday."

"And how many times have they spoken to her?"

I mentally did a recap and told him. In the absence of any comment, I continued, "Is it significant?"

"I'd say so."

"Is she a suspect?"

"Too strong," Gavin said. "The police are suspicious, that's all."

It sounded like one and the same to me.

"So I'm jumping the gun?"

"A little." He paused.

"But?"

"If more information comes to light implicating her, they might make an arrest."

"Dear God, what happens then?"

"Don't you remember?" It was supposed to be sardonic. I wasn't in the mood. Silence ballooned down the line. "Sorry, crass of me," Gavin said, clearing his throat. "If an arrest is made, they'll formally interview her on tape."

"She's already given a video statement."

"This is quite different."

"What sort of information could trigger an arrest?"

"Anything that provides a strong motive for murder."

I remembered Monica's face, protruding eyes, thin lips, and rage against a legal system that had, to her mind, removed her children from her. Jesus.

"Why did she run?" Gavin said.

"I'm not sure she did." I wanted to be scrupulously fair. "But I can see how the police might view it."

"From their perspective, she had the means and opportunity. Did you say they were looking at other leads?"

"According to my mother, yes. To be honest, it's tricky, Gavin. I'm getting all this third-hand and we don't have what could be described as a typical mother and daughter relationship."

"Whatever typical is," he snorted with dry humour.

You have absolutely no idea, I thought. "What's the next move?"

"By the police?"

"Uh-huh."

"If they haven't done so already, they'll arrange to get a life statement from next of kin, and focus on the fact that the deceased was a former judge."

"I've been thinking about that. Surely, it will be a main line of enquiry?"

"A strong line of enquiry," Gavin corrected me. "Firstly, background checks will be done on anyone who had contact with the judge within a week or so of his death and that includes your mother. Does she have any previous convictions?"

"I can't answer that."

"When was the last time you two met?"

"Over twenty years ago."

"And you have no idea of her life up until recently?"

That was the point. "No."

"Have they carried out forensic checks, DNA swabs, and so on?"

"Done." I remembered how unhappy she'd been about it.

"She didn't refuse?"

"I don't think so." Would she have told me?

"Okay." I imagined him stroking his chin in a lawyerly way, sharp eyes glinting through the lenses of his spectacles. "The police are still in evidence-gathering mode. They won't want to screw up by jumping to conclusions too soon."

"They did with me."

"Yours was a unique situation."

Good to know I was special. "What you're saying is that unless and until they make an arrest, the services of a solicitor are surplus."

"And if they do, anyone under arrest is offered a duty brief."

"You mean you wouldn't be interested in taking the job?" Dread bloomed inside me.

"Simply giving you the facts. If she needs my help, of course, Kim, I'm happy to take it on."

I felt light-headed with relief. "Thanks, Gavin, I really appreciate it."

"Keep me posted. Your mother might not need any legal representation at all."

I so hoped he was right.

TWENTY-NINE

THE COLD DAY TURNED into a vicious afternoon of driving rain. I set off early and caught a bus, my arrival timed to half an hour before the funeral.

Clobbered up in beanie hat, scarf, and thick padded jacket, a flower seller exchanged chilly greetings with me. Returning it with a half smile, I longed to change direction and retreat to my nice warm office.

Three black crows pecked in the glistening grass like a scene from a Thomas Hardy novel. I'm not superstitious but it felt like an omen, and I scurried past a stone-built lodge and through a set of open gates flanked by turrets and timid-looking purple crocuses struggling to live, and into the grounds of the sleeping dead. At once, the wind magically died down and dropped away to a lonely breeze.

Where the wide path split into three, a freshly dug grave, a wound in the earth, gaped open at me. I wondered if this were Mimi's final destination.

Hanging back near an enormous Douglas fir, I scanned as far as my eye could see for a solitary male. All I saw were gravestones and monuments to soldiers and aristocrats and those robbed of life in their prime, or before it had really got going.

Whether it was mood or delusion, once again unseen eyes skewered into me. Whipping round, my pulse jack-hammering, I scoped the graveyard for a second time but, body betraying my mind, there was no-one to see, nothing to hear, simply a vista of slimy grey and green. I stayed quite still, my gloved hands domed over my mouth, breathing slowly. Hey, everyone, there's nothing wrong with me. I'm not jumpy or sad or mad.

The South chapel loomed ahead. On my left, a wooden shelter, like the ones you find at the seaside. A place of quiet reflection for the bereaved, split into four private sections, it offered protection from the wind and rain and, more importantly for me, a perfect view. I stepped inside, sat down on a bench and let my gaze rove the church and grounds like a sniper waiting for a target to show.

Minutes passed. Stamping my boots on the unyielding ground, hands tucked underneath my armpits to generate heat, I identified a vicar, a man I thought might be an organist, and other churchy people, including two women, stolid with sensible coats and shoes, clutching orders of service. Nobody appeared resembling Nicholas Vellender.

As the hour drew near, car doors slammed. High voices piped upon the wind. Next, a surge of youngsters, school kids, supple and smiling, girls in pink shoes and dresses, lads with purple ties and jackets. Mimi's favourite colours, I guessed. There was noise and there was laughter, remembrance and celebration, cigarettes and conversation and, although it warmed me, it also made me inexpressibly sad to think of all that Mimi was missing out on, all that she'd not lived but lost.

The arrival of the funereal equivalent of the headline act caught everyone's attention. Travelling at a slow military pace, a hearse carried a light oak coffin covered in white roses followed by two funeral cars, Paris Vellender and Troy Martell in the first, the second transporting Otto Vellender. I watched as each climbed out, isolated and exiled in their grief. Resembling a Mafia widow, Paris was dressed top to toe in black and wore a pillbox hat with a net veil and large black sunglasses. The epitome of chic despair, she leant heavily on Troy Martell's arm, a man who looked hopelessly out of his depth. When she vanished inside the chapel, she looked neither left nor right. Otto, sleek and sombre in a charcoal-coloured coat, his blond hair a splash of colour in the murk, did the same. Nobody expected shocks or surprises, least of all the reappearance of a lost son.

The doors slammed shut. Organ music drifted through the chill, faint like falling leaves. I waited and watched, my breath making smoke rings in the icy air, and saw neither movement nor shadow. As each minute passed, I thought many things: that Nicholas was a ghost, a figment of Troy Martell's deluded imagination; that he lived somewhere else, far away; that the lingering fog of depression skewed my emotions and my judgement. By the time mourners emerged an hour later, I had changed my mind numerous times and I could barely feel the blood in my veins.

The funeral party eventually discharged from the chapel and trooped as one across the gravel when a sudden piercing howl soared and ricocheted like a twenty-one gun salute through the graveyard. Everyone turned, me included.

Paris Vellender sprawled facedown on the ground, her hat askew in the dirt. Unique, raw, bleeding, and visceral, the sound of grief is like no other. Her pain shot right through me and I narrowed my eyes to watch Martell and Otto run. Martell dropped down at her side, reaching out with his meaty arms, attempting to lift her. Otto Vellender had one hand outstretched to the woman he'd once loved and, for all I knew, still did. As soon as he made contact, her head jolted and she raised her face to his.

"Get away from me, you bastard," she screeched, her features contorted. "You killed them. You murdered my babies." Coarse, primal, agony stripped bare for the voyeurism of others, an arc of sound ripped through the dead, inert air.

Amid a scuffle of activity, Paris was hauled to her feet, brushed down, and guided aside.

Everyone stared. Hands cupped mouths, whisperings beneath. Embarrassed yet excited, eyes flickered and danced. I had a fleeting image of jackals surrounding wounded, bleeding prey. Alone, jaw pulsing, face white and constricted with rage, Otto Vellender straightened up, adjusted the collar of his coat, and stalked away.

THIRTY

No doubt about it, Paris Vellender's outburst changed the dynamics. Kids, clergy, and mourners sped to the graveside, the vicar leading his flock with indecent haste. Frozen and blue with cold, I waited until the last mourner had gone and the gravediggers had performed their final act. Stiff-limbed, I made a move.

Piled with soft toys, flowers, and symbols of all that had mattered to her, Mimi's grave was a monument to the freshly dead. Standing there alone, a terrible wave of grief washed over me so hard I had to steady myself from falling. I'd stood pale and tuned-out at the graveside of my lover and yet a girl I barely knew unleashed a depth of despair in me that almost crushed my soul.

When it finally passed I stooped down and studied cards that said *Love ya, babe, Forever young,* and *You're with the angels now, my mate and bestest friend.* Awkward sentiments expressed in awkward ways, but no less touching. Fingers numb with cold, I hunted through dozens in a doomed quest to find an anonymous wreath or cryptic card that might have been sent from Nicholas Vellender.

Running on empty, I straightened up and surveyed the scenery one last time. If Nicholas were to come, this would be the time to return from exile, when everyone who counted had paid respects and left. Nobody came other than an elderly couple walking hand in hand to tend a nearby grave.

I stepped across grass spongy with too much rain, the heels of my boots sinking into the earth, and back onto the wide walkway. Practically at the entrance, an acid-yellow Seat Mii driven by a dark-haired figure hurtled into the cemetery at a speed that defied the 15mph speed limit, and whipped straight past. Instinctively, I jumped back, a vapour trail of metal and benzene hitting the back of my throat like a spray of gas. Astonished, my eyes locked onto the vehicle's rear tinted windows as it burnt rubber in a wide loop up towards the chapels, gravel flying, engine revving. A joyrider, someone undone by grief, or was it meant for me, a warning? Braver souls would have chased after the car. I wasn't one of them. I fled.

In a daze, I caught the bus back to work and felt the cold embrace of melancholia. I was warned that this might occur. There's a misconception about medication that it will miraculously eliminate every symptom. In truth, despair is limited to weeks rather than months. It's still present, in other words, but I couldn't slip back, couldn't live my life without the energy to get up in the morning, couldn't allow my body's natural rhythms to be sabotaged with lethargy one minute and relentless activity the next. My high anxiety state felt as if I were walking through night in thin clothes that exposed too much of me to the elements.

Struggling to hold it together, I plastered a false smile upon my lips, and saw my one and only client of the afternoon, and drove home. I poured myself a soft drink, ignored the answering machine announcing I had two messages, lit the fire, and curled up on the sofa, my legs tucked up tight, shoulders hunched, both hands clutching the glass as if it were a crystal ball. A soundtrack of Paris Vellender's screams and accusations played through my head alongside Otto's stout retreat while the visual part of my brain focused on the Seat, how it came within an inch of chewing me up beneath its wheels, and…

I put my drink aside and grabbed hold of my laptop. Switching it on, I scrolled through and found the Missing People website. Run by volunteers, it was a charitable organisation that didn't charge for its services. According to the blurb, every two minutes someone disappears, most found within seventy-two hours, yet an astonishing number were missing for longer; some of them, like Nicholas Vellender, for years. Browsing the database of relaxed and smiling faces, young and old, black and white, foreign and British men and women, made me feel spectacularly intrusive. I couldn't help but wonder what had driven them away, or, more darkly, what might have befallen them.

Pressing a link to a more selective search, I punched in Nicholas's age range and gender, narrowed it down to the category of missing for greater than three years and selected the Cheltenham area. A raft of faces came up, but Nicholas Vellender's was not among them. With a creep of unease, I sat back, kicked off my shoes and asked myself for the hundredth time why he had upped and gone, stayed away, and where he might live?

I heated up a casserole I'd had the presence of mind to take from the freezer that morning and ate it mechanically, not really tasting, washed and dried up the debris and put back pans and bowl in the cupboard, cutlery in the drawer. I rinsed my glass, cleaned and wiped a cloth over the draining board, put a wash in the machine.

Busy, busy, wired and going through the motions, then my mobile rang, ramming my thoughts sideways.

"Kim, it's me."

I wanted to shout with joy. "Kyle, how are you doing?"

"You sound peculiar," he said. "You're not normally this happy."

Aren't I? I remembered once he'd told me not to be sad. It seemed a lifetime ago. "I'm pleased to hear from you. You sound so well," I said, recovering.

"That wouldn't be difficult. The swelling's subsided a little and I'm onto soft solids or, to the uninitiated, baby food as opposed to no food. Did you get your ma sorted?"

"Thank you, yes. It's perfect." Even if Monica didn't think so.

"Good. So what's new in the hood?"

"*In the hood?* How long have you been in the States?"

"At least I didn't call you bitch."

I burst out laughing.

"Glad I can still amuse," he said, warmth in his voice. "So what's cooking?"

"Nothing."

"And I'm a brain surgeon. Any developments in the Vellender case?"

"Kyle, it's not a case."

"Thought you mentioned murder."

No, you did that. "Jesus, Kyle, an allegation of murder is not the same as *murder* murder."

"But the two are often intertwined."

"Look, I really don't think anyone has been killed." Obliterating Paris Vellender's accusation from my mind, I forced myself to sound more upbeat than I felt. "When emotions run high people say things they don't mean."

"So you keep telling me."

I dropped my voice. Ridiculous, really. It wasn't as if our conversation was being taped. "It's dangerous to leap to conclusions is all I'm saying."

"So the jury's out."

"Did I ever mention that you have a ghoulish streak?"

Kyle snorted a protest. I attempted to change the subject but he wasn't deflected. "I've been doing some research."

"Thought you were supposed to be taking it easy."

"Moving a finger doesn't require a lot of energy."

I grimaced, wishing I'd never mentioned a single word to Stannard about the Vellenders.

"I want to ask you a question."

Must you? "Go on."

"Why did it take six weeks before Nicholas Vellender was reported missing?"

"How the hell did you find that out?"

"A simple mathematical deduction based on news reports. Fishy, don't you think?"

THIRTY-ONE

I COCKED ONE EYE open, adjusted my vision to the light, and registered that my mobile was ringing. It was seven minutes to seven in the morning.

"Yes?" Drenched in sleep, my voice sounded faraway and alien.

Monica spoke in what could be described as a peremptory tone. "I've moved out of The Battledown."

"And into the flat?"

"Yes—thank you."

"Good." In the annals of stilted conversations, our exchange hovered around the number one spot. Judging from the hour, old people got up early. I pictured her drinking her first cup of tea around six, washing and dressing and eating breakfast all before seven. She'd probably consumed the day's newspaper, too. Why she'd called at such an ungodly hour, search me.

"About tomorrow," she said.

"Your visit to the police?" I propped myself up on one elbow.

"I was thinking about what you said, you know, about a lawyer."

"Right." Should I explain I'd already taken soundings, or would that vex her?

"I'm not agreeing to it, even if things turn nasty."

I quelled a stab of alarm. "Are they likely to?"

"The police do seem very focused."

Beautifully put. "Monica." I swallowed. "And please don't take this the wrong way, but is there something you haven't told me?"

"Like what?"

"Have you any prior convictions?"

"Why would you think that?" She practically screamed it.

"I'm simply asking the question."

"No."

"That's good, very good," I said, shaky. "And you've never brought a complaint against someone else?"

"Never."

Paris Vellender's theatrical display the day before streaked through my mind. Was it all for show, a way of getting a message across? "Then I honestly believe the police are simply in evidence-gathering mode," I said, cribbing a line from Gavin. "They probably need to corroborate certain details and cross-match it with other accounts."

"Which other accounts? There was only myself and Mrs. Hawkes at the house."

"Like I told you," I repeated, feeling that I was talking to a child, going over and over the same ground again and again, "the police will be speaking to all kinds of people, including anyone convicted by the judge, who might bear him a grudge."

"But that could run into hundreds."

"Exactly."

"Then why waste time on me when they should be investigating them?"

I couldn't answer. Monica niggled with her constant questions. I was tired and I was worn out of with thinking. Making some half-arsed response, I asked her to keep me informed of developments. "I'm not around at the weekend," I added in haste.

"Oh."

She sounded miserable and I promised to drop by the following evening after her next interview with the police. "I have to go," I said, throwing back the duvet. "See you tomorrow."

Work was work. I spent an hour in a practice meeting then saw Karmel, our resident dietician and all-round magician. She not only devised delicious recipes, nutritious meals that packed a calorific punch when eaten in minute quantities, she also acted as diplomat and trouble-shooter. Mealtimes held the potential for tantrums. With Karmel around, it rarely happened. The girls liked her a lot. With her tattoos and piercings and grungy clothes, she was viewed as one of them.

"Hi," I said, popping my head around her door. "Got a moment?"

Karmel flashed a smile and jangled her latest piece of ironware. "Hey," she said, "come in, and before I forget, a cute guy handed me this."

Puzzled, I took a seat and glanced at the envelope, my name scrawled on it as if written by a three-year-old.

"You're a dark horse," she said, as she handed it over.

I forced a smile. "Cute, you said?"

She rolled her eyes. "Well fit."

"Fat, thin, tall?"

"Keeps himself in shape, shaved head, strong bone structure."

Troy Martell. "American accent?"

She frowned. "Maybe a twang."

"You didn't notice?"

She broke into another wide smile, a glint of gold flashing from a tongue stud. "Too busy admiring to listen."

I thought about that. Under pressure, did Martell slip up with the phoney accent?

"When was this?"

"This morning. Sweaty and muscled-up, the guy was mid-jog." She made a big play of staring at the letter. "You're not going to read it?"

I pushed the envelope into the back pocket of my jeans. "Nah, it will keep."

I didn't remember much of the rest of our discussion. I was thinking about Martell. With Paris on his back, I guessed he had good reason not to phone me direct. It still struck me as cloak and dagger.

Back in my office, I tore open the envelope. The message was simple. *Need to talk. Meet me tonight at 8 at The Railway Inn.*

THIRTY-TWO

I'D NEVER BEEN TO The Railway before although I'd heard that it was the place to go if you like sausages and real ale. Hidden away from the town centre and not far from where I lived, it was surprising I hadn't visited before. Mustard-coloured walls, warm wood, and leather décor—my kind of place.

I ordered a Coke and took it to a corner table with a decent view of the door. A couple of minutes early, I sipped, studied the menu, checked out the wine list and beers on tap. I worked out the couple in front of me were not married to each other in spite of both wearing wedding rings. Body language suggested that he was trying to break off the relationship and she was unhappy about it.

After half an hour of no show, I risked a call to Martell's mobile phone. It didn't ring, but went straight to the messaging service. Perhaps he was driving, although, for the life of me, I couldn't think why. Bored, I took a pen from my bag and doodled on a beer mat. Guided as if by a magic hand, I drew a collection of horizontal lines, short then long, joined by three horizontals and two squiggles. My photographic memory had captured almost perfectly the image of the scar on Mimi Vellender's arm. Georgia was right. It did look Oriental. Actually, it looked Japanese. Remembering Chris's eclectic collection of books on erotic art, I had a fleeting memory of Japanese paintings with lurid depictions of octopuses engaged in sex with young women.

Parking the thought and deciding to give Troy another ten minutes, I slipped the beer mat into my bag and placed my phone on the table, watched and waited and ignored the pitying looks of those who thought I'd been stood up. About to leave, my phone rang. I grabbed it.

"Kim, it's Otto Vellender."

Surprise didn't really cover my reaction. "How did you get this number?"

"I'm sorry, have I called at a bad time?"

I glanced around the busy pub. He could probably hear the tinkle of glass and conversation. "Not especially."

"I wondered whether you'd like to have dinner with me?"

Stunned, I didn't know how to respond. If I thought he'd phoned to intimidate me, I was wrong. So what was Otto's agenda, to put the record straight, to go on some kind of charm offensive? Then again, he'd no idea I'd witnessed the grim little scene at the graveyard the day before. And what kind of guy invites a woman to dinner the same week he's buried his daughter? The type who does the same when he's buried his son, I remembered, skeletons in my family closet rattling their spectral hands at me. Hadn't my father done something similar?

"When?"

"Friday, nine thirty p.m."

I'd intended to head to Devon. "Aren't Fridays your busiest night?"

"My sous chefs will take over."

"All right," I said slowly. Instead, I'd head for the West Country first thing Saturday morning.

"Good," he said. "Is there anything you can't eat?"

I assured him I wasn't fussy or allergic to anything.

"I'll see you then."

I plodded home, spent the rest of the evening with the growing and uneasy sense of impending disaster. I told myself that I was overwrought, imagining things, viewing my world through the narrow lens of my ripped up past and getting things out of perspective. Deep down, I knew I'd been drawn into something obscure and wrong and dangerous. Monica blurred into Paris Vellender, Otto into my father.

Wired, I hunted through my bookcase and finally unearthed one of Chris's old books. Hentai is a Japanese term used to describe perverse sexual desire. The Japanese are big on octopi, and images ranged from sadistic to tasteful. Comparing what I'd drawn on the beer mat to content in the book revealed zilch. Frankly, I was relieved. Not that it helped me rest or reduce my anxiety. When a night's sleep didn't correct my thinking I upped my medication and hoped for the best.

Imogen Miller was my first client the next day. Ground made in our previous consultation had sheared off and fallen into the sea. Back the moody attitude, the *screw you* expression, the downturned mouth and downcast eyes that refused to be held by mine. I put it down to withdrawal symptoms. A client may have a breakthrough moment only to panic at the dawning reality of having to put changes of behaviour into practice. In many ways it was easier to give in to the tyranny of addiction than allow someone like me to loosen its stranglehold.

I ran through the standard *how are you*s and quickly cut to her urge to self-harm. I kidded myself that I was nothing if not professional. I didn't admit any personal interest.

"Which websites do you use?"

She shrugged one spiny shoulder.

I waited. Seconds passed like a countdown to a millennium change. "Can I show you something?"

She looked up, eyes flickering.

I took the beer mat from my bag and showed Imogen. "Does this mean anything?"

Her chin jutted out. She peered forward. I looked at her expectantly. She met my gaze, blinking and blank-eyed. "No."

"You're sure?"

"Yes."

She was lying. She knew it. I knew it.

"I think it has a Japanese connection."

"How would I frigging know?"

I waited a beat. "Are you struggling, Imogen?"

Her smile was tight and hollow. Everything about her posture was pared down and contained. "Have you spoken to my mum?"

"Not yet."

A mass of self-loathing and guilt, she drew away from me and stared deliberately at the wall. "See, you say you'll do something and then you don't."

"But I will," I assured her.

"Right," she said, disbelieving, her voice cold and detached.

"Not every negative event, like your mother asking you—"

"Ordering me—"

"To practice means that she doesn't love you."

Imogen looked at me with hard eyes. "What the fuck would you know?"

Long after she'd gone, I realised how right she was. I didn't have a clue.

THIRTY-THREE

I SAT IN MONICA's sitting room cum dining room cum kitchen area clutching a mug of tea with pink flowers on it and listened to her account of her latest interview with the police.

"The way the bag was tied around his neck implied that someone else had done it."

"Because the ..." I hesitated. "The *individual* was left-handed, you said, and the judge was right-handed."

"I didn't even notice." She frowned into the middle distance, perplexed, as though it were remiss of her.

"And?" I said, eager to keep her talking.

"Someone like me." Her voice, so normally well modulated, rose to a wail.

"Did they say that?"

"My fingerprints were on the bag and I'm left-handed." She looked glum and cornered.

"Did you do it?"

Had I shot her in the stomach at close range with a sawn-off, she couldn't have reacted with more shock.

"Sorry, but I had to ask." I also had to ask myself a dirty great question: Did I think Monica capable of murder? Honest answer: I didn't know.

She cast me a reproachful look. Circumstantial evidence was all the police appeared to have. I watched her closely. Her eyes narrowed and she tapped her fingers on the arm of the chair.

"What?"

"There's something they aren't telling me, I'm sure of it."

She'd said so before, which meant she was really bothered by it. "Like what?"

She glanced down. "I wish I knew."

I drank tea that I didn't want and tried to roll back the timeframe. I needed to get a handle on the missing bits of my mother's life, to gather up the fragments and place them into a picture I could understand.

"Where did you go with Steven after you left Devon?"

She flinched. "What's that got to do with this?"

"I'm interested."

"Shropshire."

"What did he do for a living?"

"He was in print and design."

"And afterwards?"

She looked at me blankly.

"After Steven died, where did you go?" I pressed.

"London."

She dropped her gaze once more and I wondered why. "Brave move."

"Yes, well I thought there'd be more work there. I already told you," she said with emphasis.

"So you got a job?"

"Worked in hotels, mostly. Cleaning and such."

"Hard work."

"Long hours."

"Whereabouts?"

"All over." For a third time, she looked shifty. I got the strong impression that her time in London was an unhappy episode and that she was keeping something from me. My silence betrayed me, and she suddenly looked me straight in the eye with a steady, unflinching gaze. "I've made many mistakes in my life, Kim, but murder isn't one of them."

We sipped more tea in silence. She asked if I wanted a top up. I accepted and suggested again that she talked to Luke.

Vehemently opposed, she said, "No, I don't want him involved."

"That's absurd." In danger of breaking, I no longer wished to carry the burden alone.

"Gives it too much oxygen," she protested.

"This won't go away because you will it." It came out snappier than I intended.

She sat stone-faced and fiddled with the material in her skirt. I noticed she did that a lot under pressure. Time to take the plunge and wheel out my secret weapon. "I really believe the time has come to talk to a lawyer. In fact, I've already—"

"Kim, I—"

"Hear me out." I described my conversation with Gavin Chadwick. Initially, her eyes expressed exasperation, her body language indignation and resistance. I'm not sure what it was that finally got through to her—probably my insistence. When I finished speaking, she seemed resigned, which I took to be a good sign.

"I'll talk to him tomorrow," I said, feeling more cheerful, "tell him where we're at, then you can speak to him yourself."

"Will I get legal aid?"

I very much doubted it. "We'll cross that bridge as and when." I stood up, thinking not for the first time that Luke would have to chip in. "Can I use your loo before I go?"

"You know where it is."

I went to the bathroom. Counting to ten, I flushed the lavatory, ran the hot and cold taps, and flicked open the door to the mirror-fronted medicine cabinet. I found a toothbrush, toothpaste, mouthwash, cosmetic pads, cotton buds and make-up remover, a pack of standard painkillers, and what looked like prescription drugs. Glancing at the locked door, I reached inside and pulled out a pack of Venlafaxine, a superior antidepressant used for severely anxious patients. I grimaced. *What the hell?* My mother had led me to believe that she'd been happy in her work, settled with the judge and his wife. So what had triggered the need? Obviously, her depression could spark from chemical imbalances in her brain rather than from an event so perhaps I was reading too much into it. Maybe my own anxiety state was hereditary, I now realised with surprise, but when I fished out the second pack, I felt as if I'd crashed headlong into a wall. Zopiclone was the same sleeping drug used by Judge Michael Hawkes.

My mother had lied to me. About what else had she lied?

Grim, I returned and faced her with my findings.

She jumped to her feet. "How dare you snoop—"

I cut her off before she got started. "You damn well lied to the police and then to me."

"And why do you think I did that?" Her eyes were wide and staring, the irises flecked a sudden sickly yellow.

"I dread to think." Jesus H. Christ. What was I supposed to think?

"I lied to prevent a reaction like yours. Do you honestly think I'm a murderer?"

"I have no idea." My anger—hot, burning, and wild—was like a demonic force within me. Words tunnelled out of my mouth. "You look me up after a couple of decades of complete sodding absence. You stay in touch with other people's kids and don't give a damn about your own flesh and blood. You run away from the police. You lie. What the fuck is going on?"

"How dare you swear at me and use that kind of language."

We both stood facing each other like a couple of gunslingers at noon. I was panting hard, my mother harder. The atmosphere in the tiny studio apartment was oppressive, the lighting fake and artificial as if yielding radiation. I found it difficult to see, let alone think and focus. "And why are you on antidepressants?" The words tumbled out of my mouth, accusing. Not a great endorsement of my empathetic qualities. People lied for a whole host of reasons. It didn't mean that they were guilty. Hounding someone rarely elicits the truth. I knew this in the core of my being but it was as if, with the arrival of Monica, my beliefs and normal rules of civilised behaviour, even my professional expertise and knowledge, had fled out through the nearest exit. I was no good as a daughter, even less as a clinical psychologist.

Spent and grey, she pressed a hand against her temple, probing the pressure point, half closing her eyes. Finally, she spoke, slowly, without rancour, as if each word were costing her dear. "I knew you wouldn't understand."

"How can I if you aren't honest with me?"

Tears spurted into the creases around her eyes. "Because if I'm honest you'll know the truth and you'll hate me for it."

Nausea grabbed my stomach. My hand flew to my mouth. Was this it? Was this Monica's way of telling me that she was guilty, that she'd drugged an old man, stuffed a plastic bag over his head and cut off his air supply? Were her liver-spotted hands responsible for his bruises? But, as horrible as the truth might be, I had to know. Damn it, I *had to know*.

Scrabbling for certainty, I lied. "It doesn't matter what you've done. I'll stand by you, but please," I begged, "please tell me the truth."

She looked at me then with such need and desperation, I thought my heart would explode. "Kim," she said. "I did not kill Judge Hawkes. I swear it."

I reached for a chair and sat down hard. "Okay." My voice was shaky. "But, from now on, no secrets. Do you understand?"

Her jaw clenched.

"Do you understand?" I repeated loudly.

"Yes." That damn shadow passed behind her eyes once more. That's when I knew for certain that she was holding out on me, and I was powerless to prevent the darkness from smashing in.

THIRTY-FOUR

With still no word from Martell, I did the equivalent of shoving him into my Spam folder to be automatically deleted in precisely thirty days, and cursed myself for not paying more attention to Georgia's advice.

Midway through the morning, I made an uncomfortable call to Gavin and stuck to the facts. I didn't let on about the sleeping tablets, the *something* lurking in Monica's background, or that I found her difficult to believe.

"Are you all right?" he said when I'd finished.

"Coming down with a cold or something," I sniffed. Actually, I did feel below par, which was unsurprising.

"And you're coming to Devon at the weekend?"

"Tomorrow, yes."

"Why not bring your mother with you?"

It was a good plan. It made sense. My stomach curdled. "I'll ask her."

"Excellent. Shall we say two thirty at the house?"

Secretly praying that my mother would sooner choose to run in the London Marathon, I called her and explained the situation.

"Good idea," she said.

"You won't find it too much?"

"In what way?"

"Revisiting the ..." I almost said *scene of crime.* "The place where you were so unhappy."

"I think I can manage for a couple of nights, Kim." I disliked her chiding tone, particularly as she'd already made plain her aversion to setting one foot over the cottage threshold. So much for the reference to her sooner poking pins in her eyes ...

For the rest of the day I did my best to act like a bloke and compartmentalise my life. I struggled through the afternoon, picked up the phone three times to cancel my date with Otto Vellender and, for complex, not fully processed reasons, chickened out. A handful with kerb appeal, he was the archetypal bad boy and, if I were honest with myself, exactly the kind of guy I fell for. Each time I was tempted to back out I thought of Mimi, the plea in her void eyes, her dying wish.

Propelled by guilt, I didn't go straight home after work. Risking rush hour traffic, I drove through rough streets in Alstone and Arle, looping round to Kingsditch before cutting back down the Tewkesbury Road in another doomed attempt to spot Nicholas Vellender inhabiting the shadows.

Back at the house, dispirited, I ran a bath, poured in my most expensive bath oil and, stripping off clothes and make-up, immersed myself in steamy heat for an hour. Choosing an appropriate outfit took longer. I'd never eaten at a Michelin-starred restaurant, been the guest of a stranger, or a man whose wife accused him of having blood on his hands. As fact-finding missions went, it rated a bizarre undertaking.

Settling on a classic favourite, a chic fit and flare ink-green woollen dress with skinny sleeves, I applied make-up with more care than usual. Not because I wanted to impress, but because I needed all the confidence I could mobilise. I was, after all, dining with the devil in Paris Vellender's eyes.

Slipping on a pair of black patent stilettoes, I treated myself to a cab and arrived outside the restaurant a few minutes before nine. Lights from Otto's spilled a warm glow of amber colour onto the street. As I briefly peered into shapeless spaces, it struck me that, if he were alive, night would be Nicholas Vellender's best friend, that, if I continued my search I, too, would be forced to risk the darkness. Blind. Without landmarks.

I walked inside. Every spot lit table was taken. Two serious looking waiters in suits and ties flanked me; one took my coat, the other announcing in a thick Eastern European accent that he was my waiter for the evening. It was a strange encounter, especially as there was no sign of my dinner date.

Shown to a table, I was engulfed, not by noise and chatter and music, but the low flow of conversation, the chink of ice on glass and a spiritual atmosphere bordering on reverence. I could have been in a monastery at plainsong.

A chair was pulled back. I sat down. Someone pushed my seat in and a linen napkin was laid across my lap. My personal space fully invaded, I did my best not to convey pique or embarrassment.

"Mr. Vellender sends his apologies," my waiter for the night said.
"Oh?"

"He asks that you stay and dine, at his expense, and he will join you later."

I strained in the direction of a closed door and wondered if Vellender were hiding behind it. In normal circumstances, I'd have told myself that, at least, he hadn't tried to dignify his absence with an excuse or a lie. These weren't normal circumstances.

The waiter who'd delivered the bad news, a square faced young man with pale skin and close-cropped hair, hovered, no doubt waiting for some gesture of acceptance from me. I didn't know how to react. I love good food. I love the smell, taste, and feel. I revel in the ritual; the starched tablecloth, candles and decent crystal, as much as the impromptu picnic in bed with a lover. And that's the point. To really enjoy great food, you need to share with at least one other. There is no fun in eating alone. Everything, however sublime, tastes like grit on your tongue, salt on your teeth. I wasn't looking for a date with Otto Vellender. Mine was a pragmatic meeting, a quest for information, but the thought of dining alone left me bereft. It must have shown.

As if to placate me, out of nowhere, my waiter presented me with a glass of champagne. I smiled thanks, but didn't feel the warmth. Not wishing to be part of Otto's bullshit production, churlish as it was to retreat, I shook my head and stood up to leave. As if on cue, the closed door swept open and Otto appeared in chef's whites, his face a picture of abject apology and worry. I briefly wondered how long he'd been parked on the other side, an ear straining to hear my voice and judge my reaction. All eyes in the restaurant swung in the direction of the revered one.

"Kim, I'm so sorry. We're a chef down but I really will be with you as soon as possible."

Now all eyes swivelled to me in expectation, the consensus clearly *Go on, don't be a cow.* What choice did I have?

I flicked a smile of submission, half expecting a round of applause, and sat back down. My napkin restored, I took a sip of champagne, which tasted more rounded, biscuitier, more floral, more *everything*. Booze this good was in a different league to anything I'd ever tasted. Meanwhile, satisfied with the outcome, everyone else returned to conversation and the food on their plates. Show over, normal service resumed.

"Chef has devised a special tasting menu for you," I was informed. Next my man for the night reeled off a medley of exotic dishes with culinary buzzwords so dense I tuned out and considered which hard arse question to pose first when Otto finally put in an appearance.

What happened next was part magic act, lesson in applied physics, and hallucinogenic trip even though I'd never dropped acid. I likened it to listening to an acclaimed composer's entire repertoire of work in a day.

Food had never tasted so much of itself. Nothing bore any resemblance to its original state, everything transformed into glistening, glorious taste and mind-blowing explosions, as if some weird form of transubstantiation had taken place. To my mind, Otto Vellender had pulled off the impossible. When the last of the diners had left and Otto Vellender walked towards me, casually dressed in an open-neck slate grey shirt that set off the coolness in his eyes, and with his easy smile, I smiled back, rapt with genuine adoration.

THIRTY-FIVE

My idolatry lasted seconds.

"I'm glad you came. I thought you'd blow me out for Troy Martell."

"I'm sorry?"

"You haven't spirited him away?"

"What are you talking about?"

Otto pulled out a pack of cigarettes. French, a brand I used to smoke myself once upon a time. "Do you mind?" he said, gesturing.

I told him it was fine. It amazed me how many top chefs smoked when so much emphasis was placed on taste, but this was the least of my surprises. He lit up, poured a glass of wine from the bottle on the table. Every action studied. Every gesture a set piece, controlled.

"He's disappeared."

I did my best not to roll my eyes at the news. "When?"

"Hasn't been seen since Wednesday."

Which would explain why Troy hadn't shown up at the pub. I took a sip of wine to cover my dismay. It didn't shake off Otto. He viewed me like an eagle about to take a rabbit. Was this Otto's way of warning me off? With a pang of alarm, I wondered if we were alone in the building. Would a poor kitchen porter still be slaving over the dishes next door in the kitchen?

"Paris thinks he's with you."

"Then she's mistaken."

"Not your type?"

I met his gaze. Otto let slip a stream of smoke and narrowed his eyes. "He's definitely more beefcake than cheesecake," he said with a withering smile.

"Is that supposed to be funny? The guy's gone missing."

"Oh, I'm not that bothered. They all leave her eventually. Can't stand the pace."

"Really?"

"It's the truth."

"Then he's a bastard for ditching her when she needs him most."

"Bad timing, for sure."

"Think he's simply bunked off?" I tried to make it sound casual.

"What else did you have in mind?"

I wanted to say abducted, come to harm, vanished without trace, like the fate that befell your son. It would be like surrendering to an enemy determined to ignore the Geneva Convention and kill you. I shrugged.

"I'd watch your back, if I were you," he said, taking another deep drag of his cigarette.

"Sounds like a threat."

"A word of friendly advice, nothing more. Paris is not beyond turning up at your clinic and causing a scene."

"A daily occurrence," I said with a short smile. "I work in a high-maintenance environment and we're adept at managing it."

He nodded, as though he couldn't care less either way. "Mind me asking why you and Troy boy were in touch?"

I stalled.

"Your number was on his phone."

"Paris told you that? I didn't think you were on speaking terms."

"Only because she was absolutely livid."

"Is she always this insecure?"

"Always."

"And does she make a habit of checking her lover's calls?"

"She does a lot to piss off a man, me included."

"You must have found her attractive, once upon a time."

"Good in bed," Otto snorted. "Mental women generally are."

He looked at me as if I fell into the same category. It made me feel as if I'd stripped off my dress for his delectation. I took another sip, looked at him squarely. "Why did you invite me here?"

"I want to explain."

"Explain what?"

"About Nicholas."

"You don't have to explain to me." I was on the psychological equivalent of autopilot. The moment you assure someone that they don't need to say a word, they sing.

"I do, because I know what Mimi told you." He stubbed out his cigarette in a saucer, topped up his glass. I slipped the flat of my hand over the edge of mine to prevent him refilling it, too. "Paris did a terrible thing by suggesting that I had a hand in our son's disappearance."

"It's not true then?" I said softly.

"Of course it isn't. Do I look like a murderer?"

I quashed the sound of my mother's voice ricocheting through the empty restaurant. "Murderers are me and you and the guy next door. With the right stressors, we're all capable of it." Just as with the right stressors, those who work in mental health can disintegrate.

He didn't contest the point. Soft lighting threw grotesque shadows across the wall. Spooked, I keened my ears for sound and heard a soft clatter from behind the closed door; someone washing up, I guessed. I hoped. Otto noticed.

"That's Gabriella, always the last to leave."

I smothered a hiss of relief, waited a beat, and adopted my most sympathetic tone. "Were you close to Mimi?"

He held my gaze for a moment. The stiffness in his expression returned. "She was my little girl. Paris had Nicholas and I had Mimi. Things changed as she grew up. Pressure of the business," he explained. "We'd moved from the Midlands to Cheltenham, opened a restaurant, and I wasn't at home as much as I should have been."

"I gather you argued with her the morning of her death."

"Argued? Who told you that?"

"Is it true?"

He took another drag. "Mimi was agitated about Nicholas. Paris had put ideas in her head. I refuted them. She didn't believe me and I probably raised my voice."

"Probably?"

"All right, yes, I did. It was unforgiveable, which is why it hurts so much now."

Good, I thought, not because I was vindictive, but because it showed he had healthy feelings of remorse. "What do you think happened to Nicholas?"

"I don't know."

"You must have thought about it."

"Thought, but not arrived at conclusions."

"How on earth do you deal with the uncertainty?" Not knowing was what usually killed the spirit in most people.

"While there is uncertainty, there is hope."

"You believe he's alive?"

"Probably living the high life."

"On what exactly?" According to press reports, Nicholas had left with the clothes he stood in and without money, phone, or cash cards.

"His mother would have seen that he was all right," he said in answer to my exasperated expression.

"You mean his exit was planned?"

He viewed me with slow deadly eyes. "That's not what I said."

I sipped my drink and wondered whether Otto was aware that his ambiguous response was his first mistake. Troy Martell was, perhaps, closer to the truth than I'd given him credit for. "Then why do you think he left?"

Otto plucked another cigarette from the pack and lit up. "There was something not right with him."

A master of an obscure statement, it wasn't the answer I was expecting. "In what way?"

"Obsessive and too close to his mother."

"A lot of sons are close to their mothers and obsession is often the prerequisite for success. You should know."

He smiled at this. Quietly pleased. "You may have something there."

"Paris mentioned there were tensions between you and Nicholas."

"Did she now?" The tone was circumspect.

"Were there?"

"Fathers and sons, mothers and daughters; nothing more complicated than that. Are you always this persistent, or only with me?" He half smiled. I noticed that he had a trick of diffusing the conversation with small personal asides. A useful weapon in anyone's social armoury, Otto wielded it like a professional.

"Going back to the time Nicholas disappeared, had there been any particular rows that stood out from the crowd?"

"One," Otto said, "about his gap year. I thought it a waste of time and said so. I suggested he come here." He glanced around the restaurant.

"Would that have worked?"

He tipped the side of his head as if he had a crick in his neck. "I thought so. It could have provided an opportunity to bond."

How likely was that? "What did Nicholas suggest instead?"

"He wanted to go off on some writing course in the States."

"I gather he was gifted. Didn't he have books published?"

Otto shot me an appraising, slightly cautious look.

"I read it in a newspaper," I explained.

"Why do I get the impression that you're quizzing me?"

"Because your daughter asked me to."

He nodded, unsurprised, and blew out a great plume of dove-grey smoke. It was like watching someone disappear behind a sandstorm. It occurred to me then that he had controlling, narcissistic tendencies. I briefly wondered whether Nicholas had inherited his father's traits.

"Have you read his novels?"

"He wouldn't let me."

"You could have bought a copy without him knowing."

"Vampires aren't my style. Kids' stuff," he added, blowing a perfect smoke ring.

"Weren't you curious?"

"Frankly, no."

Otto had the crushing honesty of someone suffering from autism. "Did he ask you to fund his trip to the States?"

"Yes. I refused."

"He must have been disappointed."

"And angry."

"Could be the reason he left." Could also explain what Paris meant. Otto blew another smoke ring. If we were playing tennis, I reckon he would have been a set up.

"Excuse me." He pushed back his chair and stood. I watched as he bowled towards the door, pushed it open and bawled to hard working Gabriella, "Enough!" This was followed by a torrent of Spanish, a clatter of pans, and then silence. Otto stalked back.

"Do you usually speak to your staff like that?"

"Always. It's important to leave ego outside the kitchen."

"Unless it's yours," I said.

He smiled touché and took another drag.

"How would you feel if Nicholas turned up tomorrow?" I said.

"If he couldn't be bothered to show up for his sister's funeral, he's hardly going to leap out of the blue now."

"Doesn't that worry you?"

"I'm long past it. It's like I told you once before: there's nothing you can do to change certain things or events. You have to accept them."

Accept things, but not people.

Blood pumped through my body in syncopated rhythm. I couldn't read him. A man so boxed in he was afraid to show his emotions, or did he fear what they might unleash? I wondered how he'd react if put on the spot. "But if he did turn up," I persisted.

Otto turned the full force of his blue-eyed gaze on me. "I'd knock the shit out of him."

I started in surprise.

"For being so damn selfish," he explained. "I doubt he's given a flying fuck about what his mother is going through. And you saw what happened to Mimi." He glowered.

I nodded and let the moment roll. "Dinner was fabulous, by the way, thank you."

"I'm glad," he said, more relaxed, "only sorry I didn't get to enjoy it with you."

"How do you do it?"

"Do what?"

"Perform miracles."

He opened his mouth and laughed. I caught a flash of gold. "Hard work and ruthlessness."

"Ruthlessness?"

"I head a team. You have to be really upset with people to get the best out of them."

So reminiscent of my father, it triggered a thread of irritation. "You're wrong," I said. "Do that, you only get the worst."

"If you say so." The accompanying supple smile lacked conviction. He was taunting me.

"Is this what happened with you and Nicholas? Did you bully him in the mistaken belief that you'd produce the best?" He looked genuinely taken aback. I hadn't quite realised how angry I was, but

I wasn't finished. "Is that why you took six weeks to report him missing?"

His eyes narrowed to two thin blue slits. "Who told you that?"

"Did you?" He nodded slowly, tapped ash from his cigarette onto a plate. "Why would you be so slow?" I pressed.

"Because he'd done it before."

I jolted.

"He'd run away many times, Miss Slade. Many times."

THIRTY-SIX

I GENUINELY BELIEVED I was dying.

Otto's claim that Nicholas was a seasoned runaway had astonished me. Without anything sensible to say, I'd finished my drink and he called me a taxi. While I waited for a cab, he said, "Let's do this again, properly next time." I didn't say yes. I didn't say no.

I felt well when I climbed into bed around one in the morning. Five hours later, I knew something was badly wrong. Head pounding, stomach churning, I fled to the bathroom, narrowly making it to the lavatory before emptying my guts. It should have been the end of it. Two hours later, I was still throwing up at roughly fifteen-minute intervals. My limbs ached. Sweat poured off me. Pain wrapped a vise around my head and my vision blurred. I crawled between lavatory and bed on my hands and knees because I didn't trust myself to stand, let alone drive Monica to Devon.

At ten, when I should have been picking her up, I was vomiting for the seventh time. Beige sludge poured from my insides and tunnelled out through my mouth, my body breaking down from its inner core, organ against organ, cell rebelling against cell, turning me inside out. I couldn't swallow, or drink water without my gag reflex bouncing into overdrive. Agony in my head signalled massive dehydration. Afraid, I called an ambulance. When Monica phoned minutes later I explained in halting sentences. "I've been poisoned."

"I'll come right away," she said.

I didn't argue, just gave the address.

A short run from the hospital, the ambulance with two-man crew arrived within minutes. I crawled downstairs, dragged open the front door, and, verging on collapse, let them in. I looked so ill they decided to examine me in the living room. Next, a blur of questions about when I'd last eaten and what while my vital signs were checked and assessed.

"Was any of the food raw or undercooked?" asked a portly paramedic with short hair and massively sticking out ears.

"I don't think so."

"Any pains in your tummy?"

"No." Only a matter of time.

"How long have you been vomiting?"

Forever. "Since six this morning." The mention made me want to run to the bathroom again.

"Need to be sick?" the other paramedic observed.

I nodded feebly, staggered to my feet, and crashed into the downstairs cloakroom. The room spun. Vomit shot out of my mouth and spattered the tiled floor. One hand pressed against the cool wall for balance, I heard the doorbell ring. Eventually getting my bearings, I tottered back and found Monica in the sitting room talking to the ambulance crew. A nasty case of food poisoning appeared the general consensus. I wasn't so certain. It seemed too convenient, especially as not a morsel had passed Otto's sensuous lips.

"Norovirus is the most likely culprit," the man with the big ears said. "It's a very common organism in restaurants. Where did you say you'd dined?"

"Otto's, off the Bath Road."

Monica took off her coat and slung it on the sofa. With sleeves rolled up and a steely gleam in her eye, she enquired about my prognosis.

"Should be feeling better in a few days. In the meantime bed rest and plenty of fluids, including proprietary oral rehydration drinks to sort out her electrolytes. She can take painkillers, if she can keep them down. Don't touch any carbonised drinks or beverages."

"Sounds straightforward enough," Monica chirped, a bit too jaunty, I thought.

"You'll need to take care," he warned her. "Close contact and you risk infection."

She issued a breezy, capable smile. In my dismal state, Monica seemed invincible.

The crew packed up and left. Monica helped me back upstairs to bed. My teeth chattered with fever and cold.

"Where do you keep your blankets?" she said.

I indicated a blanket box and watched as she flipped open the lid, reached one out, and snuggled it over me as if I were a little girl. "There," she said.

She disappeared back downstairs and returned, coat on, with a jug of water and a glass, which she placed on my bedside table. "Popping out to pick up some things from the chemist," she said. "I'll need the house keys."

"In the left-hand drawer of the console table."

"And I'll need to contact your lawyer friend."

God. Gavin Chadwick, I remembered. "His number is on my phone." I asked her to hand it to me.

"On speed dial," she noted, quick as electricity as I passed it back to her.

"And speakerphone," I countered, closing my eyes.

As soon as Gavin answered, Monica introduced herself, explained that I was too ill to travel and that our meeting would have to be postponed.

"I'm sorry," Gavin said. "Do send Kim my best wishes for a speedy recovery. So where are we at exactly, Mrs. Slade?"

With your eyes closed, you are more sensitive to hesitation and slight of phrase. Immediately, I was aware that Monica was uncomfortable with the question and reluctant to answer.

"I thought Kim had filled you in on the detail," she said defensively.

"She gave me the broad brushstrokes, that's all. How have the police left things with you?"

Monica stumbled an account. She didn't mention sleeping pills. She did mention the plastic bag, the way it had been tied, something that really troubled her. Obsessively so, I thought. Gavin listened and gave Monica the same précis and analysis that he'd given me.

"Have they arranged another meeting?" he said.

"No."

"Soon as they do, phone me. Irrespective of any developments, if I can find a reason to be in your neck of the woods, it would be a good idea for us to have a face-to-face discussion. Will that suit?"

"Yes," she said. "Thank you."

As Gavin hung up, I opened my eyes.

"Good," she said, brisk and businesslike. "Got everything you need?"

193

I nodded.

"Won't be a tick." She turned to go and stopped. "Kim," she said, twisting around, "what did you mean about being poisoned?"

I gave a weak smile. "Nothing."

She looked at me straight, her expression obscure. When the door clicked shut behind her, I wanted to dissolve into the pillows and disappear.

THIRTY-SEVEN

I DIDN'T IMPROVE UNTIL mid-afternoon on Sunday. Stomach cramps and watery diarrhoea replaced sickness. If I stood up quickly I felt woozy and my capacity for sleep was gargantuan. Monica had made up a bed in the spare room and, apart from one trip back to her flat to collect fresh clothes, remained a reassuring presence. A whirlwind of activity, she cleaned stuff that had never been cleaned, scrubbed, washed, pressed and ironed laundry that had lain inert in the bottom of the basket since I'd moved in. Her mood rose as mine plunged, possibly because I'd not been able to swallow my daily dose of antidepressants. Whether it was all in my mind or there was a genuine physical chain reaction, I felt as if I were going cold turkey. The more morose I became, the more convinced I was that foul play had played a part in my misfortune. Life events had changed my thinking. I'd gone from believing everyone was lovely to thinking everyone was out to get me.

And then I received a call I never expected.

"Otto," I said, forcing the chill out of my voice.

"This is rather awkward," he began. I stayed quiet. "We've had an outbreak of food poisoning at the restaurant. Don't worry," he rushed on quickly, "we're carrying out a full deep clean, but I wondered if you're all right."

"I'm not, actually."

He let out a low moan. "I'm so, so sorry. I would have called before, but it's been a bloody nightmare. We were deluged with complaints from customers and then, unsurprisingly, we received a visit from Food Standards, who closed us down."

"So I wasn't the only one?"

"God, no." He paused. I could almost hear him catching on to the way my mind was working. "You didn't think..." He briefly stalled. "You didn't think I'd done it, did you?"

"Done what exactly?"

"Well, put something in your food deliberately, I suppose," he said, clearly unhappy with the notion. The anxiety in his voice was acute. Perversely, it pleased me.

"Why on earth would I think that?"

"Jesus, Kim, you know very well why."

"Never gave it a thought."

His abrupt silence indicated I wasn't believed. Not that I much cared.

"How long will you be closed?"

He let out a weary sigh. "Until we satisfy the powers that be. We'll bleed finance, which is bad enough. My main concern is the damage to our reputation. That could take a lot longer to restore."

"Something with which you're familiar, I'd imagine."

"Must you always be so acerbic?"

I guess I was knocking him hard when he was already down. There were plenty of other restaurants in town to take Otto's crown. Rebuilding its credibility would be one long hard slog.

"I don't suppose I could have your address?" he said when I failed to reply.

Suspicious, I asked why.

"So that I can send you flowers."

"There really is no need."

"There is every need. Please, I'd like to."

"Send them to my office." I hung up as Monica sailed into the room bearing a bowl of soup on a tray. "Who was that?"

"No one important."

She gave me a wise look, placed the tray on the bedside table, and plumped up my pillows. "Mind if I sit down?"

"Be my guest." I reached across for my first attempt at anything approaching food in forty-eight hours.

"I received a call from the police an hour ago, Kim."

"Right," I said, picking up the spoon. Shit.

"They want me back again."

"Did they say why?"

"No."

"Have you called Gavin?"

"Yes."

"What did he say?"

"He's going to reschedule his diary so that he can visit sooner rather than later. He promised to call me back. Is he a reliable sort?"

"Very." I focused on the soup, which was homemade lentil, and the steady rhythm of the spoon, the heat and taste, anything to escape Monica's fractiousness. Her face grim, she twisted the throw in her fingers, a reflection of a deep internal struggle.

"Are you worried about it?"

"A bit." She continued to look wretched.

"Why exactly?"

"I did something silly."

I put down the soupspoon.

"Some time ago," she said, glancing up, making plain that her silliness, as she put it, did not refer to a recent event. Was this what she'd already alluded to, the incident for which I would hate her? "In London," she said. "It got me into a heap of trouble."

"We all do foolish things." I silently cursed. Why oh why had I spoken? Maybe, subconsciously, I didn't want to know, but by opening my mouth, I'd ruined her flow, broken the magic spell.

She got up and smiled. "You're right." Crossing the room, her gaze transferred to the painting, Stannard's gift. "What an arresting piece."

"*An Imperfect Past*," I said.

She tipped her head, appeared to come to a decision, and then just as quickly changed her mind. "Yes, of course, I see that now." Her voice sounded faraway and disjointed. And then she slipped out of the room and went downstairs.

THIRTY-EIGHT

I GASPED. I'D STAGGERED back to work on Tuesday and really wished I hadn't.

"Someone has an admirer," Karmel said.

Jim sidled next to her. "I'm surprised the courier could get it through the door. Almost worth a dose of food poisoning."

I strongly disagreed but didn't say a word, too busy gawping at the curly stemmed olive tree. The fancy container must have cost at least as much as the plant. The white silk bow with label attached read:

A small gift to say I'm sorry. Hope you're feeling better.

—Otto.

"Is it from the hunky guy in the shorts?" Karmel stood, arms crossed, big grin on her face, ripping the piss in the nicest possible way.

"Which guy in shorts?" Jim said, intrigued.

"No, it isn't." I felt hot and wrong-footed. Otto's peace offering was as crazy as it was over the top. An attack of déjà vu made my head spin. Stannard's painting had elicited a similar reaction in me, except with Stannard I knew exactly what he was after: me.

Once my mind had taken full control of my brain, I said, "How am I going to get it home?"

"No problem, I can take it in the van." Karmel and her musician boyfriend drove a converted ambulance to transport the band's gear.

"Would you?" I said, stupidly grateful.

"I'll talk to Jed tonight, see if he can nip it round to yours."

"Thanks, Karmel."

"Want me to lug it into your office?" Jim said.

"Leave it where it is," I said and fled.

First up on the client list, Imogen Miller. She sloped in, sat down and, to my surprise, asked me how I was.

"Better, thanks for asking. And you, how's it going?"

She caught my eye and smiled.

I looked at Karmel's notes and glanced up in pleased surprise. "You've put on a pound since last week."

"Uh-huh."

"That's phenomenal progress. How do you feel about it?"

Her eyes narrowed as if she were mentally checking all her limbs were in working order and was delighted to discover that they were. "All right."

"Fabulous. And the leg?" I glanced down.

"Yeah, it's good."

"Progress."

Suddenly, her mood switched and her face clouded. "What happens when I leave here?"

"You're a little way off leaving, Imogen," I assured her. "By that time, you'll be better, more stable and prepared."

"But won't I slip back?"

"Slip back into what?"

She glanced away, clicked her tongue, the signal to me that she wanted to tell me something so badly but didn't know how. I wanted to whisper one word: *websites*. I waited.

"I might not be able to give it up."

I inclined my head in question.

She gave me another shifty look. "Daughters of Yurei."

"Pardon?"

"It's a website."

"I gather that, but I don't understand the reference."

"Yurei are figures in Japanese folklore."

This got my attention. The symbol sliced into Mimi Vellender's arm materialised before my eyes. I scribbled a note. "Tell me more." I read every emotion in her face, one part reluctance, two parts a strong desire to unload.

"According to Japanese folklore, if a person dies in a violent manner, through suicide or murder, they become unquiet spirits, or yurei. There are seven different types, but they're all capable of exacting vengeance."

Oh, hell. "In what way?"

Her eyes sparked. She dropped her voice as though she was letting me in on a well-kept secret. "They cause illness. They kill. They can even create natural disasters."

"And you believe it?"

"It's not about belief. It's about belonging. It provides a place where I can be someone else."

"You think it's easier to live someone else's life than live your own?" As soon as I said it, I thought of Nicholas Vellender.

"It's my escape."

"But is it?"

She considered my question. "There, I have a different set of friends."

"Who encourage you to do horrible things to your body." I spoke in the same tone as if I'd said *who encourage you to eat five fruit and veg a day.*

"Because they care about me, because they recognise and help me control the darkness in me."

"What darkness?" Like my darkness? Do you feel it, too? The thought came from nowhere, like the unquiet spirits Imogen spoke of.

She chewed her lip and shrugged.

Afraid of losing and messing up the connection to her, I got up out of my chair and walked to Imogen's side, squatted down, and looked up into her eyes. "We all have darkness in us, Imogen, but it's only a small part of who we are. The rest is light. You have so much potential. Every time you feel darkness, look to the light." I flinched inside for sounding too much like an Evangelist. "Does that make sense?"

"Kind of."

She didn't look convinced.

———

Later, I logged on, read through, and logged out in disgust, couldn't help myself. I'd trawled numerous crappy self-harm sites before, and Daughters of Yurei was no different apart from the Oriental twist and the pictures, which were graphic, and the prose, better written and therefore more convincing. Hooking into the disturbed mind, if you believed the blurb, was hip and cool. I wondered if the creator knew that encouraging others to become self-harm groupies had cost Mimi Vellender her life.

Appetite suppressed, I took out the thermos of soup Monica insisted I take with me to work for lunch, her parting gift before she returned to her flat.

I poured out a steamy cup and thought about the olive tree. I wasn't sure what to do about Otto. Should I call to thank him for his wildly extravagant sorry present? How would that work? Unsure, I pushed the idea of contact to one side.

The afternoon session loomed. Crossing the hall on my way back from the washroom and about to head to the office, I noticed a car draw up outside. There were two occupants in suits, both men. In my bones, I knew it spelled trouble.

Jim came out to join me. "They look like coppers." I silently agreed. "What do you think they're doing here?"

"Search me." I reached for a game tone and missed it by a country mile.

We stood and watched as they climbed out of a BMW and crossed the gravelled drive. One wore small-framed spectacles, too diminutive for his slab-sided face; the other, shorter by several inches, walked ahead with concise, darting movements. He had open features, with a slightly prominent chin. His reddish-golden hair reminded me of the colour of Enville ale. He was the guy in charge, the one to watch.

They bowled inside and flashed warrant cards. The short man spoke.

"Detective Inspector Adrian Strong and DS Philip Slater, Gloucester police."

"How can we help, officer?" Jim said.

"We understand that Kim Slade works here."

"That's me," I said, averting my eyes from Jim's swivelling gaze.

"Is there anywhere we can talk in private?"

"My office." I looked at Jim. "It's okay, I know what this is about." Surprised to receive a visit from Gloucestershire, rather than West Midlands, I suspected it signalled an unhealthy development. I braced myself to be grilled about Monica.

"I'll get Cathy to hold off your appointments," Jim said, unable to extinguish the tremor of excitement in his voice.

"This way." I gestured toward the end of the corridor.

Once inside the office, I closed the door, drew up another chair, and retreated to my big power number. I was glad of the vast wooden-topped desk forming a barrier between them and me.

"So how can I help?" I said with a pleasant smile.

"We understand you know Troy Martell," Strong said.

I blinked, muddled.

"Your number is on his phone."

"Well, yes."

"So you *do* know him?"

"Not well, no." How could I explain?

The guy with the undersized specs stepped in. He'd already taken out a notebook and gripped the pen in his hand as if it were a dagger. "How well?"

It sounded an innocent enough question, but the tilt of his lips suggested intimacy. Shit, what had Paris told them? "Professionally," I stuttered.

"He's a client?"

"No. There's a perfectly reasonable explanation," I added, in response to their mega-serious expressions. "I had a client who, unfortunately, died recently as a result of complications following a diagnosis of anorexia nervosa. Her name was Mimi Vellender. I was in touch with the family and that's how my path crossed with Troy Martell. He lives with Paris Vellender, Mimi's mother." I looked from one blank face to the other and deduced that I wasn't telling them anything new.

"Martell sent you a text with an attachment regarding Nicholas Vellender. Why would he do that?" Strong said.

"To provide context."

"But neither he nor Mrs. Vellender consulted you?"

I played for time. "I'm not sure I understand the question."

"You weren't treating Mrs. Vellender, grief counselling or what have you?" Strong spoke in a tone that suggested he believed psychotherapy to be a load of baloney.

"No."

He looked perplexed. Slater frowned.

"It's an informal relationship," I added, trying to explain the unexplainable.

"With Mr. Martell?"

"Yes."

"How informal?" Slater said. "You deny a relationship of a sexual nature?"

I recoiled.

"You look surprised, Miss Slade."

"I'm surprised *and* annoyed. Has Paris Vellender filed a complaint against me?"

"Why would she do that?"

"Because she jumped to the wrong conclusions and, frankly, I'm lost."

"You're simply friends, is that right?" Strong said.

"I hardly know the man. My association was purely professional, like I said."

"But you've just told us that it was *informal*. Do your clients normally have your number on speed dial?"

Sweat popped above my top lip. "Not usually, no. My number was on Troy Martell's phone because he wanted to keep me in the loop. He was worried about Paris." It sounded flaky and they knew it.

"So there's nothing of an intimate nature between you?" Slater pressed, lenses glinting suspicion. He had the kind of jobsworth voice that made you want to reach for the nearest bottle of vodka.

"I already told you," I said as calmly as I could, "there's no relationship, intimate or otherwise, between us."

"And Otto Vellender?"

"What of him?" My words seemed to get entangled in my teeth. I reached for the glass of water I kept to hand on my desk and took a long deep swallow.

"You know him?"

"I've had a couple of conversations with him and I dined at his restaurant recently."

"How recently?"

"Last Friday."

"Do you know how he gets on with Troy Martell?"

"I don't think they had ..." I stopped and stared. "Why are you asking me these questions? Has something happened?"

The guy with the glasses looked at Strong, who nodded.

"We regret to inform you that Troy Martell was found dead on Friday night. He was murdered."

THIRTY-NINE

ALARM CHASED UP MY spine, into the base of my head, and exploded out of my ears.

"Where were you on Friday night between the hours of nine and two in the morning?" Strong said.

"I already told you. I was dining at Otto's."

"Who with?"

"No one."

"Do you normally eat alone?"

I looked to Slater, who'd asked the question. "Sometimes."

Should I tell him about Otto's invitation? If I said the wrong word, it could incriminate him. But why protect someone I didn't entirely trust? I told them. As expected, they jumped on it, hell-fire in their eyes.

"He failed to join you?"

"I wouldn't put it like that. He made his apologies because he was short-staffed."

"But you didn't actually see him?"

"I saw him before I dined. I spoke to him after service finished."

"What time was that?"

"Goodness, I don't know."

"Make an educated guess."

"Around nine, give a few minutes either side, before I ate."

"And later?"

"Otto joined me for a glass of wine approaching eleven thirty, again, maybe ten minutes either way."

Slater nodded. Strong gave no physical reaction, but I bet he salted that one away. They were thinking that Otto had time to kill. "I have no reason to believe he was anywhere other than working in the kitchen," I added, scrupulously fair. "His staff will vouch for him, won't they?"

Neither replied. I was probably exceeding boundaries. "You were about to tell us about Mr. Vellender's relationship with Troy Martell," Slater reminded me.

"That would be easy. They didn't have one."

"They were at odds?"

Believe it or not, he's not high on my talk list, Martell told me. "I can't comment."

"Why not?"

"Because I don't know."

"You believe they had little if no contact?"

"That's my impression." Hope flared inside me and guttered. During our late-night tryst, for want of a better description, Otto had homed straight in on Martell's missing status. It was the first thing he said, as if he needed to explain his disappearance and brush it off in the same way he'd talked his way out of the delay in reporting his son's disappearance with the regular-runaway story. Was I seeing patterns where there were none, or was the truth more chilling? Had Martell uncovered what happened to Nicholas Vellender and someone had shut him up for it? Was this the reason for his request to meet? Nervously, I wondered where that left me. A level-headed person would have confided this to the police. Having prior dealings with the cops on a trumped-up murder charge, I didn't fall into that category. Chris's death and the way I was treated afterwards guaranteed a lifelong aversion and distrust of those paid to protect. Thank God, Troy had resorted to pen and paper to send the note, although I found the prospect of the police talking to Karmel irrationally frightening.

And that posed a problem. I *was* irrational. It seemed odd to me that the public believe that psychologists are special and somehow immune from stress and strain. There's a peculiar belief that we have life's vicissitudes not only taped but also packed into neat and tidy parcels. Truth is, we're as susceptible to stress and the fallout from death, murder, and bereavement as the next person; the only difference is we can identify it rather more speedily.

Slater asked me to provide contact details, which I did. Two chairs scraped back against the carpet as both stood up. "We'll need to interview you again as part of our enquiry."

"Oh," I said.

They exchanged glances; some unspoken signal passed between them that put me on edge.

"I have to return to headquarters," Slater said, "but I could pop in later."

"At home?"

"Sure."

With a heavy heart, I supplied him with the address.

"About seven?" he said.

I gave a silent nod of agreement and stood up and walked them to the door. "Can I ask you something?"

Strong inclined his head and looked me in the eye. Out of the two, I preferred him. He seemed more direct and honest, less authoritarian for authority's sake.

"How did he die?"

"Stabbed in the back."

I swallowed. A metaphor? "With a knife?" It sounded as dumb as it was.

"A kitchen blade," Slater said, hawk-eyed. "Someone who knew what they were doing."

I did my best to keep my expression neutral. "Where?"

"In a derelict pub off Swindon road. A homeless guy found him. Wasn't pretty."

"What was Troy doing there?"

Strong flicked a smile. "That's what we're trying to find out."

FORTY

"Nice place you got here." Slater's tone was more conciliatory than the one he'd adopted earlier. It put me on my guard. I preferred him when he was pissy; at least I knew where I stood.

I walked him through to the living area and indicated the sofa. He sat down and pulled out a file and notebook from a briefcase and placed it in front of him on the coffee table. A sheaf of other stuff, including something shiny, poked out although I couldn't see what it was.

"Can I get you a drink?" I said.

"A glass of water, if you don't mind."

"Still, sparkling?"

"Tap is fine."

I walked across to the kitchen section, took a glass from the cupboard, and poured water from the mains into it. Rather him than me. Cheltenham water tasted foul.

"Thanks." He drank it straight down, Adam's apple bobbing in rhythm with each swallow.

I grabbed a high stool from the breakfast bar and parked myself opposite. Slater took out a pen, looked up with a meaningless smile.

"You're not under arrest or caution."

I slipped my hands underneath my thighs, a conscious effort to anchor myself while my subconscious whispered that I was hiding something, which, of course, I was.

"To recap," Slater began, "your association with Troy Martell was based on his concern for Paris Vellender. Have I got that right?"

I dug my fingers into the soft flesh and nodded.

"How long had you known him?"

"Troy? Days, a week, perhaps." Surely that fact alone would eliminate me from enquiries.

He didn't pursue it and made a note. "But you'd been involved in the Vellenders' affairs for longer?"

"I first treated Mimi, their daughter, four years ago."

"You knew Mr. Vellender then?"

"No."

"So it's a recent association?"

"Yes."

"Did either Vellender or Martell discuss the disappearance of Nicholas Vellender with you?"

So they thought there was a connection. "In passing, yes."

His eyes hooked on mine. "In passing?"

"It would be hard not to mention something like that."

"Did you draw conclusions?"

"Like what?"

"Like what might have happened to Nicholas."

"None." Let the police do their job without me. I was only interested in discovering the truth for my own satisfaction and to honour a promise to Mimi.

"You never speculated?"

"I'm not a detective."

He flicked a tight smile and studied me for an uncomfortably long moment. "You have no reason to believe that Otto Vellender bore Mr. Martell any ill will?"

"I don't think he cared enough."

"What do you mean by that?"

"To loathe or love someone you have to care. Otto didn't."

"Otto?" he said with a secret smile.

"Mr. Vellender."

"And your relationship to him?"

"There is no relationship. He simply invited me to dine and I accepted his invitation."

Slater cocked his head. The lamplight caught his lenses, briefly blinding me. "It's a little incestuous, isn't it?"

"What is?"

"Your number on Martell's phone on speed dial and you a dinner guest of Mr. Vellender's."

"I'm not sure I understand what you're implying."

The vacuous smile again. "Simply asking questions."

Which any fool could see he wasn't. Slater was trying to find out if my so-called relationship with Otto was closer than I'd led him to believe. He wanted to know whether I'd lie to protect him.

"Were you aware of anyone who intended Mr. Martell harm?" he said, more direct now.

"How could I? Like I told you, I barely knew him."

He nodded, made another note. "I wonder," he said with a grimace, "could I use your cloakroom?" He glanced at the empty glass. "Gone right through me."

"Left into the hall and first door on the right."

I waited, listened for the sound of vanishing footsteps, slipped off the stool, and darted to his briefcase, from which the corner of a photograph protruded. I glanced over my shoulder. Sweaty-fingered, I caught hold of the white shiny edge and teased it out.

Stabbed in the back, Strong had said. The initial blow that felled Martell, maybe, but this…

Had someone cut the power cables to my brain? I pressed a hand to my mouth. Breath ripped from my lungs. My eyes burnt with incredulity as I stared at Troy naked in imitation of Da Vinci's Vitruvian Man, except Troy's long-limbed and muscled corpse bore no resemblance to beauty.

I tried to trump my emotions with intellect and failed. What passed for my sanity hung like thread from a tall tree caught in a gale.

Torso sliced open. Skin peeled back. Ribs sawn through and raised like the rafters in an old, derelict house. Internal organs exposed. Glistening. Blood. Blood everywhere.

There was more.

Troy's mouth a bloody hole, his tongue cut out and placed in the palm of one hand. The message was obvious: keep silent. The same message meant for me.

I heard the lavatory flush, pushed the photograph back inside, and returned to my seat as if I hadn't moved. I recalled nothing of what either Slater or I said afterwards. I didn't remember a word.

FORTY-ONE

"I'M IN OVER MY head," I confessed to Stannard late that evening.

"Troy's killer is a nutter."

"A psychopath would be a more apt description."

"Right up your alley."

"Blood and bones, a miserable lonely death. Hardly." I made a mental note to talk to Jim.

"Well, watch your back," Stannard said without irony. "And Otto Vellender. All that chopping up in the kitchen, he has the means and, I don't care what you think, he has the motivation."

It didn't square with my thinking, but I didn't argue.

"Going back to the timing," Stannard said. "That fits, too."

"Not necessarily and only if Vellender is an illusionist."

Stannard fell briefly silent. "You say Troy wanted to meet, but failed to show up?"

"Right. Which means he could have been killed at any time between his disappearance sometime on Wednesday and when he was found." As soon as the words left my mouth, I remembered Otto's phone call at the pub. The cold, dead hand of fear struck out to grab me by the throat again.

"Do you have any clue what Martell wanted to talk to you about?"

"I assumed Nicholas."

Stannard factored it in. "Didn't you say that Otto drew your attention to Troy at dinner?"

"It was the first thing he said."

"How did he appear?"

"Relaxed."

"He would."

"I don't think Otto killed Troy on Friday night. The whole kitchen would notice him missing."

"Unless the timing was off, in which case it doesn't exactly exonerate Otto Vellender."

That's what freaked me out.

"You really do need to take care, Kim."

"I know. I am."

He thought for a moment. I could literally hear him contemplating down the line. "If not Otto, who else do you reckon could be good for it?"

"Troy Martell was a big guy, fit and strong, rippling with muscles. Whoever killed him took a risk."

"A calculated one. Stabbing a guy in the back mitigates the possibility of a counter attack, surely?"

"And that's my point—it's cowardly and sneaky, not Otto's style."

"You know him *that* well?"

Did I detect a tinge of jealousy? I thought back to the crime scene shots. There was skill in the artistry, if you could call it that.

Stannard didn't wait for a response. "What about Paris Vellender—a crime of passion?" he said.

The jealous rage scenario was tempting, but it didn't fly with me. "Not unless I discover she has a load of toy boy skeletons already in her cupboard."

"Any way you can find out?"

"I think I'll leave that to the police, if you don't mind."

"But she threatened you, remember?"

"Then why not stick a knife in *my* back?"

"Who says she won't?"

"Is that supposed to be a joke?"

"Important to keep one's sense of humour intact."

I let out a tired sigh. This was no joking matter. "You're missing the bigger picture."

"What's that?"

"Cops will be all over her." Hadn't the police done the same when Chris was murdered? They'd had me down as *numero uno* suspect from the start.

Stannard sighed. "Back to square one then. Looks like we're missing a trick."

"Or a person."

"Yeah?"

"What if the one person I can't find is off radar for a reason?"

"You mean Nicholas Vellender?" Stannard's voice sharpened.

"The mysterious missing man." People went into hiding for one of two reasons: because of what someone else has done, a view expressed by both Mimi and Troy; or because of what they've done to someone else. Had Nicholas carried out something so awful he needed to disappear? I racked my brains, trying to claw back what

217

Otto had told me about his son. *Something not right with him.* I hadn't pursued it at the time. Now I wished I had.

Stannard sliced into my thoughts. "As theories go, not bad. What's his motivation?"

"According to his father, he was obsessed with his mother. It plays into Troy's theory that she was protecting her son. Maybe Nicholas didn't like the competition."

"Kinky. Hate to be the prophet of doom but, presuming young Nicholas is still in the land of the living, you don't stand a hope in hell of finding him now. Cops will be thinking the same thing. They'll review his disappearance. Any attempt you make will draw fire from the law."

He was right and Slater's line of questioning confirmed it.

"You'd better get more sneaky and persistent."

"Thanks very much, and how do you propose I do that, oh wise one?" There were plenty of other areas of town to cover, but it wasn't exactly a scientific approach, more a question of pin the tail on the donkey.

"Talk to his mates?"

"He didn't have any, according to Troy." Which was also a worry.

"Girls?"

"Nada." My head hurt with thinking. Who was he? Nicholas the loner? Nicholas no-mates? Sensitive soul or someone sinister with deviant tendencies? Once I'd believed it would be relatively easy to track him down. In his continuing absence, I doubted his very existence. If he were alive, it would be like looking for a diamond in a swimming pool. "How's the face?" I said by way of a diversion.

"Beautiful."

"Modest as ever. When are they letting you out?"

"I *am* out. I'm convalescing in a five-star hotel with wall to wall luxury and room service."

"You're a bloody health tourist, Stannard," I said with a laugh.

"Don't knock it. I'll be back in the UK next week. Looks like you need someone to take care of you. Think you'll recognise me?"

I smiled. For someone who'd welcomed his departure, I realised how much I needed him, beautiful or not.

FORTY-TWO

I FELT JITTERY. MARTELL'S death spooked me. Monica was due at the police station at 10:30 a.m. God only knew where that would lead. She phoned after the first sparrow cheeped, long before she left for Birmingham.

"Gavin couldn't get away sooner. He's arranged to meet me tomorrow in Cheltenham."

"I'm glad. Will you be all right today?"

"Oh yes," she said, sounding inexplicably buoyant.

"You'll keep me posted about what happens?"

"I'll call you tonight."

I wished her well, dragged myself out of bed, downed pills with coffee, and dressed in my warmest clothes. Insanely early, I had two hours before I was due at the Lodge.

Shoulders tensed, I criss-crossed through a web of side streets, past The Brewery, and joined Swindon Road a fifteen-minute walk away. Dark and overcast, cold seeped into and terrorised my bones.

Wandering towards one of the University campuses seemed my best bet, but there was no sign of a derelict pub, only a tranche of terraced houses with shiny double-glazed windows.

I crossed the road and ducked into a street flanked on the left by steel mesh fencing, signs of demolition, and warning notices to stay out. A sudden gust of wind picked up and billowed underneath my padded coat. It felt like an omen. Here I was, close to a busy part of town. Streets away, people would be getting up and going to work, parents dropping kids off at nursery, college kids jacking up on coffee and fizzy drinks. Yet a single darting glance over my shoulder revealed that I was utterly alone.

And I was scared.

Banging in my head. Stammering in my chest. And something far, far worse. An image of Andy Johnson came to me—the reason for my breakdown, Chris's murderer, my stalker and assailant—his face burnt and blistered, eye bulging red then opaque and sightless. I pitched forward, doubled up, one hand pressed against my chest, open-mouthed, gasping. Grabbing hold of a lamppost to steady myself, I closed my eyes tight shut. When I opened them, the tableau of horror had vanished.

Sweat erupting under my arms and behind my knees, I broke into a frantic run. I didn't care how weird I looked. I had to get out of the narrow street, find people and colour and normality before it—whatever *it* was—swallowed me whole.

Close to the end of the street, my boots clattering in the early morning, a flutter of blue and white caught my eye. I slowed. Crime scene tape stretched across the entrance of a manky-looking building with boarded windows and entrances, the remnants of an old pub sign hanging like a gibbet in the breeze. Bouquets of flowers, pressed tight along the crumbling brickwork, huddled together from the bitter chill. This was Troy Martell's last miserable and un-inviting view of the world. Stannard and I were right. It was no random attack. Martell had come here for a reason, to collect something or meet someone. He would never have known that he was about to be butchered, his beautiful body exposed and vulnerable and broken for the entire world to see.

I didn't dwell. I legged it and sailed into work with false bravado. I had a job to do, clients to treat. The heat needed to die down. And, yes, underneath I remained terrified.

I ploughed through the day like a three-ton truck going uphill in first gear and was glad when it was time to go home. Around 6:30 p.m. Jed and Karmel delivered the olive tree and carted it through the house to my small courtyard garden.

"Best put it over by the fence out of the wind," Jed said. With his dread-locked hair, face art, and piercings, he was an eternal sunshine man. I offered them a drink.

"Nah, better bust it," Jed said. "Band practice."

They left and, disappointed and yearning for company, I set to preparing a lacklustre dinner. Since my skirmish with Norovirus, I was off food and settled for a plain omelette and salad, which I ate half of and chucked the rest. I ordered a couple of academic books online and then scrolled through Japanese symbols, comparing what I'd drawn on the beer mat with Imogen's account of Yurei. It was a lot harder than expected. Every symbol seemed similar to my untrained eye. Rubbing my face with fatigue and about to pack it in, I gasped with sudden recognition and, holding the mat up, compared it with the image on the screen. An Onryo was a mythological and most feared vengeful spirit. The apparitions of those who died in jealousy or rage, they were, according to folklore, able to return to earth to seek vengeance. This was what Mimi had been inspired to carve into her arm. Why?

When my mobile rang I almost passed out with shock. It was Otto.

"Did you get my peace offering?"

"Thank you, yes."

"You're feeling well again?"

What was it with this guy? Petulance and the knowledge that my mental wellbeing felt a universe away from my physical health made me bold. "That's not really why you called, is it?"

He let out a laugh. "You know me too well."

"I don't know you at all." I was cool and dry and flinty.

"I take it you've heard the news about Troy?"

"You take it right. I received a visit from the police yesterday afternoon."

"Really? They came to your place of work?"

"They did."

"I should be impressed with their efficiency."

Impressed or anxious? And is this why you're on the line, to check out the lay of the land?

"Why did they question you?" he continued.

"As part of the investigation."

"Sorry, I'm not making myself clear. What I—"

"I think you're very clear," I said. "You want to find out what I know."

"I'm interested in the police angle, of course." He voiced it as if it were a natural concern.

"The angle isn't rocket science. They want to find out who killed Troy. Any clues?" I sounded waspish, mainly because I was.

"I've no idea."

I stayed silent.

"I didn't give a monkey's about him."

Nor Nicholas, nor Mimi, it seemed. Who the hell did he care about? "Do you know anything about the scars on Mimi's arm?" Silence stalked the distance between us. "Do you know what they signify?"

"Signify?" he said bewildered. "I'm sorry but how does this connect to Troy?"

I ignored his question. "Last time we spoke, you mentioned that Paris's other lovers rarely stuck around. Did any of them wind up dead?"

"Don't be ridiculous. Two have settled down with girlfriends and children. Does that do it for you?"

I ignored the sarcasm and wondered how to phrase my next potentially awkward question when Otto followed up with a question of his own. "Got a horrific amount of spare time on my hands until we get the all clear. I wondered if you might be free?"

My instinct to recoil was replaced by an opportunity to investigate.

"When?"

"This weekend."

"I'm away."

"Next week then?"

"I'll check my diary and get back to you."

"Do you always play hardball?"

"Only with those I don't trust."

"I see."

I didn't know whether or not he was insulted or if my directness turned him on, the thrill of the chase and all that. By comparison to his ex-wife, I think he considered me tame fare.

"Did Nicholas have any close friends?"

"Where on earth did that come from? I thought we were talking about a date."

"Did he?" Might as well go for broke.

"You're a strange woman."

"I hate to be rude, Otto, but I'm expecting a call from my mother."

"Sorry, I'll get off the line. To prove that I'm trustworthy, talk to Ashley Mason. She lives at Rivendell in Windsor Street. She knew Nicholas as well as anyone."

FORTY-THREE

I THOUGHT THAT WOULD be the end of it. Wrong.

"What are you doing here?"

"To persuade you that I am not a bad man."

Otto gave me the full blue-eyed treatment. Mesmerising. Dangerous. I glanced down to his hands, scarred and strong. Fleetingly, I wondered what it would be like to be touched by them. I looked back up into eyes that would not let me go. I should have known better but, at a primitive level, Otto Vellender bewitched me. Wrong, a bum move, I was stupid enough to ask him in.

He didn't smile. He stepped inside. I closed the door and turned towards him. We were face-to-face, soft staccato breath on each other's skin. The air felt electric and I shivered in exactly the same way I'd trembled in the street outside Troy Martell's last resting place. I don't know who leant in first, him or me. Our kiss was not fond or tender. It was bruising and painful and desperate. My dress tore apart with such force a seam gave way. I grabbed his jacket, which dropped like a furtive smile onto the floor, and clawed at his belt. He pushed up the skirt of my dress, ripped off my knickers. His fingers marauded over me and into me, dirty and brazen. I didn't know this man. He was a stranger and that was the thrill. When he went in for the kill, up against the wall, it was like the best drunken fuck and hangover fuck combined.

"Sex and death," he gasped, as if that explained the lunacy.

Shocked, ashamed, and embarrassed, I thought, *This must never happen again. Never.* I clutched at my clothing, anxious to cover myself.

"It was great. You were great." He raised an eyebrow to match the salacious smile. I felt as if I'd passed a test of endurance.

I plunged both hands into my pockets, curved my shoulders inward, my body shrieking, *Go.*

He must have read the signal because he placed one hand on the lock, the other on the handle. "I'll call you," he said and left. I went straight upstairs and took a hot and cold shower. The whole encounter had lasted less than ten minutes. Washing him out of my system would take longer.

————

By the next morning, Monica still hadn't called, neither had she answered. Bizarre being the new normal, I squared her silence in my mind by arguing that no news was, indeed, good news, and that she was waiting to speak to Gavin, after which she'd speak to me. I had no tools with which to rationalise my one-night stand with Otto.

With still no word from Monica by lunchtime, quiet panic escalated to cliff-edge heights and I changed my mind. The police must have made an arrest and banged her up, Gavin was most likely stuck extricating her from the legal embrace of myriad enforcement agencies. Having psyched myself up to fever pitch, I spent my entire lunchtime driving around with my hands welded to the steering wheel. First I went to the studio flat, but Monica was out, then I travelled through St. Paul's, scouring the pinched, narrow streets, hoping for a sighting of Nicholas that didn't materialise.

My mobile finally buzzed five minutes after I'd seen my last client of the day. I snatched it up, convinced it would be one of those *phone a friend* calls from Monica.

"Hello?" I said anxiously.

"Gavin here. Before you ask, I have your mother's full permission to talk to you."

"Is she all right? They haven't taken her into custody, or anything?"

"Nothing like that," Gavin said. "At least, not yet."

What the hell had happened? And what the hell was happening to me? Despite my best efforts to tamp it down, foreboding echoed through my veins. I couldn't continue with this level of anxiety. I was rapidly becoming my own problem, my own worst enemy.

"There have been a couple of fresh developments," Gavin said in his usual unruffled and moderate tone, "neither of which are smoking guns, if you'll forgive the phrase, but which potentially complicate matters." I didn't like the sound of that at all. "It's come to light," Gavin continued, "that your mother gave false references to the Hawkeses."

"What, and they never found out?"

"Apparently not."

"Has she said why she falsified them?"

"She's not forthcoming on the matter, no."

I thought back to Monica's evasiveness, the awkward conversation I'd had with her about London, that lost and lonely period of her life.

"Leave it with me," I said, though whether she'd confide in me, I couldn't be sure. "And the other thing?"

"She's a beneficiary of Michael Hawkes's will."

My throat closed over in dismay. "By how much?"

"Two hundred thousand pounds."

"Oh my God," I burst out, unthinking. "A damn good motive for murder."

"Unfortunately, the police agree with you."

I rubbed my temple in a doomed effort to erase a throb of fear. Monica had worried about paying for basic accommodation, been beside herself about the cost of hiring a lawyer—I remembered the question of legal aid. She was not a rich woman. Coupled with her intense, openly stated dislike of the judiciary, had the prospect of a small fortune corrupted her? "What's the next step?"

I heard Gavin open a door. Traffic sounded down the line. I had the distinct impression that he needed to tell me something in confidence.

"It would be helpful to find out if there are any skeletons in the cupboard. The reason for the false references, for example."

"You mean before the police discover them?"

"If we can find credible answers to their questions and put together a case that makes her seem nothing but entirely innocent, it will help her cause."

There would never be a time to ask what Gavin actually believed because it would compromise his defence. "Is there anything else?"

"I'm not a great believer in hunches, but I have the strong feeling that the police are holding something back."

An Ace card—exactly what Monica had suggested and something I'd considered right from the outset. If we were all thinking the same, chances were we were right. Meant it was critical that she was straight with me about the missing years in London. "Where are you now?"

"Outside your mother's flat."

"Are you going back in before you leave?"

"Briefly."

"Tell her I'm coming round."

I drove with a distinct lack of style, like a new driver who secretly believes he's Jensen Button. I slung the car illegally on a double yellow and flew into the apartment block. Gavin stayed long enough to let me in and pat me awkwardly on the shoulder before setting off on the long journey back to Devon.

I walked inside the minute living area. Monica looked up at me with a crumpled, defeated expression, her eyes swollen and red-rimmed from crying. Smuts of mascara clung to her cheeks. She didn't look like a woman told she'd inherited 200k. I sat down beside her and took her hand. It felt small and fragile.

"What happened?"

Her account came out in random rambling pieces. It took me less time than most to piece together the way the interview had rolled. One, because I'd direct experience of Niven's formidable interview technique; and two, because of what I did for a living.

"Want a drink?" I said when Monica finished.

"There's wine in the fridge."

I poured a big glass for her and a small one for me. Her fingers twitched as she took it. I chinked her glass, sipped, and waited for her to settle.

"Are you still taking your antidepressants?" I said.

"Yes."

"You've got enough to last you?"

"I collected a prescription from Dr. Zubrzycki after I left the police station."

I sipped my drink. "Been on them long?"

She cast me a suspicious look. "Years. Why?"

"Professional interest." I didn't push it. Maybe she was addicted. Maybe she couldn't function without them. I damn well knew I couldn't.

"I'm not a fruitcake, if that's what you're thinking."

"I wasn't."

But Monica wasn't done. "And I didn't murder the judge in a fit of madness or greed." Both her hands gripped the crystal. If she didn't calm down, it would shatter.

"I hear what you say."

"Only if I shout loudly." She looked at me with undisguised ire.

"Do you want me to leave?"

"Not particularly." She snatched at her drink. "Sorry," she added as an afterthought and put her glass down on the coffee table.

"It doesn't matter. I know this is difficult for you."

She hunched forward. "The more I cooperate the worse it gets."

"I know."

"They tie you up in knots."

I gave a sympathetic nod. "Were you aware that you were to be a beneficiary?"

She shook her head. "I'd no idea. I swear."

"And the false references?"

"It was stupid of me, I realise now, but I badly needed a job."

"I get that," I said. "Lots of people big themselves up, especially when they don't have the right credentials."

"You see," she said, eyes hooking onto mine with the desperation of the condemned about to face a firing squad. "It's not such a terrible offence."

"But this isn't about credentials," I said, as gently as I could. "This is about a gap in the commentary."

She stiffened.

"Monica, what happened in London?"

A belligerent, possessive light entered her eyes. She'd rather take her chances with the police than reveal her secret, I realised with a thump. I'd witnessed the same in the consulting room and the same with myself. As soon as a person confides, he or she hands the confidante absolute power, and that's way too scary for most people.

"Look at it from the police perspective," I said, something that I never believed I'd say. "You're the last person to see the judge alive. You benefitted from his will. You weren't honest about references. You didn't tell me the truth about the sleeping pills. What?" I stopped. Her face fell in dismay and a single tear slid down her cheek.

"I told them," she sobbed.

"About the pills?"

She nodded, took a tissue from her pocket, wiped her eyes, and blew her nose. "They now know I lied in my original statement," she said in a voice barely above a whisper.

"Which is why it's important the police understand that you're on the level. You do see that?"

She nodded again, but with less commitment.

"They'll want to know everything about you, particularly the detail before you worked for the Hawkes household."

"I can't."

"You must."

She shook her head. Twisted shreds of tissue dropped like tiny broken bones onto the carpet.

"Remember what you said to me? You said that if I knew the truth I'd hate you for it?" She continued to look away. I only registered a response because her breathing quickened. "I won't hate you. You can tell me."

She looked down. Seconds skidded past. The tiny room grew smaller, as if the walls were closing in and neither of us had enough air to breathe. Still, she clung to silence.

"Monica," I said softly, "most people don't want to revisit the darkest areas of their past, but your freedom depends on it. Gavin can't help you unless he knows, and neither can I."

She looked up at me then. "You can't help me. Nobody can."

FORTY-FOUR

TROUBLED, I LEFT AN hour later, none the wiser. My mother might have left a false trail, blacked out her past, or recall it with painful clarity and vow to share it with nobody. Innocent until proven guilty, at least that's what I told Luke on the phone.

"Do you think she'd tell me?" he said.

"I have absolutely no idea." I sounded as weary as I felt.

"I'm hoping to catch a flight end of next week."

I did the mental equivalent of putting up the bunting and hoisting a flag. "Can you give it your best shot? Unless she opens up I'm afraid the police will beat us to it."

"You think she did something criminal?"

"She's not in the system."

"No report, no crime."

"Doesn't mean to say that a crime wasn't committed."

"What's your take?"

"She's guilty but I don't think of murder."

After my late-night call, I slept the deep sleep of the exhausted. With Luke around, my burden would shift if not lift.

Waking insanely early, I assembled a cold box of instant food and packed a bag for Devon with the same enthusiasm as if I were zipping over to Monaco for the weekend. Appointments finished early on Fridays, which would give me enough time to drop in to Windsor Street and talk to Ashley Mason.

The day passed with a grinding gait made a thousand times worse by Jim. I'd made a mental note to quiz him about psychopaths but I could hardly squirrel a word into the conversation. Diverted by a conference in London the day before, he couldn't wait to crash into my office, pent-up with the fire of nervous energy.

"So what were the cops doing here?"

I sketched out the headlines. Jim dug for the detail.

"This must not go any further," I confided.

He placed the flat of his hand against his chest and looked suitably solemn. "Of course."

I gave him a sketchy, highly edited account. "Whoever killed Martell mutilated him," I said.

"In what way?"

Fighting a wave of panic, I described the crime scene shot.

Jim's hairy eyebrows combined in one single frown line. "A display," he said. "Like a modern-day Jack the Ripper. Carried out before he was dead or postmortem?"

"Christ, Jim, how should I know?"

"Was it anatomically correct?"

I gaped. "I'm a clinical psychologist not a bloody surgeon."

"Roughly done by a butcher, or skilfully carried out by someone with surgical skills?" He sounded exasperated by my dull thinking and lack of detailed recall.

My mind went blank. "There was so much blood…"

"Think. What did you *intuit*?"

I saw ribs and internal organs and a tongue cut out. I told him this. "The police thought the perpetrator knew what he was doing," I said, quoting Strong.

"So whoever did it went prepared and armed."

I agreed. "That's my take, too."

"Bearing in mind the tongue cutting exercise, and the message that contains, odds-on the victim knew his killer. Any sign of sexual assault?"

I shook my head. "I haven't the faintest idea."

"Was there anything missing?"

"Like a trophy?"

"Yes."

"I can't answer that."

"And the location of the kill was a derelict pub, you said?"

"Yes." I paused. "What type of individual would carry out something like that?"

"Mutilation indicates that the perpetrator was, himself, a victim of extreme violence, possibly in childhood. He'll be someone who has never learnt to control his anger and develop the usual social skills to control it."

"A person driven by rage and bitterness?" Like one of those Japanese ghosts, I shuddered.

"*Extreme* rage and bitterness. Although that might not be the image he projects to the outside world. Superficially charming and manipulative, he'll be blistering with resentment and a sense of entitlement. The kind of guy who feels that the world owes him."

"You say *him*."

"Statistically, it's more likely. It would be a highly unusual act carried out by a woman. Not impossible, but…" He drifted off, a sagacious expression on his face.

"Right," I said, sobered and reminded of another time and another conversation in which I'd been assured that my stalker was bound to be male.

"This is a man who, deep down, feels worthless. He'll have absolutely no concern for how his behaviour impacts on others. He won't take responsibility for his actions even when it affects family members. Maybe he was jealous of someone like Martell who appeared to have the perfect body and perfect lifestyle. Simply because there was no sign of sexual assault doesn't preclude the possibility of a sexual element."

"As in the killer getting his rocks off when cutting up his victim."

"Exactly. He's probably built up to this moment. He won't have a clean rap sheet even if he has never been caught for his crimes."

Nicholas Vellender materialised before me in crashing vivid colour.

"What I don't understand is how you got involved." Jim gave me a searching look.

I trawled him the same line I'd sold the police. From the expression on his face, Jim wasn't buying. "You have to rate as the most unfortunate person I know," he said suspiciously.

"At least my name isn't Vellender."

"True. It's as if someone put a hex on them."

I didn't disagree. With what was going on with my mother, I was feeling fairly jinxed myself.

FORTY-FIVE

Rivendell was nearest to the Prestbury Road end of Windsor Street. A woman in her late fifties, who I assumed to be Mrs. Mason, opened the door. She had a wide face, wide smile, and wide hips. She wore a pink and grey rugger shirt and her cerise-coloured jeans clung to her thickset legs like sausage casings.

"Yes?"

"I wondered whether it's possible to talk to Ashley?"

"And you are?"

I pushed a smile. "This is a little convoluted. I'm a clinical psychologist. My name's Kim Slade. Mimi Vellender was one of my clients."

Her cheeks fell into folds. "I heard she died."

"Afraid so."

"Dreadful business. So how is this connected to Ash?"

"Your daughter was a friend of Mimi's brother, Nicholas."

"Ah, Nick," she said, light in her eyes.

"I'd like to talk to her about him."

"I see." She frowned.

"It would only take a few minutes of her time. I'm quite happy for you to sit in with us."

"It's not that," Mrs. Mason said. "Ash is away at Uni."

"Oh," I said, deflated that I'd fallen at the first. "Then I'm sorry to trouble you." I turned to go.

"Is there anything I can help with?"

I turned back. She looked earnest and genuine. The desire to help is one of the more attractive human traits and I got the impression that Mrs. Mason had it in spades.

"Nick spent a fair bit of time with us. I don't know what you want to ask but I'll do my best to answer."

"You're an angel," I said and genuinely meant it.

I followed Mrs. Mason through a wide corridor, past a downstairs room with an upright piano, and into a homely lounge with deep built-in bookcases flanking a Victorian fireplace. A collage of family photographs hung over the mantelpiece.

"I've made a brew. Want one?"

"That would be great."

"Milk and sugar?"

"No sugar, thanks."

"Make yourself at home."

While Mrs. Mason went to get another mug, I studied the photos. Ashley took after her mother with her blonde hair, bright blue eyes, and smiling mouth.

"That's my Ash," Mrs. Mason said with pride, handing me a mug. "She's studying medicine at Edinburgh."

"Clever girl."

"So?" she said, sitting down. "What do you want to know about Nick?"

"Is that what Ash called him?"

"That's what we all called him. Can't speak for his mum and dad, naturally."

"You say he spent time with you?"

"Almost part of the family."

A revelation. I wondered why Troy Martell had neglected to mention the Masons to me.

"Aside from his friendship with your daughter, was there a specific reason for that?"

"Common knowledge he didn't get on with Mr. Vellender."

"Do you know why?"

"They didn't understand each other. It happens in families."

I reasoned that Mrs. Mason, a nice woman, was reluctant to speak ill of others, particularly when those others have suffered as much as the Vellenders.

"They were different individuals, is that what you're saying?"

"Nick was a quiet, dreamy fellow, thin-skinned for a boy, a little bit artistic. Do you know what I mean?"

I nodded. "He enjoyed success as a writer, I believe."

"Yes." She beamed. "I'm not much of a reader but he had a couple of novels published. Always had his nose in a book, that's for sure. Wait a minute," she said, getting up. "I've got a photograph of them together somewhere." She crossed to a set of drawers, opened the bottom one, and rifled through it. "Here," she said, handing me a print of Ashley with Nicholas Vellender. He looked happy and carefree. Somehow, it made his vanishing act worse.

"So Ash clearly liked having him around?" I smiled, handing it back to her.

"She looked up to him, I think."

"Why was that?"

"He was different to the rest of her mates. A deep thinker, had a strong sense of moral steel running through his body, if you know what I mean."

Thinking back to my conversation with Jim, I wondered how that worked with Nick as potential murder suspect. Maybe he felt intimidated by his parents with their dysfunctional family dynamics and modern lifestyle. "It must have left a tremendous hole in Ash's life when he went missing."

Acute lines appeared on either side of Mrs. Mason's eyes. She spoke slowly, painfully, as if each word hurt her throat. "We thought he'd gone off on his own, to sort himself out, but when the days turned to weeks ..." She faltered. I gave her space to compose herself. "After a month," she continued, "we knew that something more serious had happened. Nick wasn't picking up his calls. Ash went to see Paris to find out, but she was told not to worry."

"His mother didn't seem concerned?"

"Not overly so."

This didn't compute with a full-scale police investigation to find him, but it certainly stacked with the delay in reporting him missing. "Was she in denial?"

"Possibly."

"Ash must have thought it odd."

Mrs. Mason flicked a smile. "The Vellenders are not like us. My husband's a plumber and I'm a carer. They lead different lives. They play by different rules."

I thought about that. Different rules meaning different values? "But as the months rolled on, didn't the Vellenders get in touch with you?"

"Once."

"And?"

Mrs. Mason, all soft cheeks and smiles, visibly stirred with anger. "They advised her to leave it."

"Leave what?" I said, baffled.

"Ash put up lots of messages on social networking sites and so on to try and find Nick. Got quite a following. Some of her mates created posters and plastered the town with them. The Vellenders didn't like the attention."

"I see. She must have been hurt."

"Livid, more like, and so were we."

"And his mother, what was your impression of that relationship?"

"He adored her." She leant forward confidentially. "Personally, I thought it wasn't that healthy."

"Do you mean it was intimate?"

Mrs. Mason broke into an expression of alarm and pressed a hand to her mouth. "Oh, nothing like that," she said. "Nothing perverse."

"Simply too close?"

"Too close for comfort for either of them." She sipped her tea.

Then why didn't Paris go crazy when he went missing? There was only one answer to that, the one I'd suspected from the beginning. They'd never lost touch. "What you said about Nick's moral streak."

"Yes?"

"How did Nick take to his mother's lovers?"

"Not well at all." Her mouth was tight with censure, as if she approved of Nick Vellender's judgement. Did Nick feel badly enough to kill, I wondered? "Some were only a few years older than him."

"Could it be a reason for his disappearance?" I thought of my own flight from home to escape my father's lovers.

"I hate that word. It's so final."

"I'm sorry."

"You're probably right," she sighed. "Your heart hopes for the best. Logic tells you something else."

"You think something bad happened?"

"No," she said. "I refuse to believe it. It wasn't the first time he'd gone astray. He used to go off to punish his parents." So that chimed with Otto's story. "Deep down, he was on a personal quest, I think."

"To find himself?"

"Goodness, no. Nick knew who he was."

"To discover happiness?"

"To find his real dad."

Astounded, I gave a start. "His biological father?" This was news to me and it shouldn't have been.

"That's right," she said with an easy smile.

FORTY-SIX

I FELT AS IF I'd walked out through the wrong door yet ended up in the right place.

"You didn't know?"

I shook my head vigorously. "So Otto's not Nick's blood father?" I had to be absolutely certain.

"He was adopted. I think Nick always suspected he was different."

It took me several seconds to process what she said. If Nick was adopted, Paris wasn't his biological mother either. How the hell didn't I know? "Was this the root of the problem with him and Otto?"

"I wouldn't like to say." She lowered her gaze. "Put it this way: his father wasn't very kind to him."

I took a gulp of tea. I knew from personal experience how destructive that could be. "When did Nick find out?"

"Not long before he went missing."

Added to the spat about the gap year, it explained everything. It was the trigger for his flight into the unknown. "Do the police know this?"

"It came up, but not until a few months after he was reported missing."

"That's when they talked to you?"

"To Ash, yes."

"And did Mimi, his sister, know?"

"I got the impression from Nick that she wasn't in the loop, which I thought a stupid mistake, particularly as Nick and Mimi are brother and sister."

Stunned and light-headed with surprise, I blinked. "*Both* Vellender children are adopted?"

"That's right."

Again, why in God's name didn't I know? I should have been informed. It should have been in Mimi's notes. But then it seemed that Mimi hadn't known either. Was it by design? Was human error responsible, a techno-glitch, or had someone excised it for a reason?

"How exactly did Nick rumble it?"

"He said that, one day, Otto had been particularly nasty."

"In what way?"

"*Intimidating* was the word Nick used. Whether or not there was truth in it, I'm not sure," she said, at pains to sound evenhanded.

I recalled Otto's eviscerating stare. "Have you ever met Mr. Vellender?"

"Twice, briefly."

"And?"

"Charming," she said tight-lipped.

"Anything else?"

"Good-looking and knows it."

Sounded about right. I blushed to my cheekbones at the thought of having sex with him in the hallway of my home. "Sorry, you were saying?"

"Nick would always go to Paris when Otto got on his case. He sounded off to her and, for reasons best known to herself, she chose that moment to tell Nick that his father was not his real dad."

Which spoke more of Paris's thirst for payback than any positive desire to inform her son about his heritage. In admitting the truth, did she come clean and confess that she was not Nick's real mother? I asked Mrs. Mason this.

"Yes."

"Must have been quite a shock."

"He was very upset but I also think he felt vindicated, if that makes sense."

"Because there was a reason behind Otto's behaviour towards him?"

"Precisely."

"Did Mrs. Vellender supply Nick with any other information?"

Mrs. Mason narrowed her eyes. "He was four years old when he and his sister were taken into care and briefly fostered."

"With only four years between them, Mimi must have been taken at birth."

"There was a protection issue. Physical abuse, I believe. Because of the mother, I think."

Grim. Dealing in child protection made what I did for a living a breeze. "Mrs. Mason—"

"Call me Lyn."

"Lyn, did Nick give any indication that he was planning to depart for good?"

"No." All the time she was talking to me, Lyn Mason looked me straight in the eye. Now she looked away. Her body language spelt evasive.

"But you harboured suspicions?" The question teetered in the air. It was like waiting for the do-or-die moment when all is won or lost in a movie, and when, at last, the truth is revealed. She finally turned and faced me.

"The Vellenders had a holiday home in Beesands, Devon."

I pitched forward on the edge of the sofa. "I know it well."

"I reckon that's where he went. I told the police when they came to talk to Ash but, of course, by the time they checked it out, he'd moved on. What happened after that, I don't know." She gave me another square look. "None of us blamed him."

FORTY-SEVEN

MY DRIVE TO DEVON after an uneventful Friday at work was a flash photography montage of roads and lights and jumbled thoughts. The only upside was that, with Gavin's intervention, Monica no longer needed to accompany me on the trip.

Nicholas—or Nick, as the Masons called him—had a perfect motive for leaving: a deep desire to find a father who, in the brief time it had taken Nick to discover the truth about his parentage, no doubt had gained mythical if not god-like status. Be careful what you wish for. My own quest to find commonality with a woman I called Monica, in reality my mother, confounded me. And what had Nick's reaction been to his biological mother's alleged abuse? Bad enough men beating their children, but when mothers lose control, they are doubly demonised. *Like mothers who abandon their families*, a shrill little voice inside my head screeched.

But why the secrecy? Why the lie?

According to the script, Nick had vanished without visible means. No phone. No draw down on funds. Paris had either spirited her son away for his own protection or for reasons nobody knew about. I needed to know what that was.

And then there was Troy. He'd argued his twelve-month slog to locate Nicholas Vellender had turned up little, yet he'd failed to carry out the most basic search. What had got him killed? Did Nick's ghost-like status provide cover for a murderer, or was I travelling too far in the wrong direction?

By the time I reached Cormorant's Reach I was tired, with a first-class headache. Recently fitted security lights flooded the drive, illuminating the house and lighting me up like a Christmas tree. I couldn't say that it was good to be back. It was different, that was all. For four years the cottage represented a time in my life when I'd been loved and cherished. Part of me still expected the door to open with Chris standing there. Here I'd been part of a couple, and now I was single. It stung. It hurt. Maybe it always would.

Flexing my legs after the long drive, I let myself into the house so empty of people and so choc full of memories. I set down my bag, walked my box of instant goodies through to the cosy kitchen with its original pig slats intact, switched on the heating, fired up the oil-fuelled Rayburn, and went straight upstairs to make the bed with fresh linen. Job done, I popped open a bottle of fizzy organic apple juice and put a pre-prepared beef in red wine sauce for one in the oven, alongside a dish of creamy mash. Green beans from the freezer took starring role as vegetable of the day.

I ate without pleasure, drank little, cleared away, checked my phone, and found I'd two missed messages from Otto. I deleted them, called Stannard, and spilled my news. Stannard's reaction was immediate and startling.

"That's it."

"What?"

"Nicholas."

"Can you be less cryptic?"

"It's blatantly obvious. He's your murderer."

Reluctantly, I was leaning heavily towards that view. It made me deeply uneasy, as if I were in some way betraying Mimi's fond memories of her brother. "Your reasoning?"

"He faked his disappearance—"

"Aided and abetted by his mother?"

"Yep, and Martell found out."

"Found out what, that Nicholas was on a quest to find his own dad? It's not a hanging offence."

"Wasting police time is."

"Your stay in hospital has softened your brain. It doesn't provide a strong motive for murder."

"Unlike you to be snippy."

"Unlike you to be dim."

He went quiet on me, feelings bruised. I started again. "I'm going to check out the cottage tomorrow. In a small community, it shouldn't take me long to find out which one and ask a few questions. You can't get away with anything here without someone noticing."

"Anything else tucked up your sleeve, Miss Marple?"

Yes, but it was unconnected to Nicholas Vellender and wholly connected to Monica. "Nothing other than enjoying the sea air."

As if Stannard read my thoughts, he said, "How's it going with your mother? You two gals spending quality time together?"

"Wonderful, thanks."

"Which is why you're in Devon and she's parked in Cheltenham."

"When did you say you were getting back?" I said, deftly changing the subject.

"Flying into Heathrow on Monday, back home Tuesday. Think you can wait that long?"

"I can wait."

FORTY-EIGHT

Deep in the South Hams, Beesands is what I call a genuine slice of Devon. With a fishing community at its heart, it's populated by locals, second homeowners, and those abandoning marriages and/ or previous lives in the spotlight. While nobody could settle unnoticed, paradoxically, as a place for exiles, it was as near perfect as you could get.

Driving down the steep hill towards the village, I was staggered by the level of storm damage. A hole punched in the rock defences had ripped out the shingle beach. Sea had invaded, making off with boats, fishing gear, and anything else it could lay its watery fingers on. Saved by the concrete sea wall, which had stood up to one mother of a battering, those living along the front must have been terrified.

I parked and walked into the Cricket Inn. A Saturday, it was flat-out packed. Using my elbows, I managed to squirrel my way towards a hardy gathering of fishermen and farmers. The conversation ran on predictable lines: folk totting up the total cost of the loss of crab and lobster pots.

At my approach, they parted. I recognised a couple of them, old friends of my dad.

"Kim Slade," Jack Oliver said. "What you having, darlin'?" Small, squat, with a deep-barrelled chest, his check coat was held together with baling twine. Beady-eyed, pinch-faced, he had a sharp hawk-like nose and his cheeks were a mass of thread veins. Jack used to have a small herd of dairy cattle that my father had tended to when they got bloat or footrot or any of the other bovine diseases that plagued cattle. I'd heard recently that he'd sold up and the new owners had got rid of the cows.

"It's fine, Jack, you don't need to put your hand in your pocket for me."

"Nonsense, any daughter of Tony Slade deserves a drink. Fine man, he was, the best of the best," he said to anyone listening. "Broke the mould when he was made."

My face froze in a rictus grin. "Straight tonic water, no ice, slice of lemon, thanks, Jack."

"Nothing stronger?"

"I'm driving."

"You stay where you are."

"So you're Tony Slade's daughter?"

I turned towards the voice, which belonged to a man with a white polo-neck sweater, blazer, and jeans. He sounded and looked different to the rest. His Devonian accent was refined and watered down with another dialect. His hands were smooth, without callouses, and the nails clean. Lined, his face was not crevassed with outdoor life. I had him down for a retired solicitor, maybe a doctor.

"Did you know him?" I said.

He shook his head. "Not well. I knew your mother."

Instantly giddy, I said, "It must have been years ago."

"Over thirty-five."

"Goodness, what are the chances of me running into you? A million to one?"

"Life is curious," he agreed.

"And you remember her?"

He nodded with an affectionate gleam in his eye. "Your mother was the kind of woman who could electrify a room with her smile."

I opened my mouth to speak but Jack was back "There you go, darlin', one tonic water, ice and slice."

I took a deep swallow. "Smashing, thanks," I said, my full attention hooked on the stranger.

"So what brings you down here?" Jack said. "I thought after that bad business, we'd never see you again. Folk said you had your dad's old place on the market."

I gave a feeble smile. "Couldn't sell it."

"That's not such a bad thing. You're a country girl, not one of those urban misses."

Jack was a deluded sweetheart. I made a placatory sound because I desperately wanted to talk to the guy who'd known my mother. "And you?" I said, looking at him. "Do you live around here?"

"Not anymore."

"Colin lives up-country," Jack said, putting on an affected accent. "Got a nice little pile in Oxford. Too posh for the likes of us now."

"Don't believe a word he says," Colin said with an amiable smile. Something or someone caught his eye, and he looked towards the door to the restaurant. "Good to meet you, Kim, but my table's ready." And he was gone.

I felt frantic and torn. My scar was itchy and scratchy, a clear sign I was floundering. I could hardly chase after him and deluge a man I'd only just met with intrusive questions. How well did you know my mother? Is she a liar? Did my father really lead her a dog's life? Did she light up *your* room with a smile? I turned to Jack, who stood grinning, pint of cider in hand, fond memory in mind, probably of my dad.

"Do you know the Vellenders, Jack?"

He took a slurp and wiped his mouth on the back of his hand. "Their cottage was last at the end." He jerked a thumb in the direction of Torcross.

"Was?"

"Sold up a couple of years ago. I heard their son went missing, or some such."

"Did you ever see them?"

"Only the mother, a nice piece of crackling," he said with a lascivious smile.

"You never saw the son?"

"Once. Someone pointed him out to me."

"He was with his mother?"

"That's right."

"Do you remember when?"

Jack took another deep drink. "Couldn't tell you, but it wasn't recent, if that's what you mean."

"Any idea how old he was?"

He grinned, playful. "You're asking a lot of questions, my girl."

I flicked a smile in apology.

"I'm not good at ages but I remember thinking at the time he was the same age as my Ben."

"Your grandson?"

"Yeah, he'd be about twenty-two or -three now. My memory's not so good."

I squeezed his arm in thanks and finished my drink.

"Don't leave it so long next time," he said as I left.

FORTY-NINE

WITH MY HOOD UP and my coat wrapped around me, I inhaled a deep lungful of ozone and trudged across the shingled mile-long beach. The sea boiled and roiled, grey as granite, a spiteful wind ravaging the water, whipping up dozens of white-crested waves.

The end house, and former Vellender holiday home, was one half of a semi. Cream pebbledash. White-painted sash windows. Palm tree in a front garden composed of lawn. There were two up-stairs rooms that I could see. Hoping to find someone in, I opened the gate of the low wicket fence, walked up the path, and rang the bell. About to try again, the front door of the next-door house slid open. A woman dressed in a waterproof jacket emerged with two terriers, bundles of fighting fur, yapping and barking and straining against their leads.

"Not down until the season," she said in a flat tone that inti-mated that she didn't approve of folk with two homes. If I had theft in mind, she'd handed me a gift.

"I don't suppose you knew the previous owners?"

"Only moved in last year. Divorced," she sniffed.

I nodded sympathy.

"See you," she said, the two dogs yanking her in the direction of the beach.

I trailed along at a distance, battling against the breeze, a strong storm brewing. When my phone went, I snatched it out of my bag, unthinking. "Yep?"

"Did you get my calls?"

"Erm…" A boisterous gust flapped underneath my jacket, practically knocking me off my feet. Light rain morphed into downpour. Less wind, more gale.

"How's Devon?"

"Lively, Otto."

"Lively is good. I was hoping for an action replay when you get back."

I pulled a face. Is that how he thought of me, a cheap readily available lay? "Can't hear you. How are things with the restaurant?"

Otto let out a groan. "You'll never believe it but the inspectors found the food chain contaminated with human faeces."

"Oh my God." I wasn't thinking about the consequences for Otto, but what the human health implications were for me.

"Could be some time before we open. We've all got to go on a Hygiene Retraining course. I blame Gabriella."

You usually do, I thought.

"Where are you? You sound as if you're standing in the middle of a hurricane."

"I am. I have to go." I didn't apologise. I didn't say that I'd talk to him later.

Returning to the car, I loitered. How long would Colin be? Was he a two-course or three-course man? Neither, as it turned out.

He stepped outside the entrance, rolled up the collar of his jacket, and looked both ways as if searching for someone, his eyeline falling on the parked row of cars. I flashed my lights and his face broke into a smile. Seconds later, he was standing next to the bonnet. I pressed down the window.

"Hello, again," he said.

"Hello, Colin. Look, I was gobsmacked after what you said about my mother. I don't suppose we could talk?"

He seemed reluctant. "I'm not sure what light I can shed. It was a very long time ago."

"I'd really appreciate it. Please."

"All right," he said slowly.

"Jump in. You must be freezing out there."

I opened the passenger door while he walked around to the other side. "Roll in," I laughed in response to his worried expression.

"You'll have to winch me out."

Good-natured, open and honest, I instantly liked him. I was also astute enough to know, that from the way he talked about my mother, he had warm feelings towards her. After the universal bad press she'd received, it made a refreshing change.

"I don't know quite where to begin," I said, which was true.

"In that case, let me start by asking you a question. How is Monica?"

What could I say? I reacted in the way most would. "She's fine."

"I'm glad. When you see her tell her that Colin Mortimer sends his regards."

"That's so nice to know. You must have thought a lot of her."

"One of the few who did."

"That's really what I want to talk about."

"I thought as much," he said with a sage expression. "I had a lot of time for your mother, but it didn't prevent me from telling her she was wrong."

Exactly how wrong? To what degree? Wrong enough in the head to kill someone? "To leave us?"

"Yes," he said. "I thought there might be another way."

"A civilised divorce, after which she could lead a life that included her children?" That was never going to happen.

He shook his head. "Unlikely, I agree, not with your dad on the scene. He'd have killed her."

I flinched. So it was true.

"I'm sorry," he said, brown eyes flashing misgiving. "I'm speaking out of turn."

"No, please. I have to know. It's really, really important."

He touched the door handle, a giveaway clue, mentally preparing for a fast getaway.

"It's important to her too," I said, need in my voice.

He looked straight ahead, seemed to weigh something up in his mind, and then twisted his body towards me. The leather seat complained.

"Your mother was extremely unhappy with your father. Anyone could see that they weren't well suited." There was a delicate pause. "Your mother had what one would describe as a febrile nature."

"Unstable."

"Crude but well put."

"How well put? I'm a psychologist," I added hastily.

He exhaled, as though he hadn't seen that one coming. "She could be dangerous." I gulped in consternation. "To herself, I mean."

"Self-destructive?" I had to be absolutely clear.

He paused. "I blamed it on her loveless marriage."

"Were you her confidant?"

"I was."

"You were in love with her?"

He flashed a fond smile. "I loved her. There is a difference. My sexual preferences lie elsewhere." I nodded that I understood.

"One day, she left you children with a babysitter and came to see me. At the time I had an office in Salcombe. I'm an accountant," he explained. "Not to put too fine a point on it, she was in agony."

"Over the affair?"

"Yes."

"Did you ever meet Steven?"

"A few times."

"Did you approve?"

"Of him? He was a nice enough chap but, however much in love two people might be, it's hard to give one's blessing when you know there will be at least another two people and numerous children whose lives will be destroyed as a consequence." He stretched across and squeezed my hand. "I never condoned your mother's actions, Kim, but I understood them."

I looked into his kind eyes and wished my dad had been more like him.

"By that time, your father had found out that she was seeing someone else. Consequently, her life became intolerable."

"He made threats?"

"Yes."

"You know for a fact?"

"Unfortunately, I do." He grimaced as if he'd remembered a nasty event in his life, one he'd prefer to forget. He paused for a second time.

"A few days after her visit, I was locking up the office. It was dark and cold. Not many people about. Your father was waiting for me outside in the car-parking bay. I knew who he was, but he didn't know me. He asked my name. I told him and he beat me half senseless."

"God, he thought you were the other man, her lover?"

"Preposterous, but yes."

"What happened, Colin?"

"When he'd got his message across, he said that if I had any big ideas about taking his children, he'd kill the pair of us."

"You believed him?"

"He broke my arm in two places. He had a shotgun in his hand. I believed him."

FIFTY

I drove back to the cottage and went indoors.

Subconsciously, I'd always recognised the simmering violence beneath the skin of the man I called Dad. He'd never raised his hand to me. No need. In the same way Otto Vellender had bullied his son, my father had cowed and controlled his children with words.

It made me remember one defiant and defining night.

A family meeting was called to discuss my aberrant behaviour. My wild child years, as I thought of them, had involved smoking, drinking, and having sex with farmer's boys every time I came home for the holidays. I'd viewed it as making the most of turning sixteen. It wasn't rocket science. I was searching for love.

The assembled included both my brothers, Luke and Guy; Luke's wife, Jessica; and Guy's latest squeeze, whose name I forget. Annette, the woman in my father's life at that time, dispensed drinks as if it were a social gathering instead of what it was: a mock-up of a Star Chamber.

We crushed into the room in which I now sat, me perched on a single upright chair, others on sofas. Luke, I remember, sat on the raised hearth and looked deeply uncomfortable. When everyone but me had strong liquor in his or her grasp, Dad took charge, as though speaking for the prosecution. My "crimes" were listed in humiliating detail: my lack of self-respect, and the family displayed and disseminated for the voyeurism of others. I was described as a tramp, a no-good, and worse. There was no defence. There were no mitigating circumstances. All that remained was to pass sentence. Before my father, as both judge and jury, pronounced, Luke stuck his hand up.

"Yes?" my father said.

"May I say something?" Luke's face was pale with strain. A thin blue vein pulsed in his neck.

I watched my father's deep-set eyes and saw him calculate the odds. Luke was the favoured one. My father expected a vote of support. He could count on him. "Of course, son. Go ahead."

Luke looked at me straight and in a way I found confusing. Afraid, I shrank inside. Tears, like thin rivulets of sulphuric acid, sprang and slid down my burning cheeks. I suffocated with shame. Dad was known to be cruel but if Luke condemned me, I was forever lost.

"No one here would tolerate this level of intrusion," he began, pausing for the full import of his words to catch on and take effect. Turning to the others, he continued, "Which one of you can, hand on heart, declare you have no vices? Do you smoke?" he said, his eyes roving the room. "Do you drink?" He raised his glass. The room crackled with tension. My heart pounded. There was a hell of a sense of a hammer blow about to fall and smash wherever it landed. White-faced, bottom lip curling, his fists knotted in a physical display of rage contained, my father stared at Luke with astonishment and venom. How far would Luke, my father's favourite child, go? All the way, as it turned out.

"Which of you act with morality and integrity in every second of your lives?" He put down his glass, stood up, and looked directly at our dad. "Don't *you* have sex with who you choose when you choose?"

I almost passed out at the accusation. My father practically choked. Blood spread like a tidal wave up from his neck to his cheeks, turning his white face purple. I sprang to my feet and crossed the room. Fists bunched, nostrils dilated, Dad swung back one arm, ready to strike. Luke didn't move. He had no need. I stood between them knowing that my father would not hit a woman and he would never hit anyone in public.

"Step aside," he glared at me.

I didn't budge.

"I said—"

"I heard what you said. Luke," I called behind me, "can I come back to yours?"

Jessica answered. "It's fine, Kim."

"You can't go. I forbid it," my father said.

We quite simply walked out, every one of us except Annette. We went back to Luke and Jessica's tiny flat and I had one of the best nights of my life. I stayed there until it was safe for my return a week or so later, by which time Annette had gone. No words, cross or otherwise, were exchanged between my dad and me about that night. The evening was never mentioned again and I stopped screwing around. But my father never forgave Luke, which was why Luke went to the States and why my father never left him a penny.

How strange that a man could leave such a legacy of pain to his family and yet be elevated to mythical proportions by those who knew him least. The fear my dad once inspired in me had long gone, although he continued to inspire it in Monica years after his death.

"Next time you're there, go up into the attic and check the floor-boards."

"Check the…?"

Her eyes flashed. "Just do it."

I climbed the stairs to the narrow landing, dropped down the hatch, and mounted the loft ladder, flicking on the light on my way up.

Before putting Cormorants on the market, I'd cleared as much as I could. All that was left was a box of vinyls, an old metal tool kit containing rusty implements, dust, and a tapestry of cobwebs clinging to the eaves. I marched up and down, flexing every inch of floor in search of a loose board. Everything seemed solid. Next I dropped to my hands and knees and, despite the splinters, tapped and carried out a forensic fingertip search, right up to the water tank.

Turning around tortoise-style, about to make another pass of the attic, I spotted a floorboard where the nails were missing. I pushed but there was little give. Taking a tissue from my pocket to mark the spot, I straightened up, crossed to the toolbox and dug around for something long and thin that I could use to lever the board. Ditching a broken hammer and selecting a file, I went back and, slipping it between, lifted and eased away the floorboard in the same way as you open a can of fish. The wood gave and, after one final dig, broke free to reveal a hollow in which sat a small canvas bag with a drawstring. I reached inside with both hands and lifted it out. The bag was bulky and whatever was in it weighed less than a bag of sugar. Loosening the drawstring, I plunged one hand in, grasped hold, and pulled out a revolver.

FIFTY-ONE

I BUMPED BACK DOWN hard on my rear. I knew nothing about the weapon in my hand. I didn't know how it worked, how it loaded or unloaded, only what it did, which was blow holes in people. The only person I could think to ask was Stannard, and that meant facing questions I had no desire to answer.

I set the gun down, put the board back in the floor, and took the weapon downstairs to the study. I gingerly laid it on the desk where it gleamed in the lamplight, clunky, mean, and threatening.

I switched on my laptop, punched in everyone's techno-friend (Google), and searched a couple of gun websites. Through a process of hit-and-miss elimination, paying attention to the butt—was that what they called it?—and comparing the weapon to pictures on the Internet, the revolver most resembled a Colt Detective Special. And it was loaded.

The implications made my skin bloom with perspiration. Monica had told the truth. My father had intended to kill his wife if she didn't comply with his wishes. This could easily have provided the spark for Monica's possible addiction to prescription pills. And what now? Did I go to the police and hand the weapon in? What might be the consequences for her of such an action? With that kind of threat in her background, would the police think her more or less likely to commit a crime and exact revenge for a legal system that had let her down?

I paced. I took out my mobile. I paced some more, punched in Monica's number and, unsure, hung up before it connected. My mind fluttered with confusion while my heart banged so hard under my ribs, I could hardly exhale. Panic attack, I realised, struggling to loosen my shirt buttons, my mind flimsy and insubstantial, running away without me.

Kim, you're losing it.

I hurried outside, took deep breaths, focused on the creek and the water, grey and still. All these disparate strands of other people's lives in my hands and I couldn't weave a picture that fitted or made sense.

As late afternoon turned into evening, I returned to the warm kitchen and made myself a cup of strong tea. I took it to the easy chair in the sitting room and sat and sipped and closed my eyes and practiced a relaxation technique I sometimes used on my more anxious clients. As I drifted, allowing my mind to go into free fall, I thought about the desperate time when Monica lived in London stuck in dead-end jobs, grieving for a lover, grieving for her missing children and...

My eyes flicked open. My mother had no criminal record. If she had, the police would have dug it out. It didn't preclude another scenario. To test my theory, I needed to convince Monica that I believed her and that, to help her, I had to know what she was running from, what silent and secretive part of her meant that she would sooner protect it than confide it to the police. Something I'd learnt early on in my professional life: when you dredge the past you end up with a lot of mud, crap, and sharp-edged stones that will cut you.

FIFTY-TWO

DECIDING TO CUT SHORT my visit, I arrived back in Cheltenham the next morning as a faraway clock sounded eleven, and drove to Monica's apartment. I didn't call ahead of my visit. I wanted to catch her unawares. The problem with surprises is that they don't always go to plan.

She wasn't in. It was a nice day, cold and crisp, with turquoise skies. Most probably, she was out making the most of the fine weather. I didn't have her down for a church-going type.

Scrawling a note on the back of a random leaflet I'd chucked in the glove compartment, I asked her to call me.

Back home, stepping over the threshold, I picked up a card on the mat from Royal Mail. I'd missed the delivery of books I'd ordered and would have to collect them in my lunch hour on Monday.

I went upstairs, took minutes to unpack. Stowing the gun took longer. I pushed it to the back of a cupboard in the corner of the bedroom, briefly paused by Stannard's gifted painting, and returned downstairs.

I checked my phone. There was one message from the cop-shop on the Lansdown Road. Slater asking to interview me at my "earliest convenience." Reluctant to comply, I took pineapple juice out of the fridge, filled a tumbler, and drank it straight down. I'd had my pills earlier before setting out. They didn't have the subduing chemical effect they normally had. Wired and hyper, like a neurological storm was brewing, I pulsed with recklessness.

Snatching up my keys, I walked straight out of the house and crossed the streets to the park. Dogs and owners and little kids with balls and...

I twisted round, scanned the vista of shops in Montpellier Walk, zoned in on faces of passers-by, as sure as I could be that someone was dogging my footsteps. We fear most the things that have already happened to us. Did I imagine that I was being stalked again, or was it for real?

Rattled, I speeded up, crossed into the park and darted along the square near the bandstand. Racing up the steps past the Gardens Gallery, skirting the tennis courts, out the other side and over the pedestrian crossing, I cut down Suffolk Parade, past The Suffolk Anthology, a bookshop, and fled towards Paris Vellender's house. I needed to know what made a mother lie. I needed to find out why Paris really would disappear her son and where Nicholas Vellender was hiding now.

I opened the gate to the house quietly, walked with a soft footfall and, tucking myself under the porch so that I could not be viewed from an upstairs room, rang the doorbell. It had a deep, sonorous, military tone.

Footsteps. Rasping sound of a security chain hitched off the latch, a door unlocked. It swung open and I was eyeball to eyeball with Paris Vellender.

Gaunt and pale, she wore a tight-fitting black and grey tracksuit, no make-up. Her hair was dishevelled. I watched her eyes, which crackled first with shock and then anger. Before I knew it, the door bounced back towards me. I reached forward and jammed my foot between it and the frame.

"You can't do this," she screamed at me. "You can't barge in."

"Mrs. Vellender, I want to talk to you." I sounded cold and calm and in control, a mile from the truth.

"Get out, you bitch, or I'll call the police." To add weight to her words, she opened the door a fraction then slammed it hard against my leg. Pain darted from my knee to my thigh.

I dropped my voice, for her ears only. "I'll tell the police how you spirited your son away to Beesands, how you faked his disappearance, how you wasted everyone's time. God only knows what they'll uncover, but you can bet your life they'll prosecute and lock you up. Where will that leave your precious son then?"

Fear shadowed her eyes. She had the look of an art collector whose most precious work had been sliced to pieces with a Stanley knife. I made the most of the moment. "Paris, I want to help you. I'm on your side. You've lost two children and now a lover. It's not possible for you to carry on like this. You have to let me in."

Fat tears flooded her eyes. With relief, frustration, or resignation, I couldn't say, but she stepped back from the door and gestured for me to walk inside.

I followed her into a grand room that had once been two and was now divided by floor to ceiling ornate bi-fold shutters. She indicated for me to sit down on one of a pair of Regency striped sofas. On the low table between us were, a glass half full of white wine, the bottle, virtually empty, and an open pack of Marlboros alongside. A lit cigarette guttered half smoked in a saucer that served as a makeshift ashtray. She hastily stubbed it out, pushed the drink aside. I wondered if clients at the fitness centre who came to Paris to improve their health knew that she smoked and drank so early in the morning.

We sat across from each other. Paris perched, knees together, demure, as if she were seeking an audience with a priest. I'd need to play it right to extract a confession. No way could I afford to mess it up. I could not launch in with demands to know why she had chosen to conceal the fact that her children were adopted. Not yet. Jittery as hell, I could easily blow it.

I forced a smile, tried to put her at ease; her reciprocal vanilla expression was an automatic response. If I didn't speak directly and soon, Paris would concoct a verbal escape plan, and the opportunity would slip through my fingers.

"I'm sorry about Troy, but there was never anything between us. Surely, you believe me? He asked for my help, that was all."

"To trace Nicholas?" Her expression was stiff and stony.

"Yes."

"That's all he was ever interested in." She looked and sounded bitter.

"Didn't you find that odd?"

"Not to start with. He'd always been fond of Mimi. It made sense, but…" she trailed off, looked down. Despondent.

"But what?"

Glancing up, she flicked another plastic smile. "Nothing."

"How long had you been together?"

"About fifteen months."

"Do you think Otto had a hand in Troy's murder?"

She bit her lip. I think she wanted to say yes in the same way she'd falsely accused Otto of murder outside the church, but she couldn't, and she recognised that I knew that. "Absurd," she said eventually, "even if the police have their suspicions."

"Why are they so fixed on him?" I wondered if she'd yield something extra.

She looked at me hard. "The way Troy was killed."

And cut up. "If not Otto, who did it?"

The hesitation was fractional. She said, "I don't know," but her eyes said something else. I waited, hoping that she would fill in the gap. She didn't.

"Do you remember when you talked to me in the corridor?" I said. "You said it was all your fault?" The muscles around her mouth flexed. "It's not an accusation, Paris."

Frozen, unsure how to react, she levelled her gaze with big pleading eyes reminiscent of her daughter even though I now knew that they were not related by blood. Did children grow to look like the parents who adopt them?

"I could have sacrificed one child to protect the other," she said, her voice low and strained. "Instead I lost both."

"You mean you could have told Mimi the truth?"

She nodded dumbly, although I'm not certain to which truth we were alluding.

"Why didn't you?"

"Because Nicholas forbade it."

And you do everything your teenage son wants? Lyn Mason's observation of the unhealthy and unnaturally close relationship between mother and son battered my brain. "But he loved his sister, surely? She certainly loved him."

"He did love her. That's why he thought it best to disappear."

I must have looked as mystified as I felt because she continued, "To protect her." As soon as the words left her mouth, panic flashed

274

across her features. To her mind, she'd given away too much. "Would you like a drink or something? Tea or coffee?"

"I'm fine. Thank you." Thoughts cantered through my mind. Nicholas had fled for two reasons: to escape Otto and to find his biological father. I believed it; what I didn't believe was what happened later.

"Did Nicholas feel betrayed?"

The wary light returned to her eyes.

"In his mind," I said, "he'd gone out of the proverbial frying pan into the fire, taken from a father who might have treated him better than Otto. I know that your children were adopted, Paris." No point in hiding it now.

Her face pinched with shock. "You knew all along?"

I shook my head. "I found out."

"How?"

"It doesn't matter."

She glared at me in a way that assured me it did.

"You said there were tensions," I persisted.

She grimaced. "You have no idea what went on." She spread her hands, as if she couldn't believe it either.

"Tell me."

"Otto tortured him."

FIFTY-THREE

I STARED BUG-EYED.

"Mentally."

I so wanted to shout at her for scaring the crap out of me I almost missed what she said next. "Otto put absurdly unrealistic expectations on Nicholas's shoulders and when he failed, Otto did a number on him. It went on for years and years."

"What are we talking here—humiliation, subjection, abuse?"

Paris let out a weary sigh. The circles under her eyes bulged. She looked more fifty than youthful forty. "Emotionally, you name it, Otto subjected him to it."

The combination of early physical abuse from his mother and extreme mental abuse from his adoptive father would leave a toxic legacy. Fuck. "What about Mimi?" I remembered what Otto had told me about his little girl.

"Mimi was inviolate." She leant forwards. "You have to understand that Nicholas was sensitive."

For this, I read *vulnerable*. Any form of abuse would have a stronger impact on him for that reason alone. "Is this why you spirited him to Devon?" I could tell from her guarded expression that she was uncomfortable with the line of questioning. "I know what happened when Nicholas disappeared, Paris."

She didn't deny it. "I helped him survive."

"Financially, put a roof over his head, that kind of thing?"

"Yes."

"What about the money trail, bank accounts, paying bills, and so on?"

In a toneless, detached manner, she continued, "Nicholas taught me how to deal with it. Online, there's a way around everything if you know how. He *had* to get out. Otto was breathing down his neck about what he should do with his life."

"It wasn't such a big deal, was it? Why the cloak-and-dagger? Why go to such extremes? He was eighteen. He could easily make his own way in the world."

She looked me in the eye. "Nicholas felt as murderous towards his father as his father felt toward him."

"Nicholas feared he'd do something he'd regret?" I had to be careful not to push too hard, to put words into her mouth and mess it up.

"We all did."

"All?"

"Me and Mimi."

Was it simply Paris's dramatic take on a bitter spat between father and son, or was the situation as dangerous as she painted it?

"Is that why you accused Otto of killing Nicholas?"

"He *did* kill him. He killed all that was good and decent in my boy."

And what had emerged in its stead? I couldn't escape the fact that Nicholas had crushed Mimi's spirit by leaving her. Would a sensitive boy who hates his father kill another man as part of a warm-up before the headline act? Had he possibly killed before? Were his parents covering for him? Stannard's warning voice murmured in my ear.

"Would Nicholas go to any length to protect his anonymity?"

Paris's laugh was as sharp as lemon juice on an open wound. "You can't mean Troy."

"Why not? He was poking around." And so was I.

"Because it's ridiculous. Because…" She broke off and looked at me for what seemed like a long time. I noticed that same reluctance and fractional hesitation she'd displayed earlier, as if she were trying to subdue an unpleasant memory.

"Paris, is Nicholas still in touch?"

She didn't answer. Her blank expression didn't tally with the light in her eyes.

"When was the last time you saw him?"

"I don't remember."

She did, but wasn't telling. "Did you see him a year ago when Mimi spotted you together?" She dropped her gaze. Her hands bunched tight. "Did you?" I pressed.

She flexed her neck and gave a barely perceptible nod.

"Why the hell did you lie to your daughter?"

Her eyes flooded with tears once more. She spread her fingers as if she didn't understand herself. Screw that.

"You accuse Otto of torturing your son. What do you think you were doing to Mimi?"

"I'm sorry," she mumbled. "I don't know how to explain."

"Try," I hissed. "Why did Nicholas meet you, Paris? What are you hiding?"

She didn't answer. The clock on the mantelpiece chimed one. Her chest rose and fell at speed. She was running out of road and she knew it.

"He was obsessed," she mumbled, "like a man on a mission."

Obsessed rang my alarm bells.

"Where is he?"

She glanced away.

"Is he in town?"

"I think so."

"Whereabouts?"

"He's moved to another address. I have no idea where. It's what Nicholas wanted," she added defensively.

"But he's still here?"

"Possibly."

I read it as *probably*. "A risk, surely?"

"I persuaded Nicholas it was better to hide in full view."

"You wanted to keep him close."

She met my eye.

"For your benefit, or his?" I demanded.

She swallowed hard, placed both her tiny hands on her temples. I noticed that the nail varnish was chipped and the little fingernail on her left hand was bitten down to the quick. Fear returned to her eyes, which fastened on the door as if she was about to make a run for it. She was plainly terrified.

"What is it, Paris? What are you so afraid of?"

She regarded me with beseeching eyes. I'd seen the same terror many times in the consulting room. *Please keep my secret safe. Please don't use it against me. Please don't probe.*

"Sometimes," she gulped, "Nicholas has episodes."

The sunshine that had flooded the room vanished behind the drapes.

"He isn't always himself," she explained.

"In what way?"

She hitched a shoulder. "Difficult to describe."

"Panic attacks?"

"Sort of."

"When did it start?"

"Around the time he was twelve. The doctor said it was connected to hormonal changes associated with puberty." She didn't sound convinced.

"How would it manifest itself?"

"He'd be manic, talkative. It never lasted very long," she added as though this somehow made it all right.

"How long? Days, hours?"

She looked vague. "Hours, and then he'd return to lethargy."

Not exactly an unusual state for an adolescent, which was what I told her, in spite of believing something else was in play.

"I guess not," she said, a doubtful note in her voice. "Then he started having bad dreams."

"Did he say about what?"

"Mostly, he couldn't remember."

"Did you ever suspect violent tendencies?"

Her voice rose in protest. "He was a sensitive boy."

"Even sensitive young men indulge in violent fantasies."

She tore away, refused to look me in the eye. "I was never frightened of him. Never."

It seemed a strange admission. "Does he have a history of delinquency?"

"Not really." I levelled my gaze. Collapsing under my stony expression, she said, "Does truanting count?"

I suspected I wasn't getting the full story, which was illuminating in itself. "Anything else?"

"He talked about seeing a woman."

"A girlfriend?"

"I don't think so. She sounded too old."

"You didn't meet her?"

"Never. Whoever she was she caused him a lot of pain. It was as if he became someone else when he was with her."

"When did the relationship start?"

"Not long after he found out about his birth mother."

"But before he disappeared?"

She chewed her lip, nodded.

I stared hard. She looked at me and then blinked with realisation at where I was going with it. "His biological mother? Impossible."

I shrugged. It seemed a long shot. "And he never confided in you?"

"That was the funny thing about it. He usually told me everything, but each time I pushed him on it, he'd become upset, tearful even."

"Is he still seeing this woman?"

"I don't know."

I thought about it. "With his quest to find his real dad, did you help with that? I'm not sure how the adoption system works."

She chewed her bottom lip. "I..." she faltered.

"It's all right, Paris, take your time. Would you like some water?"

She shook her head; eager it seemed to get it out into the open before she clammed up forever. "Both Nicholas and Mimi were the subject of placement orders. In the usual run of things, adopted children have the legal right to obtain a copy of the original birth certificate and the name of the agency that arranged the adoption."

"Can they access background details and addresses?"

"They can trace a fair amount online and, if they wish, send for a copy of the original birth certificate."

"I'm guessing it would state the birth name given to the adopted child and names of both parents."

"Name, age, address, occupation if any of parent, and address of the hospital where the child was born. We were informed that, in both instances, the father's name had not been noted on either child's birth certificates. 'Father unknown' was the phrase used."

"Do you know if it was the same father for both children?"

"I don't know. We'd always assumed so because of the familial likeness. As I said, in a routine adoption, adopted children are given an opportunity to contact their birth parents and vice-versa."

"Providing both sides agree?"

"Yes."

"But your case wasn't routine?"

"Not with the courts involved, no. Because of the court order, there was no way either parent would be allowed to make contact even if they desired it."

"I gather there was a protection issue."

"Who told you that?"

"Lyn Mason."

Paris flicked a bootleg smile, cautious, edgy.

"Did you keep paperwork relating to the adoption?"

She nodded.

"You had a social worker assigned to the case?"

"Yeah." She glanced away.

"Name?"

"It was a long time ago."

Her face told me all I needed to know. She was deliberately stalling. "I'm sure I could find out," I said, not at all sure that I could.

Paris rolled her eyes in exasperation. "A woman called Joyce Conway."

"Which you told Nicholas?"

She nodded slowly.

"And?"

The weight of silence that followed almost swallowed me up. "Paris?"

Forced to explain and unhappy about doing so, she said, "She's dead."

FIFTY-FOUR

I'M NOT THE LEAST bit superstitious but I wanted to cross my fingers and hope for the best. "From natural causes?"

A fine film of perspiration misted Paris's top lip. "She fell off a cliff. An accident," she added with emphasis.

The room spun. "When?"

"I don't know."

"Where?"

"Bolt Head. It's on—"

"I know where it is." A few miles farther along the south west coast from Beesands. "Is that what Nicholas came to tell you that night in the dark?"

"No," she exploded.

I didn't believe her. "Did he ever meet Joyce Conway?"

"I don't know."

"Did he intend to meet her?"

"I don't know."

"Where is he?"

"I told you. I don't know." Her voice was loud and vexed.

"Why not? You're in touch. You have his number."

She stared right through me.

"You received a text from him a few weeks ago."

"That's—"

"True," I said and stood up. "When you speak to him tell him I want to talk."

That got her attention. Her head jerked up. "It's not that simple." Paris was playing for time.

"Make it simple."

"And if I don't?"

"I'll go to the police and tell them everything."

———

I let myself out and cut back across the park. I'd imagined a conspiracy of silence but hadn't known until now what it meant or where it might lead. I couldn't tell whether Nicholas Vellender was a devil or victim, or both, but I disliked all of them for what they'd done. To my mind, each of them was culpable. The social worker's fall made the blood thicken in my arteries. Too many deaths in too small a familial location. The Vellenders were fast becoming like the Gettys and Kennedys and other ancestral lines dogged by misfortune down the decades.

Passing John Gordon's, the wine merchants, my phone rang.

"How was Devon?" Monica asked.

Interesting, challenging, disturbing, take your pick. "Good," I said.

"Are you in town?"

"In Montpellier."

"I'm in the café in the Courtyard."

"Café del Art?"

"Fancy a coffee? I'm sitting outside in the sun."

"Be right with you," I said.

Monica looked more relaxed than I'd seen her in a while. She wore a sleek grey cardigan over a pale blue shirt and straight-leg jeans. She had sandals on her feet and her toenails were painted fuchsia. She could easily have passed for ten years younger.

I viewed her empty cup. "Another one, or would you prefer a glass of wine?"

"Are you having one?"

"Yes." To hell with the antidepressants, I needed a drink.

She nodded in assent and I walked inside, ordered, returned to Monica, and waited until we were settled. "I bumped into an old acquaintance of yours while I was away."

"Really?"

"Colin Mortimer." I watched the moves on her face, which encompassed surprise, delight, and apprehension. She covered the latter well. "How extraordinary. He was a good friend. How did he seem?"

"Well, and he spoke highly of you." This appeared to please her. "While I was there I had time to reflect on everything."

"I see," she said, doubtful.

"It's all right," I reassured her. "I've misjudged you. You know, with Dad and what happened."

"I'm not asking you to take a side."

"I know." I was faintly uncomfortable with consuming a large slice of humble pie. If I were honest, some of it stuck in the back of my throat. "I hope we can move on."

"Of course, Kim, but with one proviso." Her eyes shone with humour, her smile warm and serene.

"Yes?"

"You must continue to call me Monica. I rather like it. All very modern, don't you think?" My admission had obviously produced an immediate effect. She looked bright and carefree, almost skittish.

I smiled back, the easy part over, and sipped my drink and stretched out in the welcome sunshine. Anyone watching would have believed we'd been comfortable with each other for years.

"So did you do anything nice while you were away?" she said.

"Walked and talked and caught some sea air. There was one thing though."

"Yes?"

"I went up into the attic."

She blinked hard twice. At first I thought the sun was dazzling her eyes. Then I understood that she was trying to evade me.

"You remember, you asked me to look?"

She half turned the way people do when they see someone they know in the street. I twisted around, but there was nobody there. The giveaway tic in her eye flickered. What was the matter with her? I was getting a rerun of the reaction I'd had from Paris.

"It's awkward," she muttered, at last.

"What is?"

"When I asked you I wasn't in the situation then that I find myself in now."

"I'm not following you, Monica."

She lowered her voice to a whisper. "The gun."

I flashed a smile. "It's okay. I get it. Dad really meant what he said about coming after you."

She looked embarrassed and awkward and refused to look at me straight. Dread bloomed in my chest and then I tumbled to it. "The gun wasn't his, was it?"

"It belonged to me," she said.

FIFTY-FIVE

"In God's name, where did you get it?" *Why?* should have been my first question, but I wasn't thinking with enough lucidity.

"A friend of Steven's."

"Jesus, what kind of company did he keep?" A nice enough man, Colin had said. Yeah. Right.

"It wasn't like that, Kim," she said, touchy.

"Then what was it like? You do realise, don't you, that it was loaded? What the hell were you planning to do, shoot your husband?"

"It was my insurance policy in case things turned nasty."

I had a surreal image of my parents with pistols at dawn. "You would have shot him?" I was astounded.

Her eyes flashed with anger. "Don't be silly, of course not. I wanted to frighten him."

"Are you crazy?"

"Don't ever call me that." She yelled so loud, a couple on the next-door table spun round.

I glanced across with an expression of apology. Her eyes bulged wide, wild and ugly. Astonished by how undone she seemed, I lowered my voice. "You must understand how this looks."

When she spoke next each word spat out of her mouth. "I was young. I was scared. I already told you. Sometimes you have to fight fire with fire."

"Spare me the homilies," I said. "This isn't about a power struggle. You possessed an illegal firearm. How the hell was that supposed to end?" She looked at me with unadulterated truculence. I felt as if someone had spirited me back into my own consulting room. "Did you actually know how to use it?"

"Of course not."

"Dear God, if the police get hold of this—"

"Which they won't."

Unless I tell them were the unspoken words between us. The similarity between my threat to Paris and now to Monica was not lost on me. What they called leverage; I intended to use it to obtain exactly what I wanted from both of them.

Monica viewed me with undisguised anger borne out of fear. Her plan to get me onside by showing how frightened she was of my father had backfired in the wake of the judge's murder. If the police found out, she'd go straight to number one on the suspect list, and I couldn't blame them. She was hovering pretty close to what I regarded as my personal number one spot, too. I strived for a more moderate approach. "What exactly happened in London?"

"I already told you."

"You told me what you wanted me to believe. There's a difference."

She snatched at her drink like it tasted of malt vinegar. I persisted. "Something went wrong. What?"

Pinpricks of colour spotted her cheeks. Her eyes watered. The tic was back with a vengeance. "I can't," she said, breathing hard, her chest rising and falling. "I simply can't."

"All right," I said, cooling things down. "Request a copy of your medical records from your doctor."

"Why?"

"So I can read them."

"It's confidential information," she blustered with alarm.

"It is."

"You don't have the right."

"I don't."

"Then…" her voice drifted.

"Either you tell me, or I'm going to find out, with or without your permission." I was bluffing, but Monica didn't know me well enough to know that.

I watched as she processed her options. She looked ready to go silent on me, but finally, cold and grim, she said. "All right, but let's have another drink, first."

I sat in frozen silence while Monica ordered. Neither of us said a word until we had fresh glasses. She took a big swallow and stooped forwards so that she could keep her voice down.

"I became homeless and desperate and ended up in a hostel."

"That's it?"

"Isn't it enough?"

"It's sad and I'm very sorry, but you once told me that I'd hate you for whatever it is you've done. Becoming homeless isn't a sin."

She took another drink. We both did. Dutch courage. "I lost the plot," she began haltingly. "I slipped through the cracks in the pavement and plummeted into the abyss beneath."

Darkness stirred inside me. "How exactly?"

"I wound up in hospital, a mental institution."

"You were sectioned?"

I knew the steps and the strategy. Either a court detained an individual after a crime was committed, or there was what was known as a civil section whereby an individual was detained for his or her own protection, or the protection of others. The latter involved medics, three of which had to be in agreement that detention was the right course of action. A nearest relative was often consulted but, in Monica's case, there was nobody.

"I'm so sorry," I said.

Her cheeks sagged. She looked utterly dismal and lost. My heart momentarily swelled for her.

"What were the grounds for your committal?"

"The first time I was a danger to myself; the second"—she paused, stumbling over her own words—"I was considered a danger to others."

We looked at each other, the truth sharp and pointy between us. "Tell me about the first time."

"What's there to tell?" she said, gloomy and sad. "I went into a slow, steady decline after Steven's death. I couldn't find work because I wasn't functioning properly. It's a kind of horrible catch-22. I had very little money. I couldn't afford to feed myself or put a roof over my head. For a short period of my life, I ended up sleeping rough. Nobody gets a job when you're in that state. I reached the stage when I couldn't make a simple decision." It was something with which I could identify. I remembered how I'd become following Chris's death. Mentally mangled.

"How long were you detained?"

"Six months the first time."

"And the second?"

"Almost two years."

I blanched.

"It wasn't great," she said, picking up on my unease. "They said I had a severe anxiety disorder. I remember feeling paranoid about everyone and everything."

"Paranoid enough to hurt someone?"

She hung her head. "A man who didn't press charges."

I bit down to prevent myself from gagging.

"Luckily for me, he was a lay preacher, believed in the power of forgiveness." She looked up. "But if the police ever get hold of that," she said, "I'm done for."

FIFTY-SIX

WE PARTED. FRACTIOUS AND out of sorts, I trudged into town. All my judgements were off. Every time I had a handle on Monica or Paris, Otto or Nicholas, it slipped, slimy and insubstantial, from my grasp. The world as I knew it had gone bonkers, and I didn't care that it was a poor professional description.

Walking along the wide pavement outside Café Rouge, I had an instant sensation of someone behind me. At first, I shrugged it off. By the time I rounded the corner into the high street, the perception intensified. Distressed, I darted into Boots and skulked among the cosmetic counters with their mirrors and manicured shop assistants. My gaze, meanwhile, remained fixed on the double-opening doors. Nobody identifiable entered. Nobody sneaked inside with a watchful gaze and sinister intent. At a loss, I returned to the street, crossed over to the other side and, hugging the shop fronts, strode towards Regent Arcade. The feeling of being under surveillance returned. I stopped to look in a shop window, the light reflecting off the glass revealing the culprit tailing me. He stood side-on, arms crossed lightly across his chest, authoritative and in command and challenging. He wore a small rucksack on his back, the flap open. An ordinary shopper in an ordinary place. Except it was a lie.

Furious, I turned and glared. Otto stared back, the suggestion of a silken, insolent smile on his face. He could have moved towards me. He could have said *Hello, how have you been?* Instead, as I stalked off, he followed, lost, engaged in his own private game of stalker and victim in which I, no doubt about it, starred as supporting actor.

Heading into the dimly lit interior of HMV, I braved the overpowering odour of students wearing clothes that hadn't dried properly, and took my time flicking through the small classical selection before drifting to the back where I feigned interest in 'Roots'. Otto mirrored my moves. Whenever I chanced a glance I found his eyes boring into mine. I didn't like it. I had no idea where he planned to take me in the script, but I wasn't prepared to play my part.

Frustrated, about to start for the exit, I noticed a couple weave through racks of music and film and make a beeline for Otto. Mid-fifties, smartly dressed with expensively acquired suntans, they didn't look happy. Private grief, I thought, as the woman tore into him about how ill she'd been following the food poisoning outbreak. Cornered, Otto had no choice but to abandon his role-play and respond, which he did with more humility than I dreamt possible. Seizing the opportunity, I picked the nearest DVD off the shelf, slid up behind Otto, silently and surreptitiously dropped it into his rucksack, and sailed out of the shop. A few minutes later, my sleight of hand was rewarded when the alarms sounded and two security guards pounced on a bewildered-looking Otto, demanding to know what he'd stolen.

I sped back home, locked the door, and shut all the windows. Fortress Slade. Sticking on some music—a compilation of Leonard Cohen because it suited my dismal four-in-the-morning mood—I called Gavin Chadwick to explain that Monica had spent time in psychiatric care. I did not mention the assault. I did not mention the revolver.

"That explains the fake reference," Chadwick said, like someone asked what he thinks of the wine and his response is to read the label aloud word for word.

"And her reluctance to fill in the gaps."

"Sectioned, you said?" Possibly unfair, but I bet my monthly wage packet that Gavin judged it with distaste. "Presumably, she wasn't sectioned by a court?"

"A civil detention." I paused. "The police don't need to know this, do they?"

"Best if they don't. Of course, if we're pushed up a corner, it could work in her favour."

"How?"

"The police may take the view that, although a witness may be capable of providing reliable evidence, a witness in your mother's position may also—without knowing or wishing to do so—be prone to supplying evidence that is unreliable, misleading, or self-incriminating."

"It might undermine the thrust of their inquiry?"

"It could wrong foot them, certainly. Alternatively..." He trailed off. I didn't need to have it spelt out.

Thinking I ought to eat, I picked a banana out of the fruit bowl, grabbed a couple of biscuits, and squirreled them to my desk. Switching on my computer, I nibbled and searched for information on Joyce Conway, the social worker who'd facilitated the Vellender children's adoption. A load of stuff came up under the heading of WOMAN FALLS TO HER DEATH FROM CLIFFS. It seemed that Conway was not alone. All around the world, people were plummeting head first, either by choice or, more often, because they were chasing runaway pets or children.

According to an early newspaper report, Conway's body was found at around 11:00 a.m. on January 5 the previous year. A witness said that she'd stumbled across a dog, believed to belong to the seventy-year-old, wandering free. Salient points: nobody saw her fall; postmortem to be carried out to determine the cause of death; police keeping an open mind. Tributes were paid to a well-liked individual who had retired to live in Salcombe ten years previously.

I scrolled to a more recent report that revealed that Joyce Conway was a regular walker and had routinely trekked along the coastal path. A postmortem revealed that she'd died instantly due to head injuries sustained after falling onto the jagged rocks below. There was no suggestion that she was assaulted prior to the descent to her death, no hint of foul play.

I knew that stretch of coastline. Around a three-mile trip from Salcombe to Bolt Head, the path was uneven and, in winter, muddy and slippery. Perhaps the dog had run off and, in her anxiety Joyce Conway lost her footing. Occasionally, the path could crumble and slip away if you strayed too close. Maybe something had caught her eye, a bird flying low, a yacht or tanker in the distance, a play of low winter light shimmering across the water, and she'd taken a curious step too near the edge. Or...

Or she'd encountered a killer on the path who knew her routines and who intended her harm for age-old reasons.

If Nicholas Vellender had met Conway and, as payback, helped her on her downward journey, he had every reason to protect his anonymity, which could also mean shutting up Martell. And Paris knew this, even if she didn't admit it, which told me one thing. She believed her son capable of murder.

I thought again about Nicholas Vellender's "episodes," as she'd described them. Had this loner really met a woman? If he had, wouldn't Lyn and Ashley Mason have known?

Several clicks through Directory Enquiries online revealed Lyn Mason's phone number. I called and put the question to her.

"He never mentioned anyone."

"Might he have wanted to keep it secret?"

"I suppose so."

"You don't sound convinced."

"He was always quite open with us. He and Ash were such good friends, he would have told her, I'm sure."

"Would you say he was disturbed?"

"You mean did he have mental health issues?"

"If you like."

She fell silent. I got the impression she was crafting her next response with care. "Nick was complicated. Some kids thrive under pressure."

"But Nick wasn't one of them?"

"Not really. He got upset. He felt things quite deeply, I think." She paused. "After your visit I talked to Ash."

"Yes?"

"She told me something. It might be irrelevant, of course, and I certainly don't wish to give the wrong impression."

"I understand."

"Nick was into things that go bump in the night."

It wasn't the kind of earth-shattering, game-changing information I was seeking. Hard to confess, but I felt a surge of disappointment. "No surprise," I said. "He wrote fantasy fiction."

She thought about it before she spoke next. "This was different, I think."

"Would you like to elaborate?"

"He had a rather strange interest in Japanese culture."

I caught my breath. The design of the scar on Mimi's arm—there had to be a connection. I asked Lyn Mason to clarify what she meant.

"You know, death rituals. I'm not sure I can remember the phrase exactly. It sounded rather gruesome to me."

I all but gasped. "Harakiri?"

"That's the one," she said.

FIFTY-SEVEN

JAPAN CONTINUED TO DOMINATE my thinking the following Monday morning. I used my lunch hour to return the phone call to the police in Cheltenham. After negotiating with "rest" days—theirs, not mine—it was agreed I would go in after work on Wednesday. Next, I headed off to the sorting office in Swindon Road to collect the books I'd ordered. It gave me plenty of time to consider Nick Vellender's interest in ritual suicide. I knew little of such things, only what I'd watched on film. Honour, machismo, and saving face seemed the principal features. A sane person would point out that the fascination might be nothing more than a typical young man's flirtation with the macabre. I wasn't feeling sane. To my mind, it represented something deadly. I couldn't subdue the thought that Nicholas Vellender was playing out a fantasy and punishing those responsible for destroying his life. Her brother had clearly been a heavy influence in Mimi's life. Why else would she have a scar, like a tattoo, of an avenging ghost on her arm?

About to negotiate road works, traffic converging from different directions, and cars slung up half on the pavement, I felt the same strange gravitational pull of someone watching me as I'd felt the day before. I swung around. All I saw was the back of a guy weaving his unsteady way on a bike, two young women walking arm in arm, and a short stout figure in a hoodie—a flash of dark eyes, nothing ostensibly remarkable and yet somehow oddly familiar. As I watched, whoever it was peeled away in the opposite direction. I could not shake off the impression that the individual was female.

Obsessively scoping the street, a wave of exhaustion washed over me. Wiped out, I wanted to lie down, in the middle of the road for all I cared, and sleep for a straight year. I wanted to make whatever was screwing with my brain stop. I wanted to get my life back on track, without thoughts of murder and mayhem and death careering after me like a star-struck lover eager to lock me in a clinch. How could I counsel others when my own runaway emotions played havoc with my head? Should I even be doing so?

On shaky legs, I crossed over and joined a queue of people waiting to pick up missed weekend deliveries. With only two collection points inside, we snaked around the small, overheated, and airless room. I could smell perfume, tobacco, stale food, and stale bodies. I fixed my eyes on the back of the person in front of me. I tuned out. I flexed the muscles in my arms and legs, tightened and relaxed, allowing the tension to seep out of me. That's when I thought I was dreaming.

He stood side-on, waiting his turn. Slim, tall, slightly stooped, he had an unmistakable air of vulnerability about him, like a refugee in a country where he did not speak the language. He wore a long dark coat over jeans and trainers, and a black beanie. In profile, his straight symmetrical features and pointed chin were more defined.

The whisper of a moustache, evident in the photograph I'd seen, had grown thicker, and there was a fashionable growth of stubble on his cheeks. I listened as he spoke to a postal worker, but his voice was so low I couldn't hear a word he said. With a parcel tucked under one arm, he turned and walked straight past me. If I had any lingering doubts, they were quickly dispelled. I caught the colour of his eyes, the intensity of his expression, that look that could slice right through a person.

I waited for the door to slam closed after him, dropped out of the queue, and followed. I didn't think of books or clients or work or appointments or letting people down. I didn't pay attention to my own mental health. Foolish, stupid, risky, I'd gone way beyond recklessness. Murderer, victim, saint, or sinner, I didn't know, but Nicholas Vellender could tell me why a young woman had faded away pining for him, and why Troy Martell deserved to die, and in the way that he had, and whether or not an elderly woman had tumbled from a clifftop through accident or malice.

Falling back a little, I watched him walking on the balls of his feet, loose-limbed and quiet. He speeded up. He slowed down. He jinked, crossed, and recrossed the road. Perhaps it was habit. I didn't believe so. I was as certain as I could be that he'd made me. Still I kept walking, inexorably drawn to follow. I'd have sooner cut off my right hand than turn back now.

A gusty wind kicked up a trail of dust and grit. The sky turned from blue to indigo to sullen grey.

I followed him as he sloped past a restaurant, a snooker club and bar, and a brasserie. I registered these by accident. I didn't rehearse what I would say or how I would react or what I felt other than that I harboured a burning, blistering anger towards him—for insinuating himself into my life, for turning me inside out, and for causing so much pain to others.

And then he stopped.

And I stopped, too.

His right hand patted the pocket of his coat, as if he'd forgotten something important, like keys or a vital document. Next, he turned on his heel and, with a purposeful stride and razor-blade smile, doubled back towards me.

I froze, glanced at the buildings up ahead, a block of apartments on my right. Tarmac and empty street stretched out before me. It was lunchtime. It was busy, except suddenly it wasn't. It was he and I in a quiet part of town. A panicked voice in my head told me to run hard and fast and never look back.

But I didn't.

FIFTY-EIGHT

"YOU MUST BE KIM Slade."

He stuck out his right hand. I clung to the strap of my bag with both hands.

"Nicholas Vellender?" I said.

"Call me Nick." His smile disarmed me. Intellect shone through his eyes. Charming, he didn't appear in the least shy or hostile. Perhaps he'd grown up. Perhaps he was innocent. A snatch of conversation marched into my mind, Jim talking about psychopaths.

"It is Kim, isn't it? Paris told me all about you."

I bet she did. "Can we talk?" I said.

"Here?"

"Somewhere more comfortable?" And busy, maybe crawling with shoppers.

"Tricky."

"Why?"

This time his smile was cool. "I don't really exist."

For a scary moment I thought I was delusional. "You're flesh and blood to me." To be sure, I stretched out stiff fingers and grazed his sleeve. He was real all right. Eyes alive, he laughed.

"You understand my situation. Cops will be all over me if I show my face."

I appreciated his dilemma. Outside in the street would have to do.

With no intention of being lured somewhere else, I walked away a little, indicating he follow, which he did. It was growing darker by the minute, rain clouds gathering, the sky dark purple at its core like an old self-inflicted bruise, done to shift the blame and turn an abuser into the abused.

A storage facility flanked by wrought iron gates set back from the pavement under a brick-built arch provided a makeshift shelter. I walked beneath it and pressed my back against the railings. Nick Vellender did the same. To the outside world, we were two friends having a chat, nothing more extraordinary than that.

"Why the deception?"

"Long story."

"I'm listening."

"Didn't Paris tell you about Otto?"

"I'm not interested in what Paris told me." I wanted to know why Nick Vellender put his sister through hell. I wanted him to explain. I wanted to find out if he was a murderer, to say the words that would condemn him.

"Otto is a tool."

"Many fathers are—"

"He's not my father." His protest cut with contempt.

"Okay, you hate him. I get it."

"No, you don't. You couldn't."

I turned to him and noticed the set of his jaw, the tendons in his neck. Was this how I appeared to others when describing the relationship with my father? Yet Nicholas Vellender's expression said so much more. His eyes shone with something akin to religious conviction, maybe mania. At that moment I believed he could kill.

"What did he do to you?"

"A total mind-fuck."

"Be more explicit?"

"Okay," he said, his voice compressed. "How about this? I'm a vegetarian. Can't stand the smell of raw meat. Makes me heave. One day, Otto brings home a dead deer, with head, antlers, hooves, and hair. The works. It had been shot and I reckoned its heart had only just stopped pumping. God knows where he got it. Under his instruction, he ordered me to butcher it in our kitchen. Do you know anything about disembowelling? The volume of blood. The stink. The crap. It took me hours to skin, gut, and carve it up. I was twelve years old. Apparently, he wanted to teach me to man up."

Troy Martell's mutilated carcass, raw and bleeding, flashed through my mind in vivid detail. Hair prickled on the back of my neck and up my arms. My throat constricted. I forced myself to speak.

"Did Otto subject Mimi to the same treatment?" I knew what Paris had told me, but I wanted to hear it from Nicholas.

"Mimi was safe."

"But she wasn't, was she?" Ditched in a dysfunctional family, she was anything but.

He frowned, not getting it.

"Why the hell didn't you let her know you'd left of your own free will, that you were alive and well?" I was angry and it showed. "How much would that have cost you?"

"Everything." He didn't shout it. His voice was low and plangent, like the sound of a lonely wind wailing across an abandoned valley.

I ignored the insistent voice in my head that told me to leg it, mainly because I couldn't move. Paralysed, in fact.

Resting the parcel down by his feet, he fumbled in his pocket. I braced, half expecting him to produce a knife. Instead he produced a pack of cigarettes. "Want one?"

"Thanks." I attempted to mask the tremor in my hand, the terror in my voice.

He took one too in his left hand, lit mine then his. I hadn't smoked in God knew how many years, and inhaled deeply, letting the cool taste and rush flood my airways. A bit like riding a bike, you never forget.

"Mimi," I said, exhaling, dragging him back to what mattered most.

"I was at her funeral."

"I didn't see you."

"But I saw you."

Too late to check my astonishment, he smiled at my surprised response. "You were sitting in that wooden shelter near the church," he said. "I watched as Paris fell to the ground and saw my prick of an excuse for an adoptive father slope off with his tail between his legs. Brilliant. That's when I split."

"Mimi needed you when she was alive, not when she was dead." I failed to mask my fury.

A zealous light briefly entered his eyes. Underneath the cool, composed exterior, there was a twitchy undertow. "It wasn't possible."

"Yeah, right."

"Honestly," he said, serious and sad. "It was for the best."

I pretended to understand. We stood and smoked, my cover for thinking up my next play. There were two reasons Nick Vellender spared me the time of day: one was straightforward protection, the second more complex. So far, he'd managed to outsmart everyone but me, and that intrigued him. I was back to psychopaths again. According to Jim's assessment, Nick Vellender ticked all the boxes.

"You're obviously close to Paris."

"She's a good person," he said. "A better mother than my birth mother, that's for sure."

"And Troy Martell?"

"He never figured."

"You realise he's dead?"

"Paris said. What's he got to do with me?" Cool and self-possessed, Nick stroked one side of his moustache with an index finger. I pushed myself upright, turned, and looked him straight in the eye.

"What?" he said with a half smile. "You think I killed him?"

I'd no idea what I'd do if he grabbed me by the throat, slipped a blade into my gut or between my ribs, or confessed. Adrenalin shot through my veins in hot spurts. Flight seemed a better option than fight. I curbed another sudden instinct to beat it.

He snickered, amused. I didn't find it funny. "Hey, I'm a pacifist, man. I don't believe in killing people. Syria and all that terrorist jackass stuff is for morons. Fuck," he chuckled, hugely amused by my preposterous idea.

"Then why the interest in Japanese death rituals?" I challenged, my face stony.

FIFTY-NINE

His laugh flipped to outrage. He really didn't like me finding out about his unusual interest. Shifty, he dropped his cigarette onto the pavement, his signal for leaving. I'd barely started on him and he was about to slither from my grasp and run.

"Tell me about Joyce Conway."

His jaw twitched and slackened.

"Tell me."

He frowned, flicked up both palms as if telling me to cool it, and shook out another cigarette, sticking it in his mouth, unlit, holding it between bared teeth. "I spoke to her once, that was all," he mumbled, his lips working around the words.

"When?"

"About eighteen months ago, maybe two years."

"Not more recently than that?"

"No."

"You're sure?"

"I said no." He lit the cigarette, all control and down to business. I had to hand it to him, he was adept at switching on and off his emotional responses. "'Course, I heard what happened." Thin streams of smoke escaped his nostrils.

"About her death?"

"Her fall."

"Think it was an accident?"

"I don't have a Scooby."

Scooby-Doo, clue. Not very witty. Nick Vellender certainly had a way with words. "And when you found out, how did you feel?"

"What was I supposed to feel? I hardly knew her."

"You weren't shocked?"

"Surprised," he admitted.

"Sad?"

"Little bit."

"You told Paris?"

"Yeah." He said it slowly, drawing out the word, as if he feared the answer might incriminate him.

"Is that why you visited her late at night last year?" I felt a quickening in my chest. That was the exact point when Paris thought her son had a connection to Conway's death. It fitted in with his "episodes." It occurred to me then that Mimi's plea to me to find her brother had taken me off in a very different direction.

He eyed me and took another snatch of his cigarette. Sweat beaded his brow. "I told Paris what had happened to her. That was all."

"How did you find Conway?"

"Tracked her down."

"I guess you had time on your hands." It sounded more acerbic than I'd intended.

"It took me a long time." He sounded hurt. "I have a job. I work from home." This had never occurred to me. He toed the parcel.

"What is it?"

"A manuscript."

"But how—"

"It's not mine. I proofread, copy edit, offer guidance sometimes."

"How does that work with protecting your anonymity?"

"Welcome to the world of the pseudonym. Online, you can be anything you want to be. Power and freedom and liberation."

Imogen Miller had quoted the same thing. Jesus. "Daughters of Yurei, is that you?"

Startled, his mouth fell open this time.

I rounded on him, poked him hard in the chest. "It *is* you! Have you any idea of the misery you caused? Your own sister signed up for it. She had a scar carved into her arm symbolic of an avenging ghoul."

"What?" He went deathly pale.

"That's right, you troll. Not so fucking liberated now, are you?"

"It was never meant to be serious. I didn't know about Mimi, honest," he said, eyes flickering. "Art house meets death wish."

"Grow up and spare me your miserable excuses. You mess with young women's lives like that, what the hell did you expect?"

"I-I'm sorry," he stammered. His left knee jack-hammered, the jittery side of his nature breaking through the surface.

"It's too late for that. You fucking kill people with that stuff."

His jaw tensed. "I'm no murderer."

My eyes locked onto his. People are rarely what they seem. Whether or not he knew about Mimi's body art was almost incidental now. I simply couldn't work out what lay beneath Nicholas

Vellender, other than he was slippery. Disturbed, for sure. Murderous, I was less certain.

"Joyce Conway," I reminded him. "You were saying?"

He tapped ash onto the ground, uneasy at me dragging him back to my pet subject. "I wanted to find my real dad. I thought she could help."

"And could she?"

He shook his head. "My quest years took me down the equivalent of a no through road." He looked at me as if he had tumbled to a basic truth. "I guess we're all looking for someone, or something."

Love and approval, mostly. Tell me about it. "Did she tell you anything useful?"

"Nothing I didn't already know."

"Which was?"

"She explained the process; that kids aren't taken away from parents without going through a screed of administrative shit."

"She spoke to you about your birth parents?" Very unorthodox, I thought. Dark-eyed and unyielding, he didn't answer. Adept at getting women to do things for him, he struck me as manipulative. "Must have been one hell of a conversation."

The drops of sweat had turned into a trickle. I'd got him on the run.

"Yeah, you're right. Now I come to think of it, there were maybe one or two chats. Nothing heavy. She was a nice lady. I liked her."

I shot him a penetrating glance. "Seriously," he said, cool-eyed.

"And? What else did you discover?"

He bridled. "What's with all the questions? Paris said you wanted a chat. You're a shrink, not a cop, right?"

"I don't think you appreciate how much shit *you're* in."

"Hey." He flicked a smile. "Take a chill pill."

"A few words from me in the right quarter and I'll blow yours and Paris's secretive little world apart."

"Okay, okay. My mother was some bitch called Stacey Walton. Can you imagine she'd called me Ryan?" He spoke as if he found the name offensive and at odds with his cosy middle class roots.

"Anything else?"

A clap of winter thunder pounded the street. Fat spots of rain splashed onto the pavement. He inhaled and exhaled. "Our placement was all signed off by a court in Birmingham, some big shot called Hawkes acted as head honcho."

SIXTY

"JUDGE MICHAEL HAWKES?" MY voice was tight and high-pitched.

"Yup. What's up?"

What was up? My mind reeled. The chance of Hawkes's connection to the Vellenders, and by association, Monica, must rate as one in a million. Suddenly, Conway and Hawkes's deaths took on a whole new meaning.

"Did you pay the judge a visit, too?"

"Some miserable old bastard? Why would I do that?"

To exact revenge for signing you away to the most abnormal family in the country? I dropped my cigarette, stubbed it out with the toe of my shoe, and edged away.

"What's with the aggro?"

"I have to go."

"It's pissing down."

"I don't care."

This time, he caught *my* arm. "Hey, what is this? You're not going to say anything, are you? You're not going to the cops about my vanishing act?"

"Let me go."

He did, fast, like he'd touched molten metal. He stuck both palms up to prove he meant no harm. I stepped away.

"You okay? You look kind of strange."

"Feel a bit tight-chested," I wheezed, which was true. My head swam and I felt dizzy. I had to get to Niven. I had to tell her everything and prove that Monica was innocent. It meant dropping Nick Vellender right in the shit and busting open the conspiracy of silence. And he knew it. It was written all over my face.

"What are you going to do?" His eyes glinted as he took a single, purposeful step towards me, his face next to mine. I had to keep him on track, not with aggression—that might trigger a violent response—but with reason, except I was incapable of it.

"Keep away." Scared, I stepped back into the gutter.

"You think I'm going to hurt you?" He appeared genuinely perplexed, unable to comprehend how someone like me could fail to be seduced by his narcissistic charm.

"I..." My legs felt like chunks of ice. Rain gushed out of the sky like a faucet turned on full. Rivulets poured down the back of my neck and soaked my jeans.

He leant in close. "It's not me you have to fear." His voice was creepy and urgent, as if he'd borrowed it from someone else. I quelled the terror erupting inside me. I didn't need to know what turned a man into this kind of a man, a murderer. Virtually handed a walking case file, I knew.

Cool and unpredictable as a spring breeze, he stooped down, picked up his parcel. "Well, if you're set on it, I guess there's nothing I can do to stop you." He straightened up, gave me a level look. "You realise, don't you, that there's nothing to be gained? Paris was only trying to protect me."

315

I hesitated, suddenly unsure. Why wasn't he following through in the way I expected? Unpredictable, impossible to read, he seemed tired, resigned and defeated when he should have been hostile. A big part of me was glad, but was I so off the mark? In my current frame of mind, it was possible.

"I'd better split too," he said with a heavy sigh. "She hates me being late."

"Who hates you being late?"

He froze. "Doesn't matter."

"It does." The woman Paris told me about. Was this her? "Who is she?"

His expression sharpened. "I can't discuss her. She wouldn't like…" His words petered out.

I darted back under cover. "What's going on, Nick?"

He looked around, anxious and searching and agitated. A ton of new questions rampaged through my brain. Was this the same person who'd practically mown me down in the graveyard? Was this the hooded figure I'd clocked only minutes before? Pieces of the picture dropped snugly into place. "Nick, is she your mother?"

Shock lightened his eyes.

"What's her name?" I said, suspicious.

Blind and afraid, he appeared to grapple with the terrifying possibility. "I don't…" He gulped and grabbed hold of my arm as if to prevent himself from falling over. Eyes glassy, his voice hushed to a terrified whisper. "Do you think she could be?"

"Take me to her."

He sprang back. "No way."

"You don't have to introduce us. Point me in the right direction, tell me where I can find her and I'll do the rest."

"I can't." He danced from one foot to the other, eager to escape.

I thought fast. "How old is she?"

"I don't know."

"Paris's age? Older, younger?"

"Younger."

"My age?"

He frowned. "I don't know how old you are."

"Thirty-six."

He tugged on his moustache, eyes flicking to the end of the street. Something had caught his attention. I looked, too. Saw a figure retreating. Different. Taller. A man, definitely a man. Possibly unconnected. "Nick," I said, encouraging him to re-engage.

"What?" he said vague and unsettled. "Maybe a bit older, say thirty-nine."

The maths stacked.

"Now I really have to split."

"Nick, you can't. You have to come with me. You—"

Collar up, head down, he took off, sprinted into the howling wind and rain and, before I could persuade him, scooted down the nearest street and away.

Frantically, I chased after him, but he was quicker and more lithe and this was his stamping ground, not mine. Two blocks later, soaked and with a vicious stitch in my side, I gave up, bent over double, and cursed.

Straightening up, I took out my phone and discovered that I had five missed calls, including three from work along the lines of *where the hell are you?* One from Stannard giving me an estimated time of arrival in the UK the following day; another, amazingly, from Niven requesting a "chat." Normally, I'd have run it past Gavin, but I was so desperate to tell her about the Vellender/Hawkes connection, I never gave it a second thought.

I returned Niven's call first. Maddeningly, her line went straight to voicemail. I skipped the chat and informed her I had important, fresh evidence, and then I ran through the watery streets. It was three o'clock in the afternoon. It would take me fifteen minutes to get back to Ellerslie Lodge and I was late.

SIXTY-ONE

"SORRY, SORRY, SORRY." I tore into the Lodge and stood in the hall. Water dripped off my nose. My clothes clung and my chafed skin stung.

"What did you do, swim here?" Jim said, unamused. "You realise that you've missed two appointments and," he said, pointedly looking at his watch, "you're about to miss the third. Where on earth have you been?"

"Family emergency," I lied.

He raised both eyebrows.

"Gotta tidy up." I headed for the cloakroom, where I stripped off my sodden coat, mopped my hair and face with a towel, and stared at the dismal results. My waterproof make-up had smudged and my scars, a fine mesh of silver and raised red, shone through. I did a quick repair job and dashed into my office. My mind operating on stereo, I had absolutely no recollection of the next two clients, my thoughts instead fastened on Martell and Hawkes, Nicholas

Vellender and Stacey Walton, knives and blood and the bitter salt taste that accompanies any dish with revenge on the menu.

I finished the day with no word from Niven.

"A moment?" Jim said, popping his head around the door.

"If it's to talk about earlier…"

"It is, but not in the way you imagine."

He walked inside, perched on the desk side-on, and crossed his arms in a typical Jim pose. Atypically, there was a steely set to his jaw. "Don't take this the wrong way, but you look terrible."

I forced a laugh. "Is there a right way to take it?"

"Seriously, I'm worried about you." I wanted to say that there was no need. It would have been another fat lie. There was every need. "What meds are you on?"

I told him.

"Dose?"

"I've upped it. I don't want to increase."

"Need a different combination? I could advise, perhaps?"

"Jim, honestly, I've said I'm sorry. It won't happen again."

"But this business with your mother—"

"The family emergency," I chipped in to be clear we were both on the same fake page.

"It occurs to me that perhaps you came back too soon."

I jolted with consternation. It was true, of course. Work was the only anchor I had right now and that wasn't fair to my clients. "Jim, what are you saying?"

"I can tackle your workload, at least for a couple of weeks. Why not take extra time out, sort out your mother, get back on track."

Normally, I'd have protested. Normally, I'd have insisted that I carry on. Things weren't normal. With a big smile of relief, I said, "Thank you, that would be marvellous."

"Good," he said, a satisfied expression on his face. "Any more developments with the police?"

Where to start? "I'm helping with enquiries," I said, quoting that catchall expression that reveals so little.

"Hmmm," he said, in a way that indicated he wanted to push it but didn't know how.

I watched as he loped out. Crazed with frustration, I called Niven once more. This time I got through.

"I picked up your message," she said. "You said you had fresh evidence."

"Which entirely eliminates my mother from your enquiries."

She fell quiet, possibly because I'd screwed her detecting. "When can you come to the station?"

"Now?"

"Fine."

"I'll be with you in an hour."

The police station was as dismal the second time around. What possessed Niven to move from Devon to Birmingham escaped me. More cut and thrust, I guessed, more likelihood of career advancement.

I spoke to the entry phone and heard Niven's voice as she buzzed me through. Her welcome smile was as false as the *missing son, presumed dead* scenario.

I followed her into a cheerless room with a picture window and grubby blinds, a desk with two chairs on either side, and other chairs parked around the room like you see in an old people's residential home. Plastic and utilitarian, it wasn't what you'd describe as conducive to conversation.

Niven gestured for me to sit down, which I did. She took up residence. Nobody else was present so I guessed it was an informal chat despite the formal surroundings.

"Like old times," she said with a superior smile.

If she hoped to draw a reaction or start a catfight, she was going to be disappointed. I remained impassive. She tried again, softening her tone with an arid smile. "I hope our past history won't have a bearing on today."

"I agree," I said, rinsing all expression from her face. "I'm guessing you've trawled the criminal cases with which Judge Hawkes was associated."

She didn't confirm or deny. Her cool expression told me to leave her to do her job while I get on with mine.

"Hawkes also worked the family court circuit," I continued. "Cases in which children are removed from their parents."

Now I had her attention. The gleam in her eye told me so. I bet they'd spent acres of time examining criminal convictions without giving a thought to family and what might be considered low-grade affairs. "One of those cases involved a woman called Stacey Walton twenty years ago. Two of her children were taken into care and later adopted. If you look into the case, you'll discover that the social worker handling it fell off a cliff last year in Devon. Her name was Joyce Conway."

"What does this have to do with anything?"

"Hear me out. Like I said, Joyce Conway fell, or"—I paused to make my point—"was pushed."

She stiffened. "How did you come by this information?"

"I treated one of the children for anorexia and the information resulted from that. Her name was Mimi Vellender."

"Was?"

"She died following complications of her condition."

Sharp and as subtle as a tsunami, she said, "Death has a habit of following you around."

I struggled to prevent a wave of nausea from bubbling up inside me. "Occupational hazard," I said, knowing it to be untrue.

She studied me for a moment. "Interesting as this is, what you're suggesting is highly speculative. How would this woman track down those handling the adoption order?"

I shrugged. "People do."

"They don't. In cases like this, all associated individuals—the judge, social workers, expert medical teams—are specifically eliminated from file notes to protect them."

"Presumably there are ways to find out?"

"Not really, no."

Conway had been particularly loose-mouthed then—unless Nicholas Vellender was lying. "Isn't it worth investigation?"

"Do you have any further evidence?"

I told Niven about Nicholas, and the death of Troy Martell resulting in an ongoing police investigation in Cheltenham. To tell the absolute truth, that I'd tracked Nicholas down, might spell disaster for me. He deserved to be shopped for creating a vile website and for the contribution he'd made to his sister's death, but Stacey was now a more likely candidate for killer status. I explained this to Niven and revealed that Nicholas had gone missing years ago but was still alive.

"There were family tensions," I stated, "which was why he walked out." As long as the police did their job properly, they'd locate Nick Vellender and his biological mother, and find out for themselves about other possible connections. Then I would be free, my dues to Mimi paid in full and, as far as I was concerned, with interest.

Niven picked up a pen, made notes on the pad in front of her, and looked back up at me. "Let's talk about your mother."

"Okay." I really wanted to push hard with my theory about Stacey Walton, but Niven was not an easy woman to finesse.

"Are you prepared to tell us what she told you?"

"What difference does that make, thirdhand information, surely?"

She gave me one of those *answer the damn question* looks. "You have been estranged for a number of years."

"Correct."

"How many exactly?"

"Most of my life." I thought of Stacey Walton and how she, too, had been separated from her kids.

"And then your mother visits you out of the blue?"

"Is this an official chat? Shouldn't you caution me, or something?"

She smiled, more of a grimace to my eyes. "You're not under arrest and are free to leave at any time you desire. I'm simply trying to create context."

I caught her eye. She smiled. I did not smile back. "Finding anyone dead is a traumatic experience, as you'll appreciate," I said. "It's not unusual for someone to contemplate their own mortality in those circumstances."

"You're saying that's the reason your mother looked you up?"

"Yes." I thought of psychiatric units, of my mother's assault on another, of loaded guns.

"You're sure?" Niven cocked her head. Her glistening blue eyes, like boiled sweets, bored into mine. It was hard not to look away.

"Absolutely."

She looked doubtful but nodded as if she bought it. *As if.* "And when did your mother tell you about Judge Hawkes?"

"As soon as we had a proper chance to talk, around a couple of days after she looked me up."

"And what did she tell you?"

I paraphrased for Niven what Monica said.

"It must have been a shock."

"More for my mother than me."

"She lost custody of you, I understand?"

Accustomed to Niven's sudden switches of emphasis, a move designed to entrap, I was ready. "Not only me, my brothers, too."

"She must feel a certain antipathy to the legal profession."

"Action speaks louder than words," I pointed out. "She worked for the judge and his wife for over a decade. It hardly smacks of someone with a grudge."

"True, but—"

"And why wait so long?"

As soon as I said it I thought of Stacey Walton. If she were guilty, why hold back so long to strike?

Niven leant towards me with another of her shark-like smiles. "Your mother had the means and motive. As soon as the judge received his terminal diagnosis, opportunity knocked."

"She doesn't have a violent bone in her body," I scoffed.

"Forgive me," she said with a smile as tight as catgut, no attempt at civility this time, "but how would you know?"

SIXTY-TWO

RATTLED AND HUNGRY, I drove away. Nothing I said appeared to shift Niven from her entrenched position. I should have known it was a doomed endeavour because the police had an almost superstitious reluctance to link separate cases.

I returned home. Too knackered to cook a proper meal, I prepared and ate cheese on toast, washed it down with a bottle of sparkling water, and changed into my pyjamas. I called Gavin at home and gave him an edited précis of how I'd come by the information and detailed my subsequent conversation with Niven.

"Niven is looking into it although she's as fixated on my mother as she was on me," I complained.

"Unless that woman has a smoking gun, she won't be happy." I almost squeaked aloud at the firearm reference. "Keep me posted," he said, before wishing me goodnight.

About to turn in, my mobile rang.

"Hi."

I bristled, immediately on my guard. "Hello, Otto."

"I guess I should congratulate you on evading me. Clever ruse of yours, took me the devil of a job to explain that I wasn't guilty of shoplifting."

"I don't like being stalked." Despite my best efforts, my voice came out thin and nervous.

"It was only a game, a little role-play. I thought you were up for it."

"You thought wrong."

"So it would seem." He sounded mortally disappointed.

"What do you want, Otto?"

"How did you get on with my tip-off?"

"If you mean the Masons, it was illuminating."

"Why do I get the feeling it counts as a black mark against me?"

"You tell me."

"Whatever has been said, don't I get the right of reply?"

"It's irrelevant. You're not answerable."

"But I'd like you to understand."

"Understand what exactly? That you were a rotten father, a failure as a husband, that you treat your employees like dirt, or have you got something else to confess?" I was bloody tired and tetchy and sick of horrible people wanting me to understand. Contact with the Vellenders was like dealing with the Borgias.

"Wow, someone's done a number on you."

"Otto, I believe you when you say you didn't murder your son," I said flatly.

"Progress," he said, "so can I take you out to dinner to celebrate? Your choice of restaurant. Or you could come round to mine, if you prefer. A night in could be fun."

"No thanks, I've got a lot on." I cut the call, switched off my phone, checked the locks, and stomped off to bed, where I slept the sleep of the pissed off. I would have snoozed all the next day too had it not been for my early-morning visit from Monica. I'd forgotten she still had a set of keys.

I rubbed my eyes with the back of my hands as she strode into the hallway. "What are you doing here?" I said.

"I wanted to catch you before you go to work."

"I'm not going to work."

"Really? Why? Are you ill again?"

"I've taken time off." I didn't add *because I'm losing the plot* or *until this all blows over* because I had no clue what would happen the next hour, never mind the next day or week.

"In that case, I'll put on the kettle."

Too weary to argue, I padded back upstairs, grabbed a dressing gown, and joined her in the kitchen. I briefly considered telling her about Stacey Walton and decided against it. Until Niven had checked out my theory, it would be unfair to raise Monica's hopes and expectations. Besides, Niven's lacklustre response didn't augur well.

"Has something happened?" I said, unable to stifle a yawn.

"Are you all right? You look peaky."

"Monica, stop fussing. What's up?"

She looked coy. "I was thinking, wondering really, have the police been in touch?"

What she really meant was had I been in touch with the police. "Why?"

"After our chat the other day..." She ground to a halt.

"If you mean have I told them anything that might incriminate you, no."

She let out a hefty sigh of relief.

"But I did explain to Gavin."

Her lips curled back. "I spoke to you in confidence. What on earth will he think?" Irritation flushed her cheeks meaty pink.

"He'll think that you falsified your references for a reason." I could hardly say that it was a good one, because it wasn't.

"What about the other thing?" She spoke low, in the way some elderly women do when talking about sex. By *other thing* she meant the gun.

"I didn't mention it."

Annoyed at my apparent power over her, she huffed and poured tea splashily into my cup, eyed me warily, and took a sip. "I've spoken to Luke. You haven't forgotten he arrives on Thursday?"

"Of course not."

"He's booked into a hotel for a week." She beamed a dreamy smile. "It will be so wonderful to see him."

Reminded of Paris and Nick Vellender, I passed no comment. What was it with mothers and sons?

"What are you doing for the rest of the day?"

The rest? It had barely got going. "Sleep looks inviting."

"Utter waste of time. When you get to my age every second—"

I scowled, tuned out, then brightened. "I've got a friend to see."

"Oh?"

"Yeah," I said, more chipper. Thank God.

SIXTY-THREE

I stood on Stannard's doorstep in Wellington Square lost in a million thoughts.

Gone were the droop, the lopsidedness, the way his left eye sloped down. Skin that had looked dull and waxy was re-oxygenated and pink, the difference in his appearance startling.

"Are you going to stand and gawp, or are you coming in?"

"Sorry," I said. "I'm knocked out with the result."

"Well, knock yourself out and come inside."

I followed him through a lavish hall and off into a massive uber-cool, high-tech kitchen with white units, granite worktops, shiny flooring, recessed lighting, island unit, and breakfast bar. Ballroom meets spaceship.

"Park your pretty rear up there." He indicated a high stool. "Fancy a drink? The downside of recuperating in the States is the rather po-faced attitude American medics have to booze."

"I shouldn't." And it was hellishly early in the day—just after noon.

"Why not?"

"Medication."

Stannard issued a teasing smile. "Just a small glass?"

"Frankly, I'd love one," I said, instantly weakening.

"Fabulous."

I watched, mesmerised, as he selected a bottle from the fridge, popped it open, and poured out two glasses. We clinked and sipped.

"It's pretty good, isn't it?"

"The wine or your face?"

He exuded gratitude, to me, to the surgeon, to the gods. All was well in Stannard's firmament. "Mind, as you can see, I've grown my hair long to cover this." He pushed a lock away to reveal a livid scar, which to my eyes was no big deal.

"It will heal. How does it feel?"

"Tingly."

"I meant—"

"I know what you meant," he flashed a wide grin. "Amazing. I can now look in the mirror without feeling the need to put a bag over my head."

"It wasn't that bad."

"It was and you know it. Anyway, less of me, how's things? You're looking knackered, if you don't mind my saying."

I did, particularly as I'd gone to a lot of trouble with my appearance. I'd styled my hair differently and worn the ritzy new hair clip I'd been saving. I'd taken ages over my make-up and put on a new soft angora sweater over my jeans. "Pity they didn't sew up your prefrontal cortex while they were at it."

"Not a clue what you mean, but I get the impression it isn't a compliment. I only commented because I care about you." He arched an eyebrow, his voice dangerously low and seductive. I averted my gaze and took another sip. "So what's happened with the whole Vellender deal?" he continued.

"It's a lot more complicated."

"Fire away." He sprang up onto the stool next to mine. His warm knee touched my thigh. I felt a dart of pleasure.

I told him everything. About Monica, Joyce Conway, Nick Vellender, Stacey Walton, and how the Vellender case crossed and connected with Judge Michael Hawkes. I told him that Nick Vellender had never really disappeared, that he had a warped sense of right and wrong, and that he and his adoptive mother had led a lie and deceived everyone for years. I also told him the reason why and flagged up Otto's mistreatment of his son from an early age.

Stannard frowned in disbelief.

"You're not convinced?" I said.

"Last time we spoke, I had Nicholas Vellender down for prime suspect in the murder stakes."

"And now?"

"I'm even more persuaded after the *Bambi getting it* story." I should have felt the same. A shrewd light entered his eyes. "You're one big softie when it comes to young men, Slade. It's your blind spot."

He was right. I was too young to notice my brothers' pain when Monica upped and left, but I was aware of their suffering in subsequent years. Adrift, I watched them struggle without her, and it saddened me. Somewhere along the line the angels had forgotten to pray for us. Stannard cut into my thoughts. "Is there more?"

I mumbled about Nick's obsession with Japanese suicide ritual, avenging ghouls, and the website. I did not mention his "episodes."

"God, how much more proof do you need?"

"It's not proof. It's speculation."

"So is the *mother coming back to kill* story."

I blanched. "Which one?"

"The Walton woman, of course. Jesus, you didn't think I meant *your* mother, did you?"

I rubbed my eyes. It was hard to know what I thought. He took a ruminative sip. "Must be weird for you to have your ma back in your life."

"You could say that."

"And you really believe the Vellenders' biological mother responsible for murder and mayhem?"

I'd had time to think about it. "If she can knock about her son, she's perfectly at home with violence. It's not such a huge step to imagine a scenario in which she seeks vengeance."

"How does Troy Martell fit?"

I had to admit he was a loose end. "Perhaps he doesn't."

"You mean he was killed for an entirely different reason?"

"That's my guess."

"*You're* not in the frame, I hope."

"With Troy?"

"Uh-huh."

"Are you serious?"

"Probably not, although I imagine it would please Niven enormously." He flashed a mischievous grin. I realised how much his physical disfigurement had damped down his natural exuberance. With the transformation in his appearance, Stannard was unstoppable. The thought caught me unawares. It also knocked me off balance. It was a foregone conclusion that he would move on, inhabit different circles and I'd lose him. "Only joking," he said, responding to my pensive expression. "From where I'm sitting, Nicholas V has a stronger motive for murder than his long-estranged mother."

"If that were the case, why the hell hasn't he stuck a knife through Otto's heart?"

"Maybe he's building up to it."

I paled at the thought. Perhaps the mystery woman was a convenient figment of Nick Vellender's imagination, designed to throw me off the scent. In which case, Otto was in genuine danger. I told Stannard this.

"Don't you think you should warn him?"

"But what if Niven—" My phone rang. I stepped down from the stool and reached for my bag. "Talk of the devil," I said, glancing at the withheld number. "Hi."

"We've checked out Stacey Walton," Niven announced.

"Yes?" I said, expectant, the defining revelation seconds away.

"She drowned off the coast of Tenerife five years ago."

"She's dead?" I looked at Stannard who was listening to my every word.

"Presumed. Her body was never recovered."

"Which means she could be alive," I insisted.

"Possible but, in this instance, unlikely."

"Why?"

"Extremely strong currents in the area."

I felt mulish and stubborn and had no words to counter Niven's argument.

What about the damn son? Stannard mouthed at me. I shook my head and walked away.

"So there you have it," Niven told me in a tone that suggested I'd wasted enough of her time already.

"Why the hell didn't you tell her?" Stannard demanded when I got off the line.

"Because I don't buy it and I'm not sure about Nick."

"You weren't sure about Stacey but that didn't stop you."

Which was true. However there was another perverse reason for keeping silent—Monica's survival. "How's it going to look to someone like Niven if, after pointing the finger of suspicion in the wrong direction, I repoint it at someone else?" I remembered doing something similar before and it had landed me in a heap of trouble. I'd ended up isolated and friendless.

"Shouldn't you let Niven make that judgement for herself? Shouldn't you lay it on thick about Troy Martell, who, incidentally, looks less like a loose end if you put Nick Vellender in the driving seat?"

I couldn't fault Stannard's logic, yet my gut reaction remained resistant. "Niven is part of West Midlands, not Gloucestershire. She won't link cases."

"A bit sweeping, if you don't mind my saying, even though my stepfather would agree with you." Gerald the QC, I remembered, tumbling to an idea.

"Would Gerald agree to talk to me?"

From Stannard's startled expression, I got the impression he thought I'd finally flipped. "What about?"

"Placement orders."

"I don't even know if he has experience in that field."

"Worth a punt?"

"If you say so." Stannard didn't look particularly enthusiastic, "Better let me prepare the ground first."

SIXTY-FOUR

HE SWIPED HIS PHONE from the worktop and placed a call. Stannard went through a raft of pleasantries and then hit him with it.

"In what context?" I heard Gerald bark.

"Background stuff, to help with a case she's dealing with," Stannard said meeting my eye.

"Put her on."

Stannard passed me the phone. I did my best to scrub out our last bad-tempered exchange. Time and events had moved on. I hoped Gerald had evolved from dinosaur to ape, too.

"Thanks so much for agreeing to talk," I gushed. "Really appreciate it."

He didn't say *not at all*. He didn't put me at my ease. When I outlined what I needed to know, he plunged straight in. "Do you know anything about the workings of family courts?"

"Not from a legal perspective," I said.

"Welcome to the world of the secret state." Something deep inside me snagged. Gerald continued, "Family courts operate *in camera*."

"They're highly secretive?"

"That's what *in camera* means," Gerald said testily. "Once a parent gets locked into the system, it's a roller-coaster ride and there isn't much they can do to prevent losing their children."

"You sound as though you don't approve."

"I dislike the fact that family courts have a lower standard of proof than criminal courts. No criminal conviction is required to remove a child. Only an indeterminate life sentence is more drastic. Sledgehammer and nut springs to mind," he said as though it deeply offended him. "The emotional cost to families is immense, the financial cost to the taxpayer titanic. Fortunately, we've become rather more enlightened in recent years."

"Oh?"

"With the creation of the FDAC, the Family Drug and Alcohol Court. Designed to work with mothers, specialist social workers are drafted in to help rebuild confidence while at the same time monitoring substance abuse. Nine times out of ten, children are removed because of a parent's drug and alcohol problems," he explained.

"And violence?"

"Not much hope of success with those cases."

As with Mimi and Nicholas. "I'm guessing some women will repeatedly have children removed."

"Regrettably. It's not uncommon for two, three, and four children to be taken. One judge I know took thirteen from the same woman."

"God," I exclaimed.

"I'm not prepared to defend a violent parent," Gerald said without my prompting.

I sensed something more. "But?"

"For the same reason I don't approve of capital punishment, I worry about the forcible removal of children from their biological parents."

"In case a mistake is made," I surmised.

"Unfortunately, it's rather more common than you'd think," Gerald said. "Ricketts is back and X-Rays can't always detect abnormalities in young children. Social workers," he opined with ill-disguised venom, "will often maintain guilty verdicts even when a second medical opinion states otherwise."

Then it dawned on me and my heart soared with understanding. Mimi had suffered from a vitamin D deficiency as a baby. It could lead to hairline fractures. Odds on, Nicholas had suffered from the same condition. Any breaks he'd sustained were not necessarily as a result of beatings. To an inexperienced eye, damage to bones could look like abuse, and paediatricians didn't always make the right call.

If it were true, I could only imagine the rage Stacey Walton must have felt against the system. But she was dead. That left only one other person in the frame: Nicholas. Stannard was right.

Dear God, had a monumental error been made followed by a grave miscarriage of justice? If so, did Conway know? Did anyone else know?

I thanked Gerald and handed the phone back to Stannard, who signed off. "Well?" He threw me such an accusing look that I caved in. If Niven wouldn't listen, maybe Strong in the Gloucester constabulary would.

"I'll call the police handling Martell's murder."

"Now," he said, tiger-eyes gleaming.

I did. Using the log number given to me, I got straight through. I'd wanted to talk to Strong. Instead, I got Slater. Taking a breath, I explained that I believed Nick Vellender was alive and well and that he also had a prime motive for murder. That's as far as I got.

"I understand you've been in touch with Detective Superintendent Hayley Niven from West Mids," Slater said, cutting right across me.

Quick work. "I have."

"You didn't think to come to us first with this information?"

"Initially, it didn't seem relevant."

"Really?" His tone was excoriating.

"What I mean is that I had concerns about my mother."

"So I gather." The tone didn't lighten. "You've actually seen Nicholas Vellender then?"

"Yes."

"When?"

"Yesterday."

"Where."

I told him.

"You're sure it was him?"

"Yes."

"You spoke to him?"

"I did."

"Why?"

"Because…" I faltered and pulled a floundering face at Stannard, "because I felt a responsibility to the family, to Mimi Vellender."

I don't know whether I'd swear Slater clicked his tongue or not, but the silence that followed wasn't encouraging.

"Did he confess to the murder of Troy Martell?" he said eventually.

"He denied it." Which meant nothing at all. He was hardly going to confess either to Martell's murder or anyone else's.

Slater let out a sigh. "You see, Miss Slade, I'm having trouble following you. You give a false lead to my colleague at West Midlands in another unrelated—"

"It was not false. It was given in good fai—"

"Let me finish and please don't raise your voice at me, madam."

Vexed, I ground my teeth and threw Stannard a *told you so* look.

"And now you purport to have seen a man missing for the past five years and who you allege has never strayed further than his hometown."

"I don't remember saying that."

"In the same vein, you didn't think to reveal this when you had an opportunity. There is a penalty for wasting police time."

"In that case, I won't trouble you further." I hung up.

"That went well," Stannard said through pursed lips. "Now what?"

I had no time to consider it. A text came through on my phone. Cryptic, it was from Nick Vellender. *Meet me at Paris's.*

SIXTY-FIVE

"ARE YOU CRAZY? YOU can't go," Stannard protested. "It could be a trap. You said yourself that Paris Vellender will do anything to protect her son."

"I don't have a choice."

Stannard reached for his jacket. "I'm coming with you."

"Don't be daft. How will I explain you away?"

He shrugged. "You'll think of something."

I put the flat of my hand against his chest. His heart pumped through his shirt and vibrated across my fingers. "No."

"How about I skulk around outside? If anything happens or you're in there for too long, I could come to the rescue."

"Like the cavalry?"

"SWAT sounds more twenty-first century."

I briefly thought of the gun belonging to my mother. Not the most appealing idea. "All right, and how about you follow Nick Vellender when he leaves, find out where he hangs out?"

"I like your thinking," he said with a wolfish grin. "Unless," he said, smile vanishing, "he's already chopped you up into lots of little pieces."

I didn't dignify Stannard's weak attempt at humour with a reaction. I knew only too well the personal risk I ran.

Together we set off. It took us twenty-five minutes to walk from Stannard's to Paris's house. I suggested that Stannard planted himself in a café opposite, where he'd have a perfect view. He squeezed my arm and whispered "Good luck" in my ear.

Paris answered the door. Pale, strained, and sunken-eyed, she ushered me through the hall and into a vast kitchen that fulfilled a multitude of functions.

Nicholas sat hunched over a refectory table, monotonously running one finger over the grain. An ashtray choked with butts sat beside him. He had a cigarette on the go in his free hand, and tendrils of smoke curled up through the dead atmosphere. He didn't look up as I entered.

"He's been like that for the past hour," Paris said, lowering her voice.

I nodded, pulled up a chair, and sat down opposite him. I hoped to reach out, engage, then keep him lucid.

"Hi, Nick."

His finger stopped. He glanced up. His eyes were empty.

"What's up?" I said.

"She says things to me. Nasty, vicious things."

"Who?"

He took a drag of his cigarette. "It's stupid but I don't know."

I exchanged a glance with Paris, who stood in the doorway, arms tightly crossed as if by doing so she'd hold herself together. Inclining my head in the direction of the corridor, she got the unspoken message, nodded, turned, and retreated.

"How did you two meet, Nick?"

"I don't remember. She was simply there." He shook his head slowly. "Materialised out of nowhere."

Materialised out of nowhere... "Nick, is she someone in your imagination?"

He sucked on his cigarette. "You really think she's not real?"

"I don't know."

"Can you help?"

I hesitated. He looked exposed and vulnerable. A real person making Nicholas's life hell was beyond my scope. Hallucinations, psychoses, dissociated states were my bag. What really bothered me was the possibility that this imaginary person was so real to Nicholas Vellender that she controlled his actions. If I'd wanted to pass my days in places like Broadmoor, I'd have specialised in forensic psychology.

"Nick, I want you to relax. Can you do that for me?"

He stubbed out his cigarette.

"How about you stretch out on the sofa?"

He pushed back his chair, stood up, walked to the sofa, and lay down. I waited until he was comfortable then told him to close his eyes. "I'm going to talk you through a detailed relaxation technique."

He followed my instructions obediently. Less agitated now, he became still and calm.

"That's right," I said. "Breathe and let your lungs fill with air. Take a deep breath, hold, hold and strain," I repeated, "then let out the tension. Let it flow..."

Without warning, Nicholas Vellender's face contorted. His lips curled back in a snarl and he bared his teeth. His body and limbs went rigid. In the space of seconds, he physically aged by several decades. I watched in alarm as his chest filled and expanded. Next, out of his mouth erupted a high-pitched voice. "He's mine, bitch, not yours."

Cold penetrated my skin, my blood, my bones. My emotional response was *demons.* Intellectually, that was nonsense.

The taunting voice continued. "I can beat him whenever I like. I can crush him and there's nothing you can do to stop me." White-faced and alien, Nicholas's eyes rolled. "What's a fruit loop like you going to do about that?"

I gasped. I don't believe in spirits and possession, yet in that split-second I was convinced that I was in the presence of evil. I could taste, touch, and feel it breathing in the same air as me. As if to confirm my terror, Nicholas's body bucked and reared and the voice rang out with victorious laughter.

I jumped. In imminent danger of mentally slipping off the picture, of losing my mind, I exerted every sinew to cling on to reality, to prevent myself from dislocating and becoming unhinged. This was as much about me as about Nicholas Vellender. I wanted to shake him awake, to shout at the voice, tell it to shut the fuck up. But it would be the wrong thing to do and potentially dangerous. With only one way to go, I forced myself to regain the ground and take control. Panic rising, I did my best to tamp down the hysteria that threatened to boil over inside me. It was as if I were doing battle with sinister forces outside myself, the occult, maybe those elusive Japanese spirits with which Nicholas was obsessed, grappling with an unseen enemy. Grasping the tattered remains of my courage, I shouted in a loud voice, "Who are you?"

"Don't you know?" The voice was wheedling, mocking, insinuating. A chisel in my head.

"I wouldn't ask if I knew."

"Very clever, very smart."

"Smarter than you, that's for sure."

The voice dropped to a low growl. "Fuck you."

"Fuck you, too."

Nicholas lay stiff and doll-like on the sofa. Only his face, which was unrecognisable, moved.

"You're Stacey Walton, aren't you?" I said.

"So what if I am?"

I wrestled with my intellect. I was neither trading insults with a malevolent spirit nor negotiating with a ghost. I was fighting the split part of Nicholas Vellender's personality and I needed to wrest him away from it.

"What's Nick ever done to you?"

"He left me. He shouldn't have done that."

"It wasn't his fault. He was only a child."

"He pissed off when I needed him most." The voice broke into a self-pitying sob.

"But he's all grown up now and has his own life to lead."

"He abandoned me."

"That's not true."

"Filthy fucking liar." All trace of self-pity disappeared. She was back to her poisonous self.

"The truth is you abandoned him the moment you laid a finger on him." She didn't argue with my analysis.

"Fucker, fruitcake, head case."

"What a classy description of yourself."

"Cunt. You think you can have him, but he's not yours. He belongs to me."

"He doesn't. He never did."

"I brought him into the world," the voice screamed. "I'll take him out, one way or another."

"By killing him?"

"If I have to."

"Like you killed the others?"

Silence. With his eyes still closed, Nicholas Vellender's face seemed caught in a paralysis of confusion. Objectively, my curved ball had strayed wide. 'She' seemed ignorant and innocent.

"Joyce Conway, Judge Hawkes," I prompted.

"You're mental."

"I've never been more sane. But you—"

"Screw you. He's coming with me. HE'S MINE."

"Hands off him. You try and take him I'll hunt you down. You won't have anywhere to hide. I'll drag you out screaming and kicking into the light."

"You threaten me?" the voice roared, outraged.

"I'm promising you. Now get the fuck out!"

The room fell silent, as if a malevolent spirit had split the air with a thunderous sound and departed to Hades.

I panted, fear battering me senseless. Slowly, the contours of Nicholas Vellender's face softened. He opened his eyes and looked around him as if viewing the world for the very first time.

"Is it over?" he whispered.

"Almost," I replied, more shaken than I let on.

Nicholas Vellender sat up, scratched his head, and rubbed his chin. He looked a lot less zoned out than when I first sat down.

"What do you remember?" I asked.

"Absolutely nothing. It's a total blank."

I described what happened.

He looked incredulous. "Why would I fixate on my mother? I've never wanted to find her, only my dad."

"You were with her until the age of four. Perhaps something happened during that time, something you blocked out." Perhaps he was beaten after all, I thought, less sure of my ground than I was when I spoke to Gerald. "It's the mind's way of protecting from greater damage."

"Blocked out? You mean when she hit me?"

I hesitated. I wished Paris had kept him in the dark about the alleged abuse. I could think of no good reason why she thought it would help him. "You need to talk it through with Paris."

"And now?"

"You're free."

"I don't know what to say." His eyes briefly shone with insight then clouded. "Do you think it's possible that I committed a crime when I was her?"

My skin crawled with anxiety. "Do you?"

"I don't know."

"What sort of crime?"

"Dunno. Troy Martell's murder, I guess."

"Supposing you did, how did you evade detection? What did you do with your bloodstained clothes? Did you wash yourself clean? How did you dispose of the weapon?" And if Nick Vellender had a problem carving up a deer, how would he deal with a man's body?

"Yes, I see," he said, more hopeful. "I really never had a problem with Troy. I felt glad Paris had someone."

"Is he all right?" Her voice travelled from the hallway. She appeared and looked from me to her son and caught the change.

"I believe so."

"I thought you were arguing."

"Nicholas will explain."

Except I wasn't certain he would. He seemed distant, like a man who has thrown all his cards up in the air and doesn't yet know where they will land.

"I think you both need to seriously think about the future. It's time for Nicholas to come in from the cold."

About to protest, Paris opened her mouth to speak but her son beat her to it. "She's right. I can't keep hiding forever."

"But, Nicholas," she said, scrubbing at her temple with her fingers.

"I'll leave you to it," I said, easing myself out of the room.

Back outside, I switched on my phone and discovered a missed call from Otto. I listened to the message and crossed over to Boho, where Stannard was parked in the café window. He looked relieved to see me. I told him what happened.

"Is exorcism usually part of your remit?"

I pulled a face.

"You really think Nicholas Vellender is on the level?"

"I don't think he has Troy's blood on his hands." Which wasn't the same as saying I thought him innocent.

"Sounds to me more like a case of *not criminally liable and destined to wind up in a secure unit.*"

I thought about it, questioned myself for the zillionth time. "He didn't kill Martell."

"Right," Stannard said unconvinced. "I'm still going to follow him and find out where he lives. What are you going to do?"

"Otto Vellender has asked me to meet him."

"Oh yeah?" Stannard said, deeply suspicious.

"I'll let you know what gives."

"Make sure you do."

We agreed to stay in close contact. I then phoned Otto, who sounded as delighted as he was surprised to hear from me.

"I'm famished," he announced. "I was heading towards Moran's. Care to join me?"

"See you in ten." I speeded up. A blade of low winter sun struck me straight in the eye. I hoped it wasn't an omen.

SIXTY-SIX

WHEN OTTO SMILED HE magnetized.

"What do you fancy to eat? I would have ordered if I'd known and put it on my tab."

"I'm not hungry." Which was true.

"Let me pour you a drink. You look as if you need one."

I couldn't argue with that but I declined wine and asked for soda water. When he returned from the bar he picked up his glass and clinked it against mine. "Got you to myself, at last," he said with another blinding smile.

I fended off the sinking feeling in the pit of my stomach. I trusted Otto about as much as I trusted politicians and the police. "What did you want to talk about?"

"Nicholas."

"What of him?"

"I know."

I played dumb and frowned.

"And so do you," he said with a penetrating gaze. "What I want to find out is why you were talking to him."

I took another sip of water. Had Otto spoken to Paris? "When?" I said, acting vague.

"In the street."

"You followed me again?" I recalled the retreating male figure, how Nick had reacted. So that was Otto. That still left me with a question: who was the hooded female?

"I've a lot of free time on my hands. So what did he say?"

"It's confidential."

"Do you normally conduct consultations in the middle of the road?"

I ignored the jibe. "The more obvious question would be, where can I find my boy? Instead you want to find another reason to castigate him."

Otto flashed an expansive smile. "I never really believed he was dead."

Bet you wished it. "Tell me, why do you hate him so much?"

"What makes you think that?"

Where to start? "Did he take up too much of Paris's precious time?"

Colour glanced across the tops of his cheekbones. I had an image of a bloodstain spreading across a pavement. "That's absurd."

Keen to press another nerve, I leant towards him, my voice several degrees south of freezing. "He told me about you, about what you did to him."

"Then you've only heard one side of the story."

"Corroborated by two other people."

"You shouldn't believe all you hear."

"I generally don't, but in your case, lack of action speaks volumes. You'd rather pursue me than find your own damn son."

"You should be flattered."

"I'm not. The only reason we're sitting here having a drink is because I wanted to find out what makes you tick."

"You consider it sport." There was an ugly twist to his lips. He was remembering fucking me.

"If I want sport I go for a swim," I fired back. "Most people have a different side to the personality they project to others, but with you, what you see is what you get. You treat everyone with contempt."

"If you're referring to Gabriella Perona—"

"Gabriella?" I felt as if I'd been kicked in the gut.

"Kitchen staff," he explained, a contemptuous ring in his voice, "she has never once complained to me about my treatment of her."

"Probably because she's too ..." I stopped.

"What?"

"Scared," I burst out, careful to keep my expression neutral and contain the random thoughts flickering like a guttering pilot light in the inner recesses of my brain. Gabriella Perona's name suggested that she was of Spanish origin. She spoke the language. But what if it was a blind?

By virtue of her job in the kitchen, she was in the perfect position to eavesdrop on Otto's conversations, to contaminate the food in the restaurant. Now I came to think of it, and although she had what I'd describe as a lived-in face, there were facial similarities with Mimi and Nick. Stacey Walton had allegedly perished off the coast of Tenerife, the biggest of the Spanish islands and most popular tourist destinations. Was Gabriella Perona in fact Stacey Walton? Had she infiltrated Otto's inner circle with the sole purpose of getting close to the children she lost, only to discover that one was missing and the other dying? I blinked. Otto glared, took another stab at his food.

"How old is Gabriella?"

"What?"

I repeated the question.

"I don't know, pushing forty."

"How long has she worked for you?"

"For God's sake, will you stop banging on about my kitchen staff? If you must know, too long," he said, bad-tempered with it. "She shows me nothing but disrespect. Got a lot in common with Paris."

"Respect has to be earned. No wonder Paris conspired to put your son into hiding well out of your reach."

"Bullshit. My ex-wife specialises in hysteria and histrionics."

"If your ex is prone to mental instability, that's down to you; same goes for Nicholas."

The smile didn't slip. It didn't move a centimetre. "I told you the first time we met that Nicholas wasn't quite right in the head. Now you know."

"But he didn't murder Troy Martell."

"And neither did I." He speared a piece of chicken, popped the meat into his mouth, and chewed in a less discerning way than I imagined a top-class chef would usually eat. Under the onslaught of my verbal assault, perhaps he was past caring.

"The same person who killed Martell pushed a social worker off a cliff and killed a judge in Birmingham."

"Now you've lost me." He dug into his salad, forked in a mouthful, stared me out, chewed and swallowed.

"Joyce Conway," I said.

Recognition flickered in his eyes. "The woman who facilitated the adoption?"

"You remember?"

"Unlikely to forget. With the arrival of Conway, Paris had her heart's desire fulfilled."

"You didn't want kids?"

"Not especially."

"But..." I broke away, bewildered.

"I went along with it."

"How?" I said in amazement. "The adoption process is rigorous. Your reluctance would have been spotted."

He shrugged. "I'm very good at playing whatever role is deemed expedient." Cold and business-like, he bit into another piece of meat.

I regarded him with loathing and stood up. "Wrong. You're a despicable father and a lousy lover. Thanks for the drink." Before he could react I stormed out.

SIXTY-SEVEN

HURTLING DOWN THE ROAD, I called Paris. How I could have missed it for so long defied me.

As soon as she picked up the call, she screamed at me. "What the hell did you say to my son? Did you quiz him about Troy's murder, about Joyce Conway?"

"I'm sorry, I..."

"Whatever you told him has resulted in the biggest row of my life. He blames me for talking to you about family business. He's gone. Cleared out. For good this time."

"I doubt it. He's upset. Give him time. He'll calm..."

The sound of Paris Vellender breaking her heart drowned out my voice. Unnerved, I waited until her sobs subsided before I spoke. "Did Nicholas suffer from the same bone condition as Mimi?"

She didn't answer straightaway. When she did her voice was a whisper. "I knew all along. I lied to him."

"Why?"

"Because I only wanted him to love *me*."

I closed my eyes in dismay. It wasn't right what Paris did, yet I understood. "I'll talk to him. It will be all right, Mrs. Vellender."

"It will never be all right."

Dismally, I recalled a time when I'd busted open the truth on another family. It had saved a girl from self-destruction. I never found out what happened to her parents and brothers, although I knew the fallout would have been massive. Had I done the right thing this time? Had my desire for truth destroyed the bigger picture? I waited a respectful beat before I asked, "Where does Gabriella Perona live?"

"St. Paul's. Why?"

"Can you give me her address?"

She gave a name and number mechanically. "I think Troy said she—"

"Troy? He knew Gabriella?"

"Acted as her personal trainer, not that it lasted beyond two sessions."

I reeled at the connection and again thought back to my conversation with Niven, who claimed that Stacey Walton had drowned, but her body never found. "Is that what he told you?"

"Yes, it was ages ago," she said halting. "Is something wrong?"

"Bolt the doors and stay inside. Don't move and don't answer the door to Gabriella."

I hung up, went home, and let myself into the house to check that everything was as it should be. Nothing seemed disturbed, which didn't surprise me; I wasn't the target. Stand in the crosshairs of the killer and that would change.

I went straight to the cupboard in which I'd stowed Monica's gun, took it out, and held it in my hand. I was taking a crazy risk.

Weighed against a murderer who had killed three times and was hell-bent on a finale, it was a risk worth taking.

It didn't take me long to locate Gabriella's house. I noticed the car first, the vile acid yellow of the paintwork blinding my eyes. I flashed with the memory of nearly being mown down in the graveyard.

Private, in a quiet location, the apartment had its own entrance. I rang the bell. No answer. I knocked at the door. The same. Cupping a hand over my eyes, I peered through the front window like a Peeping Tom. Inside wasn't particularly remarkable. About to step back, something caught my eye: a chest expander used by bodybuilders to sculpt and tone chest and shoulder muscles. Hardly the kind of equipment used by a woman who'd lasted two sessions with a private trainer.

With her history of working in kitchens, Gabriella would be adept at wielding a knife, expert at filleting animals—including a human cadaver.

Fear thrummed in my chest.

If I were right, I would be cornering a dangerous woman who was hardly going to come quietly and do the equivalent of putting her hands up, *it's a fair cop, yep I dunnit.* I was under no illusion that she would be difficult to crack. Deceitful and an accomplished liar, a woman who had faked her own death, she would play me and maybe attempt to kill me.

About to call the police, my phone bleeped. I'd received a text from Stannard. Meet me outside that house where the Banksy used to be. You're never going to believe what I've found.

SIXTY-EIGHT

Two spooks with shades wearing gabardine macs with rolled up collars. Long destroyed and scribbled over, Banksy's creation on the crumbly walls of a house was, nevertheless, in rhythm with my mood.

In silence, Stannard caught hold of my elbow and propelled me down the road and through a narrow alleyway that was easy to miss. Passing several tiny houses on either side, he walked me right to the end, where he turned left into a small front garden with a woodshed. Behind was a dwelling so ditzy it could have housed a family of Hobbits. Despite the cuddly exterior, I held back.

"This is Nicholas Vellender's home," Stannard informed me. "Five minutes after he returned, he tore out of the alleyway with a phone pinned to his ear."

"Any idea where he went?"

"He headed back towards town. You told me to locate the house, not the guy."

"You didn't see him with a short dark-haired Spanish-looking woman?"

"Should I have done?"

"You're absolutely certain he wasn't followed?"

"I'd have noticed." Probably dismissing my persistence as febrile femininity, he said, "Shall we?"

I followed him up the paved path to a bolted stable-style door. To the right was a window, curtains semi drawn in a permanent expression of ennui. I pressed my nose against the glass, adjusted my line of vision, and jumped back with a start.

Stannard snickered. "I did exactly the same. It's not real."

"Are you sure?"

"Positive."

I peered again at the mannequin. White-faced with geisha red lips, it had wild black hair, an indigo fringe, and blue shadow around the eyes.

"Blue represents negative emotions," Stannard murmured next to me.

"How do you know that?"

"A monthlong visit to Japan," he said. "The white kimono is a burial costume."

My eyes spun to the wall on which hung a Samurai sword. "Shit," I said.

"Freely available on the Internet," Stannard informed me. "Still think our boy's as clean as a monk in a monastery?"

I stepped back, tried to shake my thoughts into some kind of order. It was as if I were standing on an empty beach at night listening to the lonely cry of the sea. Stannard favoured Nick for a murderer. Up until that moment, I'd favoured Stacey. Unless...

"Kim?" I heard Stannard say, his voice low and distant.

Blankly, I turned towards him. "Do you think we could break in?"

"Why use brute force when you have one of these?" Stannard produced a wallet from which he selected what I took to be a lock pick. "A property developer's best friend," he explained.

"Is that legal?"

He hiked his recently fixed eyebrow, a triumph of surgery over disfigurement. "What do you think?"

I stood back as Stannard pried and fiddled with the lock. I reckoned it took him less than a minute to open the upper half of the stable door. Ten seconds to stick his arm inside and push across the bolt. "Easy when you know how," he announced with an easy smile. "After you."

Straight ahead there was a short dark corridor housing a washing machine. An overflowing laundry basket of clothes stood in front of it, the tang of dirty garments pervading the close air. "You go in," I said. "I want to check through this."

I pulled out underwear, sweatshirts, jumpers, jeans, and socks, none of which showed recent signs of staining with blood or human tissue. The contents of the washing machine yielded no extra clues. If Nicholas Vellender had killed Troy Martell I very much doubted it would be that easy to remove all traces. To double-check, I walked back outside and rifled through the contents of the dustbin and discovered nothing out of the ordinary.

Returning to the house, Stannard clomping about upstairs, I stood in the living room and started at the sight of three Japanese helmets squatting on custom-designed stands. The scariest was bowl-shaped with a facemask depicting a snarling open mouth with sharp teeth below a thick bulbous nose. The deadliest, finished in black hammered steel, was as wide as it was deep. Out of the top sprouted two immensely long wooden horns. Forbidding and, at a guess weighing several pounds, the helmet inhabited the room as if on guard.

I sniffed the air, caught the aroma of wood smoke and coal, the source an old Swedish wood-burner that jutted out from a deeply recessed fireplace on the outside wall. Above it hung the sword.

Stannard bowled back downstairs. "Nothing of interest; typical young man's gaffe. Had a good gawp at the weapon of mass destruction?"

I gave him a dry look.

"It's a fine specimen," Stannard said knowledgeably. He pointed to the blade. "It's called a ken. Exceptionally long, held in both hands, it allows greater control and cutting power."

Unbidden, Troy Martell's mutilated body flashed before my eyes. Blood and pain and dying. I noticed that the blade had a blackened edge; the hilt was wrapped around with brown cord.

"This baby can cut through bone," Stannard continued, eyes sparking with enthusiasm. "Hand-forged in high carbon steel, it's monstrously powerful. See the tip? It's rounded to better thrust into the enemy. Beautifully ornate under the cut-guard."

I blinked and strained forward. Fire-breathing dragons with grotesque features glared back at me.

"And these?" I indicated the helmets.

"Wouldn't want to be on the sharp end," Stannard agreed. "Fabulous as they are."

I wasn't sure I shared his artistic appreciation. "How much would they cost?"

"Anything between four and seven hundred pounds, particularly with a menpo."

"A what?"

"Technical term for the facemask."

I'd seen enough. "Let's get out of here."

"Convinced?" Stannard said.

"Absolutely."

"So do we shop pretty boy to the cops now?"

"No."

"Why not?"

"He didn't do it, Kyle."

"Are you nuts? He had all this," Stannard said, sweeping the room with a glance.

"Nick Vellender has a heavy interest in Japanese death rituals. He writes fantasy fiction and horror. He is disturbed, but it's his mother who is the killer."

"Paris?"

"His biological mother, Stacey Walton."

"How many more times do you need to hear it? Stacey Walton is dead. Niven said so."

"Niven said that she was *presumed* dead. There's a difference."

"You're saying Stacey faked her own death?"

"Played dead, yes, just like Nick Vellender. Stacey reinvented herself as Gabriella Perona, the woman who works in Otto's kitchen. Her only quest was to find her kids. She'd been searching for them for years. What she found were the broken remains of her family."

"And now she wants vengeance," Stannard said, eyes alight with sudden realisation. "If she tracked the case as far as Otto and Paris, she knew about everyone. She could have killed the social worker Joyce Conway and the judge."

"Exactly. The point is I've led her straight to her own son and, if we don't hurry, there will be at least two more bodies on her revenge list: Otto and Paris Vellender."

SIXTY-NINE

With Paris and Otto in genuine danger, I called each. Neither picked up.

"You go to Paris's house," I told Stannard.

"She doesn't know me."

"Tell her I sent you." Then I remembered how I'd ruined it all for her. "Second thoughts," I said. "Don't mention me. Use your charm. I'll head for the restaurant."

"Think Stacey's there?"

"Fits perfectly with her plans."

"Is this a good idea?"

"You have a better one?"

"Call the cops?"

His trust was touching, but I didn't share it. "Tried that, remember? They won't believe me. They think I'm delusional."

"But this is life and death, Kim."

"I know, so *you* call them as soon as you've checked that Paris is safe."

"But that will take time. You can't go alone."

"I'm not." Plunging my hand into the bag, I took out the revolver. Alien and uncompromising, it rested clumsy and heavy against my fingers like a misshapen lump of wet coal.

"Fuck me, Slade, where did you get that?"

"My mother." His eyebrows shot to within an inch of his newly established hairline. "Long story," I said.

"Do you actually know how to use it?"

"I'm not going to use it. I want to scare, that's all." Hadn't Monica used the same argument? I'd thought it lame, I recalled.

"*That's all?* Are you mad?"

"Not anymore." I turned to go. I felt clear and focused and determined. Any residual ennui from my depression was sorted the moment I did what I did best. Like Stannard, I'd rejoined the real world, although Stannard didn't know me well enough to understand that yet.

He clamped a hand over my arm. "Kim, I'm serious, you can't. You're in a lose-lose situation."

"Not if I do it right." I twisted and sprinted away. "Call me," I shouted over my shoulder. In my heart, I knew that Stannard would shout long and loud for backup. It was why I needed to beat the police to it.

I ran. I didn't deviate. I bombed it until my heart clattered, my lungs burnt, and I had a crucifying stitch in my side.

But the restaurant was all locked up. Nobody around.

Undefeated, I hailed a cab and returned to Gabriella/Stacey's place in St. Paul's. This time she was in. Was I afraid? You bet.

With a client, I'd take down an extensive family history, build a rapport, and subtly enquire about relationships and friends, the devil in the details. I didn't have the luxury now. I didn't have the time. Somehow I had to gather Stacey's side of the story without judgement or opinion, let her talk like she'd never talked before. It boiled down to a few minutes in which every second counted, a few minutes to nail the truth and save Monica from a life sentence. In saving my mother, I was saving myself.

And if I failed…

Stacey wore a shapeless T-shirt over dull navy jogging bottoms and trainers. Her arms, strong and roped with muscle, strained against the sleeves, which led me to believe that she'd made full use of the exercise regime Troy Martell had introduced her to. Her eyes, in contrast to her drab clothing, gleamed sharp and alive.

"I've been expecting you," she said. Gone was the Spanish intonation and back was the West Midlands accent. She opened the door wide, my invitation to step over the threshold. I followed her into the plain sitting room and gingerly perched on the edge of an easy chair. Stacey sat opposite me. She was nothing like a killer. Cool and polite, she surveyed me and I surveyed her. Doubt assailed me.

"How did you work it out?" she said.

"About your real identity?"

Her eyes flickered. She nodded.

I smiled, heading her off. "Why not tell me what happened with your children?"

"Do you have kids?"

I shook my head. A black mark against me, disappointment settled over her expression. The creases deepened around her mouth. She moved the chair back a space and folded her arms as if to ram home the point.

My eyes flicked from her to the door and back again. "Help me understand."

In answer, she turned her sullen gaze to the wall. Precious seconds trickled through my fingers like fine sand. "Please, for Nicholas's sake."

She rounded on me. "Ryan," she spat. "His name's Ryan."

"Of course," I soothed. "Ryan. You've spoken to him?"

She didn't answer.

"Stacey?"

She looked so deeply into my eyes it hurt. "He doesn't want to know."

"If you tell me what really happened, I could talk to him, persuade him to listen to you." Shameless of me, I knew.

"You'd do that for me?" Suspicion dredged her voice coupled with barely conceived hope.

"Isn't that why I'm here? To hear your story, to put the record straight, to make it all right with Ryan?" The urge to enlighten her about Monica and her status as suspect in the judge's murder hung like a threat. A little voice inside told me to shut up. Not the right time.

Her face darkened. "The reason you're here is to save your mother, not to save me. I thought you were different, but you're like all the rest. You're a taker, not a giver."

My heart sank. She was going to hold out on me in a primitive version of payback. "How do you know about my mother?"

"Been watching, haven't I?"

"You were outside the post office." I recalled the small figure in the hoodie. And I was following Nicholas, aka Ryan, and Otto was following me. Circles within circles and all stuck in the same dysfunctional groove. "As soon as Ryan split, you went after him?"

"I did."

"You talked to him?"

"Not immediately. Later."

"When later?" Silent voices spun around me. I had a really bad feeling.

"Next morning."

That would be the same day Nicholas asked me to meet him at Paris's. In his more lucid moments, why hadn't he mentioned a solitary word about Stacey Walton? Either he had trouble making a distinction between reality and fantasy—not good; or they were working in tandem—not good at all. Stacey was still talking. "He wasn't well. Any fool could see it. All that Japanese stuff in his house."

"You went inside? He let you in?"

"He knew me, sort of. He recognised me from the restaurant."

I'd assumed that Nicholas Vellender had swum right out of the flow, kept his head below the waterline. I was wrong. Why would he risk being seen at the restaurant? Was he plotting Otto's downfall? Then I thought about the food poisoning outbreak. Had Nicholas stolen inside and contaminated the food? No, of course not, Stacey was responsible. I *thought*.

"What did you tell him?"

"I told him I was his mother."

I was aghast.

"Didn't believe me. Couldn't blame him. I wasn't what he expected. I told him I'd devoted my every waking hour to finding him and that I'd never given up. I explained how I'd pretended to be good old Gabriella, his father's faithful slave."

"How did he react?"

"He got upset at first, then he asked me about his dad, his real dad."

"And you told him?" God alone knew what that would do to a broken mind.

"Not much to tell. At first he seemed all right, even gave me his number, said he wanted to talk to his father. Fat chance of that. Haven't seen Fabio in years, although I didn't tell Ryan that."

"Fabio's a Spanish national?"

"Yes." A distant expression closed down her features. To avoid losing her, I reeled back the conversation.

"I know that your children were taken from you because of a flawed child protection system."

"*You've* done your homework. It's a bit fucking late now."

"They should never have been put on a child register."

"You say that, but you don't know." She viewed me with contempt.

I ordered myself to stay calm. I told myself that it would be all right. I simply needed to forget about saving Monica and tread more delicately with Stacey. I decided to tell her what I knew.

"I know that Ryan and his sister—"

"Anita," she said. "That's what I called her. She wasn't christened or anything like that, not like Ryan. It's a pretty name, isn't it? Better than Mimi. Sounds like the sort of crap name you give a poodle." I smiled in assent as if we were on the same side. I don't think she noticed. "They had two social workers hanging around outside the labour ward for ten hours, waiting to pounce and take my babe. Soon as I'd pushed her out, that was it. I couldn't cuddle her. Took her away. Court order, they said." Stricken, she bunched up as tears rolled down her cheeks and pooled underneath her chin.

I swallowed at the unimaginable pain she'd endured. In that brief moment, I saw a wronged mother and a damaged individual. It was like viewing an exercise in agony. In loss.

I reached out to her but she recoiled and shook me away, in the same way she had rejected a life without her kids.

With the back of her hand, she wiped away her tears, her eyes aflame with sudden anger. Did her fast recovery make her a killer? Wasn't I simply sitting down with a woman betrayed by the system, a system that destroyed so many lives?

I still didn't know.

SEVENTY

"Talk to me," I said softly, wondering if Stannard had got hold of the police. "From the beginning, tell me how you wound up without your kids."

Wary and tentative, Stacey said, "I took Ryan to the hospital because he wouldn't stop crying. I did what any mother would do when they see their child in pain.

"Doctors examined him and thought he should have an X-ray. That's when the nightmare began." Her face went pale with remembered fear. "Ryan had multiple hairline fractures to his ribs and legs. It's easier to explain away clean breaks, they told me. Tiny cracks are less easy. I knew straightaway they blamed me."

"Where was Ryan's dad?"

"Fabio? Back in Spain."

"Okay," I said indicating for her to continue.

"The doctors called social workers, who called the cops. They tried to get me to confess. They said I'd lose my child if I didn't. How could I confess to something I hadn't done?"

"You never struck him?" I watched her carefully.

"Never."

Did that word connect to her eyes? Honestly, I couldn't be sure. Perhaps she had smacked her child on a couple of occasions. Not great, but it didn't equate to the beating social workers had suggested. "So they took Ryan?"

"And because I was already pregnant . . ." Her voice petered out.

"They warned you that Anita would also be taken?" I said, remembering Gerald's words.

She nodded, as blindsided by the thought now as she'd been then. "As soon as I knew what their game was I tried to escape with Ryan, but they picked me up at the border. Even contacted Interpol."

"You didn't appeal?"

"Fuck's sake, it costs tens of thousands of pounds. I didn't have that kind of loot. Even if a parent is proven to be innocent on appeal, if the child has already been adopted, it's too late. You can't challenge the quacks."

"But surely—"

"You don't even know who half of them are," she said, eyes darting, agitated. "All kinds of people—radiologists, paediatricians, psychiatrists and so-called la-di-dah experts—are wheeled out, faceless nobodies with posh jobs and the right lingo. Every one of them can overrule a parent. It's a clique. It's a con. And the speed," she gulped, frenzied now. "Kids with you one minute, gone the next. Did you know the courts don't need a criminal conviction to remove a child? Local authorities swoop in with a court order and court orders are never refused."

What an utterly inadequate response to the indescribable injustice of her situation. Gerald was right to be contemptuous of the system.

"When you lose your kids," she continued, wrenching each word from the back of her throat, "you lose them for good. Forced adoption is irreversible. There's no going back. There wasn't a fucking thing I could do about it. They might as well have handed me a death sentence."

She leant towards me, her thin lips centimetres from my face. "Have you any idea what it feels like to know that your baby calls someone else mummy?" Spit from her mouth flecked my cheek.

"I'm so sorry." It was horrific. My head throbbed. Here was a woman who had desperately wanted to mother her children, while my own mother took a different choice.

She cracked a sad smile. "Nobody has ever apologised for what they did to me, to us."

I wanted to ask what she did next, but feared any sound I made would shut her down. A glance at the clock on the wall told me twenty minutes had passed.

With a haunted expression, she continued, "Afterwards, I fled to Spain and worked in kitchens." She held my gaze. It's how she'd learnt to wield a knife, how she learnt her trade, her eyes told me. Christ, if she were responsible, the exposure of Martell's ribs suddenly made sense. Accused of breaking her son's ribs, she was making a statement with Troy's. I ought to get out of there. Yet I stayed put.

"You took Fabio's name?"

"After I'd officially drowned, yeah," she said with a sly look. "We weren't married or living together, nothing like that. Not much good at picking men." She clicked her tongue, smiling at her own failure. Fearing a detour, I risked a direct question.

"How did you trace the Vellenders?"

"Contacts," she said stone-faced. "Took me years. I paid hard cash to some dodgy bastards. I got beaten up on more than one occasion, my hard-earned stolen money. Once, I was ra—" Her voice broke at the memory of something too unspeakable and raw to put into words. She swallowed, gathered momentum again, and drove herself on just the same as she must have driven herself through the many dark and empty years. "That's what you do if you love someone. I'd have sold my own soul."

I believed her. The way she said it made me realise how much she'd crossed over to the other side. Could that explain how she had been able to butcher Troy Martell without missing a beat? Although I still didn't understand what specific beef she had with him.

"And you found Judge Hawkes?" I did my best to keep my voice controlled.

She cocked her head with a *one step ahead of you* expression. Double fuck. She knew where I was going with it. She was toying with me. I told myself to rein back.

"Tell me about Troy Martell." I aimed to smooth the urgent rasp in my voice. Not sure I achieved it.

She fell quiet. The light in her eyes changed to one of decay and smashed dreams. I recognised the deadly intoxication of revenge. I had the feeling that she was going over in her mind what she'd done to him, enjoying and extracting the essence of it. Taking pleasure. For a woman to whom power was the ultimate aphrodisiac, exercising it helped her regain control over all those aspects of her life that were in chaos. In this regard, she was exactly like my clients. Food, or the lack of it, was the weapon used by anorexics to create order in their disordered lives. More than this, the subliminal message with each pound they lost was *See, look what you've done to me.* In the same vein, Martell's mutilated corpse was designed to grab attention.

"How did you meet him?"

She visibly relaxed. "Like I said, you get to hook up with a lot of nasty people when you're desperate. Met this conman, a Yank—or so I thought. Found out later he'd changed his name. We became partners."

"Sexual partners?"

"Sometimes," she said with a slow, *So what if we were?* blink. "By then, I'd discovered that my daughter was a bag of bones and my son had disappeared."

"So you hatched a plan?"

She nodded again. "Troy's job was to get close to Paris Vellender and find out what had happened to my son. I took a job with that bastard Otto. Rumour had it that Otto had done away with him. In a way, he had."

Pulse racing, I crouched in the sticky silence once more. "Did you ever approach Anita?"

She shook her head. "If I'd done that, the Vellenders would have been down on me like a landslide. I'd have lost all hope of finding Ryan." She tugged at the fabric of her jogging pants with nails bitten to the quick. "And then my baby died." Her shoulders hunched. Her head sank into her neck, like an injured animal that has lost the will to live. "Hit Troy surprisingly hard," she said, as if talking to the floor. "Think he had a thing for her, dirty bugger." She paused, no doubt contemplating it. "Trouble with him, he was lazy, cut corners. Thought he was smart when he used *you*. He was certain you'd do all the legwork while he stood back and took the credit. He was convinced you'd find Ryan."

And I did. "You fell out with Troy. Why?" I said.

"Tried to blackmail me. Said he'd tell the Vellenders who I was if I didn't give him money—a lot of money," she said, emphasising the point.

So you killed him. "And Joyce Conway?"

"Who?" Her fingers stopped moving. She looked up, her blank expression so spontaneous it couldn't have been fabricated.

"The social worker that facilitated the adoption."

"Never heard of her."

I raked her face for lies. She stared straight back.

"But you've heard of Judge Michael Hawkes."

She continued to stare, a faint smile flickering on her lips.

"My mother is facing a murder charge," I exploded.

"So?"

"She didn't kill him."

"And neither did I. Had him in my sights, but someone beat me to it. Did me a favour."

I blanched. "You didn't shove a bag over his head?"

"Not my style."

The room bled silence and threat. I was fast running out of time. And Stacey Walton knew it.

I should have seen it coming. I didn't.

SEVENTY-ONE

I REMEMBERED A RUSH of energy, the sudden force of the blow, the flash of pain—white, vicious, and blinding—and not much else.

Coming to, my eyes refused to focus. I'd no idea how long I'd been out cold. Sick and sweaty, enveloped in pitch black, my first impulse was to scream. I've never been good in confined spaces, and here I was caged in a cramped room that felt no bigger than a cupboard. My bag containing the gun and my phone was no longer within reach. My head ached and a tentative exploration with my fingers told me what I already knew. On impact, the new hairpin had dug into my head and my swollen scalp oozed blood.

I had to get out. I had to raise the alarm. The only reason Stacey hadn't killed me was because there were more important people on her hit list. I didn't doubt that she'd return to clear up later.

I staggered to my feet. My arm extended, I felt around my cell. It took seconds to identify a door, toilet and sink, and a cupboard on the wall. There was no window and the light switch didn't work. Squinting against a shudder of pain, I tore open the cupboard and, fingers bumping up against packets and bottles, found absolutely nothing that could aid my escape.

I edged my way back to the door, grabbed hold of the knob, and wrenched. It wouldn't budge. I beat the wood with my fist, shouted and yelled; my voice was sucked into the thick, cloying wall of silence. Darkness clung to my nose and mouth as readily as the plastic bag used to suffocate Judge Michael Hawkes. Frustration rippled through me.

I tried the doorknob again, wishing I had Stannard's lock-pick. My hands flew to my head in despair. I wanted to yowl. In that desperate moment, I thought of my dad. Practical by nature, he taught me everything I knew about survival. I could never take that away from him. *Electric thinking* was his watchword. As if guided by his spirit, my fingers touched my new hairpin and inspiration struck.

I patted the door down and ran my fingers over the hole in front of the knob. Inserting the flat side of the pin, I jiggled, felt it connect, turned it once, and the door sprang open.

Flying out into the street, I saw that Stacey's car had gone. Now what? I thought about what Stannard had said. *Nicholas Vellender came back. Five minutes later, he tore out of the alleyway with a phone pinned to his ear.*

Finding his real father was all Nick Vellender had ever thought about and needed. It had driven him away, consumed him, and, ultimately, propelled him back. How simple it would be for Stacey to draw him out under the pretext of giving him news that would lead him to his real dad. But what blew my mind more was that she no longer needed to hold back. Having approached her son after years of searching, he'd rejected her. Twisted and crippled with disappointment, she would seek to punish for her loss. With these thoughts in mind, I didn't stop. I ran.

I didn't know where Stacey would go next, but the restaurant was my only and best guess.

Mean streets and sleek streets roared past me; homes with chipped window frames and grimy curtains; take-away restaurants, hairdressers, and people, lots of people, all shapes and sizes and colours and creeds, yet none registered. Blood pumped through my veins and unquiet ghosts clamoured around me like a seething, restless crowd about to riot.

The entrance locked, I pushed open the wrought-iron gate and stole down the narrow alley leading to the back of the kitchen. The rear door ajar, a drift of raised voices echoed in my ears.

Breathless, I slipped inside. I passed a prepping area; racks of pots and pans and plates, and followed a maze of narrow workstations where two chefs could work back-to-back, in tandem. Gleam and steel, edge and fire. As instruments of torture went, Stacey had alighted on the perfect place to indulge her sadistic side.

An agonised scream ricocheted and bounced off machinery and inhabited all the hollow spaces. I ducked, ears ringing, crouched low and edged my way past vents and sous vide, burners and griddles, a massive charcoal oven, and hobs.

Stacey's voice rang out. "Hurts, doesn't it, you fucker?"

I raised my head enough to have a clear view of Otto sitting slumped, barely conscious and restrained. Blood seeped from his mouth and nose. There was livid bruising on one cheek and his right eye was a swollen slit. Bare-chested, his torso was a mess of criss-cross bleeding slashes, the meaty part of the tops of his arms were raw, scorched and bleeding. My gaze briefly caught the flare of blue flame from a blowtorch. I swallowed. Fire had always been my enemy to tame.

Behind Otto stood Stacey Walton. Zoned out with self-righteousness, she held a boning knife in one hand like a dagger. In the other, a filleting knife with a slimmer curved blade but no less deadly. It glinted with fresh blood. Nicholas Vellender had his back to me. I couldn't see his face. His shoulders stooped, body braced, arms rigid at his side, hands tightly clenched.

"Give the word, Ryan, and I'll kill him."

I had no idea whether or not Nicholas had egged on Stacey, whether he was working with her, whether he enjoyed the pain she'd inflicted upon Otto, whether she had turned his moral compass south. I didn't wait to find out. I burst out of my hiding place, smacked him hard sideways, and dropped him to the floor.

She slow-blinked, regarding me with no more concern than if I'd delivered a fresh consignment of fruit and vegetables. Scrambling back onto his feet, Nicholas looked wan and sickly.

Frantic, I took a step forward and grabbed the nearest implement, a meat cleaver. Irrationally, it made me feel safer.

"Ignore her," Stacey ordered him. "She's nothing. This is you and me, family, like it always was. You were such a good little boy. Together, we're going to turn back the past. I can be a real mom to you again."

"Nick, look at me," I said, desperate to break Stacey's hold. "Look at me. You don't have to sanction this."

He turned, eyes vacant, unfocused as though drugged. We stood there, the two of us. I wanted to reach out, tell him the truth: that he would never get those years back, that time had stolen them for good, that all he could do was move on. He shook his head sadly.

"See," Stacey hollered, a wild triumphant glint in her eye. "He knows what's right. It's time for justice."

My voice rang with protest. "This isn't justice. It's an execution. Nick," I said, appealing to him, desperate now, "you don't want to be part of this. You'll be an accessory to murder. You'll be throwing your life away."

He looked from me to Stacey and back to me. Confusion tightened the corners of his mouth. I moved another step towards him.

"I understand your desire for revenge, but this isn't the way. Be courageous, Nick. Do the right thing. Enough people have died."

"Shut up." Stacey sliced the air dangerously close to Otto's right eye with the shorter blade. "Ryan, you know this is what we've both been waiting a lifetime for. Think of what this man did to you, how he made you suffer. Think of what he did to Mimi."

At the mention of his sister's name, Nick Vellender put his hands to his temple and roared. Colour leached from my face. The meat cleaver trembled in my hand. I had to break through and rescue him. With Stacey stoking his demons, he was out of reach and lost to me.

"Nick, come to me," I shouted. "Walk this way."

Pressing a blade against Otto's throat, Stacey snarled, "You fucking touch my son, I'll gut Otto right before your eyes."

Seconds thumped past. The kitchen seemed to shrink in size. My thoughts felt clogged and sticky. Otto was going to die if I didn't act. I spread the fingers of my free hand. "Okay," I said, backing down, lowering my makeshift weapon. "It's fine. Nick, stay where you are."

"He took my babies from me." Stacey's voice thickened with emotion. "He deserves this."

"Nobody deserves it," I said, "no more than you deserved to lose your children. You never abused them. You were a victim of a gross miscarriage of justice. I know about your children's vitamin deficiency, Stacey, the condition that led to those tiny fractures. As soon as your children were adopted, they were diagnosed and treated."

Shock twisted her features. She let out a small cry. I was, perhaps, the only person ever to declare out loud that it was not her fault and explain why.

Everything stopped. Her face froze. Eyes the colour of jet locked on to mine. The blade in her hand, which was raised, lowered a fraction. She stood motionless.

"But Paris said—" Nick began.

"She made a mistake."

"No. She—"

"I'm sorry."

Despair inhabited and creased every feature on his face. "I don't understand. Paris knew all along but said nothing? She lied to me?"

At the mention of his ex-wife's name, Otto stirred.

"Ask him," Nick yelled, nostrils flaring.

Otto's eyes half opened, confused and bewildered. Stacey leant in, pressed her mouth close to his bloodied left ear. "Tell your boy what you knew, what you did."

Otto blinked. I watched helpless, tried to see inside his mind, tried to gauge how he would react. Any sane person would beg forgiveness, express contrition. Not Otto.

"Fuck you." He tilted his head, jutted out his jaw. "And fuck you, too," he snarled at Nick. Otto's eyes moved to mine in a blizzard of electric blue. I swear they were smiling.

"He bloody betrayed us," Nick gasped.

"They both did," Stacey said, smug and victorious.

I could hear sirens in the distance. Why the hell had it taken so long? Stacey heard them, too. Any second and it would all be over.

"He didn't mean it," I pleaded. "He doesn't know what he's saying. Tell her, Nick. Tell her to drop the knives."

"I don't know. I … Jesus," he uttered, shaking his head.

"Put down the knives, Stacey," I begged. "You have to."

She hesitated. Did I imagine the fight draining from her?

"Nick?" I said, spreading my hands, pleading. *Please.*

The light in his eyes changed but I couldn't gauge them. Locked in combat, on the edge, he straightened up, got into the zone, prepared to give the order. Despair rampaged through me. I didn't move, didn't speak. I'd run out of words. Suddenly Nick's shoulders slumped, his head bowed. He couldn't comply. Thank God.

Stacey hesitated, confusion haunting her face, and then she smiled and the boning knife clattered to the floor. Most would believe she'd reached a moment of resignation and acceptance. I knew differently. It was like watching a train about to hit a pedestrian who strayed onto a crossing. I was powerless to do anything to stop it. I let out a scream. The blade from the filleting knife flashed silver as it hurtled through space and time and plunged deep into Otto's throat. Red, so very red it hurt my eyes, spurted then flowed free, sheeting in a cascade and onto the floor. Smell of copper and fear and ordure, rank and raw. Death, in all its sovereignty, broke loose and ran free. I started forward, grabbed Nicholas Vellender, and hauled him away.

SEVENTY-TWO

Detective Strong viewed me as if I'd raised Nicholas Vellender from the dead. Slater stood next to him, hatchet-faced and belligerent, like a female version of Niven. "Stacey Walton is inside," I gasped.

"And Otto Vellender?" Strong said.

I quickly shook my head. Strong gave the order for the police to move in. Surging forward, boots in unison, they sounded like an invading army.

"You okay?" Strong murmured, giving me a slow sideways look. "There's blood in your hair."

I nodded, distracted. I didn't think I was okay, but it was easier to blag it. Unlike Nicholas Vellender. Virtually catatonic, he'd not put up any resistance when I hustled him out of the building now surrounded by a wall of police. He stood mute, hands on his head, as if he were shielding himself from attack.

"Thing is, she killed them all. It means my mother is innocent." I looked to Strong and then to Slater. Remote and detached, neither reacted in the way I expected. *Outside our remit* seemed to be the company line.

"We'll need to talk to you both," Slater said as if I'd never spoken. Severe and challenging, he rounded on Nicholas. "And you, you have a lot of explaining to do."

"Can't you see the boy's in shock?" I protested. "He needs hospital treatment."

Slater glowered and jerked his head towards a WPC, told her to see to it. Someone slammed a blanket around Nicholas's shoulders. I was offered one too and declined. A paramedic tried to persuade me to go to hospital. I should have agreed, but flatly refused. My head ached. I felt hellishly sick. Wired, all I could think of was Monica and her proven innocence, that I needed to get an urgent message to Chadwick, that I should phone Luke, except he'd pitch a host of questions at me that I didn't feel in the mood for answering. Tipping up on my toes, searching, I pinpointed Stannard among a crowd of onlookers held back at the end of the street. I raised a hand. Our eyes met and, in an instant, I knew something was wrong.

Noise behind me, I turned to see Stacey Walton handcuffed, flanked by police officers, her clothing and hands stained with fresh blood. Nicholas Vellender watched too, pale and sheened with sweat and misery, before a WPC led him away and helped him into an ambulance destined for the hospital.

"I'll take it from here," Strong said, moving off, leaving me with Slater, who said, "I'll need a full statement from you."

"Now?" Anxiously, I remembered the gun. What the hell had Stacey done with it? If it were found, I was in trouble.

"Preferably."

"I need a moment."

"I can come to you, if that's easier."

It wasn't and I didn't want Slater's officious and lingering presence in my home. "I'll come to the station." Later, I thought.

"As you wish." His voice was curt. His eyes hardened.

"Is Niven aware of developments?" I said.

"Not her case."

"But they're connected."

"You don't know that."

"I do." I sounded as indignant as I felt. "You'll inform Niven? You'll talk to her. Please."

He didn't say yes or no. The mutinous expression on his face worried me. "Do you need a car?" he said.

I looked over to Stannard. "I'll make my own way."

I pushed through cops and paramedics on legs that felt as if they were made of stone and wood and metal. Numbers on the street had swelled. Police cars and vans and sniffer dogs were everywhere. Someone shoved a microphone in my face and asked me to comment. A tanned hand shot out and grabbed my sleeve.

"She's got nothing to say," Stannard said, frog-marching me through the rest of the crowd and down the street. "You look as white as—"

"For Chrissakes, will you stop telling me what I look like?"

He jumped, as dumbfounded by my rage as I was. Brittle and sorry, I burst into furious tears.

———

We sat in a pub reminiscent of a smoky old boozer. The walls were partly tiled and the colour of nicotine. Stannard ordered brandy. I never drink the stuff but didn't argue. It tasted hot and soothing. Proper booze.

"I have to call Gavin," I said. "Can I borrow your phone? Monica is in the clear. This proves it. The police want me to give a statement, but I need to let him know first. Oh, and I've lost my gun," I admitted, shamefaced.

"Slow down and calm down." Stannard spoke in a voice I'd never heard him use before. "Have another drink."

I did. My head swam. It wasn't an unpleasant sensation.

"Now tell me what happened, from the beginning."

I gave him a stumbling, rambling, and random account.

"You need saving from yourself," he concluded, a reproachful note in his voice. "So what followed next?"

I told him. Nothing had taken place in my head in quite the same way as it had happened in the kitchen. Words did not accurately describe the scene—the horror, gore, and violence. I'd have to improve my delivery for the statement, I reminded myself, downing another glug of brandy that would wreak havoc with my medication.

"Fuck," Stannard said open-eyed. I blinked, tried to shake off the intensity of the memory. "And Nicholas Vellender watched?"

"He had no choice," I explained. "There was a second when I thought she might stop, but it was no good."

I remembered Nicholas talking about the number Otto had done on him. *A total mind fuck,* he'd said. I hadn't quite believed him. Made me feel like a hypocrite. Hadn't I been quick to judge both my father and mother?

"Kim?"

"Sorry," I said. "You alerted the cops, right?"

"Eventually." He cradled the brandy balloon in both his hands, the liquid rolling around like a slick of treacle.

"What took you so long?"

He had a cagey expression. "Did you argue with Paris Vellender?"

"Paris?" I said.

His eyes drifted away from mine.

I lowered my voice and looked around the pub, and noticed for the first time that there were people in it, most of them gawping at me. "She's dead, isn't she?"

He nodded, snatched at his drink.

"How on earth did Stacey get to her so fast?"

"She didn't." A haunting chill settled over my skin like a shroud. "I went to the house like you said," he explained. "Couldn't get in so I went around the back." He cleared his throat. "She was on the ground."

I thought of the four-storey drop. "She jumped?"

"She did."

I imagined Paris's lithe body awkward and broken. Death would have been instant and obliterating. Small consolation. My stomach felt heavy with heat and blame.

I could have blamed it on her fear of Stacey Walton. I could have held her high-strung and febrile nature responsible, but I knew it was my fault; I'd tipped the balance by threatening to expose her deceit, a deceit I'd later revealed to her only son. If I hadn't openly nailed her for telling her son his birth mother had abused him when she hadn't, Paris would still be alive. It was my fault that she'd jumped from four storeys to her death.

I made a grab for Stannard's phone. I couldn't let down another woman, least of all my own mother. I had to call Gavin. I had to tell him everything.

He picked up as soon as my call connected. "Yes?"

I began to talk but he cut me off.

"Kim," he said gravely. He neither paused nor hesitated. He gave it to me straight. "Monica's been arrested for the murder of Judge Michael Hawkes."

SEVENTY-THREE

DUMB AND UNCOMPREHENDING, I uttered one word: "Impossible." Next I gave Gavin a garbled account of recent events in Cheltenham to support my reaction. "Can you use it?"

"I'll definitely pass on the information. Meanwhile, sit tight."

"I can't," I said, promising to drive to Birmingham, ignoring the fact I should be heading directly to the police station in Gloucester.

"Waste of your time. The custody clock is ticking. The police have twenty-four hours in which to charge or they might go for an extension. Either way, you won't be able to see her. I've only dashed outside to use the lavatory before the next round."

"But how has it come to this? I don't understand." My bottom lip quivered.

"They've unearthed a new piece of information about an event that took place years before." Dizzy, nauseous, I felt the air punch out of my lungs. "A serious assault, I'm afraid."

I remembered. "But no charges were pressed. The man was a lay preacher."

"You knew?" Gavin's tone was accusing.

"Not in detail."

"Did you know the victim was also a former judge before he saw the light?"

I closed my eyes. When people describe their blood running cold, you think it's a figure of speech. You believe you know what it feels like. It's not true. My veins felt packed with sharp slivers of ice that would shred me to pieces. Was this the piece of information that Niven had held back? Had she known all along?

"What exactly did Monica do?" My voice sounded borrowed from someone much older.

"She put a bag over the old man's head and attempted to suffocate him."

Stunned, my throat went into lockdown. Black and yellow spots whizzed in front of my eyes. If I weren't sitting down, I would have fallen and fallen and fallen.

"Kim, are you still there?" Gavin said.

I wanted to howl, to shout at the sun, the moon and stars, to curse Fate and deities, and scream. Stannard, grave and sombre, extended a hand and offered to take the phone from me. I shook him off. I still would not believe it. Flatly refused.

"She wasn't in her right mind," I said, my voice a rasp. "She was mentally ill. She didn't attempt to kill anyone."

"That's not how the police view it, I'm afraid."

I didn't need to ask whether or not Gavin believed her. He was already in the mind-set of damage limitation. But not me. This was my mother. I'd waited and waited and she'd come back. I'd lost my past. My present was in chaos. I couldn't forfeit my future, too. She couldn't desert me for a second time. She couldn't.

Through a mist of tears, I asked, "How is she?"

"Not good."

"Send her my love. Tell her I'm thinking of her."

"I will."

"You'll call me?"

"As soon as there's anything to report. Now I really have to go."

He cut the call. Half crazed, I turned to Stannard, who looked guilty. "You knew?"

"Caught the news on my phone. It said a woman had been arrested. I put two and..." He trailed off. "Kim, I don't know what to say. Want another drink?"

I shook my head and vacantly slid down into the settee to make myself as inconspicuous as possible. I needed to shrink back inside myself, to think, to capture a rare moment of stillness and serenity. Yes, Monica was maddening. Stupid enough to purchase a gun with all those potentially fatal consequences attached. She stayed in touch with her lover's children but not her own. I could not begin to imagine what had possessed her to act in the way that she had, or understand what had triggered such a violent action. Flawed, so flawed, but impossibly human, too. More strongly, I recalled her shame: *You'll hate me for it*, she'd said. I flickered with insight. Shame is good. Shame is redemptive. It reminds us not to repeat past mistakes.

A shadow fell across the wooden table, Stannard returning with a fresh glass of brandy for himself.

"What did Gavin say exactly?"

I told him.

"Doesn't look good."

"That's the point. Doesn't *look*."

"It's a helluva coincidence, Kim. Maybe now is the time to face up to reality."

"Fuck," I said, standing up. "Fuck."

"What?" Stannard flinched in consternation.

"I need to get out of here."

"What are you going to do?"

I was almost out of the double doors. "Raise my game," I shouted.

SEVENTY-FOUR

Tick-tock, the race was on.

I sped outside into the night, ran down a street distorted with lights and shadows, and hailed the first cab coming off the Bath Road.

"Police station," I said. The cabbie stepped on it. No small talk. No conversation at all. I called Slater en route.

"I'm coming in," I told him. "But I need to speak to Strong first."

"That's not possible. He's interviewing a suspect." I presumed he meant *the* suspect.

"I'm not making a statement until I speak to him." I spoke with more poise than I'd felt in the past twelve months.

"And I already told you—"

"Sorry, lost signal," I said and hung up.

Slater was already outside when I handed money to the taxi driver and told him to keep the change. As I slammed the cab door shut, Slater started towards me, his lips twisted in an ugly show of annoyance. "Who the hell do you think you are? You can't dictate terms to me."

"I'm not prepared to stand idly by even if you refuse to see the connection between the murders in Cheltenham and the murder of a judge in Birmingham."

"You have a duty."

"And so do you." I looked over his shoulder and jerked my chin in the direction of the building. "Is Strong available, or shall I go back home until he's prepared to see me?" *Your call* my expression said.

His hands balled into fists as if tempted to take a swing at me. What really narked him was the fact I preferred his boss to him. Eventually he spoke. "All right," he said, his jaw grinding with tooth-shattering intensity. "I'll see what I can do. I suppose you'd better come inside."

I sat in a foyer while Slater strode through a door and disappeared from view. One minute rolled into another. He was gone for at least an hour, maybe more, and during that time the thing I dreaded most threatened to overwhelm me: doubt.

Was Monica like the client who left false trails? These were individuals adept at the art of manipulation. They gave every impression of cooperation, every appearance of friendliness. Occasionally, when you broke through the endless psychological diversion, they'd come clean and confess, and you got a ringside view of the real persona underneath layers of gamesmanship and obfuscation.

"Miss Slade?"

I turned towards the voice, which belonged to Strong. There was no sign of Slater. He probably couldn't bear the sight of me. I stood up. Strong held a door open.

He took me into a room and invited me to sit down. There was no hostility, no pressure for me to hurry up and say what I came for so that he could get on with his very important job. He pulled up a chair and sat back, his arms loose at his side, in listening mode. He was sympathetic, which rated as a first for me when it came to dealing with the police.

"You wanted to talk," he said. "Before you do, Stacey Walton alleges that you had a gun."

"Me, a gun?" I said wide-eyed. "That's preposterous."

"She was vociferous about it."

"Do I seem the type of person to carry a firearm? I wouldn't know one end of a gun from the other." But my prints would be all over it, I remembered with a jag of realisation. From hours in the consulting room, I'd discovered that, to be a convincing liar, all you needed to do was play dumb and mix truth with the lie. "Stacey waved a firearm at me," I said boldly. "I made a grab for it and that's when she hit me." I pointed to the blood on my head. Strong held my gaze for a moment and appeared to relax.

"We'll need to take your fingerprints to corroborate."

I resisted the urge to inform him that my prints were already on file.

"The floor is yours," he said.

"Have you questioned Stacey about Hawkes?"

"Claims to know nothing about it."

I choked back a groan. "That's it?" The thought of my mother remaining in the frame killed me.

"Not quite. She's pleading not guilty to Otto Vellender's murder."

"She shows no remorse?"

"None."

I fell silent. In Stacey's eyes, she'd meted out her own brand of justice so a not guilty plea was consistent with that, but why was she giving Strong the run-around about Hawkes? *Because she didn't do it?* a spectral voice said inside me. "Have you spoken to Nicholas Vellender?"

"As soon as he was discharged from hospital, Vellender gave Slater a statement."

"Are you going to prosecute him?"

"For what?"

"Wasting police time?"

"Paris Vellender would have been a more likely candidate. With her death…" He didn't finish. Didn't need to.

Uncomfortable with it, I asked, "What happens next?"

"Stacey appears at the magistrates court tomorrow."

"And after that?"

"She'll be held on remand until the case goes to Crown court."

"When will that be?"

"Hard to say. Ten months, a year, maybe."

"I take it bail isn't an issue?"

"Correct."

"That's something, I guess."

Strong tipped his head and smiled. "Why don't you tell me what's troubling you?" So I did.

I told him the whole story. Finally, I explained to Strong about the judge and Joyce Conway and the connection to Stacey Walton.

"Stacey killed Martell," I finished.

He accepted this because Stacey had presumably admitted it. When I confessed to the part I'd really played in Martell's life, his mouth slanted down, his open features darkened.

"Didn't you think it odd that Martell was keen to find Nicholas?" he said.

"I believed Martell was doing it for Mimi's sake. In fact he was doing it for the usual reason: rank greed. Whatever the truth, Monica, my mother, had nothing to do with Judge Hawkes's death."

"Even though she'd displayed a similar pattern of behaviour some years before? Come on, you're the psychologist."

I shifted in my seat. "It's tempting to draw comparisons."

"But you don't buy it?"

"No."

Strong stroked his chin thoughtfully. "You could be wrong, and we still need your statement regarding Walton."

"But that won't save my mother."

He hitched a shoulder in a *nothing I can do about that* gesture. I believe he thought, as a daughter, I was blind to the truth. "West Mids will see that justice is done." I didn't share his confidence.

"Let me talk to Stacey," I said.

"Out of the question."

"It could be legit. I'm a professional. You have cameras in the interview rooms, don't you? You could even sit in."

"You're a witness. I can't allow you anywhere near her until the trial is finished and even then it would only be with her agreement."

"But—"

"You've been watching too much television. She wouldn't talk to you even if it were possible."

"She would. I formed a connection with her in that place. Truly. Give me a chance."

I watched his eyes, saw him compute, skirmish with temptation and then doubt so weighty you could have used it to crush rock. My stomach lurched. "*Please.*"

Strong cocked his head to one side as though he were viewing an endangered species. I didn't dare move. I didn't want to screw up.

"No," he said. "To allow you to talk to her at this critical stage is not only unorthodox, it could compromise the entire investigation. More than my job's worth, frankly. Sorry."

A wave of desolation swept over me so strong I thought I'd never recover from it.

SEVENTY-FIVE

I GAVE A STATEMENT that night. It was after three by the time I got home, crashed into bed, and slept the sleep of the dispossessed. Morning dawned with a sun the colour of lemon curd.

Out on a limb and out of synch, one half of my brain registered that, in less than forty-eight hours, Luke would be touching down in the UK, while my mother was still incarcerated with Niven in a police station; the other half remembered blood and fear, helplessness and supplication, and the death of hope. I wondered how Nicholas was and where he was. In the course of twenty-four hours, the remains of his entire family had been wiped out and he was left a ruin.

I got up, used the bathroom, made tea, and took it back to bed. I felt ill, slightly feverish, as if I were coming down with something virulent. At some stage I must have fallen into a scratchy sleep until the doorbell erupted and woke me. It was past noon.

I dragged myself out of bed, padded downstairs, and opened the door a crack. A woman thrust a vast bouquet of flowers at me.

"Kim Slade?" she said.

"That's me." I signed and took them, mystified, the cellophane crackling in my hands. Walking back down the hall, into the kitchen, I plucked out the small envelope attached to the stems. The card made me smile, although the accompanying pang of guilt was less easy to banish.

Filling the sink with water, I rested the bouquet in it and called Stannard.

"You are the sweetest and kindest guy."

"Wrong on both counts, but thanks. How are you doing?"

"Iffy."

"What happened after your dramatic exit?"

"It wasn't dramatic."

"Not the consensus in the pub."

I pulled a face. "I gave a statement to Strong."

"Is this part of your *stepping up to the plate* strategy?"

"Forget my bravado and foolish enthusiasm."

"Would you like to elaborate over a bottle of wine?"

"Can't. I'm expecting a call from Gavin, in which case I'll have to go to Birmingham."

"Want me to come over, keep you company? We could sip tea."

I hovered from one foot to the other. I didn't want to disappoint, but I needed to be alone, to go at my own pace. I wasn't even dressed. "Can I call you in an hour? I might have a clearer picture by then."

"Sure. I'll stay on standby."

"And Kyle?"

"Yeah?"

"Thank you again."

I showered, bathed my face, rinsed the blood from my hair, washed it, and selected fresh clothes. Against my will, snapshots of the last twenty-four hours materialised in my mind: Otto's face as the blade struck; Nick, mute and uncomprehending; the dead, those apparitions that had followed me around for a lifetime, some I knew intimately and some I didn't. I remembered Joyce Conway, seemingly forgotten and insignificant. Perhaps she'd slipped and fallen from the cliff after all.

When Gavin finally rang and told me the news, I couldn't comprehend what he said and asked him to repeat it.

"Your mother has confessed."

"What? No, I don't believe it."

"It's true, Kim. She murdered Judge Michael Hawkes. She had the means, motive, and opportunity. She said so."

Sounded like a borrowed line to me. With Niven breathing fire at her, Monica had understandably crumbled under pressure. And there were other factors at play. She felt that she deserved her fate because of the previously unreported crime, an offence so serious that it had punched me hard in the gut. I got it. There was logic in her actions. It ticked the box on a psychological level. This is what I told myself because the alternative was too harrowing. What I couldn't bear was her refusal to see me or Luke.

"She told you that, you're sure?"

"Positive. She was most insistent on the subject," he replied in his customary direct manner.

"What the hell do I tell my brother?"

"The truth?"

I swallowed a sigh. "Did Niven put pressure on her?"

"No more than was put on you."

I remembered how that had felt. You had to have titanium-coated mental muscles to deal with the police once you're a suspect in their sights. Forget the *you have nothing to fear if you haven't done anything wrong* argument trotted out by those who've never received so much as a parking ticket. "You're certain she wasn't forced to confess?"

"Honestly, Kim, there was no coercion. Your mother asked to speak to me in private, told me she'd decided to recant her original statement, and that was it."

Pain shot through my body as raw and real as if I'd set myself alight. I think I let out a moan because Gavin asked whether I had someone with me. I told him I hadn't.

"Make sure you do." He continued to tell me about what happened next. I didn't stop him. Proceedings for my mother mirrored those for Stacey Walton. "She'll probably be sent on remand to Brockhill Women's jail in Worcestershire."

"What's it like?"

"Like the rest."

A picture flashed into my mind of women self-harming, of violent behaviour and abuse. "Okay," I said, numbed.

"I've raised the question of MH issues." Mental health, I registered. "The judge will order psychiatric reports to be carried out by the Prosecution. I'll do the same in case the Prosecution take a different view to the one we'd like."

"She's not so disturbed, Gavin, that she doesn't know what she's doing."

"Let's take a rather more open view."

"You mean it would serve her purpose if she were found to be mentally unfit?" I failed to keep the cynical note from my voice.

"We all want what is in your mother's best interests, Kim."

I drew a deep breath. "Where will the reports be done?"

"Either in prison or the judge will admit the defendant to a psychiatric hospital."

"'Jesus, that can't happen. She has a morbid fear of those places. It will destroy her."

"In which case she won't be fit enough to stand trial."

Why was it that Gavin saw a situation as win-win when I only saw it as lose-lose? Fear took me in its arms, embraced me, whispered in my ear, and held me close. If it were true and Monica was a murderer, where did that leave me? Did her guilt recalibrate my past? Did it mean that my judgement of my father was neither fair nor deserved?

I thanked Gavin for his time, cut the call, and pressed speed dial. "Kyle, can I take you up on your offer?"

"Fresh developments?"

"Of the worst kind."

SEVENTY-SIX

WE GOT HAMMERED.

Sitting absurdly close to each other on the sofa, Stannard was more tactile than usual. It made me feel awkward because the spectre of Otto Vellender sat between us like a bolster down the middle of a double bed. Loose-mouthed with alcohol, I had a crushing desire to confess all about sex in the hallway. Self-preservation kicked in. I stuck out my glass for a refill. "More wine, please." Having already consumed enough to negate the power of my medication, one more would make little difference. Might as well go for broke.

He topped up our glasses. "Do you think the shrinks will come down on the side of your ma being mentally unfit to stand?"

"According to Gavin, it's our last hope."

"Slim?"

"Infinitesimal."

"And Nicholas Vellender?"

I hesitated. "What about him?"

"You don't think he's guilty?" Stannard probed.

"Of what?"

"Online assault?"

"Is there such a crime?"

"Difficult to prove, granted, but his online activities indicate criminality, surely?"

"It indicates mental illness, which is hardly surprising when you consider how he was brought up."

"Two fuck-ups for parents isn't exactly an original state of affairs."

"Ouch."

He flashed an impish smile. "All that terrible upbringing stuff, well, it's simply not my bag."

"You sound like my boss," I said, feeling immensely tired. "So what is your bag?" Our eyes met and I wanted to claw back the words, the intonation, the tone, everything. There was no doubt in my mind of the chemistry between us, but I didn't want to risk our friendship by introducing a complicated emotional dimension.

He took my glass and set it down on the table next to his own. "You," he said, his eyes melting into mine. No, I thought. Not because I didn't want him to, not because of Otto, but because of Chris. With Otto, it had been nothing more than sex; with Stannard, I felt as if I were betraying my dead partner.

He leant in towards me. And then the doorbell blared and we sprung apart like startled teenagers caught snogging by their parents.

I jumped to my feet, fled down the hallway, and tore open the front door. My big brother stood on the doorstep.

"Luke." I flung my arms around him. He felt solid and brotherly and in command.

"I got an earlier flight," he said hugging me tight. "Sheesh, you smell of booze," he said, laughing.

"Come on in." I grinned. "I've got a friend I'd like you to meet."

Luke strode in, stuck down his bag, and shook hands with Stannard. "I could use a drink myself," he said. "So where's Monica? Is she here?"

I looked from my brother to Stannard, euphoria at my brother's return turning to gloom as quickly as a May blossom shrivelling in frost.

———

Stannard made his excuses, kissed me lightly on the cheek, and left. I don't know what I felt about that. Probably relief had the edge on disappointment.

I handed Luke a drink and told him everything. I was certain I'd left out bits that would return to me later, probably around the middle of the night, but I gave him the broad picture. When I finished he sat grave and sombre and dark-eyed.

I hadn't seen my brother for a few years. He'd aged in the way that affluent men do. While his clothes were expensive and spoke of wealth, there was, somehow, something less of him as a person, as if the values he'd once held dear were neither relevant nor coincided with his carefully created image and lifestyle. His girth had expanded. His face was fleshy, slightly pouched below his eyes, and the resemblance to my father was striking. Clean-shaven, Luke had the same mouth and dominant jawline, thin hair balding on top, grey at the temples. Two lines lay on either side of his eyebrows like stray accents in need of a vowel. I remembered those lines on my father's face, how they would deepen when he was vexed or irritated. I recalled how much they disturbed me.

"Did the police lean on her to force a confession?" His Transatlantic accent was stronger now he was sitting alone with me in my home.

"Not according to her lawyer."

"And this guy, Chadwick, he's good?"

"He handled my case, remember?"

"Sure thing," he said, rubbing his eyes. "Jet lag screwing with my brain," he apologised. "But if you're right, why confess to something she hadn't done?"

I paused. As fast as a flame setting light to petrol, Luke pounced on the gap in my response. "What haven't you told me, Kim?"

Crumbling under his austere gaze in exactly the same way I used to capitulate to my dad, I told him about the incident that had put Monica into a secure unit for a second time.

"Jeez, she's done it before? Why the hell didn't you say?"

"Because it doesn't mean she's a murderer."

He stared at me as if I'd offered to sleep with him. "Where I come from it's a slam dunk. She's dangerous and devious."

No, no, no. "She's lost." I pitched forward. "Think about it, why wait twelve years to strike? Why risk the life she's carefully created, the future she's built for herself after all that's happened to her? She maintained she was happy in the Hawkes household."

Luke rolled his eyes at my obvious naivety. "She would say that. It was part of the deception. She needed you to believe her story and you fell for it, don't you understand?"

Astringent, penetrating, his eyes bored into mine. I broke away first, scooped up Stannard's glass along with a couple of empty wine bottles, and dumped them on the draining board. The clatter made my brain ache.

"Do you think she'll change her mind?" he said when I sat back down.

"About what?"

"Seeing us."

"I hope so."

He looked mournful. Perhaps he was counting the cost of a wasted journey. He leant back on the sofa, closed his eyes, and massaged the lids with his index fingers. "What should I do?"

"I'll give you her lawyer's number. You could liaise with him." We sat in silence, neither of us thinking of anything useful to say. "Monica said that you're staying at a hotel, is that right?" I said at last.

He nodded. Weary and blind-sided, he seemed reluctant to make a move. I didn't blame him and actually didn't want him to go. "Want to stay here tonight?"

He opened his eyes and his mouth relaxed into a semblance of a smile. "That would be good. I'm only sorry it's not in better circumstances."

I remembered he'd said the same when our father died. Too often, our lives seemed punctuated by loss.

I sprang to my feet. "Won't be a second. I'll make up the bed. Help yourself to a drink. Do you want anything to eat? There's plenty of food in the fridge."

He tilted his glass. "This is fine."

I took fresh sheets and towels from the cupboard on the landing, made up the bed in the spare room, and went downstairs. We talked some more, about Luke's wife, Jessica, and children who I'd only seen as toddlers. He asked me about my health, to which I gave a pat response. I asked him about work, to which he gave a similarly bland reply. We were like strangers in a crowded room, our differences more apparent than they ever were during countless phone calls over the years. We were each playing parts, neither willing to give ground, to reveal what we really thought or felt for fear of dismaying or, worse, vexing the other.

Heavy-lidded, grey with fatigue and disappointment, he decided to turn in. We stood up, embraced clumsily, and went our separate ways. Our parents have done this to us, I thought as I climbed into bed dog-tired, the irony of flying in the face of what I preached to my clients not lost on me.

SEVENTY-SEVEN

Wordless, we shuffled around each other the next morning. I felt like hell due to the volume of alcohol I'd necked the night before. The veins in my head thumped with excess heat. My exhausted brother looked like I felt. To compound it, I'd run out of fresh coffee, a disaster in Luke's eyes, so I took the opportunity to escape, hotfooting it to the nearby supermarket.

Coffee bought along with fresh croissants, Cornish butter, and orange juice, I cut back through a small area of park where grey squirrels scampered through the trees.

My mobile rang. It was Strong.

"Stacey Walton has been remanded to Eastwood Park at Wotton Under Edge."

I thanked him and went back home, downed two Nurofen with juice, and made proper coffee with shaky hands. While we ate our late breakfast we discussed the weather, the European Union, its relationship to America, and house prices. We did not discuss old times because there weren't many that didn't come locked and loaded with emotional baggage.

Around noon, Gavin called to relay the news that Monica had appeared at Gloucester Magistrates' court. She'd confirmed her name and her temporary address as Stannard's flat in Pittville and was put on remand at Brockhill. She still refused to see us or withdraw her confession. I could see from Luke's pained response that he found it more difficult than me. Unlike my brother, I'd had an opportunity to talk to and get to know her before things turned sour. My thoughts were vague and insubstantial, yet I clung to the possibility that something good and decent and lasting would emerge. I don't think Luke could see that yet. We were split into two distinct camps and it grated on the pair of us. To tell the truth, I was relieved when he said he would head out to the hotel and check in.

"We'll keep in touch, yeah?" he said, loitering by the front door.

"Sure, do you fancy coming here for dinner tonight?"

He was evasive. "Maybe tomorrow. I need to catch up on sleep."

I flicked a smile. "Fine." Secretly, I was glad.

I didn't get in touch with Stannard, and Stannard didn't get in touch with me. Our non-amorous encounter was nothing more than a result of us being pissed, which deep down I knew was a lie. I spent a couple of hours curbing waves of drink-induced nausea and tidied and cleaned the house as a form of penance.

And then there was Paris Vellender and her leap into infinity.

Her death gnawed at my conscience. Racked with guilt, I grabbed a coat and slipped out of the house into a sunless, grey, and still afternoon.

I have no recollection of where I went. One street blended into another. I walked unseeing and thought about my father once more, how his influence had moulded me.

Most men have their secrets. Some lead dual lives. What you see is not always what you get. My father's influence had made me who I was and I often wished it hadn't. I mourned the fact that my hard edges had not been softened by a woman's touch. I yearned to reconcile myself to him, to remember him for his generosity, his mischievous nature, the steel he put in my backbone. Only my father had done those things for me, not Monica or anyone else.

And yet I could only remember him for his lack of care and occasional cruelty. I doubted that would ever change. Not now.

So consumed in thought was I that when Nicholas Vellender called for the first time since I'd dragged him from the restaurant, I didn't react positively.

"I'm so sorry, Nick, but this isn't a good time."

"I really need to see you."

He sounded desperate and lonely and I felt for him and all that he'd gone through. "How about I swing by yours in an hour or so? Would that do?"

"Thanks, Kim."

The day dimmed to the colour of slate. Gusts of wind battered the street. Rain was in the air. My mind returned to Stacey. Did she always have it in her to kill, or had life experiences corrupted her entirely? I thought over our conversation in her sitting room—so strained, so polite, so dangerous. I'd pushed her about Judge Hawkes.

"Had him in my sights, but someone beat me to it."

"You didn't shove a bag over his head?"

"Not my style."

I stopped walking. No, it wasn't. And that, I realised, was the point.

Suddenly, I felt like a successful musician who, after years of playing with bands, goes it alone and settles for a pared down, unplugged version of his song, piano accompaniment only, no strings, no drums, the essential truth of the vocals exposed.

I called Strong and, frustratingly, got his voicemail. I did the talk and walk thing you see in movies. "Stacey Walton didn't kill Hawkes. Nicholas Vellender did. You have to tell Niven. Get her to switch the focus of her investigation, find the evidence. My mother didn't do it. She only confessed as a form of misplaced guilt," I gabbled. "You have to do something. Now. I'm on my way to Nicholas Vellender's house," I bellowed and cut the call.

And why put myself in danger? If Nick Vellender went to ground for a second time, he would never be found. Monica would serve a life sentence for a crime she didn't commit. Nick was so mentally disturbed only I was capable of reaching him. Call it professional pride. This was what I sold myself as I hurried down Hobbit's Alley, as I'd nicknamed it, and crossed the cobbled path and straggly front garden to the house. The stable door was ajar and I went straight into the living room.

"Nick," I called, tentatively at first. Silence enveloped me. I called again, noticed something different. The facing wall, where the Samurai sword hung, was empty. And the helmet with the scary facemask was also absent. It took me mere seconds to process what I should do: *Run.*

Noise behind me, I twisted round and every hair on my body revolted and stood erect. An enormous figure in full Japanese body armour blocked my escape. The suit was made from oblong plates of steel and leather, lacquered to a deadly black sheen. Enormous shoulder, thigh, and calf guards in a semblance of chain mail offered the ultimate protection. His feet, ridiculous in trainers, did not lessen the effect. Held in two hands was a sword of fire-breathing dragons and a blade of exceptional length that could cut through bone. Designed to terrify, I was terrified. I could barely move. As fearsome as my assailant was, it was the face that most disturbed me. Above a snarling open mouth with snaggled teeth were eyes devoid of expression and yet so horribly alive.

"Stop it, Nick," I shouted in a shaky voice. "Snap out of it. Don't make things worse for yourself."

"You bitch, with your voodoo psychobabble. You screwed everything. It's your fault Paris is dead. You killed her."

The sword flashed through the air and carved straight through a wooden side table, splitting it in half. I ducked. I didn't think of tactics or strategy, phoning for help or screaming, or whether I could run upstairs, lock myself in a bathroom, or jump from a bedroom window. I was too paralysed to think at all. I was running on raw adrenalin and instinct. If only I had the gun. If only I had something I could use against him.

"I know about Hawkes," I bawled at him.

"So what? He deserved to die. Sneaked into his house, hid in one of those big posh wardrobes until it was quiet and shoved a plastic bag over his head. Squeezed the life out of the fucker. Satisfied?"

The blade fell again, the trajectory so powerful I felt the air part in front of my face. Light on his feet, younger than me by over a decade, motor skills superior, he attacked once more. Caught in a tangle of fear, I failed to move out of the way. A scream of pain scythed up my left arm, burning bright. Volcanic heat and light. Panting, I backed up toward the fireplace and felt the warm, viscous sensation of blood soaking into the sleeve of my jacket and dripping off the ends of my fingers.

My eyes flicked to the right. A piece of advice whistled through my mind, my father's distant voice murmuring in my ear. I obeyed and turned my body side-on to give Nicholas Vellender less of a target. Again, I was too slow. Another swathe of pain echoed through my outer thigh as my jeans ripped from my hipbone to my knee.

Everything happened so fast, yet time slowed and plodded to a standstill. My heart pounded, nerve endings scorched. It hurt to inhale and exhale. Destroying realisation confirmed that, armed, Nicholas needed no skill at all against me. *Please God, let the police get my message. Please let them arrive. Please. I'll be good. I'll do anything you want. Devote my life to good works...*

He feinted with his left arm and lunged again, the point missing me by an eyelash. Grabbing hold of a poker, with a loud cry borne of desperation, I smashed it against the blade as hard as I could. My arm vibrated on impact, sending painful shockwaves up my neck to my jaw, making my teeth rattle. I couldn't hold him off. I couldn't see a way. Death was inevitable and I wasn't ready. I had so much I wanted to do, a life to live, a relationship to forge with the woman who I called Monica and who was my mother. I thought of Stannard and Luke and the girls in my charge and how it would be too silly, too stupid, too horrible to die like this, chopped into pieces, blood and gore and...

I swung the poker once more, striking his unprotected elbow. I heard the crunch and howl of pain.

Fired up, he let out a tremendous battle cry, unintelligible but unmistakable, and lashed out. I stumbled back, collided with one of the stands. Both me, and a helmet of black hammered steel crashed to the floor. A shadow loomed overhead. Nicholas's heavy breathing echoed through the room as if the dragons, not he, breathed fire. I glanced up and saw the blade shimmer and rise, his arms fully extended, the dragons taunting me one final time as they prepared for the kill. Desperate, I grabbed the helmet with the lethal wooden horns and, with both hands, drove it down, puncturing the thin material of his trainer. I felt give as the points met skin, soft tissue, and flesh. And then abrupt resistance. Applying my whole body weight, my hands juddered on unyielding bone. Still, I did not let up. With a grunt of exertion, I powered through and continued down, giving no quarter. Not as blood blossomed. Not as Nicholas Vellender's screams battered the room, high-pitched and intense. I did not stop until, impaled and pinioned to the floor, his head and body jerked. As the sword clattered, I rolled away, scrabbled to my feet, headed for the exit, throwing myself back outside, and ran. I kept on running, blood pouring from my wounds, until I saw the revolving light of a police car and Stannard pounding towards me.

SEVENTY-EIGHT

THE WHEELS OF JUSTICE grind slowly. Monica was not instantly released. Weeks passed.

My arm bandaged and in a sling, my thigh embroidered with scars, I stood outside Brockhill Women's Jail with Luke. In the intervening time, Nicholas Vellender had been arrested for the murder of Judge Michael Hawkes and the attempted murder of me. As expected, he didn't come clean as an act of contrition. He bragged about it, which as far as Monica was concerned, was a good thing.

"You okay?" Luke said, glancing at me.

I nodded. I'd had fifteen stitches overall. Physically sore even weeks later, my mind felt fine, more sorted and serene than I'd felt in a long time. Stannard took the credit for my more docile state, as he put it. Following my collapse into his arms, he had never left my side. He sat with me while I stayed overnight in hospital and accompanied me to the police station the following day. He wouldn't let me be alone and insisted I stay at his place. I'd been spoilt. Each evening Luke came round and we'd watch Stannard cook, the three of us drinking, shrieking a lot with that peculiar high-octane laughter that comes from those who have encountered some of the worst life can throw at them. When the noise and hilarity got too much, I would disappear to another room and cry. And they let me.

I tilted my head and watched Monica emerge from the entrance. A stray glimmer of sunshine peeped out from behind the clouds in a display of solidarity. She looked wan and frail, the smile on her face as tentative as the faltering light in her eye. Like a woman given another crack at life, watchful and in awe, she took uneven steps. It was as if she were learning to walk all over again after a period of paralysis, learning to live and dream and hope.

I let Luke go first. He strode toward her in that purposeful way of his, slipped his arm through hers, held her tight, and whispered something in her ear that made her face light up. In that unique moment, I thought how much I resembled her and it pleased me to a ridiculous degree. As they walked back to me, her warm gaze fell on mine.

Sometimes words are not enough. Sometimes, like false prophets, they strike an inaccurate note, puncture the truth and create the wrong impression. This was no time for conversation. I did the simplest thing of all. I stretched out my hand. She caught it and held it tight. The three of us walked to the car. My mum and me climbed into the rear, close and side-by-side, and Luke drove us home.

EPILOGUE

"My name is Nicholas Vellender. I'm twenty-four years old and I'm a writer. I specialise in fantasy and horror. My real mother abandoned me when I was four. My adoptive mother is dead. Kim Slade killed her. My adoptive father and my sister are also dead—the former because he deserved it, the latter through no fault of her own. Rarely, but sometimes, I kill people."

"Like Michael Hawkes?"

"And Joyce Conway."

"She didn't fall?"

"I pushed her to her death."

"Does it scare you?"

He looked straight ahead at me with soulless eyes. "Never."

© Kenneth James Photography

ABOUT THE AUTHOR

Eve Seymour (England) has published articles in *Devon Today* magazine and had a number of her short stories broadcast on BBC Radio Devon. She has also written nine thrillers. You can visit her at eveseymour.co.uk and eveseymour.wordpress.com.

WWW.MIDNIGHTINKBOOKS.COM

From the gritty streets of New York City to sacred tombs in the Middle East, it's always midnight somewhere. Join us online at any hour for fresh new voices in mystery fiction. At midnightinkbooks.com you'll also find our author blog, new and upcoming books, events, book club questions, excerpts, mystery resources, and more.

MIDNIGHT INK ORDERING INFORMATION

Order Online:
• Visit our website www.midnightinkbooks.com, select your books, and order them on our secure server.

Order by Phone:
• Call toll-free within the U.S. and Canada at
  1-888-NITE-INK (1-888-648-3465)
• We accept VISA, MasterCard, American Express, and Discover

Order by Mail:
Send the full price of your order (MN residents add 6.875% sales tax) in U.S. funds, plus postage & handling to:

> Midnight Ink
> 2143 Wooddale Drive
> Woodbury, MN 55125-2989

Postage & Handling:
Standard (U.S. & Canada). If your order is:
> $30.00 and under, add $4.00
> $30.01 and over, FREE STANDARD SHIPPING

International Orders:
> $16.00 for one book plus $3.00 for each additional book

Orders are processed within 12 business days. Please allow for normal shipping time.
Postage and handling rates subject to change.